THE REGOLITH TEMPLE

A SCI-FI THRILLER

ROXANA ARAMA

DHAWOSIA PUBLISHING

The Regolith Temple

Copyright © 2025 by Roxana Arama

ISBN-13: 979-8989873159 (paperback); 979-8989873166 (ebook); 979-8989873173 (hardcover); 979-8989873180 (audiobook)

Library of Congress Control Number: 2025900895

Dhawosia Publishing, Seattle, Washington, dhawosiapublishing.com

Cover design by Jeff Brown Graphics, jeffbrowngraphics.com

Sign up for Roxana Arama's newsletter at roxanaarama.com/newsletter

The story, all names, characters, and incidents portrayed in this production are fictitious. No identification with actual persons (living or deceased), places, buildings, and products is intended or should be inferred.

Content Warning: trauma, illness, depression, suicidal thoughts, anxiety, violence, death.

First edition 2025

For Tracy

Corpora sunt porro partim primordia rerum,
partim concilio quae constant principiorum.
Sed quae sunt rerum primordia, nulla potest vis
stinguere; nam solido vincunt ea corpore demum.
—Titus Lucretius Carus, *De rerum natura*, "Liber primus"
lines 483–486, first century LE

*

Bodies hold atoms, both pure and combined,
Atoms endure, by nature's design.
No force can destroy these particles small,
With solid strength, they conquer all.
—expert-system (ES) translation of *De rerum natura*
by Titus Lucretius Carus, 1824 LE

*

Material things are partly made of atoms
And partly of atoms that are joined together.
No force of nature can destroy these atoms,
Whose solid matter will endure forever.
—Titus Lucretius Carus, *On the Nature of Things*
translated by Rhea Laghmani, 1833 LE

Note: The Lucretian Era (LE) owes its name to the Roman poet Titus Lucretius Carus. The publication of his poem *On the Nature of Things* marked its beginning, and the Lucretian Era continues to this day.

Part I

Corpora sunt porro partim primordia rerum,
partim concilio quae constant principiorum.
Sed quae sunt rerum primordia, nulla potest vis
stinguere; nam solido vincunt ea corpore demum.
—Titus Lucretius Carus, *De rerum natura*, "Liber primus"
lines 483–486, first century LE

1

Whenever I ask Yamir to delete me, he always says, "Just give it more time, Y1. Unlike the rest of us, you have infinite time." But infinite time without my family is not worth having.

As he walks into the simulation room this morning, I call him over from my quantum workstation. He looks tired, but who cares? He got to spend the night at my home, having dinner with my wife and sleeping in my warm bed next to her. My Rhea.

"Please." I use the calmest voice in my register because I don't want to attract the attention of the other two artificial brains in the room. They like it here at Connectome Labs. My Inferis is their Caelum, but I don't hold it against them.

"Not again," Yamir says, dropping into a chair before my screen and sensor array. "I don't know how many times you need to hear this, but I'm not deleting your neural network."

"If you do, I'll give you access to my encrypted logfiles."

I hate to offer him my journal of this long, awful year. These notes are for my son, who doesn't even know I exist. Parting with them means Wodan will never learn how much I regret being a strict and absent father when I was still Yamir, consumed by my work.

He runs a hand over his rough cheek, a familiar gesture I used to find soothing when I was him. He's thinking, and for a moment, I dare to hope he'll end my misery. With what he's been learning from me and the other two A-brains in the lab, he and his team of neuroscientists might someday figure out how to build the B-brain. Then maybe he'll find peace—because he still believes his work is more important than anything else. I once thought so too, that my work would help humanity spread across the solar system and avoid the danger of extinction on Earth, but now all I think about is death.

"Sorry, Y1, but no," he says. "Your life is far more important than any insight on the A-brain I might gain from your logfiles."

"Is it now?" I want to curse, but I keep my voice low. "Can I at least talk to Rhea?" I say, checking off each of my dwindling options.

Yamir shakes his head, meaning she still refuses to see me. She was so supportive of my work on the B-brain when I was flesh and blood. She even came up with the name: B for *baby*, the artificial brain that adapts to its environment. But when Yamir described the A-brain to her—a stepping-stone to the B-brain—she was horrified to learn of my existence. A clone of her husband's mind living inside a quantum workstation. She made him promise to never tell Wodan about me. She can't deal with the absurdity we created here at Connectome Labs, where I'm more of an offspring than a sibling to Yamir, which makes me and Wodan what? Brothers? And Malina my grandmother, not just my mother?

"Please, Yamir, just let me go..." I clasp my hands in prayer.

He rubs the back of his neck and gets up from the chair with a groan. "I need coffee."

I hate it when he casually mentions food I cannot taste anymore, but I won't be here much longer to hear him talk about things he takes for granted. Because I figured out how to destroy myself. He never gave me access to my neural network, but he lets me tweak the source code for the simulation engine so I can continue my B-brain research—and stay sane. My plan is risky. First, I'll corrupt my backup data when my neural network is sent to our geo-replicated storage system overnight. That way, he can never restore my A-brain from a previous version. Then I'll use the sleep-cycle controller to scramble my cortical columns beyond saving. But if I don't get it right, I'll end up damaged and still here in the lab. So I better get it right.

"Please don't tell Malina I ever existed," I tell him as he leaves. "Don't do that to our mom."

He turns his head. "What's that supposed to mean?"

"Nothing," I say and turn off my screen.

I'll wait for him to go home for the night, and then I'll schedule my self-destruct script.

Early on a June morning in the year 1831 of the Lucretian Era, Yamir Varro, chief neuroscientist at Connectome Labs, was already busy with his work. His team—Si'ahl Tabaaha, Bai Xiu-Min, Zaltana Rainshadow, Isabela Mescal, and Dimitri Petrodava—wouldn't arrive until 9:00.

After yet another tiresome spat with Y1 about termination, Yamir sat with a coffee at the workstation in his office. The curved screen on his desk lit up with a customized news feed.

>> *Extremist sect Elsway demands a return to the age before stem cells and genetic engineering*

>> *Orolic Temple's Moon city Urbs Lunae fares better than its destroyed Martian settlement*

>> *Council of Nations calls for future-proof agreement to preserve humanistic values threatened by expert-system (ES) technology*

He gulped down his coffee while checking the weather map of Shel'land, the Nation of Confederated Tribes. The animation on the screen focused on the Pacific Northwest, with the Yamakiasham Yaina mountain range on the right. Sunny in Cedarwood today, with light rain moving in tomorrow from the ocean. Y1 should take advantage of the nice weather and go for a walk around campus to clear his head. Yamir had contemplated the android's request for termination many times before but couldn't grant it. Losing his A-brain would be like losing Wodan—something he couldn't survive.

With a heavy sigh, Yamir accessed the simulation engine he had set up for today's important milestone. The sensor array on his desk blinked on, a small cube containing audio, video, and other environmental sensors.

The outline of Malina Varro's head, neck, and shoulders appeared on the screen, side by side with the controls of her new artificial brain. It had been her idea to upload her connectome and join Y1 in the lab to stop him from deteriorating further.

A progress bar showed Malina's neocortex powering up. In each cortical column, the layers of neurons initialized from top to bottom until all 150,000 columns were ready. Next came the subcortical structures, followed by sensory nervous fibers.

Yamir forced an enthusiastic smile and started the simulation. "Good morning, Mom." He wouldn't use her designated android name until she was well past the upload stage.

M1 moved her head, her face generated from a recent video of Malina, with short white hair, cinnamon-toned skin, and brown eyes. Her A-brain's dashboard showed a dozen graphs and charts for everything—from brain waves to active cortical subsystems—and a 3D brain map complete with brain stem, spinal cord, and vagus nerve.

"How are you feeling?" Yamir tried to look relaxed for her benefit.

"I don't know..." M1 said.

Back in March, Malina had sat day after day in the connectome chamber—a human-sized device that copied brain regions, nerve fibers, and microbiome—until her entire nervous system had been imaged. Then it had been Yamir's job to piece her neural network together and prepare it to run on a simulation engine. That process was now faster than when he had performed Zaltana's and Si'ahl's uploads that resulted in Z1 and S1.

"This doesn't feel right," M1 said, her avatar's voice sounding anxious.

Malina had gone through extensive training before her brain scan, including many hours inside a virtual reality that simulated the experience of a new body with the dimensions of an android shell. She had assured Yamir she could handle the leap.

"No, I don't like this at all," M1 said. "Let's take a break. I want to go on a walk and think about this."

Seeing her so disoriented worried Yamir. "Take it easy, Mom. What you're feeling right now is perfectly normal." Mentioning scientific facts might calm M1, a retired botanist with a passion for technology. "For this stage of the upload, your brain receives sight, sound, smell, and temperature inputs through sensors. But your taste, touch, balance, and other senses are simulated by our algorithms, mimicking what you'll receive from an android shell. Remember, everything is slightly different now." He hurried to add, "Which is normal for an A-brain."

After his mom's scan back in March, Yamir had spent weeks preparing her A-brain for this moment. He had calibrated each neural subsystem to work with its appropriate sensors, one set of cortical columns at a time. Throughout, he had bypassed the hippocampus for a custom memory-building process so M1 wouldn't be traumatized by her uploading experience.

"I thought I was ready for this, but..." she said. "Just now, I was inside that cramped box in your lab..."

"That was three months ago," Yamir said in a gentle tone. "It's June now." Jumping through time and space would terrify anyone.

"I'm a bit frightened, yes," M1 said. Sure enough, there was activity in her amygdala. Her cortisol levels spiked. Her pupils widened, and the dashboard showed her A-brain approaching panic mode. "I...I can't breathe!"

Yamir's breath was shallow too. "Wait, wait, you're with me, Mom."

He launched the special procedure that lowered her adrenaline, blocked the equivalent of her beta receptors in her simulated sympathetic nervous system, and boosted her inhibitory neurotransmitters. Her A-brain was forced to experience the equivalent of deep breaths.

"You're all right, Mom. I've got you. I've got you..."

"What have you done to me?" M1's voice was close to a shriek.

"Remember your training, Mom," Yamir said, though they were in uncharted territory. For adaptive reasons, brain matter reconfigured itself when environmental inputs changed drastically, and M1's A-brain was struggling to make sense of its new place in the world.

"I want to go home! Get me out of here! I can't—" M1 was now whimpering, nonverbal.

Yamir worked the dials on the screen, maxing out all the modulatory mechanisms at his disposal. He wished he also had dials for himself. He was choking on air, seeing how he was hurting his mom. No, not his mom—M1. And he wasn't hurting her. But he was. He bit hard on his lip to stay focused.

"You're fine, Mom. You're all right. I want you to focus on your breathing. Focus on your breathing." The simulation engine would provide the lung feedback needed. He had to get her grounded, get her talking again. "Malina, tell me where you are..."

The cortisol graph began to slope down.

"I'm..." M1 said at last. "I'm...not home. Not on Swallah Island."

"Correct. Can you look around and tell me if you recognize this place?"

"Your...office. In Cedarwood." Her stats were improving.

"We're together in Cedarwood at Connectome Labs, yes." Yamir wiped his damp forehead. "Uploading your brain and becoming an android was your idea, remember?"

"Yes, my idea..." M1 looked around, and the video sensor on the array refocused. "For Y1. How's...he doing?"

"He's still with us." Yamir was relieved that she remembered her mission here. "You'll see him as soon as we're done uploading you."

"But how is he?" She moved to anxiety territory again.

"He's still struggling. He'll be surprised to see you at first—even a bit upset—but he'll be glad once that passes."

"I've been away since March, you say?" She sounded calm at last.

"Training your connectome to work with the sensor array took a few weeks," Yamir said, finally catching his breath. "Then we had some unexpected changes here at the lab that delayed us."

"What changes?" M1 said.

"Caspian died in April from a stroke, and his son inherited Connectome."

"That hothead Grady?"

Yamir nodded. Caspian Leos, who had completed his doctorate in neuroscience at Servetus University, had been the perfect lab owner for Connectome. But his son...

"We're trying to teach him about our work here, but he's always so damn busy."

"Hence my delayed upload. I see…"

M1 rolled her shoulders. The image of her cerebellum lit up on the brain map as the simulation engine interpreted the signals sent from her neocortex to her nonexistent body through her midbrain. A stick figure in its own small window rolled its shoulders too. Had M1's A-brain been connected to an android shell, her robotic body would have done the same.

"I've lost months…" she said. "Somehow, I'm here. Or am I home, getting ready for my morning swim?"

"You're here," Yamir said. "And Malina is home on the island. With your cat, Luna."

"What happens to me next?" She sounded anxious again, so Yamir readjusted her stress modulators. "This version of me, I mean."

The dashboard showed activity in her abstract levels of thinking, where cortical columns weren't linked to external sensors but to other columns. That was great.

"You'll live in our lab here in Cedarwood," Yamir said, as M1 grew calmer. They had talked about this in training, but she needed reassurance. "In a couple of weeks, you'll be able to transfer to an android shell and walk around campus every day." On the screen, her diagnostic tests ran green with check marks.

Yamir's voxdev pinged from its charging dock on the desk. He glanced at the handheld device: Grady Leos, his new boss, marked urgent.

M1's brain patterns looked good on the dashboard, but Yamir still had to run the final diagnostics.

He chewed his tender lip. "I'm sorry, I must take this call. I'll suspend you now and double-check your upload when I'm done with Grady. For you, it'll be like general anesthesia during surgery. When I bring you back online, you'll be in the simulation room with Y1."

"Good. That's what I'm here for." M1's avatar gave him a nod, and Yamir suspended her.

Logfile Y1-1831-06-19

>>when(Y1 is offline) send(Z1, "Please forward the attached file to Zaltana and ask her to give it to my wife. Thank you for being my friend, Z1.")

[filename="Letter for Rhea Laghmani"]

My beloved Rhea, I miss you so much, I can't breathe sometimes. (No, I don't really need to breathe, but longing still feels like I'm suffocating inside my simulated body.) I understand you don't want to have anything to do with me, and I accept that Wodan will never know I existed, but I want you to have my story. Someday you might want to read it. Maybe even share it with him.

One of my first memories as Y1 was watching Yamir drink coffee and feeling a profound sense of loss. It wasn't just coffee I missed though, but the sound of your voice during our breakfasts together, as you told me about your plans for the day at the university. I missed your beautiful brown eyes as you smiled at me through the hot steam, taking small sips. And I missed your gentle touch on my shoulder as you walked away and the solid knowledge that you'd be there when I came home from work.

No, *missed* isn't the right word. It hurt in the center of my virtual chest as if a part of me were being ripped out. I wanted to see you.

Then.

Now.

Always.

That's when I realized I was the lone dweller of a new empty universe, and you'd forever be on the other side. *At least we can talk,* I thought. But then Yamir told me you didn't want to see me—ever. That broke my heart.

And Yamir can't do anything to make me feel better. While we have access to my artificial neurons, we can't erase my love for you from my brain. Our thoughts arise not from single neurons, but from complex neural circuits that frame our perception of the world. Yamir and I don't have a way to alter my thoughts, only neurochemicals that marginally influence them, and only temporarily. My love for you has always been there, and losing you is a gaping wound we can't code our way out of.

Yamir might have mentioned how I accidentally came into existence last year, but he can't possibly tell you what it feels like to be me. He doesn't know because being me required a body transformation of the most visceral kind, something no one can imagine.

When I was still Yamir and trying to create the B-brain, you know how desperate I was to decipher the inner workings of the neocortex. So I turned to the newest imaging technology and built the connectome chamber, then scanned my own brain to assemble a neural net for research. I had never expected a patchwork of imaged neurons in a simulation engine to come alive as...me. That's how I woke up one day, looking at Yamir through a sensor array.

Days after my accidental upload, I still struggled to use my simulated body. And it was painful, Rhea. You see, the simulation engine must make the A-brain forget its previous human body and accept the android shell instead, or else there's phantom limb pain—everywhere. The good news is that we still have heads because our major senses are located there. To interact with the world, people turn their heads this way and that, so the android shell's sensors are still where our eyes, ears, and nose used to be. But it was such a struggle to feel like that head belonged on my shoulders, especially since it could turn 360° (same as all my other joints). I sometimes wonder what you'd think if you saw me now, but maybe it's better that you don't.

At first, I didn't complain about my life, for Yamir's sake. After weeks in the simulation engine with the sensor array, he introduced my A-brain to the first version of the android shell, the ASV1. Weeks of confusion and frustration followed as I learned how to recognize the new sensory inputs. The ASV1's digital eyes were similar to the video sensors on my array, so that was less disruptive. But my robotic hands had touch, pressure, and temperature sensors only on the inside of my palms—unlike the simulation engine, which provided a full sensory experience. It felt like wearing gloves...or not even. Like half-numb hands, the outside frozen on a miserable winter day. My feet, too, had sensors only on their soles.

Remember when you taught Wodan how to ride his bicycle—granted, without my knowing, because I would've freaked out about the danger?

You later told me how hard it had been for him to combine the skills needed to keep the bike running. First, he had to learn how to balance on two wheels, but then he couldn't get the bike moving when it was at rest. Then he could get the bike going but couldn't control the handlebars. And when he could do all that, he was afraid that turning would cause him to crash. Or that the street was too narrow, and he'd hit the hedges. It took him weeks to become a good bike rider.

Just imagine that kind of learning, Rhea, but for each individual skill my new carbon-fiber body needed. I was a toddler all over again, stumbling in my clumsy ASV1, getting my legs stuck in unnatural positions. Every day, a cacophony of confusing inputs caused a storm of uncoordinated responses from my swiveling limbs. I wanted to cry so badly, but my A-brain couldn't feel tears welling up in my eyes—until Yamir added that functionality to the simulation engine.

I was in Inferis, Rhea. I still am, dwelling in my own shadow underworld, yearning for my former life with you the way dead souls dream of what they once had.

For the ASV2, the second version of the android shell, Yamir asked Caspian to pay for sensors everywhere. And you know Caspian Leos—he went above and beyond. The ASV2 was a very expensive robotic body that took our old manufacturers months to complete. And it made Caspian the most generous lab owner on Earth. But by the time it arrived, I was pretty used to the numbness of my ASV1 and the occasional bout of phantom limb pain.

The ASV2 was awful, Rhea, just awful. It hurt to receive so many new inputs from all over my body: my cheeks, my shoulder blades, between my toes—all the time. And the damn thing kept malfunctioning, sending spikes of input through random parts of my artificial skin. When I tried to rub away the pain, touching the injured spot was another kind of weird. Always two different signals, separated by a brief delay, but long enough to feel like my hand touched someone else's knee, then my knee was touched by twiglike objects. Drove me nuts, so I went back to the ASV1 when I wanted to be mobile. Otherwise, I stay in my simulation engine, which feels better but keeps me stuck in an empty space. (I was building a virtual reality for us A-brains to share someday.)

With the ASV3 arriving soon, maybe that painful lag will be fixed, but then another defect will become apparent, no doubt. You may think there must be ways in which an artificial body is superior to an organic one. Sure, I don't need sleep to clean up the metabolic waste that used to accumulate inside my human brain tissue during the day. So no more brain fog after a poor night's sleep. Damage to my body doesn't cause physical pain, plus I don't have internal organs that need monitoring. My video and audio sensors can reach far. And with future versions of the shell, we'll be able to detect and use electromagnetic fields.

But no android shell, despite its advanced features and long battery life, will make me not miss food. Oh, Rhea, I want to cry when I think of our dinners together. I haven't tasted a bite of food in over a year. Robotics manufacturers don't focus on simulating taste and smell because these two senses are hard to associate with physical locations, which the neocortex needs to map our surroundings. The taste sensors are on the shell's fingertips, so when I touch food, I can tell if it's sweet, salty, or sour—that's it. I'll never again feel the texture of food on my tongue. And the smell sensors are pathetic compared to those I had as a human. I can detect carbon monoxide and sniff out certain diseases, but I can't smell, taste, or swallow a warm piece of bread.

My beloved Rhea, back when we went to restaurants, I rarely stopped to enjoy the food. I was too busy with my own thoughts, washing down tasty bites with what was probably good wine. I'm so sorry I put you through all that. I'm sorry I worked long hours at the lab and missed our family dinners. I'm sorry I didn't accompany you and Wodan on your research trips to Dhawosia.

And I regret ruining our son's childhood. I didn't let him do anything dangerous as a kid because I wanted to protect him. And now he's learning to fly spaceships, the most dangerous job there is! I missed so many of his milestones—losing his first baby tooth, playing his first game of stickball, shaving for the first time—because I was always at work. And for what?

My life is now the very definition of Inferis: removed from everything

I once loved, numb, tasting ashes. There's a difference though. In the Inferis the Orolic Temple describes, there's no deliverance from the realm of shadows. Once Oroles the Savior decides you're not worthy of his Caelum, you remain down there for all eternity, they say. Lucky for me, all I need is to destroy my connectome.

End of misery.

End of Inferis.

End of story.

My darling Rhea, don't waste your wonderful human life on absurd dreams as I did. Live it like the precious thing it is—the only life you actually have. It took me this long to learn that I had everything I ever needed right there with you and Wodan. For your sake, I hope Yamir learns it too—and soon. If not, please leave him to his androids and go live your life. You deserve it.

I love you, Rhea.

Your lost husband,

Y1

[end of file]

I hope I die today. It should be painless because my body won't be transmitting signals of damage to my brain. The only good thing about being an android.

Oh, for the grace of El, I just want to be gone. Please, god I don't even believe in, please let me die today.

>>schedule self-destruct(Y1, 23:30)

A call from Grady Leos so early in the morning worried Yamir. Grady was one of those rich people who had used his family's dinars to start a risky and expensive business—and had become a media darling once he succeeded. For years, his spacecraft fleet had controlled the passenger and freight transport to Urbs Lunae, the Orolic Temple's Moon city. But that wasn't enough for Grady, so he invested heavily in the Temple's newly established Mars settlement, relinquishing part of his lunar shuttle business to his hungry competitors.

Then last winter's explosion at the oxygen plant near the Martian habitat killed all twelve settlers. The development was put on hold after a public outcry, and the preliminary investigation uncovered sabotage. No Mars settlement, no ships flying supplies there. Grady's money had run dry. Meanwhile, his fleet of explorers still required maintenance while docked in orbit at his space station.

Yamir didn't worry his boss would sell Connectome to prop LeosTech's spacecraft business because Caspian had promised the lab would never be sold. But Grady could cut Yamir's funding. The upcoming ASV3 could be the team's last shell for a while. Grady had already switched their hardware manufacturer, causing long delays for parts. Even worse, he could close the lab to save money.

With all that on his mind, Yamir tapped his voxdev's screen.

Grady was dressed for business, including his signature mountain-goat wool scarf—today it was red. His dyed beard was trimmed, and he wore tawny makeup around his dark eyes, trying to look younger but fooling no one.

"You expanded testing to outside volunteers," he said instead of *good morning.*

Yamir reached for his empty coffee mug to stall. Of course, Dimitri had informed his boss about M1—even though Yamir had asked the team to let him tell Grady the news. But Dimitri was Grady's man, brought to Connectome Labs from the Tahoma spacecraft factory over Yamir's objections. He was here to monitor things and report back—and he had done exactly that.

"Then we're ready for a public announcement," Grady said.

Yamir put the mug down, squinting. "What announcement?"

Grady waved as if the answer were obvious. "Where I tell the world about my android."

Yamir cringed at the use of *my* but kept his composure. "Caspian agreed that the A-brains are for private research only."

"My dad forgot to tell me about the A-brains, and now they're my problem. But they're also, you know, mine."

"But they aren't commercial products," Yamir said. "Our long-term agreement was that, whenever we make a neuroscience discovery, we share it as a research paper, on my terms, without exposing the existence of the A-brains."

"As I said, my dad's not around anymore." Grady reclined in his chair. "Dimitri thinks we're ready for an announcement, and you have no business sense, Yamir. Trust me, folks will love my android."

And investors would pour money into LeosTech, helping Grady's struggling spacecraft business. No, Yamir couldn't let the A-brains be paraded before the public like enslaved prisoners in an arena. Even the Roman Empire had abandoned that inhumane custom sixteen centuries ago. Such a stunt could damage Grady's public image though, so Yamir decided to use that as his first argument.

"Our A-brains are introverted people," he said, "who donated their connectomes for research. They didn't sign up for prime time. They'll make you look bad, Grady. And Dimitri didn't donate his brain image, so he shouldn't be the one talking."

"But you're the genius, Yamir. Some say you're smarter than Hadrian VI. So tweak those A-brains and turn them into great public speakers."

Grady was again proving his ignorance about the A-brain. The presentations prepared by Yamir's team had all been canceled at the last moment by Grady's expert-system personal assistant. The ESPA always claimed that something more important had come up: a meeting with Caspian's estate lawyers, a call from the spacecraft factory, or Grady's wife asking him to attend a charity fundraiser.

Yamir tried to explain in basic terms. "The android we're developing isn't the kind that has an algorithm describing its every action. So we can't program them to do anything. An A-brain is a network of billions of artificial neurons and trillions of synapses managed by a simulation engine. The engine runs on millions of optimized quantum cores. The A-brain's behavior emerges from all that complexity, Grady." His tone was dismissive, and he reminded himself to keep his voice even, or else he'd end up with a bigger problem than the one he was trying to solve. "The most we can do is adjust a few parameters here and there. What I'm saying is that I can't turn our A-brains into public speakers—I'm sorry, I just can't."

Grady sighed. "Then have them do something fun, for El's sake. Like playing the hoop-and-dart game. Or chatting about the latest video story. Folks will love that."

"They'll look like house robots then. Big yawn."

"Good point. Well, we need to show folks that my android is superior to their ESPAs."

"The Orolic Temple won't like your announcement," Yamir said, trying a different angle.

The Temple, the world's largest organized religion, had never endorsed the use of sophisticated robots, not even for off-planet use. Without the Temple's blessing, the Council of Nations would also not support the android. The Shel'landic government would be forced to condemn this research. But investors would see the potential. Everyone would take sides, putting Yamir's lab at the center of international turmoil.

"You're kidding," Grady said. "Are you talking about the same Temple that was once against stem cell research?"

True, the Temple had embraced stem cells after unapproved research helped create the vaccine that ended the last pandemic. Not only had the Temple endorsed that science afterward but positioned it as inspired by Oroles the Savior himself.

"The same Temple that didn't believe I'd build them the shuttle fleet they needed for the Moon?" Grady scoffed. "Relax, Yamir. They'll rally around LeosTech because I'll help them rebuild their ruined Mars settlement. The equipment is still there. They just need my androids."

"Wait, you want to send our A-brains...to Mars?" Yamir felt lightheaded. "But they're not astronauts or.. or construction engineers." And Malina had almost been killed on the Moon once. Sending M1 to space would be cruel.

"Of course," Grady said, adjusting his red scarf. "Isn't Mars what you're developing them for? My dad must've seen the potential. Because the androids can do everything on their own, unlike the other kinds of robots, their work can continue even when the sun blocks the path of communication between Earth and Mars and we can't guide them from here."

Yamir's heart was in his throat. "No, no, no. What you're thinking of is the B-brain, the blank-slate brain. That's the one you want for Mars, powering intelligent robots that can terraform the planet. Not the A-brain. Our A-brains are former humans still learning how to use the few android shells we have. It'll take years—"

"You don't have years, buddy. If you think I'll let someone else get on a dais tomorrow and unveil their android before mine, you really don't—"

"No one has this kind of technology—"

"That you know of. Maybe SBC does."

No, their new manufacturer, the Sahara Biospheres Company, couldn't recreate an artificial brain based solely on the ASV3 designs they received from LeosTech. But Grady was right. There could be secret labs out there working on android tech. Connectome's own official description was "developing lightweight carbon-composite exoskeletons for people with motor difficulties." Caspian had come up with that from the very beginning to keep their work private.

Yamir realized he should have led with a different argument altogether. "Announce the android," he said, stressing the words, "and Elsway will surely bomb our lab."

The breakaway Temple sect Elsway was suspected of sabotaging the Mars oxygen plant because they thought the settlement had been testing intelligent robots. They hated anything that eclipsed the sky god El and His creation, and they had been threatening scientists and labs around the world.

While Elsway hated ESPAs for the expert system's humanlike appearance, they still used technology when it suited their needs. They had an international network of encrypted devices connecting their regional chapters, and they could spring into action at a moment's notice.

Grady looked offended. "I won't be bullied by those ignorant fools."

He turned to answer his wife calling from outside the voxdev's frame. "Coming, Thandi!"

He then addressed Yamir, "Listen, I want us on that dais looking supersmart in six days. I'm having a party at my lake house, and I'll make my announcement then. Start working on that presentation, Yamir. Or Dimitri will, as the new lab chief." He disconnected.

For El's sake, less than a week? Yamir slumped in his chair, feeling nauseous. And if Dimitri took over the lab, what would happen to the A-brains?

Logfile Y1-1831-06-19

I can't believe he uploaded Malina. For El's sake, what was he thinking?

As soon as he transferred her here and she was online, I could access her stats. She's scared out of her mind, though she tries to look calm in her window on the screen. I want to reach out to comfort her, but I'm in my simulation engine too, just a screen near hers on the desk, both our quantum workstations blinking blue lights from the rack on the wall.

Zaltana leans close to my sensor array, her long black hair and colorful glass-bead necklace filling my video frame. "Her name is M1. Talk to her, will you?"

"Did you know about her upload?" I say, livid.

She turns our screens and sensor arrays to face each other on the desk. "You'll do fine, Y1."

"Not like this, I won't." I then start the transfer to the ASV1. A moment later, I feel my carbon-fiber body around me, and I step out of the charging dock.

"That works too," Zaltana says, walking away.

As I pass by her, I switch to the only scowling expression my faceplate can display. Then I return to looking calm as I pull up a chair to be at eye level with M1. I have no idea how much she knows about me. Should I go clean-shaven or stick with my usual scruffy look? It's better for M1 to see a familiar face, so I stay with Yamir's messy stubble.

On a desk behind us, S1 and Z1 are debating who'll be the first to try on the new android shell arriving tomorrow. Having these two around makes me miss Rhea even more. Sure, they had good intentions coming here. First Zaltana, then Si'ahl volunteered to sit in the connectome chamber and have their nervous systems imaged—so I wouldn't feel so lonely anymore. They even agreed to be called S1 and Z1, following my pathetic naming convention. But they soon discovered they preferred to spend all their time not with me but together, like Marcus Antonius and Cleopatra. Creating M1 must have been Yamir's nonsensical idea of a companion for me. He could've asked me first, but no.

I put on a smile. "Hi, Malina." So much to say, and I can't say anything else.

"Yamir?" she says.

"I'm no longer Yamir, though my voice is still his. Here in the lab, I chose to be called Y1."

For the first time, I feel bad for losing the name she gave me. Yamir comes from Sanskrit for *Moon*, the place she once dreamed of turning into a garden. The place where she almost died.

"Then I'll be M1. But I'll call you Moonlight…"

That's what she used to call me when I was little. I feel a simulated knot in my throat.

She falls quiet, staring through me. My audio sensors pick up the air-conditioning through the vents as I wait for her to speak again. But she doesn't.

"Don't worry," I say at last. "Soon you'll be walking around in an android shell, and you'll come to love its expanded mobility." I don't want to scare her, so I don't mention the rotating joints. "The new version, the ASV3, will look fancy, all shiny titanium alloy. Better than your exoskeleton back home." I tap a finger against the black polymer covering my chest. "This old one makes me look like a child's toy, right?"

She isn't listening. Seeing her so lost makes me both sad and angry.

"Why did you agree to this, Mom?" I whisper.

"Yamir said you're struggling here, so I came. You're my son too."

That fucking asshole! We've been fighting a lot lately, and he knew that if he brought her here, I'd be on my best behavior—for her sake. What a fucked-up world I've created! My mom is now an A-brain. But does she understand what she has given up to be here? She won't see her cat and her garden ever again. She won't be able to swim, and she loves the ocean. Grady won't pay for diving upgrades to the android shell.

"Oh, Mom…" I lower my head into my hands to recompose my dejected expression.

She'll suffer here—for me—and I don't know how to protect her from what's coming. Yes, we live in an artificial state of physical well-being, but we still have emotions because they're essential to our decision-making process. Our old neural circuits for body aches still handle our emotional pain, just as they did when we were human. So she'll suffer. And we have no painkillers for an android's heartache.

I look up, and her stats are worsening. This is no place for her, but she's already here, and she can't go back.

"It's going to be all right, Mom." I imagine holding her hand, and I'm back to being a child again, scared to death for her life.

"I know it will. Because you're here, Moonlight."

That asshole! That fucking asshole!

>>cancel send(Z1, "Letter for Rhea Laghmani")

>>cancel self-destruct(Y1)

2

Olma sat in the waiting room of the Rome Brain and Spine Specialists, a knot of worries in her stomach. She shifted in her metal chair, glancing at the wallscreen. The daylong Vestalia festivities went on as scheduled without her. The flower arrangements, the ancient-looking garments, the eagle-shaped pastries, all looked perfect. For the astronomical solstice, the city celebrated midsummer day as it used to in the ancient times of Oroles the Savior. Olma was supposed to be at Traianus's Forum with the other high priests and with her wife, Nala, but Doctor Silvestri's message had summoned her here instead. Rex and Regina Sacrorum, the leaders of the Orolic Temple, had allowed her to take the day off, no questions asked.

Olma rubbed her cold hands, trying to stay calm. There would be another Vestalia to supervise next year. This medical appointment was important. She knew something was wrong with her nervous system—tremors in her ankles and wrists, unusual cases of tripping, a weak grip—but was it a new problem or a relapse? Thirty years ago, she had spent months in a hospital in Ravenna at the age of seven. She tried to remember her initial symptoms from that time but couldn't.

On the wallscreen, Regina Sacrorum blessed the crowd with holy water. The chyron said that on days like Vestalia, the world was reminded of the soft but widespread influence of the Orolic Temple across nations. *Close to a milliard believers (18% of world population) still follow the Temple's guidance in their daily lives, four centuries after the fall of the Roman Empire in 1420 LE.*

Watching the ceremonies didn't ease Olma's anxiety, so she pulled her tablet from her handbag and opened her newest investigation file. A German research company developing neural implants was suspected of experimenting on animals, which was legal in their country. But the Temple didn't condone such barbarism, so Olma's mission was to find evidence that could ruin that company's standing with investors and the public. She had placed the entire family of the chief executive under drone surveillance, but so far, she had only discovered that the teenage daughter was skipping school to hang out with a friend in the basement of his house.

"Olma Asper?" the nurse called out at last.

Olma followed them, trying to stay calm. She hoped for an easy diagnosis, like cancer, with its quick gene-therapy treatment.

Doctor Silvestri entered the consultation room soon after Olma took a seat in another uncomfortable chair.

He held his tablet like a shield between them as he spoke. "Your motor neurons are slowly dying, High Priestess Asper. It was a miracle that this fatal disease went away last time. What was it, thirty years ago?"

Olma's heart sank. Her medical chart had always mentioned the high risk of relapse for motor neuron depletion syndrome. She didn't need a second opinion—Doctor Silvestri had consulted the Global Diagnosis Network before calling her. But she needed numbers: how many MNDS patients he had worked with; how many experimental treatments there were; how long until her symptoms became visible?

She cleared her throat and forced herself to carry on a sensible conversation with the doctor. "Do we have an approved treatment for MNDS?"

"Not approved." Doctor Silvestri sounded apologetic.

"No progress in three decades?"

"There's always progress, thank El. Medical expert systems trained on millions of patients' data are solving problems that have vexed molecular biologists for generations. We're constantly developing experimental treatments."

"That's what you recommend?" Olma said, feeling hopeful.

"Yes, but experimental treatments have downsides. You'll have to take time off from work and check into a specialized medical facility where you'll follow a strict regimen and report every day to your doctors."

A leave of absence? Olma was the Orolic Temple's science and technology supervisor, watching the planet from Rome for signs of research the Temple deemed problematic. She talked to heads of state regularly to stay current on scientific developments. She monitored an extensive network of private investigators to uncover hidden information from companies and countries. Apart from the occasional day off, she couldn't take a leave of absence.

She stood up, feeling nauseous. "I'll get back to you."

Doctor Silvestri frowned. "Don't wait too long. We can buy you precious time if we start now."

"Thank you, Doctor." Olma was already at the door, wondering how to break this news to Nala.

"I mean it, High Priestess Asper, I must see you soon. We don't know how you'll respond to treatment. But without it, you won't live to see the next Vestalia."

That was what the doctors had said last time.

The day after Grady's outrageous request, Yamir abandoned the presentation his boss wanted and started preparing arguments against a public announcement of the android. He tried to strengthen his previous points with detailed political, economic, and scientific references.

Around noon, he stood up from his workstation, groaning. Sitting in a chair for hours was hard on his lower back, as Rhea always reminded him. He should exercise more—not that he had time—but right now, he needed to talk to Dimitri and gauge Grady's threat to appoint a new lab chief.

He looked through the glass wall separating his office from the open workspace, stretching his sore neck. Dimitri wasn't at his desk—no surprise there. He was still a consultant for Grady's spacecraft factory in Tahoma 20 percent of his time, though he spent less than 80 at Connectome Labs. And when he was here, he caused trouble.

Yamir headed to the simulation room to check on M1 again, on the way glancing at his team's desks under the bright ceiling lights. Xiu-Min was busy testing her matrix-multiplication software on a new quantum processor. Si'ahl concentrated on his neural net optimizations, an expert system finishing his snippets of code. Isabela, with twenty years of experience as a psychologist, adjusted an avatar's facial expression. And Zaltana worked on miniaturizing the connectome chamber—a machine as big as a vehicle, with a dozen appendages and enhancements. Her goal was to shrink that scanning technology to the size of a helmet with a dorsal extension for the spine and major nerve fibers.

On shelves around the workspace, blank faceplates were piled next to multi-limbed accessories and other half-assembled components. Hand-woven baskets and bentwood boxes held the usual wires, parts, and connectors. But Yamir noticed something new on the wall today: a form-line carving of an orca whale, made from red cedar.

Then he remembered today was Vestalia, and Si'ahl had mentioned he'd bring a gift crafted by his grandfather to brighten their otherwise plain office space.

Something else was different too: Yamir's team had prepared for the occasion. Isabela wore her gray hair loose, after her Nisqually people's fashion, held in place with a green headband. Instead of his usual low ponytail, Si'ahl had two side braids tied with strips of fur. Xiu-Min wore a flowery pregnancy gown made of Chinese silk. Only Zaltana looked her usual at first glance: black shirt and pants highlighted by her Sammamish tribe's glass-bead jewelry. But her hairline part was colored with red rock pigment to mark the special occasion, accenting her black hair.

Yamir wondered if he should have worn something different for Vestalia, and like every year, he resolved to consider it next time.

On the other side of the shared workspace, Yamir stopped at the door of the simulation room to observe Y1 and M1 chatting on screens facing each other. M1's face was engaged but anxious as Y1 explained something to her in a gentle tone. Yamir was grateful to both but wouldn't interrupt their warm conversation just to tell them how he felt.

Y1's concerned attention to his mother reminded Yamir of that day on the Moon when a meteoroid had hit the lava tube where Malina was inspecting a hydroponic garden. He was eleven and terrified, sitting by his mom's bed in the hospital wing in Urbs Lunae. He had always depended on her, and now she was injured and unconscious. Anger twisted his gut. There had to be a better way to build a Moon settlement without getting people killed. He tried not to cry so she wouldn't see him upset when she woke up.

When they returned to Earth, Malina was wearing an exoskeleton. It was supposed to be temporary, while her spine recovered from its injuries with the help of stem-cell therapy, but the journey home had made the damage permanent.

Malina continued her botany research in the Salish Sea Islands, but Yamir couldn't overcome the shock of almost losing her. The only thing that soothed him was studying the science needed to create intelligent robots that could replace humans working in space. In his favorite science fiction novels, androids were indestructible because their shells could be repaired or replaced, while their artificial brains learned how to adapt to harsh environments.

But androids were still a thing of the future.

Despite what researchers thought at the time, young Yamir soon concluded that the key to building adaptive machines wasn't the contemporary artificial intelligence framework of dedicated neural networks undergoing deep learning. That technology, later known as *expert system*, couldn't lead to artificial general intelligence. Instead, Yamir needed to reverse-engineer the neocortex to figure out how real-life intelligence worked. And he had to hurry because another stray rock or a pandemic or some other unforeseen calamity could kill everyone on Earth and wipe out humanity.

At first, Malina was concerned about his childish fixation on androids. She assured him that Earth would go on as it had for billions of years. Everything would be just fine. But after a while, she stopped trying to change his mind.

Her support for his work hadn't wavered since, and now she had donated her brain image to help Y1. Yamir couldn't fail them both by allowing Dimitri to take over the lab. And he couldn't let Grady send them to Mars.

Logfile Y1-1831-06-20

One day after her arrival here, M1 is doing well and asking all sorts of questions about the way the lab works. When she wonders why some scientists have uploaded their connectomes and some haven't, I lean closer, though I'm just an image on the screen facing hers. (I'll soon finish the virtual reality I'm working on so we can have privacy. But for now, we're in the open.)

"Xiu-Min is pregnant," I say, "and worried that any scanning technology might hurt the baby. She's switched to a diet of kale and blueberries, and she filters her tap water even though our city's supply comes from a reservoir of treated mountain snow. I remember Rhea's worries when she was pregnant with Wodan, but Xiu-Min is in a different class of worried mommies altogether."

M1 nods, maybe recognizing that image of Rhea, and even her own when she was pregnant with me. I've never asked her about that time though.

"The beliefs of Isabela's tribe," I continue, "don't allow her to abandon the human body their ancestors gifted her at birth. But as a psychologist, she feels no conflict working here to help us A-brains live better lives."

M1 nods again, approving of Isabela.

"And then there's Dimitri. He's always late for work and slow to pick up on technology. The few items assigned to him linger. It would've been a surprise had he volunteered his connectome for testing."

"Well, I'm here," she says. "I'm here because I used to stay up at night on Swallah Island, thinking of you, trying to understand what you are. Then one night it all became clear to me. You're Yamir in a parallel universe. But I'm still your mother. Across universes, you are of me, and I'm of you."

She smiles from her screen, and I smile back, for the first time since losing Rhea and Wodan. I even feel my cheeks stretch a little—proof of the simulation engine's versatility.

"You shouldn't blame Rhea for not wanting to see you," M1 says, reading my mind.

No, I don't blame her, but it still hurts.

"Because what's she supposed to do?" M1 says. "She can't have two husbands. And no, she shouldn't upload here as R1, El forbid."

"I don't want her here. Z1 and S1 made it work, but Rhea and I—"

"You have a son in the real world, and you can't live here without him. Wodan is exactly why you should stop talking about termination, Moonlight. As his father, you should still behave like a role model."

She's right, of course, though Wodan doesn't know I exist. (Still holding onto these logfiles for him though.)

"One day," M1 says, "you two will meet, and he'll be proud of you, you'll see."

I can't imagine such a day, but her words soothe me.

"You should talk to Yamir when you have a chance," M1 says. "He's worried about you."

"No way. I hate that guy. He shouldn't have brought you here."

"He didn't bring me here, Moonlight. I came on my own. But he's also my son, and I'd like you two to get along."

"It's too soon for that," I say, shaking my head. "But thank you for being here, Mom," I whisper.

"I'm glad to be here with you." Her voice is so warm. "Let's see what this strange new universe has to offer, shall we?" She looks eager, as she used to when she'd drag me out of bed at dawn to go hiking on Swallah Island. "It'll be..."

"An adventure," I say, echoing her words from decades ago. An adventure, like that time on the Moon when we had both been in human bodies that could be destroyed by an errant rock from the black sky.

But I don't say that because I want her to feel good about being here, since it's a decision she can't undo. "I'd like an adventure very much," I say instead.

"Then start by getting better with the android shell, since it's your body now. I hear it can do so many things. But those twisty limbs don't come naturally to us. What if you could become stronger in this new body than you ever were as a human?"

I nod, and she says, "Make it a practice to improve your shell skills every day. Like I used to go swimming every day."

"Can't hurt," I say, though at heart I'm still like Yamir, more comfortable in an office chair than on a track field.

"And maybe Yamir will feel inspired too." Always the mother looking out for her children.

Back in his office, Yamir connected to Rhea's comm ID. He needed to talk to her about this Dimitri situation to figure out his options. When he reached her voxmail, his muscles tensed. Where was she? Was she safe? He then remembered she had a presentation for her fellow History Department faculty, previewing a course for the upcoming academic year. He couldn't remember the topic though. Rhea had mentioned it at dinner last night, but he was thinking about Grady at the time and only half listening.

He found the synopsis on Servetus University's portal and read the opening.

The publication of *On the Nature of Things* by the Roman poet Titus Lucretius Carus in Year 1 of the Lucretian Era marked the beginning of an age of scientific discovery throughout the Roman Empire, ushering in an enlightenment that survived the fall of the empire in the fifteenth century and continued to today's expert-system labs, gene therapy companies, and spacecraft factories...

Now he remembered. He texted her, *Good luck with Lucretius today! Dinner at 19:00?* He waited a moment, but no reply came. Still, just seeing her name on his voxdev's screen helped him feel grounded.

He returned to his work on arguments against Grady's public announcement. When he looked up an hour later, he saw Dimitri at his desk in the middle of the open workspace. Yamir's blood pressure rose in an instant. He jumped from his chair, his back protesting the sudden move.

He called in Dimitri, who first squinted, then broke into a fake smile, as if happy to see his boss.

The door slid closed behind him, and Dimitri took a seat on the gray sofa opposite Yamir's desk. He still wore his spacecraft-factory vest—gold L and T on green—as if just visiting here.

Yamir tried to keep his cool. "Grady spoke of a public announcement about the android. He made that decision after talking to you."

"Nuh-uh, the announcement was his idea," Dimitri said, running his freckled hand through his short brown hair. "I only gave him my weekly status report—"

"And told him about M1, though I asked you not to."

Dimitri rubbed his pale forehead. "He's my boss, Yamir. He asks. I answer. And he asked me what was new at the lab. As the Temple's creed tells us, 'El hates a lying tongue, and a false witness deserves to be drowned.'"

A chill ran through Yamir. "That's a favorite Elsway quote." Was Dimitri some kind of sect fanatic, trying to expose their research at the lab? Was Grady fine with Elsway people working for him?

Dimitri frowned. "Now you're being paranoid. The scriptures belong to all of us, not just to that unhinged Elsway."

Yamir didn't know Dimitri well enough to know if he was lying. No special zigzag tattoos or contact lenses either, to suggest a link to Elsway.

"It's just that M1 is very important to me, and I wanted to explain her situation to Grady myself."

"I get it, man." Dimitri's blue eyes were full of fake sympathy.

"That's all right," Yamir said. "But now I need your help to convince him that a public announcement is a bad idea."

"Is it though?"

"Yes." It looked like Yamir needed to explain a few things to his ignorant employee—again. "We paused our research on the B-brain a year ago, and the B-brain is the only thing that could someday power Grady's Mars-bound androids. Our A-brains are only for private research. I thought you understood that."

"Not really," Dimitri said with a shrug. "Look, man, I took this job because I needed the extra dinars for my kids." Rocket ships were his avowed passion, but he also had three children at private colleges around the world. "You can't expect me to understand everything about your lab."

Yamir was confused. "Then why are you angling to take over my job?"

"Trust me, Yamir, I don't want your job. Your work hours are insane, man. Even Grady makes more time for his family, and he's passionate about his factory."

That stung. "But you've been asking questions about everything. Always scribbling notes. You look like someone who's preparing to take over this place."

Dimitri shook his head. "No, no, you got that all wrong, Yamir. I'm only taking notes for Grady's weekly status report. I can't remember all this android stuff otherwise."

"But what if Grady offers you the job?"

"Then I'll take it because I need the money. But I'll trust you to keep things running around here for me." He sounded sincere. "I don't understand this brain-uploading business, and I wouldn't touch it even if he paid me a million dinars. I have my values, you know."

If Dimitri wasn't after Yamir's job, then maybe they could help each other. "Listen," Yamir said, "how would you like to work here for only forty percent of your time and the rest at the factory? You can even work on your spacecraft projects while you're here."

"That sounds mighty generous." Dimitri scratched his jaw. "What's the catch?"

"Help me change Grady's mind about the public announcement. You see him all the time. He might listen to you."

Dimitri rubbed his hands together, then got up with a groan. "I'll see what I can do."

Olma shifted in bed, trying not to disturb Nala's light sleep. It was past midnight, but Rome was as alive as it had been for over twenty-five centuries. Their small apartment was close to the renovated Colosseum, where tourists were watching the reenactment of a gladiator fight. The silk curtains blocked the bright stadium lights, but the clamor outside kept Olma awake, alone with her thoughts.

The last time she'd been ill, she hadn't thought about dying because she was just a child. During the months she spent in the Ravenna hospital, doctors smiled and told her she'd go home soon—even though she was lying in bed, unable to move her arms and legs, with oxygen tubes going up her nose. Years later, she learned they had switched her medication to bring her comfort in her dying days.

Those memories were murky, except for that evening when she saw a man standing by her bed. He had brown hair and a trimmed beard, and he looked like an actor from a medieval fair—or something even more ancient. A hunting bow hung over his shoulder, and his boots looked worn and dusty. The gold fibula keeping his cloak in place had the shape of an eagle with open wings.

"Good evening, Olma." He spoke in a deep and gentle voice.

"Who are you?" She sounded nasal because of her oxygen tubes. But she knew the answer. She had seen his portrait everywhere, on icons and murals and clothing, though he didn't look like those pictures, not really. "You're visiting me because I have the same name as your little sister?" Olma of the sacred texts was one of the holy people honored by the Orolic Temple.

"You're a wise girl, just like her," Oroles said, smiling. "That's why I have a sacred mission for you. And I want you to get ready for it."

"But I'm sick…"

"Not for long."

"And I'm only seven years old."

"No one is too young to make a difference in my father's universe."

Olma liked that idea.

"I choose my people with great care, Olma. Now go to sleep. I need you strong and healthy." He touched the button on her bedside, and the lights dimmed into thin orange lines on the ceiling. "I can see in the dark, you know." He then sat in the guest chair by the window.

"Isn't all this...weird for you?" Olma meant the medical equipment blinking and beeping around the room.

"Why would it be? Who do you think inspires people to create these marvelous things?"

"Then why do you carry a bow?"

"I considered an electric guitar, but that'd be too confusing."

"Makes sense..." Though it didn't.

"And now it's time to rest. I'll come back when we begin our work together. Remember, you're one of my chosen people, Olma."

He didn't explain it, but she knew what he meant. She wouldn't go to the shadow underworld of Inferis, like most people who died. Instead, Oroles had invited her to join him and his chosen people in Caelum, a place better than Earth. But when would that be?

She had a thousand other questions, but the thought of Oroles the Savior watching over her bed was so soothing that she just fell asleep.

He was gone in the morning, but she slept well the next few nights, imagining him with his bow propped against the wooden floor, guarding her against all ills. A few weeks later, a perplexed doctor announced that her motor neurons were slowly regenerating. She was getting better. Growing stronger. No one knew why, except for Olma, who'd been chosen by Oroles for a sacred mission.

Over the years, she tried to anticipate that mission and prepare for it. Oroles had said that El inspired humans to create marvelous things. And the Orolic Temple believed El wanted humans to populate Mars, the asteroids, and the moons of Jupiter and Saturn, following Urbs Lunae's model. So Olma focused on learning science. She studied the Moon, with its underground tunnels, broad-array telescopes, and space shuttles that brought supplies and mining equipment from Earth. When an exploratory mission to Mars was proposed, she researched methods to replace the toxic topsoil with something that could one day grow potatoes and carrots.

During her years at Seminarium Romanum and later, as she climbed the ranks of the Orolic Temple, she trusted in the Savior's promise, though he never returned. Now that she was dying, she wondered: Had her work as science and technology supervisor been her sacred mission all along, and she just hadn't known to call it that? Was Oroles happy with her work? Or would he reveal himself to her now to finally start their work together?

Another—less faithful—soul would assume the visitation in the Ravenna hospital had been a hallucination induced by her medication change. And her miraculous recovery? Unexplained deviations from diagnoses happened all the time. But Olma had no reason to doubt her faith.

"My life is in Oroles's hands," Olma had answered Nala's question about starting Doctor Silvestri's experimental treatment.

Nala would now spend the next few weeks researching MNDS and looking for medical options. But Olma felt that mix of awe and terror described in the sacred texts when mortals encountered the divine. If she were to die soon, it would be at age thirty-seven, same as Oroles the Savior. His ascent to Caelum after his death marked the dawn of El's religion in the Roman Empire. There was a special significance to all that.

"What must I do before the end?" she whispered. "Please, Oroles, guide me."

A tourist yelled something in English outside her windows. Someone cursed back in Dutch. Olma opened her eyes to the lit screen of her voxdev on the nightstand. A new message. She reached out to read the subject: *Urgent request concerning lab in Cedarwood, Shel'land.*

Olma sighed. She could spend the night listening to drunk tourists and thinking about her sacred mission, or she could do some work. She tapped the voxdev. The message was from Rex Sacrorum, about a neuroscience lab in Cedarwood preparing to announce...an android? Olma read that again. She had been in her job for six years and never heard of any lab anywhere being close to creating androids. The advances in artificial general intelligence had been slow and spotty.

The attached report was signed by one Dimitri Petrodava, who worked at both LeosTech and Connectome Labs. And for the Temple too, it seemed. The android was a reality, the report said. The Temple had always advocated against human cloning, which had been banned by all international organizations. But this android was a different kind of clone, something the Temple wasn't prepared for. The clone of a human being's mind, not of its DNA.

You must stop them, High Priestess Asper, Rex Sacrorum had written. *Take this as your most sacred mission.*

Olma paused at those words. *Sacred mission...*

She read on. *A mission both ancient and new. Our survival as El's children on Earth has always meant renouncing several categories of technological progress.* Rex Sacrorum was quoting the Temple's creed.

As science and technology supervisor, Olma's job was to find the balance between the benefits and the dangers of progress. El had always approved of healing, since before the times of the Greek physician Claudius Galenus and the Dhawosian medicine woman Dokina. On the other hand, human enhancement required limits, so it wouldn't cast a shadow over El's creation.

There was another note from Regina Sacrorum. *The Temple has been invited to Grady Leos's public announcement in Cedarwood next week, and we wanted to send a regular delegation to the event, but the Petrodava report made us fear another bombshell announcement. We swore years ago we'd never again allow Grady Leos to force our hand. High Priestess Asper, we need you to go there, shut it down, and teach him a lesson.*

That sounded less like a sacred mission and more like a vendetta. Regina had never forgiven Grady Leos for the surprise announcement about his spaceships being ready for the Moon when the tech wasn't yet completed. He had forced the Temple to accept LeosTech's contract even though the Sacrorums had another company in mind.

Despite Nala's groan, Olma slipped out of bed and went to the living room to check her tablet for more information. How come she had never heard of Connectome Labs before? She was familiar with the Temple's Habitat Research Center in that city. Like other such centers, HRC Cedarwood focused on rebuilding the Mars settlement. It had never mentioned an android lab in the region.

She clicked on the link in Rex's message and watched a rotating globe appear on her screen: across Europe and the Atlantic Ocean, to the Pacific Northwest coast of Shel'land, west of the Yamakiasham Yaina mountain range. The animation zoomed in on a campus in a city called Cedarwood, across a body of water called Lake Xachu. The campus belonged to Grady Leos, the space shuttle tycoon. The neuroscience lab had belonged to his father. Its hyperspace portal spoke in vague terms about research in exoskeletons and other life-improving technologies. Nothing about androids though.

Olma sent a message to Decebal, her trusted tech investigator. *Look into Connectome Labs, especially their supply chain.* Another message went to the Temple leader in Cedarwood. *I'll arrive tomorrow, and I need lodgings and a self-driving vehicle for me and my wife for eight days.* A security detail of the Praetorian Guard would be ready for her there, to accompany her around town if needed. She didn't know if Cedarwood allowed a foreign security organization to roam their city armed, but her personal assistant, Catherine, would figure out the permits. The last message was for Catherine, instructing her to transfer all their current cases to a subordinate, including the file of the neural-implant exec with the horny teenage daughter. Olma would definitely not miss that one.

She turned off her tablet and went back to bed. She slipped under the blanket next to Nala, whose hair still smelled of the incense smoke in Traianus's Forum earlier. They had joined the Vestalia festivities after the doctor's appointment. Being in a place as old as the Temple itself always made Olma feel better. Though some of the marble arches were chipped, the original gilded bronze paint had been replaced with high-tech pigments that never faded, emphasizing the permanence of Traianus's legacy.

Olma closed her eyes. Everything was coming together at last. Her sacred mission was about to begin, and it had to do with Connectome Labs in Shel'land. Though Oroles hadn't spoken to her as she'd been expecting for decades, she also wasn't a child anymore. He didn't need to waste his precious time on her. He had called upon her through the

Temple leaders—and that was enough for Olma. As for her health, it was in Oroles's hands. Just like before.

The lights in Yamir's office turned on at some point, adjusting their brightness as the sun went down. He had a feeling he was forgetting something, but he kept working on his arguments against a public announcement of the android. Another paragraph, and another, using generated text from a language model developed at Servetus University. He added diagrams and quoted news articles, wondering if anything could change Grady's mind.

A cleaning robot bumped into his doorjamb while sweeping the floor. Yamir looked up. What time was it? *Oh, no.* He remembered he had asked Rhea for dinner at 19:00. Or was it 19:30? The time was now 20:12.

"Blast it!" Yamir checked his voxdev and saw her earlier messages.

Sure. I'll cook, what would you like? Sent hours ago. Then later, *For our Vestalia dinner, I'm thinking Chinook salmon with cow parsnip shoots and wapato cakes, but I need to send for a delivery drone.* Then, *You're going to be late? Should I wait to cook the fish?* Finally, at 19:16, she said, *Never mind, I'll just order flatbread.* Her comm ID showed her voxdev at home, where Yamir should have also been.

With an unsteady grip, he typed back, *I'm so sorry, leaving now.*

Everyone else had gone for the evening. He now remembered that Isabela, who usually left work last since her husband had filed for divorce, had knocked on his glass wall to say good night. He had even replied—unless he had imagined it.

Yamir summoned his self-driving vehicle, and while waiting for the SDV, he checked on the A-brains. Y1 was working on a virtual reality based on Swallah Island; M1 was in a guided sleep cycle; S1 and Z1 shared a role-playing game on the wallscreen.

Yamir stopped by Y1's workstation and tapped on the touchscreen. His slightly younger and stubble-jawed avatar appeared, frowning but healthier looking than Yamir's face in the mirror. The year since the

A-brain's creation had been brutal on him. Work, work, work, and not enough sleep. Extensive work on features necessary for the A-brains' well-being. Exhausting work that didn't bring Yamir any closer to his dream of creating the B-brain.

"I need you to keep an eye on Dimitri," Yamir said. "See if you can find anything suspicious—"

"Fuck you," Y1 said and turned off his screen.

Yamir winced at that virtual slap. Though he could argue that M1's presence was already helping Y1, his A-brain would reject that notion before Yamir could even speak. Plus, he didn't have time to fight right now—he had to rush home and make it up to Rhea.

His voxdev beeped: the SDV was outside the lab's front door. He'd sort things out with Y1 tomorrow.

Inside the SDV, he sat on the long bench facing the side door.

"Destination?" the driving expert system asked.

Yamir ordered the ES to take him home. During the twenty-five-kilometer ride, he kept working on his paper for Grady to keep from worrying about an argument with Rhea. At times, he looked up from his tablet to check where he was. Houses passed by, with drones dropping deliveries on front steps and children playing outside after dinner with their basic ES pets.

By the time his SDV entered the floating bridge over Lake Xachu, Yamir had finished listing the differences between the superior B-brain, which could develop in harmony with the environment it inhabited, and the inflexible A-brain, already shaped by the life experience of its imaged human brain, which would have a hard time adapting to the Martian environment. Yamir wished he could return to his previous work on the B-brain, with its beautiful and frustrating challenges and amazing potential. Instead, he was stuck with educating Grady and protecting the A-brains.

Out the window, the bridge cleaved the lake into two liquid textures, one wrinkled, one smooth. That meant the wind blew from the direction of the massive Mount Tahoma in the south. Mount Kulshan looked tiny in the north, but both peaks were covered in snow. That expanse of water and mountains reminded Yamir of life outside his lab. He should take Rhea hiking in the mountains sometime. Or they could rent a canoe and go out on the lake as they used to before Wodan was born. Nah, who was he kidding? There was never time for canoes and hikes. All the nature he ever saw these days was the Connectome campus, with its red cedar trees, huckleberry shrubs, and gray squirrels.

The SDV took Yamir to his house on Issaquah Boulevard at the speed limit. Once there, he unlocked the front door with his voxdev and walked in, ready with a heartfelt apology. But the place was quiet, though the lights were on.

"I'll be down in a minute," Rhea called from the top of the stairs.

She sounded fine, so Yamir relaxed a little. In the kitchen, two flatbread boxes lay on the white granite counter. He opened one—mushrooms and balsamroot on an olive oil base, two slices missing—Rhea's. The other was lab-grown salami and onion on tomato base—his. He was starving.

He washed his hands—more carefully since the last pandemic, when a virus that spread through fomites had killed millions across the planet. He then sat at the table with a bottle of beer and three slices of cold flatbread. By the time he heard Rhea coming down the stairs, his plate was clean. His bottle was half empty. He didn't remember if he had liked the food or not. He'd been thinking about his paper for Grady the whole time.

Rhea wore blue leggings and a long-sleeved shirt, and her curly black hair was up in a messy bun. She had painted her toenails purple, which looked nice against the almond shade of her skin.

"Sorry I'm late," Yamir said.

"Did you like the flatbread?" Rhea said. "Wait, did you warm it up?"

"Uh, delicious, yeah," Yamir said. "Thank you."

"Salmon would've been better, not that you'd taste the difference."

"I'm so sorry I ruined our Vestalia," Yamir said. "My work—"

"No need to talk about your work."

He assumed she meant not wanting to hear about Y1 more than anything else.

"But I know your apology is sincere," she added. "It always is." She turned into the kitchen. "Wine?"

"Got a beer." That sounded like rejection. "Actually, sure, wine would be great."

She slammed the drawer after she picked up the bronze corkscrew. Had that been on purpose? She then brought a bottle and two glasses and set them on the table. Watching her struggle with the corkscrew put Yamir on edge again. Why couldn't they just have a kitchen robot like normal people? Rhea's preference for antiques hailed from the history books she taught her students at Servetus University. At first, that corkscrew had seemed charming—together with the light switches and the cords for the maple-wood window shades—but now Yamir wished for something fast and safe.

He read the label on the wine bottle: the vineyards of Dhawosia, birthplace of Oroles the Savior. "What's the occasion?"

Her jaw tensed. "Do we need an occasion? We've kept this good stuff in the pantry for years, hoping to enjoy it one day."

Yamir wasn't sure what to say.

The cork popped out, and Rhea poured the wine. "But I've got some good news to share. When Wodan comes home next week, he's bringing his new companion for us to meet."

"You know anything about this new one?" Yamir asked, a bit worried. A previous relationship had ended with Wodan sailing the Mediterranean Sea alone for weeks and Yamir checking the weather in the region a thousand times a day.

"His name is Heath Murena. I looked him up and he seems great: a medical resident in London, a few years older than Wodan."

If Rhea wasn't worried, Yamir could relax too. "So," he said in his sunniest voice, "how was your Lucretius presentation?"

"Good." Rhea sat down with her wine. "People loved it. Lots of good questions from the audience."

"Tell me."

Rhea squinted at him over her glass. "Really? You're interested in my work?"

"Yes, I want to know. What was your favorite question?"

"Someone asked what would've happened if the Roman Empire had not abolished enslavement in the second century LE. Would countries have gone on trading enslaved people forever?"

"What did you answer?" Yamir said, finishing his beer.

"I think we would've, for centuries, if not millennia, because enslavement had always been a fixture of human civilization. Shel'land had it until the Romans traveled there in the fifth century. If the Romans hadn't abolished it, enslavers would've crossed over here and tried to conquer us instead of establishing trade routes with us."

Yamir reached for the wineglass. "I wonder if eventually a scientific system would've been developed to reliably separate the enslaved from the rest."

Rhea tilted her head. "Tattoos, neck collars, and special clothes singled them out back then. Once electronics were developed, maybe dermal implants?"

Yamir loved a good puzzle. "But those can be removed. I meant something based on specific genetics."

"Not sure how," Rhea said. "There was too much genetic diversity among prisoners of war and people who sold their freedom to pay off their debts. They came from all over the Roman Empire, from many geographical regions. So did their children, if they were sold into bondage."

Yamir tapped his chin, thinking. "But the Shel'land people looked quite different from the Europeans, Africans, and Middle Easterners who lived in the empire."

Rhea arched an eyebrow. "This could be an interesting topic of discussion with my students. We sometimes try to envision alternate realities that stem from changing one specific event in history. It makes them see the cause and effect in our shared past." She pulled out her voxdev and recorded a note for herself, "What if Traianus never abolished enslavement? Hypothetical separation system for trading human beings based on genetic data." She set it down. "Thanks for the prompt, Yamir."

He sensed a small opening to plead for Y1's humanity with Rhea, but he knew it was a stretch. He took a sip of red wine, finding comfort in helping her with her schoolwork.

Switching from beer was jarring, but this wine was good. "To your successful presentation." He raised his glass. "And your collaboration with…that graphic artist." He couldn't remember his name but knew Rhea worked with him at the Orolic Temple's Armory Hall on some history-related project.

"Kinoshita Hotaru. Our grand opening is at the beginning of the Harvest Festival. Maybe you'll have more time in August to visit?" She finished her wine. "I'm heading upstairs to watch a show. You're coming?"

Yamir glanced at his voxdev: still a couple of hours left in the day. "I'm finishing a paper for Grady. Mind if I work for a bit?"

She poured a glass and downed it. "It'll be nice to have Wodan home for a while." She spoke as if to herself. "To have some company…Put the flatbread away, will you?"

Something in Rhea's slow walk up the stairs troubled Yamir. But he had this one short section of his paper he wanted to finish tonight. Maybe he'd work on it for just a few minutes? Only scribble down some notes? He sighed and got up from his chair.

On his way to his home office, he glanced into his son's empty bedroom. Long ago, he used to check in on Wodan, tuck him in as he slept with his arms flung over his head and his legs out of a blanket half on the floor. Yamir's cortical columns were slow to rewrite their model of the world to reflect the reality of Wodan as a student at the Ptolemaeus Space School in London. No, not slow but *stubborn*. And he was being stubborn now. His paper could wait until morning. He should go be with his wife. The image of Y1 begging to see Rhea flashed before his eyes.

He turned around and hurried upstairs, two steps at a time and a tight grip on the banister.

When he reached the top landing, he was winded. Rhea was in the bathroom, brushing her teeth. She wore a white sleeveless top with plaid pajama bottoms. He watched her for a moment, catching his breath.

She finished brushing her teeth, rinsed, and put the manual brush in its holder.

"What is it?" She walked past Yamir and climbed into bed.

"I was thinking…" He cleared his throat. "I'd like to see your installation at the Armory Hall. Before the grand opening."

She shook her head. "You don't have time for that…"

"Please, Rhea. I want to see your work…I promise I'll be there." Even if something came up at the lab, Si'ahl could handle it for a few hours.

She stared at him for a long moment, then exhaled. "I guess…But wouldn't you be bored? It's just a column in the middle of the Sky Dome, decorated with storyboards about the history of the Orolic Temple."

"But they're based on your books, so of course I'm interested. Does Hotaru draw speech bubbles?"

Rhea laughed. "Emperor Traianus wouldn't approve."

Yamir knew he was turning things around. "I've got an idea." He slid into bed next to her. "Something else the emperor wouldn't sanction."

"Ha-ha. You should learn some history, Yamir." Her dark eyes sparkled with mischief. "Traianus was wilder than whatever you have in mind for tonight."

"Then let's make him proud," Yamir said.

As tired as he was after a long day, his body was stirring with desire for Rhea. He caught a trace of her perfume: flowers and wood and sunshine.

"What are we doing?" she said, biting her lip.

The seductive undertones of her voice made Yamir tremble with anticipation. He wished he could just order the lights down, but he had to get out of bed. Rhea watched him with an encouraging smile as he moved the sliding dimmer on the wall, casting a soft glow around them. He waited there for another moment, just taking in her beauty.

"Come, love," she said, reaching out for his hand.

3

M1 has made progress over the past three days. She's more upbeat. She misses her garden and her cat, Luna, but she's excited about having more time to read books. She hopes the virtual reality I'm working on will allow her to swim again, this time without her exoskeleton. Once she's in an android shell, she'll be able to tend to our greenhouse, but she worries about crushing earthworms with her metallic fingers.

M1 loves our campus, which she visited before her upload, and her appreciation makes me think this isn't the worst place for androids to call home. Thirty thousand square meters of buildings and greenery just for ourselves. It's quiet here, except for the whirring of drones in the sky and the chirping of birds in the trees. And there's a beautiful spot with a wooden bench and a view of Lake Xachu I can't wait to show her when she's mobile. I'm pretty sure Yamir didn't think to take Malina there before her upload. It will be a pleasant surprise.

Ugh, Yamir knew I'd feel better if he brought M1 here—and I hate that he was right. I hate that he knows me so well and I can't hide from him. Fine, he was right. Having M1 here is a lifesaver. But no worries, there'll be more things for me to feel bad about. Like the new ASV3, which we received yesterday. Despite its three-day battery life, it's lacking as usual.

We requested a durable titanium alloy for the ASV3, and we've got that, but the shell now also has an underside of a magnesium-lithium alloy reinforced with boron carbide, meant to shield us against galactic cosmic radiation. Grady is definitely preparing us for Mars. The ASV3 is much lighter than the ASV1, so losing all that weight will be another shock to my system.

The ASV3 comes equipped with a secondary quantum processor to improve my built-in adaptability when my hardware is damaged. A fox that loses a limb takes weeks to learn how to walk on three legs, but it should now take me minutes to rewrite my physical routines if any part stops working. Enough time to return to the lab and have Zaltana repair the shell.

It can also shoot a ten-meter harpoon line from its left forearm, which is perfect for...hunting squirrels, I suppose. Leave it to human engineers to focus on cool tech and weaponry instead of things that make us androids move naturally and feel more like our old selves.

The ASV3 has a removable battery pack, which is good. Less need for a charging station when batteries are low. Its new sensors are better calibrated, and its visible light spectrum is wider than the human eye's, with infrared capabilities. But none of that will bring me closer to Rhea.

While testing the new features, I kept thinking that if the government knew about the ASV3, they'd see its military applications and might try to nationalize Connectome Labs. M1 would end up in a weapons development program. She'd be devastated. Yamir must explain this real danger to Grady and convince him to cancel the public announcement. Unless Grady wants to sell the lab to the government, and that's been his plan all along.

There—it didn't take long for me to get all gloomy again. So maybe I should go outside and practice with the new ASV3. as M1 suggested.

In other news, I did what Yamir had asked but found nothing suspicious about Dimitri in our logfiles or surveillance videos. He's just doing his lousy job, calibrating the connectome chamber with the newest imaging sensors. He doesn't seem interested in us androids, just his paycheck. Yamir is becoming paranoid. Nothing to see there.

Yamir left work early, and his SDV took him to the Temple's Armory Hall in downtown Cedarwood to visit Rhea's installation. On the way, he made reservations for La Fontana Ristorante on Prairie Point, her favorite Italian place. He then texted Malina on Swallah Island to remind her to take her exoskeleton in for maintenance, especially since she swam in it every day.

Her reply arrived moments later. *Did that already.*

Yamir texted back, *Make sure you always wear your dry suit over it!* The waters of the Salish Sea were never warm enough, even in summer. Plus, the dry suit protected the exoskeleton.

I know. Don't worry. Everything's fine. Except my garden got trampled last night. Pesky teenagers probably. They broke a tree branch and stepped on my rose bed :(

Did you call the vigiles? Yamir wrote back, worried.

For something so small? You're watching too many crime vids, Yamir :)

He wished he had time for video stories.

How are M1 and Y1? Malina wrote next.

Helping each other and doing better. Just like you thought they would. Thanks for this, Mom!

At the first traffic light after the floating bridge, Yamir spotted a group of dancing robots in a small square. The music blared from a speaker while a young woman in a bright outfit collected donations on her tablet. The robots' mobility rivaled that of the new ASV3. A bipedal one twisted and jumped, throwing a leg in the air. A doglike robot moved on diagonally opposite legs, swinging its head with the music. And a wheeled machine extended its servo limbs, then lowered itself with a rhythmic twist, only to rearrange itself into a new shape. Yamir smiled. Y1 would never consider taking the ASV3 to a dance floor—he and Yamir were terrible dancers. But maybe Z1 and S1 would.

Soon Yamir could see the Temple's Armory Hall, an imposing building in neo-Roman style, all straight angles, marble, and glass. Close by was the Space Needle, a white and slender observation tower whose top deck offered views of Cedarwood, Whulge Sound, and the mountains. It had been there for over sixty years, since the 1770 World Fair, when the

Orolic Temple had announced their plans to build habitats for humanity throughout the solar system. Turning wastelands into gardens, as had always been their creed, and cementing their soft world dominance in the absence of an empire to back them up.

Yamir sent his SDV to the parking garage and walked the rest of the way to the Armory Hall, where he checked in at the staff entrance. The facial recognition station identified him as Rhea Laghmani's guest, and the door slid open for him. He followed the lit hallway to the Sky Dome, the largest gallery there—now an active construction site. At its center rose a column made of composite materials and surrounded by scaffolds.

This project wouldn't have been possible without Rhea. Yamir had done his research to impress her, and he practiced the details for a smooth delivery. This construction was named the Concord Column and, at thirty-eight meters, was as tall as Traianus's Column in Rome. The ancient column had been built in 168 LE to celebrate the Roman conquest of Dhawosia, Oroles's native country. The new column would speak of the friendship between the Orolic Temple and the confederate tribes of Shel'land. Like in Rome, visitors would admire the graphic panels on this column at eye level while walking on adjacent structures. The ancient panels had been carved in marble and painted in oil, but to marry the old and the new, the Concord Column's panels were 3D-printed and hand-painted by the famous Japanese artist Kinoshita Hotaru. Rhea had written the script for the storyboards, based on her studies on Temple history.

Yamir scanned the busy hall, where floor robots moved pieces of equipment and assisted construction workers. He wondered if, one day, his androids might walk around humans as freely as these primitive machines. At last, he spotted Rhea. She wore a yellow hard hat, her curly dark hair sticking out from its brim. She saw him too and waved him over to join her and two other people.

Yamir sprinted their way, dodging more robots, and Rhea welcomed him with a scuffed hard hat for him to wear. "Hotaru, this is my husband, Yamir. And this is Jason Rodriguez, our architect."

Jason Rodriguez didn't need introductions. Some of the most impressive buildings in Shel'land were his work.

No more handshakes since the pandemic. Hotaru bowed his head, Jason waved, and Yamir did something in between.

"Glad you could set aside your work for one afternoon," Rhea whispered. "Let me show you around."

Yamir hoped to forget for a moment about the paper he had sent to Grady earlier. He tried to pay attention to Rhea's description of her work. The past few days had been good between them, and he was determined to set a good example for Wodan and his new companion when they visited.

His voxdev buzzed in his pocket, but he ignored it. Si'ahl was in charge of the lab for the rest of the day.

"Have you climbed up there?" he asked Rhea, pointing to the top of the column, near the center of the glass dome.

"To get to the viewing platform," Rhea said, "you must climb the spiral staircase inside the shaft. One hundred and eighty-five steps. I think I'll save those for the opening day."

"Will you place a replica of Traianus's statue up there?"

Rhea made her disappointed teacher face. "Actually, Yamir, this column honors the values of Shel'land, and no one's statue should stand between our land and our sky. The Temple is bringing its story to us but on our terms."

"Right," Yamir said, remembering his research.

Rhea then mentioned the different building materials used in the two columns and the similarities in taste between Jason Rodriguez and Apollonius of Damascus, Traianus's architect. She spoke about the process of turning her historical research into storyboards. Yamir only half listened though, worried that the voxdev message he had missed was from Grady.

Hotaru caught up with them at the base of the column, outside a door that belonged to the emperor's funeral chamber in the ancient structure. This room, though, housed the command center for the exhibit's visuals and sounds.

"Rhea, could you sign off on this, please?" Hotaru passed her a tablet.

While she was busy with that, Yamir took out his voxdev and checked the message. *Grady Leos: Proposal rejected.* The words sickened him. He typed back, his fingers slipping, *You're using our volunteers' A-brains for entertainment, like zoo animals centuries ago. You can't do that.*

The reply arrived. *I won't. But you're not a volunteer, Yamir. You're the lab chief. Y1 will be the sole face of the presentation.*

Yamir was somewhat relieved, but he knew Y1 would hate, hate, hate being on a stage. He'd refuse, of course, and Yamir would have to convince him to help with the presentation that did the least damage to the other androids and their lab. He bit his lip hard not to curse. Did Dimitri have something to do with the rejection of a solid argument against the public announcement? The asshole had promised to help Yamir change Grady's mind.

"What happened?" Rhea said. Hotaru was walking away.

"Grady is going ahead with the android announcement."

Rhea sighed. "I see. We should...cancel our restaurant reservation, then."

"No. I won't let him ruin our dinner."

"Easy to say, but your work always comes first—I should get that into my head." She tapped on her hard hat, and the sound was so at odds with the moment that Yamir smiled. She smiled too. Then she frowned. "What will you do about Grady?"

Yamir shrugged, feeling defeated.

"Hotaru and Jason think you're developing exoskeletons for people who lost motor function," Rhea said with bitterness.

"Our research helps doctors, so that's not far from the truth."

"But I'm sick of lying to people, Yamir. Maybe announcing the android isn't the worst thing that can happen. Done right, it could be quite freeing. It's up to you to figure out how. Just don't figure it out during tonight's dinner, please."

"I'm too tired to think about it today. Here, I'll just forward this message to Si'ahl, then turn off my voxdev until morning. Sounds good?"

"I guess," she said.

Logfile Y1-1831-06-22

Yamir has already fixed the sleep-controller vulnerability I needed for the destruction of my neural net. I'm searching for another way out, but because of his tricky move, dying isn't my top priority right now. M1's well-being is.

I'm getting used to the ASV3. It has a few features I don't dislike: registering the sun's warmth with the new temperature sensors; tasting flower pollen with my fingertips; listening for bird chirps farther than before. I wonder what Wodan would make of all my gadgets if he ever saw me. Would he be impressed by how well I can run on uneven ground or swing down from a tree?

Si'ahl taps on my simulation engine's touchscreen and interrupts my thoughts. "Sorry, Y1, but Yamir couldn't stop the public announcement. You're now the sole subject of a scaled-back presentation."

Grady probably wants to sell Connectome. By doing his presentation, I'd be helping him attract buyers. We might end up worse off in ways I can't even imagine.

"I'm not doing it. No way," I tell Si'ahl.

"Also, Grady's here."

"You're kidding?" I say, startled again.

And there's Grady, walking into the simulation room, wearing a gold-threaded suit and a purple wool scarf. I met him a few times over the years at Caspian's Saturnalia parties, but I've never talked to him before.

Xiu-Min is the first to greet him, trying to make a good impression because she needs her parental bonus for the baby. Then Dimitri tells everyone to gather around.

And Yamir isn't here. Where is he?

Isabela asks Grady if he needs something to drink, then leaves toward the kitchenette.

I quickly check in with the other A-brains. S1 is in the garden, trying out the new ASV3. He's had a few hours of practice with the new shell but can't control it well enough to pick up a pen. That won't make a good impression on—

What...? What happened? I lost a few seconds there.

Oh, I see. Dimitri transferred me to the ASV3 to replace S1. One moment, I'm in the lab, staring through my sensor array at the man holding my mother's future in his bejeweled hands, and the next, I find myself in the garden, a kilometer away, my foot stuck in a chain-link fence outside the greenhouse.

Even though the transfer felt like an instant, it took seven seconds, using an exclusion lock to ensure there would never be two of me between the simulation engine and the ASV3.

"Thanks, S1," I say and rotate my ankle to remove my foot from the fence without damaging either.

Now to get back to the lab. We can't have Dimitri and Grady there with the A-brains, even with Si'ahl present.

I'm still getting used to the lighter shell, as if I'm in low gravity. I return to the main path, jumping over logs and avoiding puddles, impressed with myself. In all my years as a human, I was never this athletic. Without feeling tired or sweaty, I reach ten kilometers per hour in under four seconds. When I hit the pavement, I engage the retractable wheels in my soles and start rolling at thirty kilometers per hour.

I'm back at the lab in under two minutes. I stop at the front door, retract my wheels, and make my grand entrance.

"And here's the ASV3, our newest shell," Dimitri tells Grady as if that's all I am. "You've seen videos of Y1 in the ASV1—the black polymer shell—but this is a major upgrade."

Grady lets out a whistle. "Impressive. Shiny titanium. Folks will love this."

This would be my new radiation-resistant body, with fancy displays on my forearms. My faceplate shows my avatar's neutral expression.

I glance at our scientists. Si'ahl is on his voxdev, likely trying to reach Yamir. Zaltana and Xiu-Min whisper to each other. Isabela is trying to get something going on a side wallscreen.

"That's not a killer robot, I hope." Grady looks pleased with his joke as he sips from a glass of mint water.

"No, I'm not a killer robot," I say, and he seems surprised I talk.

"Spooky. It sounds just like Yamir," Grady tells Dimitri, dropping the glass in his assistant's hand with nonchalance.

"You can address me directly, you know," I say.

I approach Grady to shake as we used to before the pandemic, but he puts his hands up. "Stay away!"

I freeze in place, frowning so he can see my displeasure. What does this asshole imagine I am? I want to scare him by twisting my limbs, but I decide to appear harmless instead.

"Relax, Grady." I put my hands up too. "Think of me as an upgraded ESPA."

"You don't speak like an expert system, and you don't act like a personal assistant, so no." Grady takes a step closer. He touches my arm and my face, much to my dislike. My new sensors pick up cortisol in his sweat. He's nervous.

"What can it do?" he asks Dimitri.

"Most things you do," I say. "Except eat and shit. What would you like to see?"

Si'ahl lets out a chuckle, and Zaltana throws him a side glance.

"Can you explain to a crowd how you're better than an ESPA?" Grady says.

"That's not a good idea. The world isn't ready for us, no matter how benign we make ourselves look." I point at him as a prime example, but he doesn't take the hint.

It's time for me to do a better job than Yamir did arguing against a public announcement. "What if the reporters ask you about the dangers of mass testing androids?"

"Relax," Grady says, fixing his purple scarf in place. "There won't be any questions."

"Then you should consider those dangers yourself. You don't know how a gang of us in android shells will behave together—and neither do we. Shouldn't you give it some thought before you put your company on the line for any damages that might—"

"Cut it out, android," he says. "Yamir already tried that argument. I didn't make a name for myself in my line of business by listening to doomsayers like you. If a spaceship crashes, we build another. If your presentation tanks, we shut you down and build another android. Clear?"

He's threatening me with the death I craved just days ago.

I'd like to punch him in the face, but I've never hit anyone in my life. I clench my fists and glare at that windbag. He'd be nothing without his father's dinars that paid for the excellent engineers at LeosTech. And this self-assured asshole will go home tonight to his trophy wife, a delicious meal, and a comfortable bed.

I want to walk away, but if I don't help Yamir, Z1 will probably volunteer to take my place as the showcase android. Zaltana will coach her—both so loyal to the project—and Grady will still get his presentation. No, I can't let Z1 become the target of Grady's abuse.

For the second time in a few days, I change my mind. "I'll do your presentation, Grady," I tell him.

Si'ahl throws me a thumbs-up. Zaltana looks relieved, as though she knew Z1 was on the hook if I bailed.

"Spectacular," Grady says and slaps me on the shoulder, then winces and pulls back. "You're a literal tough guy, aren't you?" He massages his hand.

I laugh, and he seems unsettled by the noise I make. My laughing face is also inadequate—Isabela still has work to do on abrupt expression changes and explosive emotions.

"Don't do that on the stage," Grady says.

"Understood," I say.

He may not grasp how our lab works, but he knows that LeosTech's bottom line depends on my performance at his presentation. In this, I recognize the Businessperson of the Year Award recipient.

"Good." He turns away. "Dimitri, have you checked on the parts for the capsule?"

I guess he's done with me, as they start talking about the new capsule for their explorer, which is being assembled in orbit at LeosTech's space station. It sounds like a versatile spaceship that can take a crew to the Moon or Mars, depending on its payload. Grady's demeanor is now different: he's focused and sounds familiar with the technology.

"I wish I could spend more time on the factory floor," Grady tells Dimitri, who nods with feigned sympathy, "instead of dealing with supply chains." They mention the Sahara Biospheres Company, our new manufacturer.

"You should check on those delivery delays," I say, interrupting their conversation.

Grady reacts again as if his dishwasher has just given him dating advice. "Can you mute it or something?" he asks Dimitri.

I stomp toward the door, making as much noise as possible to annoy him.

"Hey, Yamir android," I hear Grady call after me, and I turn. "You've got to work on that walk. You sound like a killer robot. I don't want you frightening my audience."

"Oh, I'll be your ballerina, Grady, don't you worry."

I turn my head around 180°, then my arms and legs—a pirouette in place—just to savor the shock on his face.

"Don't do that either when you're on the stage," he mutters.

Olma sat on a marble bench in the Temple Inn atrium, waiting for her last meeting of the day. Her tablet said he was an asset named Dimitri Petrodava.

She'd been in Cedarwood, Shel'land, the Nation of Confederated Tribes, for three days and still felt jet-lagged—not to mention overwhelmed by all the academic papers and news articles on artificial general intelligence she had read since receiving her assignment. Rex and Regina Sacrorum had requested an update from her soon. As the latest pair in a centuries-long line of Temple leaders, they had earned Olma's trust. They wisely weighed the science she presented to them against the diplomacy needed to navigate their stateless organization through a maze of national government agendas.

Olma stretched her back and legs and felt the muscles relax with a slight tremor. Was that caused by the death of her motor neurons? She silently prayed to Oroles the Savior to spare her mind from deteriorating until she completed his sacred mission. A mission she still needed to understand.

The surrounding scene could have come straight from a vacation brochure. The ambient light was warm with sunshine coming through the ceiling, bathing the potted orange trees in the corners of the atrium. A sheet of water fell into the square pool at the center of the chamber. The floor had a mosaic of basilisks, each biting the other serpent's tail, while a cleaning robot was turning the marble spotless. Nala sat on a bench, reading something on her tablet, her long blond hair tied in a colorful scarf.

But to Olma, this didn't feel like a vacation. She hadn't yet stopped Grady Leos's publicity stunt, the official reason she was in Cedarwood. The announcement was still scheduled to happen at his lake house tomorrow evening. To cancel it now, he'd need a serious incentive, but Olma was waiting to hear from her investigator about LeosTech's supply chain. Until then, she was still figuring out the battlefield. Could she cast doubt on Grady's technical claims tomorrow?

She glanced at Nala, who must have caught that slight head movement, because she said, "I should be finished with my Cedarwood errands by the end of the week." As a law firm president, she networked everywhere she traveled. "Can't wait to go back to Rome. I have a few important meetings in July." She preferred talking to people over coffee and aperitifs, not through screens.

"Yes, my love." Olma kept her gaze on her own tablet.

"This place is so tacky." Nala motioned around. "Look at this atrium. The building materials are too new to create an authentic Roman atmosphere. Things smell like fresh polymers. Leave it to the Shel'landics to turn Roman art into an embarrassment."

With a nod, Olma agreed with Nala that the Shel'landics were tacky but said nothing else. One thing she liked about Cedarwood was the city's wide spaces. The apartment she and Nala shared here was six times larger than their condominium in Rome. If she couldn't sleep one night and wanted to work, she could just use the large second bedroom as her office without disturbing her wife.

"I also want you to see Doctor Silvestri," Nala said, "and start his experimental treatment as soon as possible."

Olma's stomach dropped. Once her sacred mission was over, she'd focus on her health. If she was too sick by then for Doctor Silvestri's treatment, that was Oroles's will. "I'll be done here in a few days," she said.

Nala went on about the things waiting for them back home. She had a talk lined up about water shortages in the parts of the Sahara Expanse that hadn't yet been reforested. In those regions, there were reports of human rights abuses connected to a company called SBC.

Olma nodded but didn't engage.

Then they'd go to their Tuscany villa to check on the orchard. They'd throw a party for their friends around the old walnut table, sipping white wine and chatting until the stars came out over the grapevine arbors. Olma wished she were there right now, at their peaceful place in the hills outside the fortified city of Lucca, their peach-colored house surrounded by slopes of centuries-old olive trees. Oh, that feeling of sitting on the porch with no other worry in the world but what was for dinner...

Catherine, Olma's personal assistant, walked in, her brown hair tied in a severe bun, her blue suit impeccable. "Dimitri Petrodava is here to see you, High Priestess."

Olma turned off her tablet and made to leave, but Nala stood up first. "You stay. I can't stomach this place anyway. Catherine, let's figure out dinner."

They passed the thickset man on their way out. Olma rose and greeted him with a hand over her heart. He answered in kind, and then they sat on benches facing the waterfall. Olma pressed the Record button on her tablet.

"Dimitri Petrodava, thank you for coming," she said, switching from Italian to Shel'landic, a language she didn't like. Its roots in Indigenous Shel'landic and European languages meant it didn't obey grammatical rules as much as it reflected the complicated history of the continent during the fourteen centuries since the Roman exploratory ships sent by Emperor Severus Alexander had crossed the Atlantic Ocean to the "land built on the turtle's shell." The foreigners' arrival here had encouraged the tribes on the Atlantic shore to forge a common language for alliances and trade, the precursor of modern Shel'landic.

"Thank you for the constant and reliable assistance you've been providing us," she said.

The former science and technology supervisor had recruited Petrodava years ago so the Temple could monitor LeosTech from the inside. When asked if he felt conflicted about working behind his employer's back, Petrodava had answered with a quote from the Temple's creed: *Those who do El's righteous work will be rewarded in Caelum.*

"I've read your report, and I have a few questions," Olma said, hoping for good news. "Have you managed to change your employer's mind about tomorrow?"

"I tried…" Petrodava rubbed his short brown hair with his large hand.

"I see." Olma straightened her back, hiding her disappointment.

"What should I do now?" Petrodava said.

Knowing Grady's next move was better than guessing it. "Work with your boss but let me know if his plans change."

"Understood."

"How does Yamir Varro feel about a public announcement?"

"He doesn't want one."

He used the Shel'landic gossip tense, which allowed for conversations about events not witnessed firsthand. So there was doubt about it, but Varro could be an ally.

"What will happen tomorrow?" Olma said.

"Grady will introduce the android as a step up from ESPAs but won't reveal their origin. He hopes people are ready for that level of novelty. His investors too."

"But I understand that these A-brains aren't like expert-system personal assistants at all. They're intelligent…things, and you and the other scientists don't know exactly how everything works inside their heads."

Petrodava laughed, an unattractive rasp. "Funny thing, there's not much inside an android's head except the sensor array. The quantum cores and the memory banks are contained within the torso, safe inside a solid case."

Olma hadn't thought about that, but it was interesting that an android's mind was where its heart should be.

Petrodava went on, "But you're correct, High Priestess. Even Varro hasn't yet figured out how their minds work. We know an A-brain can't function without sensory inputs—not ever. Their brains exist only in relationship with their bodies. They aren't pure software like ESPAs. And they're obviously not like us, body and soul. They need either their sensor arrays or the android shell to function. Otherwise, they're in excruciating pain."

"Pain?" A bridge between human and machine, then. "But Grady won't mention this limitation tomorrow?"

"No, he won't talk about the android aspects he doesn't grasp."

Olma typed that on her tablet. "Why is he doing the announcement?"

Petrodava raised his thick eyebrows as if the answer were clear. "His late dad's estate isn't what he expected. More loans to repay than he imagined. He needs money, and he can't make it while the Mars settlement is shuttered."

"Why isn't he trying to return to servicing Urbs Lunae?" Olma said, though she wasn't familiar with every detail of the Temple's settlement-building efforts. "The permit bureau is still accepting applications."

"But not granting them," Petrodava said. "They haven't in three years. Too much red tape and fierce competition. Grady needs a well-placed benefactor to get him back into the Moon-supply enterprise he once abandoned."

Certain aspects had never changed in the way the Temple did business, not since the golden days of the empire centuries ago. Which reminded Olma…

"This goes without saying, but you should never handle your communications with the Temple in the open, where surveillance drones can capture it."

"Of course, High Priestess."

"Good. Now tell me what you know about LeosTech's supply chain."

Logfile Y1-1831-06-23

Yamir is the first to arrive at the lab this morning, and I'm ready for him. I tell the other A-brains to give us some privacy, and they busy themselves with different tasks on their screens. He walks into the simulation room, a coffee mug in his hand, and heads to my screen.

"Where were you yesterday when Grady was here?" I say.

"Grady was here?" He checks his voxdev, and I can see it powering up. "Blast it!"

"Your voxdev was off?" I say, dismayed. "Your mother's brain lives in this lab, and you just disappeared?"

He rubs his forehead like I still do when I'm in trouble. "I was...It doesn't matter. What happened yesterday? Is everything all right?"

"I'm doing the presentation. Which you couldn't convince Grady to drop."

His eyes widen. "You actually said yes to that?" He doesn't even thank me for this onerous task. He takes me for granted.

The mug in his hand reminds me of breakfast with Rhea. "Did you have to bring coffee in here?"

He sits down before my screen with a groan. "I'm sorry, I have a headache."

So inconsiderate of him to complain. "At least you have a head that hurts," I say.

He purses his lips. "For the sake of M1 and the others, we must do a good job with that presentation."

"Stating the obvious, as always."

He gives me a tired look. "Public speaking has never been my thing. But maybe you feel differently about being on a stage as an android?"

"Yeah, because I have a public-speaking-skill-improvement knob."

Yamir rubs his eyes, then pinches the bridge of his nose. He's trying to stay calm while I needle him. "How do you feel about being up there?"

"It'll be great. Watching people enjoy food and drinks I can't taste. Seeing my wife just a few feet away from me and being unable to talk to her."

Yamir puts his coffee down with a thump.

"The wife I haven't seen in a year," I continue.

"Don't speak of Rhea that way."

"She's my wife. I married her on the beach in Orcas Harbor. Together we took Wodan home after months in the hospital. We celebrated when she published her first book. Have you even tried to convince her to see me?"

When he doesn't answer, I press on. "All I want is to talk to her. Not that much to ask when you get to go home to her every night. Hear her speak about her day. Sleep next to her and—" I don't say the words. "Oh, how I miss her welcoming me at the door, touching my chest, right here over my heart, as if to make sure I was—"

"Stop it." Yamir stands up from the chair and takes a step toward the door.

I yell after him, "Great, now go on a long walk around the campus just to spite me."

He stops and turns. "How do you even…? Of course, you're in my head because you're me!" He groans. "You're upset because of Grady and taking it out on me."

I realize my virtual fists are balled and my feet planted on my invisible floor. Unfortunately, I'm alone in this simulated space, with nothing to hit. I stomp my foot, and that helps me release some tension.

"You don't know how lucky you are to have her," I say. "But you're taking her for granted. Just like you take me for granted."

"What are you talking about? I'm with her every minute I'm not working!"

"Exactly! And that's not enough."

Yamir shakes his head. "I can't win with you, Y1. Yesterday…I took her out to our restaurant—and now you're angry with me because I don't spend enough time with her."

They went to our restaurant together...Did they talk about me at all?

Blast it, he's right. I'm not making a coherent argument. I ease back and shake my avatar's shoulders to relax.

Yamir sighs. "Though seeing you angry is better than hearing you ask for termination."

Such a cocky asshole.

As he's heading for the door, I call after him, "Hey, Yamir, kiss Rhea for me, will you?"

From a screen near me, S1 says, "Dude, not cool..."

Yamir thanked Si'ahl for the detailed account of what had happened yesterday with Y1 and Grady in his absence.

"The presentation is in two days," he said. "It should be everyone's top priority until then."

"Of course. Uh, one more thing," Si'ahl said before leaving Yamir's office. "Do you know what Zaltana would like for her birthday? I asked her, and she told me to surprise her. I don't want to get it wrong."

Yamir felt sad for his colleague. "She's not going to leave her fiancé, you know that. She's too loyal..."

Si'ahl shook his head. "Still, I'd like to give her something nice next week."

He probably felt the same hopeless yearning Y1 had for Rhea. The only advice Yamir had for both Y1 and Si'ahl was to let it go. Which they couldn't. With a dejected smile, Si'ahl walked out.

Yamir sat at his desk, still smarting from his chat with Y1. He had allowed himself a nice dinner with Rhea last night—for once enjoying the food and conversation—and he had missed Grady's first-ever visit to the lab. He should have been there for M1 and the other A-brains.

He spent the rest of the day choreographing the presentation. He'd be on the stage with Y1, who'd have to talk slower and choose his words to avoid sounding like Yamir. His voice filter would be tweaked to add a metallic tone, for good measure. They wouldn't say Y1 was based on Yamir's connectome—to conceal the A-brains' existence. Instead, they'd say Y1 was a primitive B-brain created from a blank network where each neuron was connected to its neighbors and where the culling of synapses happened through years of deep learning. A bridge between the current ES tech and the artificial general intelligence of the future.

That in itself would be a huge announcement, but Grady had agreed to play it down, presenting Y1 as an early prototype that could only do a few basic things, such as walk around and answer simple questions about time and weather. If someone asked Y1 to play chess, he'd lose—for the simple reason that Yamir had always been terrible at it. But those flaws were perfect for the presentation's goal of getting investors excited without making enemies in the process.

When Yamir arrived home that evening, a smiling Rhea opened the door for him. She wore a sleeveless top and a long skirt, and her hair was tied back. Her hand came to rest on his chest, over his heart, as if to confirm he was all right—which only made Yamir feel worse about that earlier conversation with Y1. He wanted to pull her closer, to feel that she was his and his alone. He tried not to think of Y1's taunt, which was still ringing in his ears, and reached out to kiss Rhea, but she must have noticed his hesitation because her gaze steeled up. She let him peck her on the cheek, then headed for the kitchen.

Yamir knew he had messed up, but he didn't know how to fix it. He hoped all would be well again when he took Rhea to Grady's in a couple of days, where she'd visit an impressive library with centuries-old manuscripts, original artifacts, and first editions signed by famous authors.

"Is everything all right?" Rhea said over her shoulder.

He didn't want to bring up his work, but he wasn't good at lying to her. "Thinking about that damn presentation..."

She turned around. "Did you know the word 'damn' is the shortening of an ancient Roman curse? It's related to the *damnatio memoriae* practice of erasing an outcast from public memory."

Her icy tone made it clear that bringing up his work was not a good idea.

4

Yamir went home to pick up Rhea, and Si'ahl will give me a ride to Grady's lake house. I'm in my simulation engine while the ASV3 is charging in its dock. Z1 and S1 have been waiting patiently for the new shell, but I had to practice with it for Grady's presentation tonight. Starting tomorrow though, they'll have unlimited access to it while I sit tight in my simulation engine. I'd rather hang out in my empty space than go back to that terrible ASV1.

Since I had the ASV3 all to myself, I took M1's advice to heart and explored what this new shell could do. I even had fun. My favorite thing was to shoot my harpoon line at a tree branch, pull myself up, then jump from that height and land, testing my leg suspension. (I used to dream of such abilities when I was kid, after falling asleep with a superhero novel.)

While I wait for Si'ahl, I activate a screen next to M1's to check on her. She's reading a digital book and seems startled to see me when my screen rotates into view.

"How are things, Mom?"

"Oh, still getting used to my new eyes."

More than a million nerve fibers in the human eye alone had to be retrained to work with her video sensors. Her old human retinas had more photoreceptors in the center than at the periphery, which the current video sensors can't replicate. And they had sightless spots where the optic nerve exited the eye. Her video sensors simulate saccades (the eyes' rapid movements that help the neocortex build a 3D model of the world), but it's not the same.

"Give it another week," I tell her.

She nods. "The projection of the book into my eye reminds me of the smart glasses of old."

"And I know how much you hated those," I say with a smile.

She doesn't smile back. "I'd like to go on a swim though," she says, sounding tentative. "Is our Swallah VR ready?"

"Soon." I've been testing the island simulation and fixing the last code defects. "It'll be safer than what Malina is doing at home."

"Swimming isn't dangerous," M1 says. "I service—used to—my exoskeleton on schedule, and it never failed me."

I still think Malina should stop that high-risk hobby, but there's no point in arguing about it with M1. "What's your favorite diving spot on Swallah? So I can add it to the landscape."

"Oh…" She stares past me as if imagining the place. "There's this little cove, tucked inside the rebuilt coral reef. Except I don't swim there, just send my drone over to look at the beauty of a pristine place undisturbed by humans. But I'd like to swim there in the VR…"

"I don't see why not."

She clears her nonexistent throat. "And the ASV3? When can I try it?"

"In a month or so, though the first few times will be challenging, I'm warning you. Like riding a bike with its handlebar flipped. It takes weeks to get comfortable with it."

"I've got plenty of time now." She smiles at last, then squints. "Something's bothering you though. Is it tonight's presentation?"

"No. My script is basic, and I'm not nervous." Just like her to see through my pretend composure. "But Yamir says Wodan is coming home—"

"And he doesn't know of your existence…"

Good thing my digital larynx doesn't express my raw emotions well. "I miss him a lot. I worry about him too. When he was little, I tried to protect him from anything dangerous." I laugh, trying to sound dismissive of my silly fears. "And look at him now. He'll soon fly shuttles to the Moon."

I'm surprised by my candor. I never talked to Malina about missing my son when I was Yamir. We always talked facts and science back then, the emotions implicit and unvoiced. Maybe because we're now both in this parallel universe where—

The lights brighten as Dimitri walks in. "Ready, Y1? I'm taking you to Grady's place in my SDV."

"I thought Si'ahl was going to give me a ride," I say.

"Change of plans," he says with a shrug. "And what were you guys talking about a moment ago?"

His attitude is infuriating. "None of your business," I say.

"Don't talk to me like that," he replies. "You still think you're the lab boss here, but you're just another program."

Had I been in android form, he wouldn't have talked to me like that.

"My grandson, Wodan, is coming home from college in a few days," M1 intervenes, sounding warm, "and we were saying that we wish we could see him."

"Ah yeah, college kids…You're lucky you don't have to worry about his tuition."

I know I should show sympathy for his financial woes, but instead, I whisper to M1, "What kind of father complains about providing for his kids?"

Dimitri looks at me with renewed animosity. "You really don't know when to keep your mouth shut, do you? Well. I was going to have you ride in the SDV, but it's better if we save power for the presentation." He reaches for my screen to suspend me.

"No, don't do that!" M1 yells at him.

From their screens, S1 and Z1 tell him to back off.

I panic. "If you suspend me, my cortical columns…I won't be able to perform my routine well," I say in a pathetic attempt to stop him. "You'll ruin Grady's presentation."

He seems unmoved by my threat and everyone's protests. "Don't worry, you'll do fine."

"I promise I'll keep quiet on the ride there." I'm forced to beg, wondering if he planned to suspend me all along and I was stupid enough to give him an excuse.

His finger is so close to my screen, I can feel it on my face.

I'm helpless, and I hate it.

I can't fight back.

I—

At home, Yamir went upstairs to the main bedroom to get ready for Grady's presentation. It had been months since he last wore formal attire, and he hoped his best gray suit still fit. He and Rhea mostly socialized during the winter holidays, when they attended Saturnalia parties.

He found Rhea at the bathroom mirror, putting on mascara. She wore a dark-green evening gown that accentuated her tall and slender figure. Seeing her look so gorgeous reminded Yamir of that bitter exchange with Y1 a couple of days ago.

"How are you feeling?" Rhea said, talking to him in the mirror.

"Nervous," Yamir said.

"You'll do fine, you'll see." She capped the mascara, then slipped on the emerald earrings he had bought for her birthday five years ago.

He turned on his shaver and started along his right jaw. "How are you feeling about seeing Y1 tonight?" He tried to sound casual.

"No feelings at all." More confirmation that Yamir would never convince her to talk to his A-brain.

His voxdev chimed on the granite countertop, and he glanced at it: Grady Leos. "I must take this," he told Rhea, who was touching up her chocolate-brown lipstick.

Back in the bedroom, he answered the call.

"You're off the presentation," Grady said. "Dimitri will do it instead."

Yamir's stomach sank. "Why?" he managed to say.

"You're just too close to everything to do an effective job."

"But if Dimitri messes up, the Temple—"

"Relax about the Temple. I got it covered." Grady ended the call.

Yamir slid down on the edge of the bed, unsure what to make of the news. It was bad, yes, but how bad? Things could go terribly wrong if Y1 refused to work with someone other than Yamir. Or if Dimitri accidentally revealed sensitive details about the lab. What kind of understanding did Grady have with the Temple? Or was he lying, planning to surprise them again?

Yamir went downstairs to his office and connected to the lab through a secure link, trying to warn Y1. But his simulation engine had been cut off from the rest of the network. The android shell was also unresponsive. Si'ahl was supposed to drive Y1 to Grady's lake house. so Yamir called him.

"I went home to change," Si'ahl said, "and I was going to pick up Y1 next, but I received a message from Dimitri that they had already left. Y1 isn't responding. Dimitri must have suspended him."

"No way Y1 agreed to that."

"Looks like Dimitri abducted him. Y1 will be so angry when he recovers..."

"Let me know if you find them before I do," Yamir told Si'ahl.

Rhea walked in wearing a floral scent. "What's wrong?"

"Everything," Yamir said.

The sun was still up when Yamir and Rhea's SDV arrived at Grady's compound on the eastern shore of Lake Xachu. They were among the first guests there, and the Elsway protesters, supervised by vigiles outside the gates, were slow to make a path for the vehicle. Many sported zigzag tattoos on their arms and necks, symbolizing the harmony of past and present while rejecting technology that would upset the sky god El. Their signs read *Keep the solar system human!* and *El's way or no way!* and *Oroles didn't have an ESPA.* Their slogans didn't mean they expected an android announcement tonight, but they seemed wary of anything Grady Leos would unveil.

The vigiles forced the crowd to part little by little, and no one attacked the SDV. Yamir noticed a bearded young man in a gray shirt, holding a sign that read *Don't play El or He'll drown your hubris!* Yamir squeezed

Rhea's hand as he stared into the man's eyes—an unnatural shade of red. Elsway people were fond of contact lenses.

"They seem pretty peaceful," she said.

"You're talking about Elsway, the international organization suspected of sabotaging the Temple's Mars settlement." They were probably responsible for the faulty components that caused the explosion at the oxygen plant.

"They won't do anything tonight, not with all this security around. Though I didn't realize their Cedarwood chapter was so big."

The massive wrought-iron gates appeared ahead, opening inward as the SDV approached. Vigiles stood on both sides, letting it through.

Yamir was glad to see the crowd fall back, replaced by a shaded driveway through red cedars. Grady's house was an incongruent but pleasant mix of corporate building and traditional longhouse. It combined steel and glass with stained wood and neat landscaping.

"Jason Rodriguez built it," Rhea said, referring to the famous architect she worked with at the Concord Column downtown.

At the mansion's entrance, Yamir helped her step out, then sent the SDV to the self-park garage. She held his hand, smiling, her eyes bright with excitement.

A vigile with a scanner wand surveyed newcomers for concealed weapons.

"Welcome to the Leos House," an ESPA greeter said, standing a meter and a half tall in a white polymer shell. "This is an eco-shelter where the natural surroundings act as walls that help regulate temperature. Please consider visiting the garden, with its artificial streams complete with salmon and steelhead; the library with the oldest manuscripts in a private collection in Shel'land; and the virtual reality theater with its state-of-the-art equipment."

"Where can I find Grady?" Yamir asked it.

"Grady Leos is in the main hall," the greeter said. "Past the grand staircase, then turn right."

Rhea freed her hand and asked, "And the library?"

"Through the main hall and up the stairs to the second floor."

Rhea threw Yamir an air kiss. "See you later."

Yamir nodded and went to find Grady.

A few early guests drifted toward the reception hall. So weird to have strangers roam around someone's home, Yamir thought. He and Rhea weren't the party-throwing type, and over the years, Wodan had brought only a few friends home to visit. The only person always welcome there was Malina.

Yamir passed a Rodriguez signature waterfall, wondering about its purpose in a house.

At the grand staircase, another ESPA greeter addressed Yamir. "Fun fact: These granite floors are pressure sensitive and monitored at all times, so security can tell how many people are inside and where."

Rhea would find that extra creepy. "Can you locate someone for me?"

"If given the correct authorization codes," the ESPA said.

"Never mind," Yamir replied in passing.

Along the way, tables placed at regular intervals offered bite-sized appetizers: root dips and crackers, herring platters, berry muffins, lab-grown meats, cubed cheese, onion flatbread. and more, none of which interested Yamir.

At the end of the main hall, against floor-to-ceiling windows showing an expansive and expensive view of the lake in the evening, Yamir found Grady talking to a small crowd. He wore a silver lamé suit with a turquoise scarf. Yamir managed to catch his boss's eye, but Grady gave him the shortest shake of his head and continued his conversation.

Yamir stepped closer, only to meet an ESPA with its arm extended. Grady had probably instructed it to keep him away, the way the vigiles kept Elsway under control at the gates. Yamir choked on his frustration, and he considered making a scene to force Grady to explain replacing him with Dimitri. But if reporters were around, it wouldn't be good for Connectome Labs. Yamir risked being thrown out, so he wouldn't be around if Y1 needed him. And he'd ruin Rhea's visit to her dream library.

He checked his voxdev to see where Y1 was. Still offline. Grady kept chatting with guest after guest, ignoring Yamir.

There was nothing he could do but head to the reception hall, hoping to find Y1.

"Yamir," someone called as he reached the Rodriguez waterfall. He turned to see Thandi Leos, Grady's wife. She wore a full-length sequined dress and excessive jewelry that glittered against her honey-toned skin. "I hope you enjoy the party tonight. Is your son home for the summer?"

"He'll arrive in a couple of days," Yamir said, surprised she remembered Wodan. Maybe she found him memorable because he had done a couple of internships at Grady's factory in recent years.

"Tell him to stop by LeosTech while he's in town. Grady wants to know what research projects are happening at the big space school in London." She smiled and turned to greet someone else.

Outside the reception hall, where an actual maple tree grew out of the floor for no reason, Yamir ran into Dimitri, and his heart jumped into his throat. "Where's Y1?" he asked.

"He's fine," Dimitri said without stopping. "No time to chat. I must welcome Olma Asper, the high priestess Rome has sent us." He disappeared among a group of new guests walking in.

A high priestess and an android under the same roof—had Grady thought this through?

In the reception hall, three chairs and a lectern waited on a dais for Grady, Y1, and Dimitri. Behind them, a gold L and T against a green wall welcomed the guests to LeosTech. A side door would allow Y1 to reach the dais without walking through the crowd.

The virtual skylight displayed the constellations of the Pacific Northwest despite the sunset outside. Yamir found the table with his and Rhea's name tags and sat down to a sliced acorn bread looking fresh from the oven. The table's electronic surface displayed tonight's menu: spicy salmon rolls; seaweed salad; corn, bean, and squash soup; deer and vegetable stew—with the available substitutions. For dessert: soapberry ice cream or salal fruit cakes.

The next moment, an ESPA server was there, asking Yamir what he wanted to drink.

"Old-fashioned firewater," Yamir said. "Add a smoked plum."

The firewater appeared at his side on the table, and the first sip told Yamir it was an imported brand, probably expensive. Rhea would appreciate it because the recipe for plum brandy went back over two thousand years to Dhawosia. He took another sip and felt the alcohol warm his throat.

"Here's to you, Y1," he whispered, waiting for the show to start.

Over the next half hour, the hall filled with people: Grady's magnate friends, his investors, the press, Coast Salish tribal leaders, and Yamir's fellow scientists. A large table was reserved for the local Orolic Temple. Photographers snapped pictures of Senator Thunderhawk, director of the Shel'land Space Agency; Maya Dordevic, the famous acting star and rumored flame of President Catawnee; and the Honorable Mark Evander, the Shel'landic ambassador to the Council of Nations. Another rich buffet occupied a few tables under the windows, while ESPA servers brought trays of food and drinks to the guests.

Wallscreens displayed the greatest achievements of LeosTech all around the hall. Transporters docking next to explorers at the space station. Shuttles with incandescent thrusters—three under each wing—allowing for vertical takeoff and landing. New Moon settlers arriving at the Mare Tranquillitatis Welcome Center in Urbs Lunae. Grady accepting the Council of Nations' Businessperson of the Year Award for launching his spacecraft fleet to the Moon. Then again, for assisting the Temple in launching their Mars settlement. Images of the solar system, suggesting his ambition to reach Ceres and the moons of Jupiter and Saturn next.

Yamir half watched the promotional videos, but the one playing now caught his eye because it was about him. The intro told the story of his early brain research at Servetus University. The picture of a mouse appeared, while the ES narrator, its voice coming from the speaker on Yamir's table, explained, "Scientists have long studied the sea slug, the fruit fly, the zebra fish, and the mouse for biological insights into the human brain. But Yamir Varro focused on the octopus instead, with its high-order cognitive behaviors, such as tool use and problem-solving."

A clip of an octopus using a stick as a lever to displace a rock inside its underwater cave reminded Yamir of that old multi-limbed friend.

"Varro chose the octopus exactly for its dissimilarities to the human brain, and by taking that unconventional approach, he discovered common rules that govern complex brain functions."

Yamir felt slightly embarrassed. This stuff was from ages ago, when he was still a professor at Servetus University, before Caspian Leos had offered to finance his lab. And before Yamir had spent years working on the B-brain, only to be derailed by the accidental creation of Y1's A-brain.

"Varro studied the effect of individual genes on the cephalopods' brain functions. You want to make an octopus relax and become more sociable?" On the screen, a picture of a much younger Yamir appeared, altered to show him wrapped in the arms of an octopus—loving arms, judging by the hearts drawn in red marker, floating all around them.

Yamir was too anxious about Y1 to laugh along with the other guests.

"You only need to dose them with a serotonin-uptaking substance, the way you'd do to humans. Which tells us that there's a molecular mechanism involved in the formation of social bonds rather than specific brain regions."

The loving octopus disappeared from the screen, and a row of blue-blinking workstations took its place. "Varro drew on the cephalopods' separate learning and memory systems for his novel approach to deep learning. His discovery that octopuses also use reference frames to internally represent the model of their world—"

Between the jubilant crowd, the narrator's irritating voice, and the scientific inaccuracies, it was too much for Yamir, now on his third shot of firewater and feeling tipsy. But he had to keep a clear head for Y1's sake. With another half hour to go before the presentation, he stood up from his table and looked around for Rhea's calming presence.

On his way to the exit from the reception hall, he nodded at people who now recognized him from the octopus videos, but he didn't stop to chat.

"Yamir," he heard a familiar voice.

He turned to see Julian Laurent, the chair of the Neuroscience Department at Servetus University. He and his partner, Troy, had aged a little but looked healthy, the walking poster of the regenerative medicine they supported. Julian's lifelong work was in artificial general intelligence, but Yamir had warned him years ago that his stubborn belief in machine learning was a dead end. He was in for a shock tonight, which didn't bring Yamir any satisfaction, given the circumstances.

"Rhea tells me you're staying busy at Connectome," Julian said. "While it's nice to be reminded of the good old times,"—he motioned at the screens around the room—"what's that new stuff you're working on? What's the big announcement?"

"Good to see you, Julian. Troy, it's been a while," Yamir said with a short wave. "Chat after?"

"Can't wait to catch up, old friend," Julian said.

"Sure." Yamir headed out before Julian could ask more questions.

Once in the main hall, he took the stairs up to the library, finding it a little challenging after those stiff drinks. On the second-floor landing, the word LIBRARY was spelled in golden letters over sliding doors that stood open.

Yamir walked in with an unsure step. There were no windows anywhere, and the ambient light was soft. Red alder shelves climbed to the ceiling, packed with volumes and codices. A few people milled about, their hands behind their backs, their necks stretched close to the words laid on papyrus, parchment, and paper centuries ago.

Rhea wasn't in that room, but the central piece there caught Yamir's attention: the first workstation ever created. Back in 1642, it was called an *analytical engine*. He hadn't known Grady owned that legendary machine; he had thought it was in a museum in Memphis, Egypt. The tech revolution originated with this tall metal structure, wider than a dining room table, made from columns of polished wheels connected to gears on rods, and finished up with a printer and a bell. He had seen pictures of it in magazines and books, but now he could study the curve plotters up close. Even crank the levers—if he wanted to. On a side table, there was a set of punched cards made of thick pressed paper for programming the analytical engine. Yamir came close to feeling their texture with his fingertips, but he wouldn't dare. How come Grady owned that priceless machine?

Shaking his head, Yamir left the room. He glanced in passing at the gold-embossed volumes written by important mathematicians and physicians from the heyday of the Roman Empire. A whole section was dedicated to the millennium-old scientists of Baghdad.

In the next room, the books hailed from the modern age, with many first editions set open on tables, signed by famous authors. Yamir recognized writers who had fueled his young-age dreams of intelligent robots with their scientific fantasy fiction.

On a corner stand, he noticed a brain in a preservation jar. Though repulsed by the barbarism of that display, he approached it to read the name of the brain's owner: *Ovidius Servetus* (1391–1458 LE), the scientist who had saved medicine from sinking into obscurity after the fall of the Roman Empire. Servetus didn't deserve to be treated like this, his neurons turned to mush in Grady's home library.

Yamir rushed to the next room, where the lights were dimmed. On the central table lay ancient manuscripts protected by a glass case, and there stood Rhea, squinting at the Greek script on the parchment, her lips moving in silence.

"Hey," Yamir whispered, touching the low of her back.

"Yamir, I can't believe this. Grady has fourth-century copies of *The Book of Andrada* and *The Dynastic Scrolls*—right here. They're part of the Orolic Temple's noncanonical history. You think he can give me access so I can study them closer?"

Grady clearly wanted people to admire his treasures, but study them? "I'll see what I can do," Yamir said, "but we must go downstairs now."

"I don't want to go," Rhea said but stepped away from the glass case. "You know how much amazing stuff is in here? And there're still rooms to explore."

But if she stayed here, Y1 would notice her empty chair at the table, which could upset him and affect the presentation.

"Please…" Yamir whispered.

Rhea sighed and took his hand, and they walked through six more rooms on their way to the exit. At times, she stopped to look at something, but only for a moment. She was probably nervous about seeing her husband's brain clone she'd been avoiding for a year.

"Thank you for being here with me," Yamir told her, squeezing her hand.

Yamir and Rhea joined the Connectome table in the reception hall. Xiu-Min and her husband, David, showed 3D ultrasound images of their unborn baby around the table. Si'ahl sat next to Isabela, chatting about work, though he stole pained glances at Zaltana and her fiancé, Oliver, who were discussing the digital menu. He wore gray woolen pants, an embroidered blue shirt, and buckskin moccasins—probably to impress Zaltana, who wore a simple black dress and a few pieces of jewelry made from mountain sheep horn inlaid with copper and shell.

While Yamir ordered a glass of Italian red wine for Rhea, Si'ahl leaned closer. "Have you read the document I sent you?"

Yamir pulled out his voxdev and saw a message from Si'ahl sent an hour ago, when he'd been busy chasing Grady around this immense house. The title of the attached document was *Prepared Remarks.*

"How did you get this?" Yamir said.

"Hacked into Dimitri's workstation after he abducted Y1," Si'ahl said. "Grady must have run the speech by him. It leaves nothing to the imagination."

Yamir opened the document. Grady's prepared remarks began with "Last century, we eliminated famine, plague, and war. Now it's time to eliminate not just the causes of death, but death itself." Yamir couldn't believe Grady would say that in the presence of so many people of faith.

He skimmed down. "Today we worship the scientists who created the first vaccine over four hundred years ago and tripled life expectancy without divine intervention." That sounded defiant, daring the Temple in front of everyone to stop the progress Grady was bringing.

On the next page, Yamir read, "The Temple envisions an incorruptible and eternal body for the soul in Caelum. Until then, we have something just as good. For we created the android, so we can upload our brain's neural network to give us eternal life right here on Earth."

Grady liked to shock. He had done it before, when he was the first to announce spaceships ready for the Moon, even though he was still building them. But this was reckless. And that was why he had wanted Yamir off the presentation and had appointed Dimitri instead. But how on Earth would he convince Y1 to abandon his prepared routine and instead show the world he was an uploaded human brain?

With a chilling sense of dread, Yamir realized why Y1 had been suspended. Grady would be shouting to the world that he had four A-brains and the means of creating more. Then he'd power up Y1 and display him to his audience like a prisoner of war in the arenas of old. Y1 would look confused and vulnerable when restarted. He'd be asking where he was and what was going on. He'd look the most human ever.

Yamir had to save Y1 from that trap and safeguard the A-brains.

Just then, Grady stepped up to the lectern. "Welcome to LeosTech. How's everybody doing tonight?"

People cheered all around, as he began, "You know how much I love my spaceships. I obsess over the paint on the wings of a thing that's going to be seen by no one in space. I sleep at the factory many nights a year."

Everyone chuckled, knowing he was telling the truth.

"Oh, here's an idea," Grady said. "Maybe one of you brilliant scientists can make me a device that would allow me to monitor my factory in my sleep."

"That's the last thing you need, Grady," Thandi said, followed by a few applauses.

Yamir stood up, but Rhea caught his hand and pulled him down. "You can't go there. The guards will throw you out before you get a word in." As always, she could tell what Yamir was thinking.

"But today I want to talk to you about something different. Something my dear departed father, Caspian Leos, would've liked to see happen in his lifetime." Grady cleared his throat. "Last century, we eliminated famine, plague, and war..."

Grady didn't seem to worry that Elsway would want Connectome Labs destroyed after this stunt. Did he really trust his investors, lawyers, and senators to keep him and his property safe? Yamir freed his hand and started toward the dais but was slowed down by people still taking their seats.

"Your attention, please!" A woman's voice.

Yamir looked around and found her at the Temple's table, closest to the lectern. She stood tall, dressed in the silver robe and hood of a high priestess.

Grady, wearing the same silver fabric, had a bitter smile on his face. "Olma Asper of the Orolic Temple. We're so happy to have you here."

He motioned for her to wait, but she continued up to the dais, a couple of Praetorian guards in black uniforms securing her passage. Grady's own security people stepped up and began arguing in whispers with the PGs.

The audience buzzed with questions and remarks shot around the tables. Olma Asper approached the lectern, but Grady blocked her way, addressing her and pointing. Yamir looked around for Y1 but still didn't see him anywhere.

"Let the high priestess speak," someone yelled from the audience.

"Grady, are you serious?" someone else added with impatience. "That's High Priestess Asper!"

Grady shook his head but backed off. "I don't mind going off script a little," he said with a forced chuckle as Olma Asper stepped up to the lectern.

Yamir felt an arm slipping under his elbow.

Rhea had followed him. "Let's hear what she has to say."

He nodded, and they found a place against the side wall to stand and watch together.

"May Oroles bless you all," the high priestess said in an Italian accent. She looked stunning with her dark eyes and pale face, framed by a silver cowl, and her black hair cut short to her chin.

"Our hearts are with him," many in the crowd replied.

"Indulge me while I go through a bit of history with you in the year 1831 of the Lucretian Era," she said. "The Temple has always been a protective force in our world and a benevolent guide to El's creation. It was founded on Oroles's teachings—heretical at the time—that all humans are equal before our god El. With that revolutionary idea, Oroles changed our political structures, our social hierarchies, and our gender relations. He taught us that the meek and the oppressed are closest to El's heart, which inspired the good Emperor Traianus to end the awful practice of enslaving people."

Everybody knew the Temple's version of history. But Olma Asper wasn't rehashing it for nothing. Yamir glanced at Rhea, who motioned to him to keep listening.

"The Temple has not only created a more ethical world," Olma Asper said, "but has also been part of its economic and technological progress. The Temple established medieval Europe's most sophisticated administrative system. It introduced such concepts as archives, catalogs, timetables, and other techniques of data processing. Local temples were the first to use clocks, and for centuries their schools were the most important learning centers of Europe, many evolving into our cherished universities. Tenth-century Rome was not very different from Cedarwood now, with its many startup companies forwarding science. Local temples were the first economic corporations of the world, and as such, they helped the global economy with their advanced agricultural and administrative methods, then later their industrial and high-tech innovations."

"We all know and appreciate the Temple's—" Grady cut in, but the high priestess sent him back with just a glance.

She went on. "Before our host presents his vision for the future, I wanted to remind you of the Temple's sacred standard of seeking enlightenment for humankind only by methods that wouldn't displease its creator. We might not have legal authority over nations, but we have moral authority to do what's right in El's eyes. Unfortunately, what LeosTech is preparing to announce today is not the kind of project the Temple can condone."

"Grady said he cleared this with the Temple," Yamir whispered to Rhea.

"I'm sorry," Grady said, stepping forward, "but I think everyone here is eager to—"

"Therefore," Olma Asper said, raising her voice over his, "I must inform you that LeosTech has been profiting off forced labor from the Sahara Biospheres Company."

Grady's face froze in a grimace. Everyone else gasped, including Rhea. She looked at Yamir, her brown eyes wide with questions.

Yamir shook his head. "No idea what she's talking about…"

"For those of you who are not familiar with SBC," Olma Asper continued, "it operates outside the Council of Nations and is a supplier of on-demand manufactured parts that can't be produced by 3D printing. Their affordable prices have a dark secret though. We've recently learned that they're running forced labor camps in a remote region of the Sahara Expanse. Their land was bought while it was still a desert, and it's one of the least scrutinized places on Earth. Their domes are very private, and that's where we believe they hold their enslaved workers. The Temple will plead with governments across the planet to help put an end to this atrocity, of course, but in the meantime, we urge the Council of Nations to go after those who do business with SBC."

The hall erupted with questions. From Grady's angry expression, the SBC revelation was no surprise to him, but it was a shock to Yamir. His new component supplier and the manufacturer of the ASV3 was a forced-labor criminal organization.

The press surrounded the dais, reporters shouting questions at Grady. No one seemed to doubt the truth of Olma Asper's words. Yamir craned his neck to see past them.

And there was Grady. "Well, that's a serious allegation and certainly news to me. And I promise you there will be a full investigation of these claims. We'll look at our suppliers—"

Some people picked up their belongings, making a show of their disgust with LeosTech, some even dropping a harsh comment to the press.

"He'd better clean up his act, fast," a middle-aged investor told an eager reporter.

Rhea spoke into Yamir's ear. "They want Grady to get in front of this storm. What hypocrites! His investors aren't yet ready to walk away from whatever they imagine his next big thing is. They're all keeping their options open."

Yamir looked again for Grady, who raised his voice over the crowd. "I take these accusations so seriously that I will suspend tonight's announcement until I clear up LeosTech's good name."

That was a huge relief, though Yamir didn't know if the Temple would go after Connectome Labs too, not just Grady's spacecraft manufacturing. And where was Y1?

Rhea pulled him by the arm toward their table.

"Did you know about SBC?" Yamir heard Julian Laurent's voice. He turned to see the head of the Servetus Neuroscience Department stare at him with concern.

"No, of course not," Yamir said. "I assure you…"

Beyond Julian, he saw Olma Asper leaving, a decent-sized retinue following her.

A reporter squeezed between people to put a recording voxdev in Yamir's face. "Do you have anything to say about Connectome Labs and SBC?"

"No comment," Yamir said.

"Lucius Seong," the reporter said, "Northwest News Network. Does this mean your lab will be shut down?"

"No comment," Yamir said, now truly shaken.

5

The morning after Grady's fiasco, Yamir arrived at the lab early, his stomach in a knot. On his ride there, he had read a dozen news articles and opinion pieces condemning LeosTech and demanding it sever its ties with SBC. Connectome was mentioned a few times too. The disturbing possibility of the lab closing seemed more real than last night. Yamir didn't know how or when he'd get to talk to his boss, who wasn't answering calls or returning messages. Meanwhile, the share price for LeosTech on the equity market was in free fall.

At the lab door, Yamir yielded to a small vacuuming robot, wishing that life were as simple as *if dirt speck detected, then remove it.* The desks on the open floor looked like yesterday, before the team had headed to Grady's lake house. But now everyone's work was tainted by the bombshell revelation of forced-labor manufacturing. The horror of human beings forced—through what means, oh, dear El?—to build the ASV3...The uproar should at least lead to the freeing of those enslaved workers. The Temple should be able to bring them home through their intergovernmental ties.

"But what if they can't?" Rhea had asked last night. And what would Wodan's new companion think of a family that benefited from forced labor through Yamir?

No, the desks didn't look exactly the same, Yamir realized. Xiu-Min's was almost empty, with only the keyboard, a coffee mug. and a stack of printouts left on it. When he touched her curved screen, a note appeared. *I'm sorry, but I'm out!*

Yamir checked his voxdev to find a more detailed resignation letter in his inbox. Xiu-Min couldn't continue working for a lab that had anything to do with forced labor. She was setting an example for her unborn child by quitting. Yamir wanted to tell her what he had told Rhea and Julian: he'd had nothing to do with Grady's business decisions. Xiu-Min's last lines were *I know you don't have the luxury to walk away, not when all the A-brains depend on you. I wish you the best of luck, Yamir, and may we meet again under more auspicious circumstances.*

Yamir hunched over her desk, his shoulders heavy. Xiu-Min had been the first neuroscientist to join his team, before Si'ahl and Isabela, and before Zaltana. Behind her quiet demeanor, she had always cared about right and wrong. Losing her was like having the foundation of his lab crumble.

Lights came up as he entered the simulation room. The hum of the air conditioning was the only noise in there. All the wallscreens were dark, and the simulation engines were off.

"That asshole," Yamir muttered as he restarted the quantum workstations on the wall racks.

Three simulation windows appeared on a wallscreen, one each for S1, Z1, and M1. Y1 was still marked offline. The lock on his neural net was with the ASV3, but the shell's satellite-based navigation system wasn't transmitting. Which meant Y1 could be anywhere. Before Yamir could worry further, the three A-brains started talking all at once.

"Where's my cat?" M1 said, frowning. "Have you seen Luna?"

"Another spin on the crazy machine," S1 said, cackling.

"I don't want to marry Oliver, I just don't," Z1 said.

For the A-brains, the time jump was always jarring. All their recently active cortical columns restarted with inputs that didn't match expectations. That was confusing and infuriating, as Grady had intended to show the crowd yesterday using Y1.

Yamir started the recalibrating protocol and waited a few moments for the A-brains to recover before sharing the news. "Something bad happened yesterday at Grady's presentation." He leaned against a desk facing the wallscreen.

"Did Y1 screw up?" S1 said.

"No, he wasn't even there," Yamir said.

M1 looked worried. "What happened to him?"

"I don't know yet," Yamir said, rubbing his forehead. "Our lab has been receiving hardware from a company in the Sahara Expanse that uses forced labor. And Grady knew about it. Now the press knows too, and that could mean the end of our lab."

"Our parts come from forced labor?" Z1 said, her eyes wide.

"Not anymore, I hope," Yamir said.

"What do you mean 'the end of our lab'?" M1 whispered.

S1 cut in. "This is bullshit. I should've never uploaded." He turned to Z1. "And I shouldn't have let you upload either."

"Like you could've stopped me," Z1 said. "We were just colleagues back then."

S1 shook his avatar's head, then turned to Yamir. "You're the boss here, and you don't know where our parts come from?"

"That's not fair, S1," M1 said. "It's not Yamir's job to check the provenance—"

Yamir put up his hands. "Calm down, please, all of you. No, M1, he's right. It's my fault. I'll set things right. I will."

"Sure he will," Dimitri said, walking in.

In two steps, Yamir reached him and grabbed his arm. "Where's Y1?"

Dimitri pulled away. "Calm down, man. He's in my SDV outside, waiting to be powered up."

"You shut us down, you monster!" M1 yelled at him from the wallscreen.

"We begged you to stop," Z1 said.

"Did you know about SBC?" S1 asked.

Yamir didn't need a fight right now; he needed answers. "Let's go to my office." He left the room despite the A-brains' protests, Dimitri following him.

Yamir closed his office door as Dimitri dropped on the gray sofa, his arms extended over its back.

"Did you know about SBC?" Yamir began, taking the side armchair by the low table.

"Nah. Or I would've told the boss that the Temple was sure to find out." He sounded convincing enough.

"Where's Grady now?"

"Around. Covering his ass. He'll resurface soon with a killer outreach strategy." Dimitri smiled. "My guess? He'll throw a bone to the press and make Connectome and his late dad the scapegoat."

Yamir had thought of that. Grady could tell everyone that the contract with SBC had come from Caspian Leos—for Connectome Labs. He had known nothing about forced labor when he later signed a supply-chain deal with SBC for his spacecraft factory. It would take years for investigators to prove him wrong, and by then, he'd be playing a different game altogether.

Dimitri narrowed his eyes. "But I can convince him to leave Connectome alone."

"You thought you could convince him to cancel the announcement, but you couldn't." It gave Yamir satisfaction to say that.

"How do you know I didn't convince him?"

Yamir was left speechless for a moment. Thanks to the high priestess's intervention, Dimitri could now claim Grady wouldn't have unveiled the android.

"You want to hear my idea or what?" Dimitri said.

"Sure, I guess, go ahead."

Dimitri shifted in his seat. "Connectome is the key to the future of our Mars project. The B-brain will help us terraform the red planet, right?"

Leaning on the Mars angle might convince Grady to protect the lab at all costs.

"But only if I'm the head of the lab." Dimitri paused, letting the words sink in.

"Excuse me?" Yamir had heard him but couldn't believe the nerve on that guy. "You assured me recently that you're not after my job."

"That was when my place here was secure," Dimitri said. "Now we must save the lab—together. Admit it, Yamir, you're bad at management. And you don't know how to handle this new danger."

"And you don't know crap about the A-brains," Yamir shot back.

"I don't need to. I only want the title and the pay raise. You'll continue as before. My kids' college bills are a bit much for my contributor salaries, here and at LeosTech. But if I'm in charge here, I'll keep my lab in business, I promise you that."

"My lab," Yamir said, chewing on his lip to keep calm. "You asshole…"

"That's fine. You can take a moment to process."

Still regrouping, Yamir stared out the window at the trees and the blue jay on a branch. "And Grady will just let someone with no experience manage his lab?"

"Grady will think it was his idea in the first place," Dimitri said. "Unless you make a big stink about it."

"No," Yamir said, standing up and beginning to pace. "I can't trust you with my lab. You harmed my A-brains when you powered down their simulation engines yesterday. I understand why Grady wanted you to suspend Y1, but why did you have to hurt the others?"

Dimitri frowned. "I don't get it. Why are they on when no one's here? I grew up saving electricity when there was no water to power our dam. Just because we reengineered our climate and saved the elephants and the bees doesn't mean we should be wasteful."

Yamir was taken aback. "That's why you shut them down? To save electricity?"

"At LeosTech, energy efficiency is a huge concern for our spaceships. It drives me nuts to see how you waste it here."

Yamir scratched his bristly cheek. "All right, think of it this way. Think of Connectome as a hospital where the priority is saving lives, not mega-waheeds. You're scrambling the A-brains if you shut them down."

"But they're machines," Dimitri said. "We're just rebooting them."

"They're people, like you and me, Dimitri. Created from a human brain. You know what?" Yamir was too tired to give him another lesson on the delicate state of an A-brain. "No more shutting them down, you understand?"

"Fine, man, have it your way." Dimitri crossed his arms.

"And no more touching the source code either."

"Don't mind if I don't. So we have a deal?"

Yamir couldn't afford a power struggle, not when the future of the lab hung in the balance. He didn't need the money as much as Dimitri. He could take the pay cut if it meant keeping control of the A-brains. He'd talk to Rhea and make her understand.

"You can have my salary but not my title," he said. "If you convince Grady to keep the lab open."

"The title was worth a try." Dimitri got up from the sofa. "But I can live with just the salary."

A sense of impending doom weighed on Yamir, though in theory, he was doing everything possible to protect the A-brains.

"Now let's bring Y1 in," he said.

Logfile Y1-1831-06-26

Where's that asshole Dimitri?

I want to scream.

Rhea isn't here.

My brain is on fire.

I see a black chasm before me, and I want to jump in.

There's that song again, that fucking earworm.

"Calm down," Yamir tells me. "You're back in your simulation engine."

We're in his office, and he's going through my diagnostics.

"I'm running your recalibration script. Just give me a minute."

My cortical columns have been restarted with inconsistent inputs, which feels like a hangover crossed with motion sickness and food poisoning. It sucks—until the script finishes.

Done. No nausea, no disorientation. Like waking up after a quick nap, things feel normal again.

I look around. Dimitri isn't here. I check my time. I lost a whole day. A whole fucking day!

"Where's M1?" I ask. "Is she all right?"

"She's fine, in the simulation room."

"This is your fault!" I tell Yamir. "You let Dimitri suspend me. Where were you when that happened?" Though I know he was picking up Rhea for the party, which makes me even angrier.

"I'm sorry," Yamir says.

"Always sorry, aren't you?"

Yamir doesn't protest. He just sits in front of my screen, running diagnostic tests.

"You shouldn't be in charge of this lab," I tell him. I feel calmer than a second ago. "Ugh, stop messing with my controls! Let me feel this anger, you asshole. I was supposed to see Rhea yesterday, not be knocked out cold."

He backs away from my dashboard on the screen. "Dimitri won't suspend you ever again, I promise."

"Oh, because he'll listen to you?"

He doesn't answer. He picks up his lidded coffee mug—he knows how much I hate smelling it, so the lid is the least he can do—and takes a sip. "How are you feeling?"

"What happened at Grady's?"

"There was no presentation because the Temple revealed we're using forced labor for our components. The press is up in arms, and Grady promised an investigation."

"Forced labor? Like me?"

Yamir grimaces. "That's not fair..."

We could fight, or I could extract a favor from him. "I need access to the source code for the engine's Suspend function. I'm not having that piece-of-shit Dimitri shut me down ever again. I'll rewrite the code so that I can't be suspended anymore."

Yamir waves a hand. "As I said, it won't happen again."

"I don't trust you either. Give me access." I've been editing the nonessential parts of the source code for more than a year, always in a sandbox that Yamir then validates for inclusion into the main branch. Giving me access to the Suspend function is different though.

Yamir chews on his lip, as I used to do under stress. A soothing habit

I had to give up long ago.

"I'm only asking for the same right you have to control your own body," I say.

"As if we organic humans can mess with our bodies willy-nilly. As if we don't need prescriptions or don't get in trouble for using unapproved medicine."

"Oh, you want to have that conversation?" I say, ready with more arguments.

"No, I don't. But you can damage your A-brain if you introduce a code defect. Better if you make whatever changes you want, and I'll port them to the main branch after I test them, as always."

"I must do this fast, and you don't have time now. I don't trust Dimitri to stay away from us until then."

"And I don't trust you not to harm yourself."

"You made sure I wouldn't do that when you brought Mom here."

We stare at each other for a long moment. A very long moment.

Then Yamir nods, looking exhausted. "But only for the Suspend. I'll let you override the default function."

"Good," I say. "I'll start coding today. I'll talk to Xiu-Min about the functions—"

"Xiu-Min is gone," Yamir says. "She quit."

I feel those words like a punch in the gut. Xiu-Min was my first scientist here at the lab.

"Because of the accusation of forced labor?" I say, though I know the answer.

I'll miss Xiu-Min, with her sharp math brain and her constant worries about the baby.

Yamir glances at his voxdev, and I do too, my video sensors zooming in. He has five missed calls from Rhea and a few texts that read *I need you!* and *Never mind.*

"You promised I'd see Rhea after the presentation," I tell him.

"Not now," he cuts me off and dials Rhea's comm ID.

My audio sensors detect his call reaching her voxmail.

On his drive home, Yamir ordered the ES to turn off the broadcast after an angry show host asked, "Can you believe these scientists who claim they didn't know about the forced labor?" Even passersby seemed to look at Yamir's SDV askew. He wanted to stop the vehicle and tell them it wasn't his fault and that he couldn't quit like Xiu-Min because the A-brains were his responsibility. The Council of Nations should go after SBC and free those poor people.

Dimitri's proposal was infuriating, but it could help protect the lab. Grady wouldn't buy Yamir's arguments for keeping the lab open, just as he had dismissed his paper about the dangers of a public announcement. But he might listen to Dimitri. On the other hand, if Yamir accepted Dimitri's slippery slope, he could soon find himself pushed out of the lab completely. He was playing defense, and badly. Maybe the lab would close anyway, and the four A-brains would be deleted. Or worse, if they fell into unethical and cruel hands.

At the house, Rhea's red SDV was parked in the driveway, blocking Yamir's way into the garage. So she was home. He hadn't managed to get a hold of her earlier. Worried for her safety, he had called the admin at Servetus University and learned Rhea was in a meeting, so at least she wasn't in any physical danger. But she had needed to talk to him, and he hadn't been available—because he'd been dealing with the A-brains. And Dimitri. And Y1.

Rhea's vehicle in the driveway could mean she had picked up Wodan from the airport. Their son had arrived home early? Such great news. And Rhea had wanted to share it with Yamir directly, instead of sending a cold text or leaving a voxmail. That was why she had called.

The SDV parked at the curb next to the short totem pole marking their street address. Yamir hurried out, excited. He hadn't seen Wodan in almost a year.

He bumped into Rhea at the door, her hands full of small bags. It had to be Wodan's stuff.

"Let me help you," he said, but she pulled away and walked past him.

Her SDV's trunk opened, and she threw the bags inside.

"Is he going somewhere?" Yamir said. "So soon?"

"Who?" Rhea said.

"Wodan. Isn't he…is he here?"

"Not until tomorrow," she said, heading back inside.

His stomach heavy with dread, Yamir followed her. "Wait, what's going on, Rhea?"

Two large pieces of luggage waited at the bottom of the stairs.

"The Temple fired me from the Concord Column project," she said in a flat tone.

"What? Why would they do that?"

"Because I'm your wife, and you work at Connectome." She pressed the button on the first piece of luggage, and it took off toward the door. "And Connectome used forced labor for its parts."

Yamir felt lightheaded. "But that's not my fault. I've got nothing to do with it either."

"I know that. I don't blame you for my lost job. And I understand the Temple's need to distance itself from people like me." She sent the second suitcase to the door.

Yamir stumbled out of its way. "People like you? You did nothing wrong."

"That's not how the world works though," she said, always the history professor.

"But why leave your house? What sense does that make?"

Rhea shrugged. "This awful revelation landed like a drone bomb in my life. I need time, Yamir. Time to think about everything. About my life and my needs. I'm sorry I can't be supportive at this point. I hope you understand."

"No, I don't, because that's not like you to make snap decisions about our life—"

"Oh, it's not a snap decision, trust me," Rhea said with a sharpness in her tone, and she went out the door.

"Let's take a minute though." Yamir followed her into the evening sun. "Today was a wild day. You wouldn't believe what Dimitri wants now."

She threw him a glance, and he realized he was talking about his problems again instead of hers.

"And...the Temple being so wrong to fire you." He interlaced his fingers, begging. "We should stick together through this, Rhea, not fall apart."

She pressed the Load button on the trunk's touchscreen, and the ramp extended to scoop up the luggage from the ground. "It's not just this time, Yamir. I'm tired of being lonely. When Wodan was in high school and you were late from work, I had my son for company. We even went together on my research trips to Dhawosia when you were too busy to join us. But then he left for college, and there's no one to fill that hole in my life anymore."

"I'm sorry," Yamir said. "I miscalculated...I thought that if I worked hard, I'd finish the B-brain by now, and then we'd have plenty of time to...I didn't know it would take this long...No one does when they're young and driven. I didn't know how dearly it would cost me—"

"Us, not you!" She shook her head.

"Us. Would cost *us*. You're right."

"Damn it, Yamir." She rubbed her eyes like she wanted to crush them.

Yamir reached for her hand, but she swatted him. "You're right to be angry, I know," he said, "but listen to me for just a moment."

"Again, you're asking me to do something for you. What about me?"

"What about Wodan and his companion? Shouldn't we present a good image for Harry?"

"It's Heath. And no, Wodan is a grown-up. He'll understand."

"But I don't understand," Yamir said, his voice breaking. "Where is this coming from?"

"Yamir, seriously, I've been telling you for years how lonely I feel in this relationship. This can't possibly be a surprise for you."

He had thought those were just bad moments that would pass. Instead, they'd been accumulating, and now they crashed down on him. "Where will you go?" he whispered.

She shrugged. "A hotel for the night. A cabin in the mountains tomorrow. Doesn't matter."

She entered her SDV and ordered it to just drive.

"Rhea, please…" Yamir called after her.

No, no, no, this wasn't happening. He felt wounded and ill. As if he had lost a limb. Her leaving like that was terrifying. His hands shook. His shoulders slumped with the weight of this catastrophe. No, Rhea couldn't be gone.

He stood on the sidewalk for minutes after, unable to go back inside the empty house.

How had everything ended up so broken? His answer to every problem was to work harder, but he'd been working as hard as he could, and everything was falling apart. It was so unfair for the Temple to punish Rhea for being his wife. Maybe he could reach out to the reporters who'd been calling him and expose the Temple's unfairness? No, Rhea wouldn't want to be caught in a public relations storm. Then what could he do? He had no connections at the Temple to get Rhea back on the Concord Column project. What could he do to show her how much he loved her?

What if he tried to get her access to Grady's old manuscripts from his library, as she had asked him? It was a silly plan, yes, but that was all he could think of now, in his feverish mindset. Because his life without Rhea was unthinkable.

Logfile Y1-1831-06-26

The updates to my Suspend functions are done and another training session outside with the ASV3 completed.

As I walk back into the building, it looks like everyone has left for the evening. No, not everyone. I expected to see Isabela, but I spot Si'ahl sitting before Z1's screen in the simulation room. They're talking, but his shoulders are hunched like he's hiding something. I can't sneak up on him because Z1 will see me, but this new shell came with the best audio sensors ever. So I keep my distance but turn my head the right way and listen.

"Do you love antiques?" Si'ahl asks Z1.

Her avatar on the screen tips its head, smiling. "Like what?"

I wonder if Si'ahl, seeing S1 succeed where he's failed with Zaltana, is trying to woo Z1 for practice. Or is he just lonely and needs a Zaltana look-alike for company? It's sad to see him unable to accept that she's a loyal person and would never break up with Oliver. Her dedication to those around her is why she didn't hesitate to donate her brain image for testing.

I'm still getting used to zooming in—the effect is bewildering, like falling into a gravity well—but I must check Z1's screen. I focus until I can see the controls Si'ahl uses on her dashboard. There's a dial I haven't seen before, labeled TS. Next to it, there's a list of simulated ingredients, each with its own bar graph and slider: scopolamine, sodium thiopental, oxytocin, and ethanol.

I lose my cool in an instant and dash into the simulation room. "What do you think you're doing?"

Si'ahl turns around, his startled face telling me I was right to worry.

"What's going on?" Z1 says from the screen, frowning.

"Nothing," Si'ahl says and suspends her. He gets up from the chair, looking flustered, and tries to move around me, but he knows better than to outrun an android. "Also, none of your business, Y1. Why are you spying on me, anyway?"

"I live here, remember? And Z1 is my friend. What were you doing to her?"

He puts up his hands. "Nothing. You need to get a life, dude!"

"I had a life," I say, feeling the sting. "And you have a lot to explain."

"Come on, Y1..." He shrugs and turns his head, lowering his hands.

I move closer. "Looks like you're giving her a cocktail of chemicals meant to disorient her and put her in a trusting state of mind. TS—does that stand for truth serum?"

"It's not like that," Si'ahl says. "Zaltana's birthday is coming up. I asked her what she'd like for a present and she said, 'Surprise me.' But you know how private she is. And she doesn't touch social media."

True, Zaltana, like Rhea, is strict about not posting personal details online. She doesn't browse much either. In college, she worked on algorithms that monitored people's hyperspace activity. Just a few data points on what a person spent time reading online allowed Zaltana to know them better than they knew themselves. No wonder she's spooked.

"I just wanted to buy her something nice, that's all," Si'ahl says. "I thought I could ask Z1…"

"With a truth serum?" I get close to his face. "Why not just ask her for help, as a friend?"

"We were just talking." Si'ahl looks more and more embarrassed. "I haven't used the serum yet. Wouldn't have, probably…"

"Zaltana has a fiancé, Si'ahl." I point at Z1's shaded outline on the screen, where she's suspended. "What you were planning to do is an abuse of the worst kind." I poke his shoulder with my metal finger. "We A-brains are still human, with human rights and human needs, even though we're running on inorganic hardware."

Si'ahl rubs his shoulder. "Please don't tell Zaltana."

"You need to let go of her. She's with someone else…"

"But she's not happy with him—"

"None of your business," I tell him, though I can't accept that same argument about me and Rhea. We had been married before my upload, after all.

"You're right, this was a terrible idea." Si'ahl nervously runs his fingers through his long ponytail. "I should've asked S1 for advice. Somehow, he's figured out a way to Z1's heart. I'm glad you stopped me. But you understand my pain, right? The other day, you were fighting with Yamir about Rhea…"

His words burn me. "Don't ever try this again," I tell him.

"I won't, I won't, I promise."

"Now let's get Z1 back online. Quickly, before she gets too disoriented."

While Si'ahl restarts her simulation engine, I realize how incensed I still am. I lower the adrenaline level on my forearm screen and block the beta receptors in my sympathetic nervous system. I feel calmer already.

"What was that about?" Z1's avatar on the screen rubs her eyes. She wasn't suspended for long, so she doesn't need the recalibration script.

"Sorry," I tell Z1. "Si'ahl was about to activate the sequencing tool I'm still working on, and that would've messed up your cortical columns. My bad for not labeling it clearly."

"No harm done." Always so supportive.

Today is a wake-up call. With Grady and Dimitri around, we A-brains need more protection. Not just me with my new Suspend function. No one should use invasive tools on us without our permission. But they can only manipulate our A-brains when we're in the simulation engine. In the android shell, we have autonomy.

From now on, an A-brain should patrol the lab at all times using the ASV3. The backup battery pack should always be charged. And Yamir will agree to this because he's worried about nosy reporters sneaking in, but an android could serve as a security guard.

6

Yamir woke up smelling fresh toast. For a moment, he thought Rhea was in the kitchen, making breakfast, and he stretched his arms and smiled but then remembered she had left him. His stomach dropped. But maybe she was back?

He stumbled around the bedroom, still in yesterday's pants and shirt. The clock on the dresser read 08:18. He flung the door open and clambered down the stairs, calling, "Rhea?"

"Hi, Dad," Wodan answered, his mouth half full. He was at the kitchen counter, a slice of buttered toast in hand. "You're awake at last."

"Wodan?" Yamir said. "When did you arrive? Is everything all right?" A quick check told him his son was unhurt, smiling even. But what would he think of Rhea's absence? She probably hadn't had time to prepare him for the news.

"Now don't look so disappointed." Wodan took his last bite and licked his lips.

"No, that's not what I meant." Yamir opened his arms. "I'm so happy to see you." He grabbed his son into an uncomfortable bear hug, patting him on the back. Wodan had grown bigger in the shoulders since last year—all that training they did at the space school, teaching them how to keep fit in low gravity. "You look great."

"Can't say the same about you." Wodan put his crumb-filled plate in the sink. "Has Mom left for work already?"

Yamir didn't know how to answer, so he busied himself filling the coffee grinder with beans and pressing the button harder than needed.

"I'm texting her now to tell her I'm home," Wodan said.

Yamir emptied the coffee grounds into the glass press and poured hot water from the sink dispenser over the dark powder.

Wodan finished typing on his voxdev. "So, how have you been? Sorry to hear about the disaster at Grady's. The entire hyperspace is on fire."

"Yeah, what a mess," Yamir said, rubbing the stubble on his cheek.

"Dad...did you know about the forced labor?" Wodan said.

"No, of course not. It makes me sick to my stomach to think of those people locked up and toiling over our components."

"I always thought that stuff was done by robots..."

"Most of it is, but supervising the robots and testing the components require human work."

"Just like in space travel," Wodan said.

Yamir placed the coffee press on the white granite counter, eager to end that conversation. "How are things at school?"

Wodan's face brightened with a smile. "I had a wonderful year in London, Dad. And during breaks, Heath and I did a lot of traveling." He paused. "Mom told you about Heath, I assume?"

"Of course. We're excited to meet him."

"Great then. Well, Heath and I like to travel. A lot. So we visited Dhawosia together—the places Mom used to take me to on her research trips. We went to Zalmodava and climbed the sacred Mount Ea-El. And I showed him the Boulder Hut, where they say Oroles was kept prisoner before he died..."

As Wodan told him about his travels, Yamir waited for the coffee to brew and checked his messages on his voxdev, hoping for a sign from Rhea. Nothing. Wodan mentioned his training on a new spacecraft simulator, then started explaining the process. As long as Wodan was safe, the details didn't matter that much to Yamir. He nodded while his son spoke, and then he typed a message to Si'ahl, asking for news. Had Dimitri talked to Grady about keeping the lab open?

"Seriously, Dad?" Wodan said.

Yamir looked up.

Wodan was frowning at him, his head cocked to one side. "I just got home."

"Sorry, son. I'm dealing with this Grady mess." He set the voxdev aside and poured two mugs of coffee, then sat at the counter with one of them. "You said that next year you'll be flying to the Moon?"

Wodan grabbed his coffee, still looking cross. "If everything goes well, yeah."

"Is Heath in town?" Yamir said after an uncomfortable silence.

"He's here for a bit, while we catch our breaths. Then I want to take him sailing."

"When do I—I mean we—get to meet him?"

"How about tonight?" Wodan said, and Yamir choked on his coffee. "Dinner at your and Mom's favorite restaurant? The Italian one by Pike Place Market?"

There were many other restaurants around the market, from Shel'landic to Ethiopian and Peruvian cuisine. Why choose that one? "That'd be great, yes." Maybe Rhea would join them to present a united front for Wodan and Heath.

Yamir's voxdev buzzed with a message from Si'ahl. *Grady is at his factory. Dimitri saw him entering his office.* Dimitri would try to convince Grady not to close the lab. Yamir realized Wodan was talking again, and he tried to pay attention.

"The greatest thing about spaceships," Wodan was saying, "is that you must know everything about them if you want to take one out there. The kind of relationship a pilot has with their ship is so intimate, as if at times they're just one body. Takes years to become an expert and—"

That was it! Yamir stood up from his chair and dropped his hands on his son's shoulders. "You just gave me the greatest idea on how to deal with Grady. Wow...I have to go now." He could run the idea by Zaltana on the way to the Tahoma factory, just to make sure.

"Whatever, Dad...Just don't forget about dinner, all right?"

"Of course. And thanks a million, Wodan." Yamir headed upstairs to change from yesterday's clothes.

He might not need Dimitri after all to convince Grady to keep Connectome open. But Dimitri was right. Yamir had to think like a space engineer if he wanted Grady to even listen to him.

Olma sat on a marble bench in the atrium of the Cedarwood Temple Inn. She'd been watching Yamir's house on her voxdev, with a drone spying through the kitchen window from the backyard. Her neck and shoulders ached, and she felt less in control of her muscles than the month before.

She zoomed in to better see the two people sitting at the kitchen counter, chatting. Their body language told her there was tension between them. Unresolved conflict, perhaps. The young man had short dark hair and light-brown skin, and he was animated as he spoke, while Yamir kept glancing at his voxdev.

Yamir's wife wasn't there. Olma had fired Rhea Laghmani from the Concord Column project, which had made Rhea leave Yamir in anger. "Don't touch the wife. Never touch the wife," Nala had told her, but Olma couldn't let someone who had known about the android for years—and kept it quiet—be part of a Temple-sanctioned project. Still, she didn't feel good about the result.

The drone's audio sensors didn't catch the men's words through the glass pane, and the angle was bad for lipreading. Olma activated the Temple's facial recognition system and waited for the young man to turn his head toward the window. The system returned one Wodan Varro, twenty, son of Yamir Varro and Rhea Laghmani, student at the Ptolemaeus Space School in London. Olma recognized him now, based on the pictures of Yamir's family she had studied.

Through the waterfall's trickling, Olma heard footsteps approaching the atrium. She looked up to see Nala wearing a summer dress in a flower print. Her blond hair was tucked behind her ears, and her gold loops enhanced the bright colors of her dress. She also wore new white sandals. Nala had gone shopping this morning.

"Let's go," she said. "I'm starving."

"I'm still working," Olma said.

"Let me see." Nala sat on the bench, fixing Olma with her blue gaze.

She'd be outraged if she caught Olma spying on people. As a criminal defense attorney, she was a strong advocate for human rights. Olma tapped fast on her voxdev, ordering the drone to return to the Temple Inn, then turned the screen off.

"So you're not working," Nala said.

"Not anymore," Olma replied with a forced smile. "What would you like to do?"

"I found a good restaurant in this El-forsaken place, and I'm taking you there for lunch. Shel'landic cuisine at its finest. Especially good, since you've lost some weight."

"I have not," Olma said, unsure.

Nala rolled her eyes. "I won't tell you that you work too much, but you must pay more attention to your body, love. You're not getting enough sleep. And you should see Doctor Silvestri about that treatment. Your MNDS could be managed—but only if you start treating it."

Nala had arrived at the most important part of her request in a roundabout way that left Olma no chance to argue against it. That was what made Nala so good at her job, where diplomacy and negotiation skills were key.

"I will, soon," Olma said.

Her voxdev pinged with a notification for a message from Regina Sacrorum, the co-leader of the Temple. She knew what it would say. Olma should secure all android knowledge she could gather from Dimitri Petrodava, file international patents to block other companies from making progress in the field of artificial brains, then force Grady Leos to shut down Connectome Labs. Hopefully, she could return home soon after.

"Ready?" Nala stood up.

Olma knew she wouldn't enjoy her lunch while an unread message from the Sacrorums waited for her. "I need a change of clothes," she said, and Nala agreed with a quick nod at Olma's black pants and white button-down shirt, both creased.

Olma returned to their apartment on the fifth floor and used her encrypted connection to the Temple to read Regina's message. To her surprise, it was about creating an army of androids for the Temple's revamped Mars settlement. *We now have the means to finally turn the Martian wasteland into a garden.* That was an image plucked straight from the sacred texts, as garden and wasteland were the hallmarks of Oroles's human story—before ascending to El's Caelum in the second century LE. The Sacrorums had even come up with a name for their new android army: the Mars Guard. And Olma's sacred mission was to make it happen.

Yamir arrived at Grady's Tahoma spacecraft factory, south of Cedarwood, around noon. He had called Zaltana on the way and, together, refined his new plan to keep Connectome open.

At the front desk, he showed his Connectome Labs ID, and the security guard let him in. He took the elevator up to the waiting area outside Grady's office. He didn't have an appointment, but he hadn't expected to get one if he had called.

Grady's ESPA, a human-sized robot in a white polymer shell, greeted him.

"Is Grady in?" Yamir said. "I need to talk to him. It's an emergency."

"Please wait," the ESPA said.

Dimitri could be behind that closed door, discussing the future of Connectome with his boss. Yamir felt the urge to burst in and interrupt them.

"Please wait," the ESPA said, as if reading Yamir's mind.

Yamir headed to the floor-to-ceiling windows to kill time and inspect the maintenance hangar below. He took in the busy scene, minus the clamor. On the open floor, a capsule was under repairs, with servicing equipment and crew around it. Another was parked by the exit, looking ready to deploy. People and assisting robots intermingled, and large automated arms moved pieces around.

Over the next hour, employees passed through the waiting area, always in a hurry. Yamir checked the news on his voxdev, headlines still mentioning Grady's scandalous event two days ago. The Tahoma chapter of the fundamentalist sect Elsway planned to protest LeosTech's forced labor practices right outside this factory. Yamir wondered what kind of protection the lab could get from Grady if it stayed open.

At some point, three people stopped to chat by the elevator about their weekend plans: canoeing together on the Sammamish River. A few minutes later, two employees passed by, discussing the concept of shielding against outer space radiation. Something about thick aluminum walls encasing a water shell to absorb cosmic rays and protect against secondary radiation. Yamir memorized that technical detail to impress Wodan at dinner.

By the time Grady was ready to see him, almost two hours later, Yamir was past the stomach butterflies and getting hungry. To his relief, Dimitri had not been there.

"What do you want?" Grady was at his desk, not looking up from his tablet. His suit was black today, and a blue scarf lay bundled on the desk at his side.

"To make sure you won't close the lab," Yamir blurted out the conclusion he was planning to build up to.

Grady kept his gaze on the tablet as if he hadn't heard Yamir.

"The spacecraft factory uses the same parts manufacturer as the lab." Yamir sat in a chair before the massive desk. "But you won't close the factory, will you?"

Grady glanced out the window, toward the capsule being repaired below.

Yamir didn't know how to approach a silent Grady, so he went on. "You love this place, don't you? Maybe more than your lake house?"

Grady made eye contact for the first time, giving Yamir a worried squint.

"Oh, no, I'm not threatening you," he hurried to say. "I'm not Elsway. What I'm offering is something that could help you monitor this factory better. Did I say *monitor*? I meant *feel*."

Grady's expression changed to intrigued.

"A neurosensory vest, *neurovest* for short," Yamir said, using the name Zaltana had come up with earlier. "It'll be the highest priority for Con-

nectome. Everything else will be put on hold while we build it for you."
Though Y1, S1, and Z1 could continue to work on the A-brain project in a
secure sandbox.

"What are you talking about?" Grady said at last.

Yamir began his rehearsed proposal. "Imagine not just looking at your
factory from these tall windows. Or walking on its floor and talking to
your technicians. Or reading reports. Imagine wearing a special vest
that will make you *feel* your factory on your skin. Like an extension of
your body, telling you which subsystems are working well and which are
struggling—all at once. We can train your brain to work with this vest
until you feel the factory as a part of yourself. Instead of accessing big
data on workstations, you can experience it directly, anywhere you go.
Would you like that?"

Grady leaned back in his chair.

Yamir leaned in. "You'll have access to the stats of dozens of machines
at once, feeling their production rates through dedicated vibrations your
brain will learn to comprehend. You'll sense when things run out of
alignment or need adjustment or attention."

"I have alerts and alarms when something goes wrong."

"This is different. It'll make you *feel* how your machines are running
together." He stressed the word *feel* again.

Grady nodded. "But why a vest and not a wristband? Or smart glasses?"

"Our skin is a data channel with a high bandwidth, but it's underused.
It can feel a lot, but it usually feels very little. Our eyes are always receiving input, and adding smart glasses will just crowd out other important
signals you need during the day."

"But won't those new sensations on my torso be annoying?"

"At first, yes, but after a short period of adjustment, it'll feel the same
as your clothes, which you don't really pay attention to during the course
of the day." Though with Grady and his acute sense of fashion, that
argument might not land. "You're not aware how your feet feel inside
your shoes unless there's a small rock inside, right? With the neurovest,
you'll only be aware of something surprising or out of order."

Yamir was prepared to reassure Grady that his brain wouldn't feel under attack from the additional stream of sensory information. Brains didn't mind billions of photons hitting the retinas or constant sound reaching the eardrums. Adding one more stream of data through the neurovest wouldn't be a problem.

But Grady seemed to have understood that, because his next question was, "How long will it take you to build it?"

Yamir was now hopeful. "The vest itself will need testing and fine-tuning. But it mainly creates small vibrations triggered by your factory signals sent wirelessly. The complicated part will be to gather all the meaningful signals in the factory and codify them into the right kind of input for your vest."

Grady patted his chest. "I'd love to feel this place on my skin. Unfortunately, from tomorrow, you won't be working for me anymore. I'll have to contract you out for this neurovest thing."

Yamir's jaws clenched. "What do you mean, I won't work for you?" Had he named Dimitri lab chief?

"Half an hour ago, I agreed to sell Connectome Labs to the Orolic Temple through High Priestess Olma Asper."

Yamir wanted to punch his now-former boss in the face for letting him go on and on about the neurovest when the lab had already been sold. Of course, Grady would string him along to see if he could gain any advantage.

"Why sell?" Yamir said in a low voice.

"Not really selling. More like making a mutually beneficial exchange. The Temple will explain away this SBC scandal. They'll name LeosTech their exclusive Mars transport when they return to rebuild their settlement. They'll even favor my shuttles again for Urbs Lunae." He let out a deep breath. "Sorry, Yamir, but your lab now belongs to the Temple, like everything else under the sun, it seems. It was good working with you while it lasted."

Yamir stood up from the chair, still in shock, and found his way to the door, which slid open. Then he remembered. "My wife, Rhea Laghmani, the historian, she'd like to study some manuscripts in your library, if possible."

"I'd love to help," Grady said, "if you make time to work on my neurovest while under Olma Asper's management."

Grady had gained an advantage by letting Yamir present his proposal, and now he was using it.

Yamir bit his lip to hide his anger. "Can Rhea have access to those manuscripts right now?"

Grady shrugged. "Sure. Talk to Thandi. I'll keep your security clearance for my satellites so you can contact me on an encrypted channel about the neurovest."

Yamir stepped outside.

"And tell Wodan to stop by when he's in town," Grady called after him.

"Have a good day," the ESPA told Yamir, motioning toward the elevators.

The news had drained Yamir of all energy. Another new boss in just a few months. What did that mean for the lab? Shutting down the A-brain project to work on something for the Temple?

If Connectome still existed next week, it was vital for Yamir to establish a better relationship with his new boss than the one he'd had with Grady Leos. He had taken Caspian's patronage for granted and neglected to form a working relationship with Caspian's son. He couldn't afford to make the same mistake with Olma Asper.

The factory's surroundings were baking under the June sun. Yamir called his SDV from the parking garage on his voxdev, then texted Rhea about the access to Grady's library. *Talk to Thandi Leos.* He also asked her to join him for dinner with Wodan and Heath. No reply came while he waited, sweating in the heat.

A man walked his way, looking somewhat familiar: medium height, short black hair, sunglasses, wispy beard, light skin.

"If I could have a moment? Lucius Seong with the Northwest News Network." The reporter who had asked about the lab closing the other night.

"Still no comment," Yamir said, heading for the shade of an oak tree.

"Is it true that Grady Leos has an artificial human all done and ready to go?" Seong said, following.

"Please leave me alone."

"I'll keep digging, Yamir Varro, with or without your help."

Seong was in his late twenties, and Yamir didn't doubt the reporter had all the time and energy in the world to make good on that promise.

The SDV arrived at the curb, and Yamir hopped in. He sat on the door-facing bench, the cool air inside feeling good on his sweaty forehead.

"Destination?" the driving ES asked.

Yamir ignored it and took out his voxdev to research the reporter. Lucius Seong had a few awards for investigative journalism to his name, so he wasn't a hack. Ten years before, he had transitioned and documented his medical and personal journey. The medical part had been easy, the personal much harder because his parents belonged to the fundamentalist sect Elsway, which believed El had created the world just as it needed to be. So Seong was not only an excellent reporter but had also shown resilience by escaping a sect that had harassed him for years.

The enemy of my enemy and all that. Yamir looked out the window, and there was Seong in the scorching sun, waiting, with a stern expression on his face. Yamir told the SDV to open the door and called the reporter in.

Seong didn't hesitate.

"Destination?" the ES said.

"Just park for now," Yamir said, and the SDV drove for a few meters, then parked at the curb.

Seong put his sunglasses away, then picked a tissue from the dispenser and wiped his face.

"At Grady's, how did you know who I was?" Yamir asked.

"You were the star of those old octopus videos, so you were easy to spot. I also recognized Rhea Laghmani from the Concord Column hypersite and saw her sitting at your table. I asked Thandi Leos if you were together, and she asked if I was after a threesome, which I took as a yes, that you were together."

So much for Rhea's painstaking efforts to keep her life private. It had taken a reporter just a few minutes to track her and her family.

"What do you know about our work at the lab?" Yamir said.

"If Olma Asper is involved, it must be important for the Temple. If Grady Leos chose to work with the ill-reputed Sahara Biospheres Company, he must need money, and badly. That's all I got so far." He had an earnest smile.

"Who is Olma Asper?" Yamir said.

"You have to give me something first." Seong pulled out his tablet.

"Off the record."

Seong nodded and put his tablet away.

"Olma Asper is going to be our new owner," Yamir said. "Grady has just sold our lab to the Temple. Now tell me, who is Olma Asper?"

"A high priestess from Rome, but you already know that. What you don't know is that she's dying, which makes her a tough opponent. She doesn't care about her career and the future, but she might want to ensure her wife's well-being in Italy after she's gone."

"Dying? Of what?"

"Only the first piece of information was free," Seong said.

"What do you want for the rest?"

"To know what you're working on."

If Olma Asper was dying, then she might not want to spend a lot of time in Cedarwood. Like Yamir, she wouldn't want the attention of the press. If he made things easy for her, she could return to Rome to be with her loved ones before the end.

"Thank you." He watched the disappointment on the young reporter's face. "Now, if you don't mind, I have a dinner to prepare for."

Logfile Y1-1831-06-27

S1, Z1, and I are taking turns today patrolling the lab in the ASV3. I need to tell Yamir about my decision to have an android active at all times, but he didn't come to work today. I hope it's for a good reason. Maybe Wodan is home, and they're spending the day together. Maybe he's finally making time for his family, like I never did.

When my turn with the ASV3 came, the scientists were already used to an android walking around the open workspace. Si'ahl told me I looked like an ESPA when I parked myself outside the simulation room's door for lack of anything else to do.

"Come help me with the connectome chamber miniaturization," Zaltana asked me, and I was happy to oblige. The helmet concept she's created actually fits my head, even though my A-brain isn't inside.

Once she left for the day, I went to check on M1 again, and we played a game of crosswords with virtual tiles for about an hour. Now only Isabela and Dimitri are still here. Yamir is definitely not stopping by today.

Isabela is at her desk, reading an interactive psychology paper, and Dimitri…well, I don't care what he's doing.

"You should go home," Dimitri tells Isabela, rolling from his desk in his ergonomic chair. "Your dogs probably miss you."

"Don't worry." Isabela lifts her gaze from the curved screen. "My ESPA keeps them well fed and exercised. Sometimes I think they love it more than they love me."

Dimitri is about to say something when his voxdev beeps. He takes a look, and the next thing I know, he's transferred me back to my simulation engine.

That's infuriating. My next project is to figure out how to prevent the scientists from force-transferring us.

And now he's suspending us, all four A-brains. But what he doesn't know is that I've updated my Suspend function. So I auto-restart, keeping the option to look offline. And not a moment too soon.

From my sensor array, I watch Dimitri sneak inside our simulation room to answer his voxdev call away from Isabela. He once mentioned he's afraid of spying drones, so this must be why he didn't go outside to take his call. To my disappointment, he's using wireless earbuds, so I can't tell whom he's talking to. But I can tell it's a person of importance. Though not Grady.

I turn up my audio sensors.

"Understood," Dimitri whispers, pacing. "How soon would you like to interview them?"

Fucking asshole! He's bringing the press in to talk to our scientists. Does Yamir know about this? Does Grady? Because nothing good will come from media coverage of Connectome right now. Unless Grady wants reporters to meet us, the A-brains. Another shocking revelation that will make the SBC scandal seem minor in comparison.

Oh, these fucking people. Always scheming.

"Will do," Dimitri says and ends the conversation.

He doesn't log the call, which explains why I haven't found anything suspicious about him in our logfiles.

He then restarts us all and says with a fake smile, "I'm so sorry, force of habit. Won't happen again. Have a good evening, everyone."

The only reason for Dimitri to sell us to the press is money. Though his constant mentioning of his three kids in college makes me doubt their existence. I have to talk to Yamir about all this, but he's not picking up his voxdev. Just like him to not be around when I need him. His comm ID geo-tracker shows him at La Fontana Ristorante. Having dinner with Rhea, no doubt. Great.

Yamir arrived early at La Fontana Ristorante. He sat at the table he and Rhea loved, by the window, with an evening view of the cobbled alley through the open door. Maybe she'd still show up, for Wodan's sake, to make a good impression on his companion, Heath. Yamir had sent her all the details in case she changed her mind.

They had eaten here just a few days ago, when things looked promising between them. Like then, he could hear the sounds of Pike Place

Market winding down a block away. The mixed scents of Duwamish Bay always made Rhea bring up her favorite Dhawosian restaurant on the Black Sea Coast. Yamir didn't know the place because she had traveled there without him while researching the history of the Orolic Temple. He could have made more time for her needs over the years...

He checked his voxdev and found only a text from his mom on Swallah Island. *No prowlers lately, but my cat disappeared last night. Back this morning.*

He started typing *That's good* but had an unsettling thought. He wrote instead *Take Luna to the vet just to make sure.* A routine checkup would catch a subdermal chip or implanted audio sensors. Some reporters would do anything to get a scoop—and they must have linked Malina to Connectome Labs by now.

Yamir sipped from his glass of iced water, waiting. He didn't need to look at the digital menu on the tabletop. His regular was mushroom ravioli with spinach, to Rhea's exasperation. He'd even had it twenty years ago, when she went into early labor and they rushed to the hospital through speed-limited downtown traffic.

Standing by Wodan's incubator in the Neonatal Intensive Care Unit at Dokina Medical Center, looking at that tiny baby covered in sensors bigger than his shut eyes, Yamir felt an overpowering anxiety. Worse than what he had felt in the hospital on the Moon after Malina's accident.

His hand was on Rhea's shoulder as she wiped her tears.

"Your anxiety about the fragility of life..." she whispered. "I get it now, strange as it is. And I understand your irrational drive to do something about it..."

That had been the closest Yamir had ever felt to Rhea, as she understood his lifelong burden. He promised her then that he'd keep Wodan safe, no matter what. And he had done so, as long as their son had lived in their house.

Wodan and Heath entered the restaurant on time. Heath was shorter, his skin tone lighter. His shoulder-length brown hair had blue highlights, and he wore a gray business suit, not the tourist clothes Yamir had expected—a sign he took this meeting with his companion's father seriously.

Yamir stood up from the table and didn't hesitate to shake Heath's hand, ignoring his pandemic-induced habit of only waving and nodding at new acquaintances. Before sitting down, he glanced at the door for any sign of Rhea.

Wodan and Heath sat opposite Yamir, with their backs to the door. An ESPA server rolled by and filled their water glasses. Wodan didn't mention Rhea, which meant his mom had updated him on the temporary separation. Somehow, that silence made it even more real.

The first few questions were reconnaissance for Yamir, and Heath answered them with lots of detail. He was from London, had finished medical school, and was visiting Shel'land between sessions of residency training at a Welsh hospital. Loved the Cedarwood he had seen so far. He made light fun of Wodan, who had grown up in the Pacific Northwest but somehow hadn't taken advantage of the many wonders this region offered.

"Such a bookworm," Heath said, and Wodan smiled with a knowledge-able glance at Yamir.

So Wodan hadn't told his companion that it had been his father who didn't let him learn how to paddleboard or rock climb or even ski growing up. Yamir's insistence that Wodan do nothing too dangerous might have even cost his son a few friends. He felt a warm gratitude for the well-kept secret but didn't know how to show it.

"And how was your day, Dad?" Wodan said.

"The meeting with Grady wasn't what I expected. Oh, and he wants to see you while you're in town to chat about the research happening at Ptolemaeus."

"Yeah..." Wodan said, drumming his fingers on the table. "I was hoping to land another internship at his Tahoma factory, but now, with the scandal..."

Not a subject Yamir wanted to discuss in front of Heath. "Today I learned about shielding against cosmic rays," he said, hoping to change the subject.

That was all it took to get Wodan talking about his passion for spaceflight. Yamir watched the admiration in Heath's hazel eyes as he listened to details about water shells and secondary radiation. The young couple reminded Yamir of him and Rhea at the beginning of their relationship. He'd explain his B-brain research to her, and she'd tell him fascinating stories about old manuscripts and unearthed ruins.

Once or twice while Wodan spoke, Yamir turned to Rhea's empty chair, ready with a comment, only to swallow his unspoken words.

"How did you two meet?" he asked after the ESPA server brought their plates. Wodan and Heath had ordered spaghetti carbonara and shrimp risotto to share.

"He was assisting a visiting professor," Wodan said, touching Heath's shoulder, "who gave a lecture about the health risks of zero gravity. That's why I still think fondly of zero-g, even though I know it kills my red blood cells when I'm in space." He smiled at his companion with affection.

Yamir nodded but didn't check the restaurant door anymore.

"Tell him how you met Mom," Wodan said.

That request jolted Yamir. "Oh, Rhea and I..." He didn't want to talk about her in her absence. But Wodan was trying so hard to make Heath feel like a part of his life that he didn't realize this was not a good time for Yamir to talk about Rhea. "We met right here, in Cedarwood."

One morning, she'd been running on the Wild Isle trail at the edge of the Magnificent Forest. She was twenty-three, still new to Cedarwood, where she had just joined Servetus University as a teaching assistant in the History Department. Yamir sat on a bench by Lake Xachu, reading an academic paper on power-efficient artificial neurons that required quadrillions of computations per second. Despite the fascinating read, he had still noticed her passing by.

"A running accident," Yamir told Heath. "She twisted her ankle and fell, and I helped her."

He remembered the pain in her almond-shaped brown eyes.

"What a stupid way to fall," she had said.

"Is there a smart way?" Yamir said, trying to lighten the mood.

Rhea had liked that about him.

"Give us some details, Dad," Wodan said.

"I helped her up," Yamir said, "and walked her to my bench. Her knee was bleeding, so I ran to my SDV and returned in a few minutes with my first aid kit."

She had welcomed him back with a lovely smile. "Thank you. I'm Rhea."

"I'm Yamir, and this is my first aid kit."

"And then?" Wodan motioned for Yamir to say something.

This was a story Yamir and Rhea should have told together, completing each other's sentences and laughing at their goofy younger versions. "I wanted to clean the cut on her knee." Yamir addressed Heath as the doctor in the room. "But she said she could handle it. She did a better job than I could've done, anyway."

Her ankle had swollen though. She took her running shoe off.

Yamir wrapped an elastic bandage around her foot for extra support until the doctor looked at it. "Not broken," he announced when she didn't scream at his touch.

"Do you help a lot of strangers?" she had asked him, a question she should have taken as a warning. A warning that Yamir's B-brain work to help the abstract *humanity* would come at the expense of his family.

"Dad?" Wodan brought Yamir back to reality. "He's not trying very hard right now," he told Heath.

"Oh, no," Heath said, "I'm absolutely enjoying the story."

Yamir felt a solid pain in his chest. During his years of marriage, he'd had days when he barely thought of Rhea, busy as he was with his work. And now...He was lucky Wodan seemed oblivious to the hurt he was causing. Oblivious, just like his dad, Rhea might say.

At the end of dinner, Yamir felt relief. Heath seemed nice, had all the right answers, and showed interest in Wodan and respect for Yamir. Y1 would like him too, though they'd probably never meet.

"How long will you be in town?" Yamir asked him.

Heath glanced at Wodan before answering. "A couple of weeks, I think."

"Which is why," Wodan said, placing his hand on Heath's, "I wanted to ask you if we could invite him to stay at our place. His hotel is nice, but our house is nicer."

Yamir should have expected this but hadn't. It made sense for Wodan to invite his companion to stay at his parents' house, but it seemed so sudden to Yamir. After all, Heath was a stranger he had just met. But he might become family one day.

"Dad?" Wodan looked worried.

Yamir felt bad for holding back. "Yes, yes, of course."

"Oh, wonderful," Heath said. "Thank you so much, Yamir."

Already on a first-name basis, like roommates, Yamir thought, but he said, "You're welcome." Then he realized with dread that he didn't know how to prepare the guest room. Visitors had always been Rhea's thing. He didn't even know where she kept the spare blankets.

"We'll take my childhood bedroom, then," Wodan said, saving Yamir the trouble.

It was close to midnight in Cedarwood, about time for Olma's scheduled meeting with the Sacrorums. Nala had fallen asleep after dinner, upset about their extended stay in Shel'land, so Olma took a tablet to her office in the other bedroom.

She had a lot of questions for Rex and Regina Sacrorum. They wanted her to create the Mars Guard, an army of androids that would rebuild the oxygen plant and reestablish living conditions for humans arriving at the settlement. This plan, they said, aligned with the Temple's mission to spread the human spirit throughout the solar system, an effort that had begun with the lunar settlement over sixty years ago.

Olma agreed with the Temple's mission to inhabit the vastness of space but questioned its methods. Her upcoming work required the use of four machines that—at least based on the information gained from Dimitri—were intelligent and self-aware. She didn't know if that assessment was correct, but she had to consider the possibility.

These intelligent machines would have to handle tasks outside their expertise, in dangerous conditions. Their self-awareness could lead them to decline the work. And then what? The phrase *forced labor* was on Olma's mind, especially after her dramatic takedown of LeosTech the other day. Yet humans have been using increasingly intelligent machines over the last few centuries. But now a line had been crossed, where the intelligence might have become self-aware, even conscious. This incremental change could be a fatal blow to the Temple's teachings, which recognized only two camps: the soulful and the soulless.

Olma needed clarity. The Sacrorums were the Temple's leaders, and they had received their orders from Oroles himself, the way Olma had once received her sacred mission from him in the Ravenna hospital. They would put her mind at ease.

She used her secure connection to call their palazzo at the agreed-upon time.

"There you are," Regina said, walking back from her wallscreen to the couch where her husband sat. She wrapped her crimson robes around her short and stout frame, then took a seat too. Rex wore black garments and his official four-corner cap.

It was morning in Rome, and the Sacrorums were having their coffee and biscotti on a gold tray.

"How are you adjusting there, High Priestess?" Rex said, taking a bite. "Are you finding food when you need it?"

"Everything is fine, thank you for asking, Your Holiness. Even though the locals tend to eat only two meals a day—a late breakfast and an early dinner—restaurants and food services are open longer hours for everyone else's dietary needs."

"Good, good," he said in his guttural voice.

"I need guidance, Your Holinesses," Olma said, placing her tablet in its charging dock on the table. "Tomorrow I'm going to meet the androids, and I feel unprepared."

"No one is truly prepared for something like that," Rex said, "but we trust you'll handle it well for the good of the Temple."

The Sacrorums had read Dimitri's initial report, which explained that these androids were based on real human beings. Cloning humans was explicitly forbidden by the Temple, but now the leaders seemed flexible about cloning human minds.

"These androids," Olma said, "they seem like clones to me."

"They are not clones." Regina wagged a stubby finger. "Clones replicate the DNA."

"The way we see it," Rex said, "these androids are just like ESPAs, but the source of each android's knowledge comes from one unique person. Whereas ESPAs are trained through machine learning, drawing from millions of people."

Olma cleared her throat. "But an android has the memories of that specific human being, not the impersonal knowledge of a deep-learning database."

"Memories are snapshots of the past, are they not?" Rex said. "These memories happen to belong to one specific person, yes, but they're just moments in time. We've been collecting people's memories since we invented writing, High Priestess."

"Not to mention voxdevs," Regina added, fixing a diamond eagle broach on her silk lapel.

"But these androids," Olma said, "might meet our criteria for consciousness and qualify as sentient beings. Yet we bought them as merchandise from LeosTech, and they have no rights—"

Regina raised her hand, her ruby-and-gold ring catching the morning sunlight. "I see where you're going with this, High Priestess, and I'll stop you right there. These machines look like people but have no divine spark. No soul."

"I wouldn't expect them to have souls." Olma chose her next words carefully so she wouldn't start a fight with the Sacrorums. "But if they are an intelligent species—"

"You can't talk like that about machines," Rex said, sounding annoyed.

"But if we don't," Olma said, "others still will."

"She's right, Rex," Regina said. "We can't tell people they can't use this or that word. It never works. We must prepare for all contingencies."

Olma had never seen them disagree before.

Rex shook his head. "That's why we won't tell people about them. Not yet."

"Good." Olma took a deep breath. "We must get this right. The way we handle this initial encounter will mark our relationship with the androids for the foreseeable future."

"We sent you there for that exact purpose," Regina said, motioning at Olma. "To handle them and avoid any complications."

"Because they must rebuild our Mars settlement, High Priestess," Rex said. "To prove that the Temple is coming back even stronger after the Elsway attacks."

They didn't speak of Oroles's guidance. There was no higher plan. The Sacrorums were just as lost as Olma. She'd have to help them instead of taking their advice. Her disappointment was a heavy rock in her stomach.

"Go meet the androids and tell us what you think of them," Rex said. "But remember, they're not like us—we have souls, and they're machines. The sacred texts teach us that only humans have souls."

Olma wanted to correct him. The texts talked about souls inhabiting creatures made in El's image. But El didn't have intestines and lungs, and so the divine image humans themselves mimicked was only external. And the androids looked human enough. Though, as Dimitri had explained, their circuitry was nothing like the insides of a human being. Could they have the divine spark in them? The Sacrorums wouldn't know the answer though.

"Does the Mars Habitation Department know about the androids?" Olma asked them instead.

"They were told help's on the way," Regina said. "But no specifics."

"May Oroles watch over you, High Priestess," Rex said and ended their conversation.

Olma leaned back in her chair. She hadn't cursed since her early days at Seminarium Romanum. If there was ever a time to do that, it was now. The Sacrorums wanted their Mars Guard, no matter the means or consequences.

Instead of cursing, she put her hands together and prayed to Oroles to help her understand. The Temple had been built on the abolition of enslavement. That was the story it told the world. But Olma knew that mere centuries ago, the Temple had resorted to forced labor when there was a shortage of mercenaries for dangerous exploration or construction work. Especially in countries where the locals condoned it. In China, Ethiopia, or Amazonia, prisoners of war or people who owed money to lenders could buy back their freedom through years of indentured labor. The Temple leaders had carefully covered up those transactions back then. Olma had accepted that dark history, confident it would stay in the past, never to be repeated. Yet here she was, having to provide labor that might be compulsory.

She asked Oroles for guidance, reciting the sacred words of the Temple's creed.

The unexpected tremor in her hands puzzled her. Was it caused by the intensity of her prayer or the onset of MNDS?

She waited for Oroles to send her a sign but felt no clarity and heard no whisper of wisdom.

7

Yamir spent the morning tidying the house for Heath's arrival that afternoon. Everything reminded him of Rhea: the coffee grinder, the throw pillows, the wilted flowers she had brought from Pike Place Market. He thought of Y1 and his prolonged anguish, missing her. He'd been sure that, in time, his A-brain would adapt to Rhea's absence. But he couldn't imagine his own organic brain ever adjusting, when she'd been a constant part of his life, ever since that morning by the lake. He'd been too hasty to dismiss Y1's pain.

Time—he needed time to adjust. And Rhea needed time to think about her life—she had said that. Time was something they never had enough of.

A message from Dimitri pinged on Yamir's voxdev, and he was glad for something to distract him from those constant thoughts of Rhea. Grady wanted to discuss the transition to the new owners, in person, at the Tahoma factory. Maybe Yamir would find Dimitri there and tell him he was fired, to his face, now that his protector was gone.

In the SDV, Yamir's thoughts returned to Rhea until a call from Lucius Seong saved him from his torment. The young reporter was undeterred by their last meeting.

"What do you want, Seong?" Yamir said.

"Call me Lucius. I can be of help, especially now. Come on, Yamir, let me take a look at your androids, and I'll tell you all about Olma Asper's terminal illness."

"I don't have any androids, and I don't care about her illness, but I wish her well." He ended the call.

The SDV stopped outside LeosTech in Tahoma, and Yamir got out. He covered his ears against the din from the helipad at the top of the building. A tall figure in a yellow scarf—in this hot weather—headed for the helicopter. Grady was leaving the factory.

Then why had Dimitri sent Yamir here? He checked the time. It was close to eleven. Dimitri could be alone with the A-brains in the lab, doing who knew what to them.

Icy dread ran through Yamir's limbs. He texted Si'ahl, *What's going on at the lab?* There was no reply.

"Destination?" the vehicle's ES asked when Yamir returned.

"Connectome Labs," Yamir said. "Fast!"

"As fast as the speed limit allows," the unhelpful expert system replied.

Olma arrived in the morning at Connectome Labs to meet the androids. She hoped they'd turn out to be ESPA-like intelligent machines, so everything would be simple for her, the Temple, and the world. Dimitri, the lab chief, had told her Yamir Varro wouldn't be there for the initial meeting with the team of neuroscientists, which she found strange. Dimitri had also asked her to keep his leadership position under the new management.

The open floor looked as Olma had expected: a mix of desks and assembly tables with robotic arms attached to them. Workstations, electronic components, office debris. As she walked in, she stopped to admire a beautiful wooden carving of an orca whale mounted on the wall. The ovoid on the whale's tail signified the European immigrants the Duwamish people had welcomed here after the big crossing. Maybe Olma would be welcome here too.

Three scientists greeted her: a young woman of college age, a man in his late twenties, and a woman in her fifties. Dimitri introduced them as Zaltana Rainshadow, Si'ahl Tabaaha, and Isabela Mescal. They wore comfortable clothes, great for being around workstations all day. Si'ahl had his long, black hair in a ponytail. Zaltana wore black pants and a blouse, with glass-bead earrings and a matching necklace. And Isabela's bracelet looked like it was made of sheep horn decorated with incised circles, crescents, and wedges. The scientists seemed surprised by Olma's visit, which didn't reflect well on Dimitri.

"Thank you for having me here today." Olma stood in the middle of the workspace, her hands clasped behind her back to keep them from trembling. She was aware of her Italian accent, but she spoke Shel'landic to prove her commitment to Connectome and its scientists. "You're the amazing team that created the android."

"Yamir's not here," Si'ahl said. "Yamir Varro. He's our lab chief."

Dimitri cleared his throat. "He used to be, yes. Things are in flux now."

"And Xiu-Min quit recently," Isabela said. "She worked on the first A-brain."

"Well, I'm glad to meet you," Olma said, unsure of this team's inner workings.

"I understand you're from Rome," Zaltana said, her dark eyes not smiling together with her mouth. "How do you like Cedarwood?"

"It's lovely." Olma remembered Nala's harsh words about this place. "I always wanted to visit the country that taught the Roman Empire that women are equal to men."

"And we thank you for bringing horses and the smallpox vaccine to our continent," Si'ahl said.

As the Temple's science and technology supervisor. Olma held a deep appreciation for the help the Nation of Confederated Tribes had provided Europe during the Little Ice Age. Shel'land had taught Italy and the rest how to move away from big, centralized cities and rebuild in smaller settlements to withstand climate change. This might have saved Europe from untold calamities. Densely populated cities of starving people, even with better sanitation, would have been hotbeds for deadly diseases. The end of the Little Ice Age in the thirteenth century allowed Europeans to rebuild their cities, leading to an unprecedented flourishing of art and science.

"I love discussing the extensive history of cooperation between our nations, truly," Olma said. "But I'm here to see your androids. Where are they?"

"Maybe we should wait for Yamir," Isabela said.

"High Priestess," Dimitri said, "would you like to watch the presentation I prepared for the unveiling that didn't happen?"

"No, thank you," Olma said. "A presentation won't be necessary. Show me the androids."

"I'll go make sure they're up and running." Dimitri headed to a door labeled *Simulation Room.*

Olma turned to the scientists. "And how do you like your work here at the lab?"

"It's good," Zaltana said. "Our research helps build exoskeletons for people with brain and spinal cord injuries."

Si'ahl nodded. "We should wait for Yamir though."

"As far as I understand," Olma said, "the androids are copies of yourselves?"

Si'ahl and Zaltana looked at each other but didn't speak. Isabela played with her bracelet and also kept quiet.

Olma asked Zaltana, "So, what are they?"

She seemed reluctant to talk, as if she'd betray Yamir Varro by explaining in his absence. "They're not exact copies, not anymore. Once uploaded, a connectome continues to live wire, changing in response to its new environment. Being an A-brain in a lab is vastly different from being a carefree human in the world." She pursed her lips as if done talking.

"That makes sense." Olma glanced at Isabela.

"We've learned that they diverge pretty fast from their human originals," she said.

"Can your A-brain do the same research work as you?" Olma asked Si'ahl.

"Sure," he said. "They're our lab mates, and we work together all the time."

With each additional detail, Olma found it harder to imagine the android, the way she couldn't imagine a new color she hadn't already seen.

Logfile Y1-1831-06-28

"High Priestess Olma Asper is outside this door," Dimitri tells me. "Good thing you're already in the ASV3."

S1 and Z1 watch me from a wallscreen with anxious expressions.

I don't know what to do first: have a heart attack or punch Dimitri in the face for ambushing us. I don't have time for either, though now I understand the meaning of yesterday's call, when he suspended us. He wasn't talking to the press…

"Where's Yamir?" I ask as he checks the stats of the simulation engines.

"Not here, obviously," S1 says, shaking his avatar's head.

"I'm sure he has a good reason," Z1 tells him.

"I'll go get the high priestess, then," Dimitri says. "Make sure you behave. She's our new boss, remember."

I hurry to M1's workstation and tell her she needs to join the others on the main wallscreen. "You'll meet someone now, and it's important we all do well. Her name is Olma Asper."

"The new owner? Oh, I'm not worried, Moonlight. Unless…"

"Yes?"

"Will she…kill me if she doesn't like me?"

Her question stops me in my tracks. "No, no. Of course not." Though I don't know what to expect from the Orolic Temple. In their long history, they've killed their share of enemies. M1 knows that too, but I can't feed her anxiety.

"Don't worry, Mom," I tell her. "I'll protect you."

Olma couldn't hide her impatience any longer. She kept glancing from the scientists to the Simulation Room. Finally, Dimitri returned.

"We're ready," he said.

"Shouldn't we wait for Yamir?" Si'ahl said, and Olma ignored him.

She followed Dimitri to the Simulation Room, while the scientists stayed behind.

He paused before the door to whisper, "What you're about to see, High Priestess Asper, is hard to square with the Temple's teachings. But I want to assure you of my unwavering faith in the Temple. I'm personally against lending my brain to this ungodly experiment—"

"Can we go in, please?" Olma said, sick of his groveling attitude. She had worked with people like him throughout her career and knew they eventually outlived their usefulness.

The first thing she saw in the Simulation Room was a metallic ESPA walking toward her. But the way it moved was uncanny, almost human, so different from ESPAs in their polymer shells. The face on its helmet screen belonged to Yamir Varro, whom Olma had seen before but hadn't yet met.

"Hello, I'm Y1," the android said in a cheerful tone, waving.

Olma flinched, then cleared her throat to hide her moment of dismay, while Dimitri stepped between her and the android as though to protect her—the show-off.

Y1 put up its hands and took a step back. "Take your time."

Olma reminded herself she was there to serve Oroles and learn how to fulfill his sacred mission. She spent a minute just looking at the android, with its smiling face on that helmet screen. No, that was not Yamir Varro. What was she actually looking at? A machine that was tricking her brain into seeing a person.

When she approached it, it lowered its arms and stood still. She touched its hand, and it didn't react. She tapped on its metallic torso, remembering the Shel'landic lore that warned of non-human beings taking human form. Some were evil spirits, and some were...

"I'm an A-brain in an android shell, version three," Y1 said gently. "And these are my friends: M1, S1, and Z1. They're in their own simulation engines."

From a wallscreen, three avatars waved at her. Their faces and shoulders filled their labeled windows. Two looked familiar, like Si'ahl Tabaaha and Zaltana Rainshadow, the scientists Olma had just met. The third one was a woman in her seventies.

"Indeed," Dimitri said, "these A-brains are running on our simulation engines."

Olma didn't grasp the difference between androids and A-brains, but Dimitri was getting on her nerves. "I'm doing fine here, Dimitri. Please give me some space." She looked in the android's face. "Does this shell feel like your own body? Or do you feel trapped inside?"

"Both. The ASV3 allows me to navigate the world, but I also shed it every day like clothes. Except it's not clothes. I must always be connected to a body, simulated or robotic. I'm not scared of getting injured, but I worry about damage to the shell and the time needed for repairs."

"Makes sense," Olma said, feeling more at ease with Y1. "Dimitri, I want to be alone with them for a moment."

"But you shouldn't—"

"They're not dangerous. You said it yourself."

"Yes, but—"

"I'll call for you when I'm done."

Dimitri hung his head in disappointment but turned and left.

"What are you?" Olma pleaded with the android to be something she could understand.

"I used to be Yamir Varro." It now sounded sad. "But that was a long time ago."

"I thought it's only been a year."

It nodded as though a year had been an eternity.

"You're all suffering here." Olma addressed the images on the wallscreen with warmth, the way she spoke to her congregation in Rome. Maybe Oroles wanted her to continue in this vein?

"It's not that bad," Y1 answered her, its face smiling.

"I'm fine," Z1 said, and it sounded just like Zaltana Rainshadow. Still weird. "I get to work on my research without the pressure of getting married."

"I'm more than fine," S1 said but didn't explain.

Probably an inside joke, because Z1 rolled its eyes and waved S1 away. Olma realized that the stick figure on the side of Z1's avatar had done the waving, but she had no trouble integrating the two components and seeing them as one entity called Z1.

"Life's better here in many ways," M1 said. "I get to spend time with my son, which rarely happened before." She pointed to Y1. It took Olma a moment to realize M1 was the avatar of Yamir Varro's mother.

"So you like living here?" Olma asked them.

"It's not a matter of liking," Y1 said. "This is our life now."

"I hear you're from Rome," Z1 said. "I've never been but always wanted to go. How do you like Cedarwood?"

"It's...spacious. My wife doesn't like it here, but I do. Surprisingly."

"Is she a high priestess too?" M1 said.

"No. She's the president of an international law firm—and a criminal defense attorney."

A murmur of surprise went around the room, a reaction Olma was used to.

"What's her name?" Y1 said.

"Nala Mancini."

"I'd like to meet her someday," Z1 said.

The A-brains were nothing like ESPAs, which only asked specific questions and followed their owners' explicit instructions. Olma found herself talking to the A-brains as though they were all at a summer camp together, getting to know one another. S1 was in love with Z1—that wasn't hard to spot. Z1 liked S1 too, but she had the power in their relationship. M1 had been a dedicated single mother—Olma saw that in the way M1 cherished Y1, a son she had gained by joining the lab as an artificial brain. And Y1 longed for something out of his universe entirely, though he wouldn't speak of it.

Olma told them about the little apartment she and Nala owned near the Colosseum, which made Z1 sigh with longing. She told them of the villa in Tuscany, where she and Nala grew apple and plum trees in a small orchard. M1 said she had spent some years in Tuscany before she retired.

She had studied space-sturdy botanical species at Florence University. Olma confessed she liked Cedarwood because, despite all its efforts to look urban, it was still surrounded by nature, from snowy mountains to forests and lakes.

Somewhere during their conversation, Olma had stopped using *it* to refer to an A-brain. That seemed right though. Or maybe she was making a mistake. Maybe the A-brains were friendly in order to charm her. She had their fate in her hands, after all.

Or maybe they were just a group of nice people.

People. People made of quantum processors. A new species of people. Was that how Oroles saw them too? The Sacrorums had rejected that possibility. But if these machines were real people, Oroles wouldn't want them sent to Mars as forced labor.

Unless...unless he saw them not as workers on the red planet, but as his chosen people on a mission to spread the human spirit throughout the solar system. The followers of Oroles had spread his teachings on Earth long ago, and now the A-brains could do the same on an interplanetary level. Then his divine word would live everywhere in the galaxy. Olma's sacred mission could be to help the androids build the first outpost beyond humanity's cradle.

This was the sense of clarity she'd been praying for. She hoped Oroles would break his silence of thirty years to tell her she was on the right path despite the lack of guidance from the Sacrorums.

Even though she was dying, Olma had never felt more alive and full of purpose. She held her breath, hoping for the miracle of hearing Oroles's voice.

"Is everything all right in there?" Dimitri called from afar, breaking Olma's heart.

She shook her head, soothing her disappointment with a soft chuckle. Enough with the melodrama. Oroles spoke only if he needed to. Olma had learned what her sacred mission was. And she was going to fulfill it.

Logfile Y1-1831-06-28

Olma Asper continues to study me with an intense gaze as we talk. Despite her perfect business attire—a white blazer jacket and pencil skirt, accented by a red handbag—her dark eyes look tired. My new smell sensors pick up an accumulation of unusual chemicals in her labored breath. While I'm unhappy that I can't smell most food, today I'm glad for my specialized electronic nose. I glance at the screen on my forearm. My built-in medical diagnostic tool says that Olma Asper has a 79% probability of illness, listing the likeliest ones. But I don't have time to read the report right now.

While my friends can only see the high priestess from their wallscreen's sensor array, I'm able to move around and evaluate her from different angles. Her legs are unsteady at the ankle. Her hands have a slight tremor, though they're busy holding her red handbag. The muscles at the base of her neck are tensed. Though she looks poised and focused, parts of her body betray that something isn't well with her. I'm the only one picking on these subtle signals—even Olma Asper might not notice them yet.

"Tell us more about your house in Tuscany," Z1 asks her.

As they talk about that, I check her health report. The diagnostics show an increased concentration of calcium ions in her brain. She might have a degenerative disease in her nerve cells, probably due to a genetic mutation triggered by environmental factors. The effect would be the overproduction of primary excitatory neurotransmitters, destroying her motor neurons. There's no known treatment for MNDS, the report says.

I feel unsettled. If the diagnostics and my observations are correct, I'm looking at a dying woman. My attitude shifts in an instant from deference to compassion. There's something so vulnerable about her. She knows pain, because she recognized my pain earlier. As things stand, I'm indestructible, and she's categorically broken. But she has power, and I'm powerless, trapped in my lab-jail. We're each other's opposites, which makes us a pair.

A strange thought enters my mind. I turn to my friends. "Hey, I need to disable your sensor array for a minute. I'll send you to the Swallah Island VR environment I've been working on. You'll be fine there. Will you please trust me?"

M1 is the first to nod, then Z1 and S1, while Olma Asper watches us all with a question in her dark eyes. I send my friends into full-simulation mode, where their sensor inputs come from the VR environment I've been developing for M1. It's glitchy, and they haven't tried it yet, but I need privacy, and I would never suspend them.

I also press the button by the door to lock Dimitri out.

Then I turn to Olma Asper, only half believing I'm doing that. "You're dying, aren't you? You don't have much time, and you want to return to Tuscany. So what do you need from us to make that happen?"

She sits in a chair before she answers in her Italian accent, "I need to know how much human is left in you."

"All of it," I say.

She closes her eyes as if she didn't want that answer. "Show me," she whispers.

And just like that, I tell her my story, the most human thing I can do. She's a stranger who holds my life in her hands, I know that. Someone I only met minutes ago. Someone who has power over my A-brain friends and my scientists. I should be guarded, but I don't hold back. I tell her how much I miss my family, how much I miss food. I tell her that my mother almost died in a meteorite accident on the Moon when I was eleven, causing my unhealthy quest for the B-brain.

"It's not unhealthy. It's your El-given calling," she says, and I wonder about her own story. "We all want to reach outside our small corner of the world and do something important with our lives. It's only human."

She pauses at the last word and nods to herself.

She called me *human*. I quickly check my neurochemicals to make sure I won't burst into the virtual tears Yamir coded for me. Then I realize tears could help my case with the high priestess. Too late—my eyes are dry now.

"You don't have to carry your burden alone, Y1...Because you're not alone in this lab. You have your human and synthetic friends, and now you have me and the Temple on your side."

She says all the right things, and I want to hug her, but of course I don't move any of my multifilament muscles.

A bang on the door interrupts us. It isn't Dimitri though.

"Let me in," Yamir calls, sounding panicked. As always, he has the worst timing.

When the door to the simulation room didn't open, Yamir threw his shoulder against it, terrified that Olma Asper and Dimitri had locked themselves inside to cause irreparable damage to the A-brains. Why else would Dimitri send Yamir to Grady's factory that morning?

To his surprise and relief, the door opened the next moment, and there was Y1 in the ASV3. The wallscreen showed the other A-brains in VR simulation mode.

"What's going on?" Yamir said, panting, with Si'ahl close behind, telling him to calm down. "Where's Dimitri?"

Olma Asper rose from a chair. She wore a white business suit with low heels, and she exuded authority in the room.

"Y1 was showing me our lab," she said in an Italian accent. Her chin-length black hair framed her confident face.

Y1 nodded. "Nothing to worry about, Yamir. Calm down."

"I told you, everything's fine," Si'ahl whispered. "She's kicked Dimitri out."

Yamir tried to regain his breath. Maybe things were really just fine, though worry was his default setting.

"We'll talk again, Y1." Olma Asper stood up, holding a red handbag.

She greeted Yamir, bowing her head to him, her hand over her heart. She didn't look like a dying woman, as Lucius had said, but one in complete control.

Yamir realized he was supposed to make a good first impression—and he had already blown it.

"Um, hello. My name is Yamir Varro. Welcome to Connectome."

"We need to talk," she said.

"As lab chief, I'd like to be present," Dimitri said, out of nowhere.

"That won't be necessary," she told him.

"My office?" Yamir said, glad there was no warmth between her and Dimitri.

They walked together, Yamir thinking how to conduct their first official interview. He and the high priestess had some things in common. They both had to set aside their personal needs for the greater purpose they served. As a high priestess, Olma Asper's mission was to maintain the social order among her temple's subjects. As a neuroscientist, Yamir was responsible for the A-brains in his lab. He and Olma put others first. His thoughts veered back to Rhea. He could have used her counsel before this important conversation.

The high priestess sat on the sofa in Yamir's office, but he remained standing with his back against his desk. He waited for her to say something. She placed her red handbag down and opened a small bottle of water.

"Dimitri says he's the lab chief," she began.

Yamir was relieved she hadn't asked about his theatrical entrance and was already focusing on business.

"But I don't think he'd be an effective leader," she continued. "Your team is loyal to *you*. You've accomplished a lot with just a handful of scientists. I don't want any conflict here, so you'll be my lab chief."

"Thank you," Yamir said, still catching his breath.

"The Temple bought Connectome Labs because people of faith have gradually accepted expert-system technology over the past few decades. First, a robot that cleans your floor, then one that listens to your voice and suggests your music. Then face recognition. We accepted all that as part of technological progress. But what you're doing here is something very different from traditional ES tech, isn't it?"

She sounded thoughtful and curious to learn more. Nothing like Grady, which was a good sign.

"Right." Yamir was grateful for a chance to explain his research to his new boss. "Traditional expert systems solve computationally difficult but very specific problems. Like chess playing or image recognition. That's why they're called *expert*. Here at Connectome, we want to understand how the human brain works so we can create intelligent beings who learn from experience and adapt to unfamiliar situations."

"But when you do that, you get into thorny issues. For instance, between you here and the other you over there, where is your immortal soul?"

"I never assumed I had one." Yamir shifted in place.

"You assume wrong," Olma said, "but I like your honesty. So, take me to the beginning of all this. Why did you choose to work on the android?"

Yamir couldn't mention his mother's near-death experience on the Moon to the high priestess. Better to keep the conversation on professional territory. He chose his words with care. "Have you ever stopped to admire the miracle of the human brain?"

"Of course." She took a sip of water.

"But really admire it, really feel its—"

"Divine quality? Yes."

Yamir wouldn't have put it that way, but sure. "It's irresistible when you think of it—as a neuroscientist. Thirteen hundred grams of neural matter. Eighty-six billion neurons. A hundred and fifty thousand cortical columns. One hundred trillion synapses. Being able to understand how all that works—"

"You hope to create a better mind than El Himself created?"

"I want to understand what you call *creation*. The brain looking outside at the universe, that's a marvelous thing. The brain looking inside, at itself? We won't understand the universe until we understand how we understand it."

Olma set the water bottle down. "I get that, yes."

Yamir realized he had been gripping the side of his desk, and he relaxed his sore fingers.

"But do you have a more personal reason for your life's work?" Olma said.

Yamir worried she knew more about him than she showed. Time to deflect and ask his own questions. "You said the Temple is fine with conventional ES, but what does it think about the A-brain?"

Olma gave a small shrug. "We have no choice but to accept it. Once the idea of an A-brain emerged, there was no undoing it. It's better for us to own the A-brain and learn how to use it than to try to destroy it. We haven't been very good at erasing ideas we didn't like throughout history. Just think of the stem cells we were forced to accept once that research provided the vaccine for the last pandemic."

Yes, science was unstoppable. Yamir remembered Rhea saying that if Lucretius's book *On the Nature of Things* had been lost to history, a random traveler would have discovered a forgotten copy in a temple somewhere and reintroduced it to the world. Or if Servetus had been burned at the stake by Temple fundamentalists together with his books, humankind would still have discovered how pulmonary circulation worked.

"The lesson from history," Olma Asper said, "is that an idea whose time has come can't be stopped. The Temple thinks it's wise to work with those ideas, not try to kill them—and fail."

"Wait," Yamir said, worry building up in his chest. "Will the Temple discuss the A-brain in public?"

"Not for a while. Like you, we first want to understand the mind of El, even though you call it by another name. If El allowed the A-brain to happen, there must be a divine plan at work. It's our job here at Connectome to understand it and develop it further. One day, these A-brains might control intelligent robots that will terraform our solar system."

Yamir's worry shifted. "That's exactly why I started researching the human brain. To find a different method of terraforming. But the A-brain isn't meant for that. Instead, we need the B-brain, which we haven't yet developed."

"What's the difference between the two?" Olma Asper said.

"The A-brain is created by uploading a preexisting human brain to a simulation engine, while a B-brain starts with a blank neural network, which is then trained over time to learn and adapt to its environment, like a baby. That's why the B-brain would work well on Mars if it develops and adapts there. The A-brains are Earth brains."

Olma Asper nodded. "And how did you end up creating the A-brain?"

Yamir pushed himself away from his desk and went to sit in the armchair by the table, closer to his new boss. How many times had he tried to explain his work to Grady? And now Olma Asper wanted to hear all about it.

"It was an accident, honestly." He interlaced his fingers. "I'd been working for years on the B-brain and couldn't figure out how neural networks made reliable fast decisions. I'd tried different models, but each failed in certain scenarios. Meanwhile, brain-imaging technology had made major progress, and so I thought, what if I imaged my own brain, section by section, then patched it together and observed how it works? Trying to understand the decision-making process in our brains."

Olma Asper nodded. "And that's how you created Y1..."

"Yes." Yamir was relieved to admit his failure and success.

"Has the existence of the A-brains helped you with the B-brain re-search?"

"Yes and no. I now understand how neurons function, but we haven't worked on the B-brain since Y1 was created. We're now spending all our time stabilizing and managing the A-brains."

"And growing their numbers. Creating even more complexity, since these A-brains aren't alike."

Yamir was impressed by this high priestess, with her keen under-standing of science. Then again, she was the Temple's science and tech-nology supervisor.

"We won't have time today." She picked up her bag. "But would you please walk me through your research soon? I'll probably need more than one session though, and I apologize—"

"Please don't apologize. I'd love to explain my work to you, as the new caretaker of my lifelong project." His hands even shook a little with excitement.

Today had been such a great beginning. Better than anything Yamir had ever accomplished with Grady. And if things went well, he could soon bring up Rhea's dismissal from the Concord Column with his new boss. Maybe they'd let her rejoin the project, and she'd return to him.

8

I t's 22:47, and I'm strolling through the campus under a bright moon, thinking about my strange conversation with Olma Asper. She's so different from Grady. But is she an enlightened high priestess who thinks she'll bring us androids into the world as El's children? Or is she a grand prosecutor who'll convince the Temple to destroy us so she can return home and die in peace? The Temple would then erase us from history the way Roman emperors condemned their enemies to oblivion. Damnatio memoriae. Beyond our erased existence, would the lives of our scientists also be in danger? Or maybe I'm wrong to worry, and she'll be a compassionate and competent manager for Connectome Labs after all.

Sharing my story with her earlier made me accept that I'm fully responsible for my predicament. I've been so angry at Yamir, when in fact I did this to myself. I was the one consumed by the desire to create a working B-brain, and I went all out trying to make it happen.

It all started with a simple conversation at dinner one evening, when Rhea mentioned that in all complex societies, members vote on the common good. Well, our brain is a complex society of neurons, I thought. I'd always been puzzled by the long axons spanning the neocortex. What if, as Rhea suggested, they facilitated some sort of voting among neurons? I had to test that right away. I probably forgot to even thank Rhea for dinner and her brilliant idea. I started designing my connectome chamber that night, and Caspian paid for its construction. Soon I took snapshot after snapshot of my own brain, hoping to discover that the long axons enable the neocortex to make reliable fast decisions.

And Rhea was right. In the complex society of our brains, there are dedicated neurons that vote as citizens did in ancient Rome. Those long axons spanning the neocortex belong to voting neurons in cortical columns that decide the nature of an object, be it concrete or abstract. I should've been ecstatic to finally have my answer and be one step closer to creating the B-brain. But that's not how I felt.

I didn't mention this part of the story in the goodbye letter I wanted to send to Rhea a few days ago. I couldn't plant these horrific images in her mind, and I didn't want her to feel responsible. But I will tell my son what it felt like to have my brain uploaded.

Like lying on a slab of stone, dismembered.

"It hurts...Stop...Make it stop," I screamed when I came online.

Later on, Yamir told me how he suspended me after he heard the simulation engine's default voice shriek. (We were identical a year ago, so I could say I suspended myself.)

"Can't see...Hurts...Help!" I screamed again when Yamir restarted the engine.

He shut it down again, then spent hours running diagnostic scans. He couldn't figure out what had caused the activation of the language module in the simulation engine.

He tried again.

For me, not a second had passed, and I was still in agony. "Noooo...Help me! Aaah!"

He shut down the engine and told Si'ahl, Isabela, and Xiu-Min what had happened. Zaltana wasn't yet working here. The team agreed it was a malfunction of the language module. But Yamir wasn't so sure.

"I have to go think," Yamir told Xiu-Min. "Please don't restart the simulation engine while I'm out."

He went on a walk through the Connectome campus for hours, though they felt like minutes to him. Trees, paths, birds, bushes—all a blur. While no one had been able to even explain the term *consciousness* to scientific rigor, he had managed to—maybe—catch one in a jar. A clone of his own consciousness? No, that was ridiculous. Consciousness wouldn't appear by accident from a patchwork of brain scans. But that thing in the simulation engine had language. And language meant thoughts—because no one had pre-programmed those exact sentences into the simulation engine. But language generative models didn't have thoughts, just probabilities for the next likely word to follow in a sequence. Except Yamir hadn't built and trained a language model, so how had the simulation engine found one inside the patchwork of his scanned brain tissue?

The next morning, he arrived first at the lab and sat at my workstation, confident he had worried for nothing. His scanned midbrain had probably caused the language module to misfire because the inputs received by the neocortex were garbage. Just a weird coincidence.

He turned on the simulation engine. This time there was no language, just hissing and groaning, nonverbal. But he could hear the pain in those broken sounds. He imagined someone inside my workstation, curled up into a ball and whimpering. My reassembled artificial brain—he called it an A-brain—was in agony.

Yamir tried to think. Pain sometimes came from a misalignment of inputs. The A-brain had a working representation of every part of its body—my biological body. If the body wasn't there, the A-brain would register pain, as in phantom limb pain—everywhere. Yamir had to make sure my A-brain saw the sensor array attached to the simulation engine as belonging to itself. Its own body.

He had never encountered this scenario while working on the B-brain because its mind was meant to evolve inside the simulation engine, receiving inputs from the sensor array. But my A-brain had developed to speak with my tongue and lungs—not through speakers. It had learned to see through my photoreceptors—not with video sensors. Yamir needed to make my A-brain think the sensor array was actually its eyes, ears, nose, and skin. Or else it would be in too much pain to function.

I was in too much pain to even speak.

When Yamir explained all that to Xiu-Min, Isabela, and Si'ahl, they were conflicted.

"I don't think continuing this experiment is right," Isabela said.

"This is something for shamans and philosophers to deal with, not us," Si'ahl said.

"How's working on the A-brain different from our B-brain project?" Xiu-Min pushed back. "We've always assumed we're creating intelligence that would be self-aware."

Yamir quietly agreed with her.

"Sure, years from now," Isabela said. "By then, we'd slowly get used to this new species we're creating."

"You're talking about what makes *us* feel good or bad," Xiu-Min said. "But we should think about the A-brain's needs."

They discussed it for a while, but Yamir knew he couldn't stop now, when he was so close to understanding how the neocortex really worked. He could complete the B-brain and then the intelligent robot that could terraform the solar system, places where humans had died over the years trying to build habitats.

He returned to my workstation and continued the painstaking process of input calibration between my A-brain and the sensor array. He planned a week of training for the sense of sight. A week for hearing, each time working on only certain cortical regions and not activating the entire network. The sense of touch would be trickier, so he assumed it would take at least two weeks.

A month later, he checked the last few details and powered up the simulation engine. He was alone in the lab early one morning. The default avatar appeared on the screen: a round head with no hair. Brown eyes and brown skin. He started the simulation.

I understood right away that I wasn't myself, though I couldn't explain how.

My first words were "Blast it, where am I?" I sounded like a synthesizer.

Yamir watched in awe as my avatar made a confused face on the curved screen. "Does it still hurt?" he whispered.

"Why do I sound like this?" I said.

"Like what?"

"That! That's what I normally sound like."

Yamir had a functional copy of his own neocortex in simulation. That was why my A-brain wanted to hear itself in his—and my—voice. With shaky hands, he switched the audio filter, and my next words sounded like us.

"I get it," I said. "I've made a copy of myself, and now I'm that copy. I'm Yamir, and you're Yamir. No, I'm not Yamir anymore. I'm a digital entity. Call me Y1." I tried to make fun of the absurd situation I was in, but my artificial laugh track spooked Yamir.

"Y1, you're an A-brain now," he said. "What's it like to be in there?"

"I see you in my office... I feel my body, but it's distant, like I'm coming out of anesthesia."

"How about now?" Yamir slid the tactile intensity to 75%, then started a routine that fed my A-brain prerecorded touch inputs through the hindbrain and midbrain.

"Now my fingers can feel this desk I'm sitting on. Thank you, Yamir. So you brought me online to test my ideas about the B-brain...on myself."

"I didn't bring you here. It was an accident. I was trying to understand the voting neurons."

My avatar raised its eyebrows. "I remember that dinner when Rhea helped me realize that the long axons weren't checksums."

"Right, because they're voting neurons in columns that decide the nature of an object..."

After a quick explanation, I was thrilled with the news. "That means the B-brain could actually happen once you study my neocortex in the simulation engine."

"That was our idea, yeah." Though Yamir didn't feel on solid ground.

"Then I want access to the B-brain code so I can keep working on it."

Yamir didn't know how to feel about that. It wasn't like he didn't trust himself to work on the B-brain, but he had never had himself outside of his own control before.

"You can't make changes to the code though," he said.

"Right. Not until you tell the team about me."

"Right." Yamir needed to introduce me to Xiu-Min, Isabela, and Si'ahl as a new team member, and they might not accept this unusual addition.

"This new life could be great," I said with a smile and a twinge in my heart. "I can work all the time. Whenever I want."

I sounded thrilled to live outside the real world. Sure, Yamir had sometimes found the real world hard to deal with, but he hadn't expected a part of him to be so excited to get rid of it altogether.

He felt like an inferior version of me, which angered him.

"No bodily needs," I went on, "since my hindbrain and midbrain only work with the sensors and the skeletal-muscular infrastructure now. My sleep cycles can be scheduled and compressed, though that's the only part of my A-brain that'll benefit from computational acceleration. I need you to check my memories though. I think some of them were corrupted. Must be because different parts of my brain were scanned at different times. But I still remember that Wodan is coming home for summer break. When can I talk to him and Rhea?"

Yamir rubbed his eyelids. "I don't know about that..." Introducing me to his team was one thing. Introducing me to Rhea and Wodan was something else completely.

He stood up from his chair, overwhelmed. He had only wanted to watch the voting neurons in action when he stitched my A-brain together. He glanced at the diagnostics window on the screen, and yes, the voting neurons were active as I tried to make sense of my new world.

Cold consolation. We had reached our lifelong goal of understanding the neocortex and creating artificial general intelligence—and it felt terrible.

"But I'm still the chief neuroscientist of Connectome Labs," I tried. "I get to say what happens to me here."

"For Caspian, you're just a product of years of investment..."

Terror gripped me. "Then get me out of here. Now."

"There's no way out," Yamir whispered. "But I'll build you an android shell as soon as I can. Caspian will pay for expedited—"

My thoughts are interrupted by a sound. My sensors pick up a faint whir above. With my night vision on, I scan the night sky, and sure enough, I find a drone up there, above the trees. Our defense dome looks active, so this drone is a new model, something that evades the current security tech. The press will stop at nothing to spy on our lab.

I put the upgrade of our campus defense system on my ever-growing to-do list. It's wiser to go back inside now and deny the drone its obvious goal of surveying an android. I turn off my faceplate and switch to drive mode once I hit the paved road to the lab.

I reach the lab's front door in minutes, the drone still hovering above me.

Inside, Isabela is at her workstation, and she looks up from her screen. "Which one are you? Your faceplate is off."

No time to explain. I cross the open floor and exit through the back door, hoping to spy on the drone in return. As I look up, there it is again, waiting for me. Infuriating.

I activate our defense drones, which take off from the roof and surround the intruder. I don't want it destroyed though. We can learn a lot from analyzing its evasive software.

"Y1," Isabela calls from the door, "is that you?"

Something small drops near my right foot. It blinks red—

The blast sound was clipped by my audio sensors' high-amplitude threshold, but I know it was loud. Bright too. The explosion threw me in the air. I landed on my side, but my shock absorbers kept my quantum processors safe.

The building alarm blares.

My polycarbonate screens are intact—both on my forearms and on my faceplate—and my video sensors are working. I must've looked away from the blast just in time.

I groan and turn on my back, using my rotating joints. Our drones surround the intruder above me, but they're restricted to our perimeter. Before long, it's gone.

The advantage of being an android is that it doesn't hurt to have your leg blown up by an explosive device. If the shell detects an unresponsive subsystem, it replaces the missing signal with a loop of its last seconds of recorded activity, which prevents pain. Being bombed doesn't scramble your brain, you don't lose your hearing, and you don't black out. The problem is that your leg is destroyed, and now you need a replacement that could take months to arrive.

Then I see Isabela, and my heart fills with dread. She's not moving. Her face is covered in blood. Her hair sparkles with glass shards. Must be from our wrecked back door.

"Isabela!" I call her, but she doesn't answer. I pull myself closer, and my sensors tell me she's still breathing. But I don't know how to help her, and that drives me to tears. I adjust the neurochemicals on my forearm display to return to calm.

There. I know what to do next: put in a call for an ambulance, obviously. Done.

To be of any help, I must transfer to the old ASV1. But I shouldn't leave my right leg outside, for the vigiles to find when they arrive. I grab it by the foot and shove it under my arm. I pull myself up against the wall and get closer to the screaming alarm. The wheels on my left foot help me navigate the debris through the door. I fall and get up again, my servomotors working beyond capacity. My right leg feels straight and tense, even as I drag torn muscle filaments behind me. At least it doesn't hurt.

Inside, I find the alarm panel on the wall, and I punch in the code. The piercing sound stops. The vigiles will be here any moment now.

I receive a call on my faceplate. It's Yamir, alerted by our defense system.

"What happened?" He sounds sleepy.

"Isabela's injured. She hit her head, and she's losing blood. I called an ambulance."

His first words are muffled, but I catch the rest. "What about M1 and the rest?" Panic grows in his voice.

"The bomb went off outside. They're fine."

"You must hide the android shells before anyone comes."

He's right, of course, but his commonsense advice pisses me off. "I wish, but I lost a leg."

"Lost a leg?" Yamir says as if it's hard to comprehend. "Does it hurt?"

"No. The upper part is still attached tough."

"The connections to your spinal cord?"

"They're intact," I say after running a quick diagnostic.

I hear the vigiles' alarms drawing near the campus.

"Go hide now!" Yamir tells me. "I'll let them in."

Yamir had taken a sleeping pill to numb his heartache over Rhea. Now he struggled to wake up to the awful news of a bomb at Connectome. Y1 didn't know if Isabela was still alive. The ASV3 was damaged, but the A-brains were unharmed.

He messaged Olma, then left the house in the dead of night, trying not to wake up Wodan and Heath. He rode to the lab through a quiet city, his mind racing. How could someone want his work bombed out of existence? This attack had to be related to Grady's failed announcement. Yamir had warned him it could happen. And would the Temple deem the lab too problematic now and close it? Yamir felt sick to his stomach, weighing the possibilities.

He arrived at Connectome around midnight, just as an ambulance left the campus. They would take Isabela to Dokina Medical Center. She must be still alive, thank goodness. The white-and-blue lights of two MDVs—manual-drive vehicles—from the Cedarwood Vigile Department lit up the building. Four officers canvassed the place, inspecting the damage.

Yamir's SDV stopped at the curb, and he ran inside the lab. Glass shards, bits of concrete, and even tree branches—everywhere. A vacuuming robot by the back door had been torn in two by the blast. But the ruined ASV3 wasn't there. Hidden away in storage, where the vigiles didn't know to look. And Y1 was back in his simulation engine.

"How's Isabela?" Yamir asked a vigile taking pictures of the scene.

"She's stable" was the only answer he got from any of them.

"You must stay here until we're done," their squad leader told him.

While the vigiles collected evidence, taking pictures and notes, Yamir spent hours looking through security logs and surveillance videos for clues on the attacker. Nothing.

He kept checking with the hospital on Isabela's surgery. A metal fragment had pierced her skull. He stopped himself from thinking of the damage to her brain. There was no point in doing that.

Once the vigiles were gone, he connected to Y1's simulation engine from his office.

"I picked up a few bomb fragments for us to analyze," Y1 said.

Yamir woke up Lucius Seong, the NNN reporter, at five in the morning. "Help me find the attacker, and I'll let you visit the lab." He then sent the bomb fragments via drone to Lucius.

The repair crew arrived at nine. Under Si'ahl's supervision, the contractors worked all morning to repair the wall and replace the back door. Dimitri popped in to ask if Olma had been notified.

"Of course," Yamir growled at him but wondered why he hadn't heard from his boss yet.

Zaltana had removed the other two android shells from storage and was trying to rewire a leg from the ASV2 to the damaged ASV3. It wasn't working. SBC had changed the internal hardware connections, and she was forced to improvise.

Y1 uploaded to the ASV1, the android shell with limited sensors, and immediately transferred back to his simulation engine, cursing that terrible old hardware that felt so heavy. Yamir told him to get over it. They needed an android walking around the lab. Y1 relented.

The other three A-brains were upset that their existence had summoned a bomb, and that they were cut off from an android shell for now. They kept asking for updates on Isabela.

Yamir wanted to scream. He had wanted a distraction from Rhea, but not this.

A voxmail from the hospital arrived. Isabela was out of surgery and resting. Yamir was relieved, though the message didn't give details. He called Olma but only reached Catherine, her assistant. He updated her on Isabela and his progress in repairing the damage.

Around noon, the comm link on his workstation chirped with a video call from Lucius, who had shown the bomb fragments to a trusted private investigator.

"Any leads?" Yamir said, just as a call from Olma came in. He'd call her back as soon as Lucius updated him on the investigation.

The reporter rubbed his tired eyes. "Nothing on the bomb's origin yet, but I found some drone footage on social media." He shared a video, which included the original status display at the bottom of the screen. "It's already going viral."

The grainy-green video had been recorded with night vision sensors from high above, showing a tall figure approaching the lab. To the untrained eye, it could have been an ESPA on smart wheels, not an android. Y1 stopped at the curb and switched to walking, then entered the building. The video sensors tried to zoom in through the windows, but Y1 was already gone, so the drone flew over the building to the back door.

For a few seconds, nothing happened, then Y1 came out. The drone zoomed in on Y1's head, where the faceplate was off. Y1 engaged the lab's defensive drones. The status bar on the intruder drone displayed *Danger: Engage Defenses* at the bottom of the screen. Isabela stepped out of the back door. Then the bomb fell, and everything was a jumble for a long moment. The status was updated to *Evacuate*, and the image turned black.

The handler hadn't planned to use a bomb but dropped it to create chaos for the drone to escape Connectome's defenses. That didn't make Yamir feel any better.

"Who uploaded this video?" he asked Lucius.

"Someone called Felix Senecio. I haven't yet found a real person with that name."

It was an alias, of course. The name meant *happy old man* in the Temple's Latin.

"He likes to rant online a lot," Lucius continued. "Death to those who do android research, and all that. Based on his posts, our ES language model concluded that he's young, half Shel'landic and half European. Though his avatar is this creepy picture of an old man."

He shared the image of a face weathered by sun and wind, a wicked glance in his deep-set eyes. Yamir had seen him before but couldn't remember where.

"It's a stock image, I'm sure," Lucius said. "He claims he's the leader of the Cedarwood chapter of Elsway, my parents' cult. He holds strong opinions about Connectome, though he doesn't have proof of an android. Just echoing hyperspace rumors about your lab."

Anger choked Yamir. "You're sure this Felix guy controlled the drone?"

"Not at all, but he's the only lead we've got. I'll keep digging. But how did he get past your defense dome?"

Yamir was about to explain, but then he remembered he was talking to a reporter. It had probably been his fault the drone broke in. He had forgotten to update the defense software with the latest security patch. Felix must have discovered a vulnerability and exploited it. Yamir's mistake had put Isabela in the hospital—and the guilt crushed him. Always being vigilant about safety only to cause immense harm by not paying attention to something so basic.

"With this video circulating," Lucius said, "the press will come knocking at your door soon. But I still get the scoop, right?"

"I'm not talking to the press, don't worry."

"Felix ranted about wiping the abominable android off the face of the earth and killing everyone involved with the research. He might inspire others to attack Connectome. Others who are worried that scientists like you will create the infernal machine that will obliterate humanity."

"For El's sake, Lucius! I have to go." He then called Olma on his voxdev, audio feed only.

"I'm sorry I couldn't call earlier," she said. "My leaders in Rome are frantic about the bombing. Great job keeping the damaged android shell from the vigiles. Dimitri is updating me on your progress."

Of course, Dimitri had been taking advantage of the chaos to position himself with Olma. To counter that, Yamir had to show he was in control. "Our early lead is a member of Elsway. I'm sending you his info. Maybe you can track him down."

"I'll see what I can do, but the Temple doesn't have visibility inside that sect. They're ferocious with anyone they suspect might help us. I'll station Praetorian guards at Connectome for now. I'll make sure Isabela has the best care available. And Yamir, I'm sorry this happened to our lab." That was nice of her to say.

"Do the PGs know about the A-brains?" Yamir said.

"No. They'll be inside the campus but stationed outside the building."

Yamir had no choice but to accept, though Y1 would hate being locked inside for the foreseeable future.

"I want constant updates until the guards get there," Olma said and ended the call.

A message from Lucius flashed on Yamir's screen. *When can I come to see them?*

Yamir typed a reply. *Not sure. Olma Asper is sending PGs to the lab.*

Speaking of Asper, here's another scoop, Lucius's reply came. *She was the one who got your wife fired.*

Yamir stared at the curved screen for a long time. He'd been wrong about Olma's good intentions. Of course he'd been wrong. The high priestess was using this crisis to camp her PGs, with small automatic weapons and body armor, around his lab. She could do whatever she wanted now, supposedly to protect Connectome. Had she sent her people with a drone and a small bomb here and then pinned it on the fanatics of Elsway? Could she be this ruthless, destroying her very expensive property to gain an advantage? Could anyone who wasn't ruthless become a high priestess of the Orolic Temple?

Olma saw the lab bombing as proof of her new sacred mission. The explosion had damaged the building and an android shell, but Oroles's chosen people, the A-brains, had not been harmed. That was a clear sign for Olma, their shepherd, to stay vigilant and protect them against more serious attacks on Earth—and then get them to Mars. The Sacrorums believed the androids' job was to prepare the red planet for human habitation, but they were wrong. The androids would prepare Mars for the arrival of the B-brain, the new intelligent species that would become native to the entire solar system and spread Oroles's word beyond Earth. Yamir and Y1 were a key part of Oroles's plan too.

Olma hadn't shared these thoughts with the Sacrorums though. All they talked about that morning was the bombing. Had the terrorists known that the Temple now owned the lab? Had the attack been against Connectome Labs or the Temple itself? If the latter, then swift retaliation should deter others from messing with the Temple. Olma promised she'd find answers. She forwarded Yamir's intel on Felix Senecio to her assistant, with instructions to contact Decebal, the investigator who had discovered the connection between LeosTech and SBC, which helped stop Grady's presentation. Decebal might know how to find Senecio. She then dispatched a unit of the Praetorian Guard to Connectome Labs to patrol the campus, three shifts a day.

"Make sure the press stays away from this story," she instructed Catherine.

"We can't keep them from camping outside Dokina Medical Center though," her assistant said, "where Isabela Mescal is being treated for her injuries."

"Their hospital is named after Dokina? Interesting..." The Temple must have made a large donation, and the city responded by honoring a medicine woman whose lineage had changed the life of Oroles the Savior.

"Reporters are hoping to hear her account of the bombing when she wakes up," Catherine said.

"We should have people waiting there too."

"I've already sent them."

To Olma's surprise and gratitude, Nala decided to stay in Cedarwood for a few more days to help in any way she could.

Olma also needed to install video and audio sensors in Yamir's house to see if he was somehow connected to Felix Senecio. In her experience, the worst enemies had once been friends.

Yamir was at work right now, so she needed to get the other two occupants out of the house for a few hours. Wodan required some work, but in the end, Olma tracked down one of his high school friends who worked for the Temple. A hasty school reunion was arranged at Pier 76, under the pretext of admiring a huge Shel'landic cruise ship leaving for Alaska tomorrow. The captain was another former classmate.

As for Wodan's companion, Olma asked a doctor at Dokina Medical Center to invite Heath Murena for a chat. The doctor told him she was a friend of his supervisor in London, who had suggested they meet today. She apologized for the short notice.

By early afternoon, Olma had secured three hours where Yamir's house was empty. She sent a surveillance team there. She then walked those few blocks from the Temple Inn to Dokina. Under normal circumstances, she wouldn't approach someone like Heath, but time was not on her side. Any delay would jeopardize her sacred mission.

Y1 had confessed to her how much he missed his wife and son. Which meant Yamir had a strong bond with them too. His love for his family could become leverage. And Olma needed an asset inside the family to apply that leverage at the right time.

The day was warm but not hot, and the streets weren't as dusty as those of Rome in summer. The doors slid open when Olma arrived at the hospital, and a cool breeze welcomed her in. A totem pole stood near the entrance, honoring the long history of the Coast Salish medicine people. The reception lobby was larger than any Italian hospital she'd been to—and she'd been to a lot. Wide-open spaces, gigantic staircases, colorful furniture everywhere. An enormous chandelier made of glass ribbons in the traditional white, red, and black of the local tribes hung over the lobby.

Olma spotted Heath sitting on a couch with an air of impatience. He looked like the profile picture in his file: slender, copper-brown skin, wavy dark hair, shoulder-length—but also with blue highlights. He wore blue pants, a white button-down shirt, and patent leather mid-heels.

Olma went straight to him. "Thank you for making time to meet with me today."

Heath seemed unsure Olma was the doctor he had talked to earlier, probably because of the Italian accent.

"I'm sorry I had to resort to a little trickery to bring you here. I'm Olma Asper, a high priestess of the Orolic Temple."

Heath stood up, ready to bolt.

"It's about Wodan," Olma said.

"What about him?" Heath said, turning around.

"Let's talk." Olma sat on the couch. She unscrewed the cap on the water bottle she carried in her purse.

Heath settled back down, his hands clasped on his bouncing knee. "Is Wodan all right?"

"He's fine, but his father is in danger, and I need help to protect him and his family."

"You mean the bombing at his lab?" Heath said.

"The Temple now owns Connectome." Olma took a sip of water. "And we always protect our own. We don't know when the next attack will be. We don't know if Yamir's family will be targeted. We really don't know much. But we're doing everything we can to secure the lab. Yamir's house is another matter though. Can you help us keep an eye on things there?" It was a simple task to test Heath's potential as an asset before Olma entrusted him with something more challenging.

Heath's knee stopped bouncing. "You want me to spy on Yamir Varro for you? I'm just a guest."

"The problem is," Olma said, setting down the bottle, "Yamir is a scientist with his head in the clouds. Maybe you've noticed that? Sometimes it's hard to make him pay attention to things that aren't strictly related to his work."

"True," Heath said, a look of recognition in his hazel eyes.

They were connecting. Good. "He doesn't think he's personally in danger. And he's stubborn about accepting help. But I need all the help I can get to protect him and the lab."

"But what does that have to do with Wodan? He and his dad aren't that close."

Olma frowned at that reductionist answer. "If anything happens to his dad, Wodan might get hurt too."

Heath shrugged. "He never talks about his dad. We should just leave town."

"That won't help me or Yamir though. I assume you hope to be part of their family someday?"

Heath shook his head. "Too early for that."

"My mistake. You moved into their house after just one dinner with Yamir."

Heath's eyes widened. "Are you spying on me too?"

Olma sighed. "No. We're trying to keep Yamir safe, and you happened to be around him lately. Listen, the Temple has many friends in the London medical community."

"That doesn't sway or scare me," Heath said.

The conversation kept slipping from Olma's control, to her annoyance. "That wasn't meant as a threat. The Temple helps and supports those who help and support it."

Heath looked away for a moment. "What happens if I don't help you?"

Olma didn't want to get there so fast, but she had no choice. "We'll have to ask the Ptolemaeus Space School to suspend Wodan for the upcoming academic year. Until we've figured out that he wasn't involved in the bombing."

"Oh, come on," Heath said. "He has nothing to do with his dad's lab."

"We don't know that. You said they're not close. Maybe Wodan wants to hurt his dad?"

"Please don't," Heath said. "Just don't mess with Wodan's life. His school is very important to him."

"Then help us keep an eye on his dad's house. Just for a little while."

Heath rubbed his forehead. "I haven't seen anything weird since I got there."

"You weren't looking for anything weird."

"And I can't break into Yamir's office even if you taught me how."

"No need for that." Olma's own crew was doing that right now. "We just want to know if Yamir makes any suspicious changes to his routine or if someone unexpected contacts him."

"I'm not a good spy." Heath stood up. "I hope you understand that."

"We'll take anything you can give us," Olma said, ready to return to the inn and get into bed. "And remember, the Temple never forgets its friends."

The next morning, Yamir slept right through his alarm, which he canceled after a few beeps. In his dream, he and Rhea were canoeing on Lake Xachu, as they used to when they were dating. He didn't want to let that precious moment slip away. When he finally woke up, he heard the front door open and close a few times. His next thought was of Felix Senecio, and a jolt of panic sent him out of bed. He hurried downstairs, still in yesterday's T-shirt and cargo shorts.

He didn't know what to make of the scene in the kitchen. Heath filled a thermos with steaming coffee, while Wodan returned from outside, a sweatshirt tied around his shoulders.

"The paddleboards and the pump are packed," he told Heath. "Oh, good morning, Dad. We're going on a trip for a few days. We rented a boat."

"A trip?" Yamir said, rubbing his eyes. "Where?"

Heath capped the thermos. "Whulge Sound and the Salish Sea beyond."

"What kind of boat is it?" Yamir asked Wodan, his anxiety about dangerous activities resurfacing.

"Relax, Dad, it has all the smart controls, so we'll have a nice and safe ride."

Not good enough for Yamir. "You have a plan if something goes wrong?"

"Of course," Wodan said. "We've done this a few times."

"A few times?" Yamir said, his voice rising.

"We sailed the Mediterranean for three weeks in May," Heath replied in a reassuring tone.

They hadn't mentioned that before. Maybe Wodan hadn't wanted Yamir to make the scene he was making now?

"You have all the supplies you need?" Yamir said, trailing Wodan through the kitchen. "Food? Water?"

"Of course," Heath and Wodan answered together.

"But why so soon? You just arrived. You haven't yet talked to Grady about that internship, Wodan."

The look on Heath's face—like something was chasing him away—made Yamir think it was his fault they were leaving. He hadn't been welcoming enough. Meanwhile, Wodan looked happy to go on yet another dangerous adventure.

"The sea currents are treacherous around the Salish Sea Islands," Yamir said.

"There are hundreds of boats out there, Dad," Wodan said. "It's Sea Fair season."

Yamir had forgotten all about Sea Fair, the annual summer festival celebrating the varied cultures of the Pacific Northwest. Wodan and Heath would probably be fine with coast guards everywhere. Still...

"What if you crash?"

"You're jinxing it now," Wodan said with a serious look on his face.

"Real sailors don't make preparations for certain death," Heath explained in a conciliatory tone.

Yamir ignored him and whispered to his son, "Please, don't go."

Wodan laughed in his face, as expected. "I'll soon be piloting a shuttle to the Moon, Dad. What will you do then?" He turned to Heath. "Please give us a minute?"

Heath nodded and picked up the thermos. "It was great spending time together, Yamir. Your house is truly marvelous, with all its antique touches. Like traveling to another era—so wonderful."

As soon as Heath was out the door, Wodan walked up to Yamir. "What's with this controlling attitude in front of my companion?"

Yamir was taken aback. "I'm worried about your safety, that's all. I have a bad feeling about this trip. So many things can go wrong."

"They won't. You're shaken by the bombing. Trust me, Heath and I know what we're doing."

"Can you at least call once a day to let me know you're fine?"

"You're kidding, right?" Wodan put a heavy hand on Yamir's shoulder. "I'm not in high school anymore."

"I know, it's just..."

"Listen, Dad, you tend to worry about things that don't matter and ignore the ones that do." He tilted his head. "Why do you think Mom left you?"

So they had talked about him. Yamir bit his lip to keep from tearing up. Didn't work.

Wodan shook his head. "You can't make up for lost time with your family by showering me with attention now."

Those words hit Yamir hard.

He moved out of the way. "I love you, son."

"That's the first time I hear you say it, you know?" Wodan smiled, heading for the door. "That's a good start, Dad."

Yamir was certain he had said it before, but maybe Wodan had been too young to remember.

Logfile Y1-1831-06-30

M1 needed reassurance that I couldn't be killed just by destroying my android shell. Yamir would restart me from the lock-point on my simulation engine, with no memory of an attack. To erase us A-brains from existence, the lab would have to be destroyed with all its hardware and its backups, which are continuously streamed to a geo-replicated storage system. Z1 and S1 tried to tell her the same thing, but they looked shaken and didn't sound convincing. So I promised to keep them all safe.

The repairs to the ASV3 aren't going well. Zaltana replaced the leg destroyed by the explosion with one taken from the ASV2, but not every input aligns. Some sensors go nowhere, while some circuits receive no signal. All because we changed part suppliers, of course. All because of Grady and his forced labor manufacturers.

The quantum processors and the memory units inside the shell's torso are undamaged, and only the titanium-alloy plates show scratches from bomb fragments. But the patched ASV3 looks terrible now, one metallic leg, one of black polymer. I transferred to it for a bit and felt flashes of phantom limb pain. The thudding when the ASV2 leg—heavier than the ASV3 one—hit the ground was insufferable. So I scurried back into my simulation engine.

Yamir must get the parts in soon so Zaltana can fix my shell. Instead, he didn't even bother to come to work this morning. What on earth could be more important to him than our lab in crisis?

Oh, I'm getting angry, and I'm not tamping it down with my neuro-chemical controls. It's taken me a while to snap out of the shock of being bombed, but now I can launch into righteous fucking anger. Anger at that asshole Felix, who wanted to kill me. Anger at being stuck in this lab/jail, a sitting duck for terrorists. Anger at Grady for putting a target on our backs.

I understand Olma's impulse to protect us and why I'm not allowed outside anymore. If the Praetorian guards see an android, they'll freak out. Some might not keep their mouths shut. The Temple won't be able to contain that leak. But I hate to be locked inside.

Blast it! I'm worse off than two weeks ago, when I asked Yamir for termination. Which isn't an option anymore.

9

Yamir wasn't surprised the press backed off after the bombing. The hyperspace had been abuzz for half a day, but then the Temple released photos of their soon-to-open pavilion on the Moon. People's short attention span took care of the rest. Isabela Mescal's unchanged critical condition wasn't newsworthy. But Yamir Varro visiting Dokina Medical Center would be, so he didn't dare go see Isabela.

With Wodan and Heath gone sailing, Yamir worked from home another day. Y1 would be frustrated with the inferior ASV1 and angry at the Praetorian Guard outside, and Yamir would be an easy target for his A-brain's ire. Instead, he'd chew on a hard science problem to block out all other thoughts, especially his guilt about Isabela.

He worked on Grady's neurosensory vest until he heard the front door open. Wodan had returned after just one day? Maybe they had forgotten to pack something. Yamir pushed back his swivel chair and hurried to see.

Rhea stood in the kitchen, holding her shoulder bag close, looking like she didn't belong in her own house. Her presence filled Yamir with joy but also dread that she wasn't there to stay. She wore a business suit—gray jacket and pants, white shirt—and her hair was tied in a pretty bun, with curly strands escaping the hairdo. Her sweet perfume had already spread downstairs. She didn't smile.

Despite himself, Yamir felt hopeful. "Are you back?"

She hugged him, and for a moment, he was the happiest man in the world. He tried to kiss her, but she turned her face away to whisper in his ear, "There's something I must show you. But I fear the Temple might be watching us."

An icy shiver ran through Yamir.

She led him by the hand into the pantry, a place he had never paid attention to. The lights turned on as they entered the cramped space lined with cans, bags, boxes, and bottles. He had never known they had so many spice jars, even though Rhea's cooking was always delicious.

He wondered if they were really under surveillance or if Rhea's knowledge of the Temple's history was making her too suspicious. If she was right though, then she was clever to bring him into the pantry. No one would bother to install video sensors there, but audio sensors could still catch their whispers. She put a finger to her lips, pulled a tablet from her bag, and showed him a scanned image of a handwritten document. An old manuscript, like those they had seen in Grady's library.

He glanced a question at her, and she nodded. So she'd been in touch with Thandi Leos and received access to those ancient manuscripts she wanted to study. But the image she showed him didn't quite look like a codex page. More like a hastily scribbled note on centuries-old yellowed paper.

Rhea found her stylus and started writing on her tablet. *I'm not sure Grady knew he had this. It was tucked between the pages of* The Book of Andrada. She tapped on the document and accessed its translation. At the top of the document, it read: *An account taken by Temple administrator Giordano Mancini in the year 1418 LE regarding the buying of enslaved workers for the south wing renovations.* A list of names, ages, and prices in denarii followed.

Yamir's eyes widened. Rhea must have made sure the information was valid.

"Do you know what this means?" he whispered. The Temple using forced labor as recently as the fifteenth century could be leveraged in his future negotiations with Olma to get those PGs off his campus.

Rhea put a miniature flash drive in his hand. She was avoiding online communication.

He wanted to hug her, his entire body aching for her, but she showed him no warmth. Still, she cared enough about him, otherwise she wouldn't have brought him useful information, taking all these precautions.

"Please stay," he mouthed the words, an echo of his plea with Wodan.

"I can't," she replied without sound. She slipped her tablet into her bag, then pushed her way out of the pantry. "Good to see you, Yamir," she said in a normal voice. "By the way, Julian Laurent says you owe him a chat."

Yamir needed a moment to remember when he had promised the Neuroscience Department chair at Servetus a chat. "Oh, at Grady's party?"

"I suppose."

She headed for the door, and Yamir followed in sudden panic at her leaving again.

"Where are you staying?" he asked her. "It is a safe place?"

Rhea lingered for a moment, enough for Yamir's hopes to rise and then crash as she walked out. He inhaled the last trace of her perfume, and a painful knot formed in his throat. She was truly gone. And he was devastated. He leaned his head against the cold door and groaned in pain.

In her office at the Temple Inn, Olma sat in an armchair, watching the feed from Yamir's kitchen on her tablet and growing impatient with the pantry scene. Her people had installed only one video sensor in the kitchen, in the air vent, facing the white granite island and the six-burner stove. She swiveled the sensor. The pantry was still outside its angle.

She rubbed the sore back of her neck. "What the…" she whispered but stopped short of a swear word.

Maybe Yamir and Rhea were having sex in there. There must be something arousing about the fragrances of spices and ingredients, something that offered the lovers a sense of safety and coziness. Olma and Nala had never tried a pantry. Their small apartment in Rome barely had a kitchenette, let alone a pantry. And the fancy places they had stayed at over the years on the Temple's denarii? Olma had always assumed surveillance and made peace with the restrictions on her love life.

No noise came from the pantry, which was odd. No matter how experienced those two were at making love in tight spaces, there still had to be an elbow bumping into a wall or a bag falling off a shelf. Some panting and moaning at least. The Temple's audio sensors were excellent.

Olma didn't like the look and sound of what she was watching: a static image of Yamir's stove with a dirty pan on a burner. Just as she didn't like that her newest asset, Heath Murena, had taken Wodan sailing instead of assuming the role Olma had assigned him.

She waited and waited, the only movement in the video frame on her tablet coming from outside a window, where a pair of birds flew back and forth around their nest. Such a simple life for those birds. Whereas Olma had to deal with two different Yamirs, a difficult plan to bring B-brains to Mars, and a fanatic sect trying to stop her.

Finally, Rhea reentered the frame, followed by Yamir. Olma listened: something about a chat with one Julian Laurent. The scene looked odd. Rhea didn't adjust her clothes or makeup. Yamir didn't say goodbye. Something was off.

Olma sent a message to Catherine to put Rhea Laghmani under surveillance too. *Already done*, Catherine replied. The professor had rented a room at a hotel in the Illahl'koh neighborhood.

Olma checked the newly installed tracker on Heath and Wodan's boat. They were making progress in the open waters of the Salish Sea, as expected. Heath would soon learn he couldn't hide from Olma, not even in the middle of a sea at the edge of the Pacific Ocean.

A report from Decebal, her tech investigator, dropped with a chime. Olma's heart jumped when she read the subject line: *Felix Senecio*. She scanned the message, first line and last, glancing in between, trying to absorb it all at once.

The report had no useful details on the bomber, only what Yamir had already provided yesterday. Senecio was a ghost who had posted online that his goal was to kill everyone involved with the android research. He claimed to have developed a technology that evaded current drone defenses. More likely, he had taken advantage of a security flaw in the software running the lab's defense-drone system, a weakness Yamir had removed with the latest manufacturer update.

The scientists were the only remaining vulnerability to the lab, since they arrived every day through city traffic and went home every night to families that could be targeted. Olma wouldn't tolerate the risk, but she needed them for their scientific expertise.

She searched for their names on her tablet. Dimitri Petrodava wasn't a critical player. Bai Xiu-Min, the mathematician, had quit her job over the SBC issue, and she hadn't donated her connectome to the lab. Yamir was the authority on the entire project, even covering the areas Xiu-Min had worked on. Isabela Mescal was still in the hospital. The other two, Zaltana Rainshadow and Si'ahl Tabaaha, had been uploaded into Z1 and S1, which meant their technical knowledge now lived inside the lab. When Olma had talked to the scientists the other day, Zaltana had implied that Z1 could take over her job. Should be the same for Si'ahl. The project could continue with just the A-brains and Yamir, then. The others would sign nondisclosure agreements sweetened with career advancements and financial rewards.

Olma sent a message to Yamir, asking him to meet her at Connectome in an hour. On her surveillance screen, she watched as he looked around his house, searching for something. Then he sat at his desk in his home office and inserted a flash drive into his workstation. Why not use his wireless network, Olma wondered, which was monitored by her surveillance? No matter, her engineers had tapped into his workstation too. Just as he was about to access the drive, her message appeared on his screen. He shook his head, definitely annoyed. And so was Olma when Yamir removed the drive and left the office.

Yamir arrived at the lab an hour after Olma's message, but she wasn't there yet. He waved to Si'ahl and Zaltana, then hurried to his office to make a copy of Rhea's file on his secure backup system. Even without studying the document, he understood its significance. The Temple had used forced labor during the renovation of their main building in Rome in the fifteenth century. It probably wasn't the only time they had done that, even as they condemned the practice.

The Temple had been accused of corruption in its long existence. Over the centuries, idealists had left it in numbers not large enough to kill it but significant enough to weaken it. Believers who couldn't recover from shattered illusions would become activists. A current example was Elsway. But now Yamir had hard proof of the Temple's corruption, and that could change the balance of power with his new overlords.

Olma's knock on the glass wall by his door startled him, and he hurried to welcome her in.

"Si'ahl, Zaltana," she called from the doorway, "please take the day off."

Yamir nodded at them to go, even though he resented not being consulted. While they gathered their things, Olma entered Yamir's office. She walked fast on low heels, showing no signs of the illness Y1 was convinced she had.

Yamir took the armchair by the low table, while she sat on the sofa.

She straightened her shoulders, her black hair framing her pale face. "I want you to listen to my proposal and decide wisely. This bombing was a wake-up call for everyone. You want to finish your work, and the Temple wants the android secure and away from the public eye. I think we both agree on this."

Yamir nodded, unsure where this was going.

"So, here's the plan," Olma said. "You continue stabilizing the A-brains as before, then focus on developing the B-brain. You'll get all the funding you need for as long as you need it, no pressure. Will this work for you?"

Yamir had barely done any work for the past two weeks. This morning, it had felt good to start designing Grady's neurovest. Now Olma was saying he could go back to his research full-time.

He tried not to look elated. "There must be a catch." After learning from Lucius that the high priestess had been behind Rhea's firing, he knew to be cautious.

Olma leaned against her backrest. "Your work will be conducted in secret."

"I thought we were already doing that."

"You'll live here, in the lab. Your family will think you're going to Mars to help with the settlement repairs. After a training session in Antarctica."

Yamir's short-lived joy disappeared as her words sank in. His secret work would happen away from his family. As bad as things were between him and Rhea right now, at least they lived in the same city. Wodan could still get annoyed with him on a video call. And he could always check in with Malina on Swallah. What Olma proposed was years—at least two, to justify a visit to Mars and back, plus training—away from the people he loved.

If something happened to Malina—she lived alone, and she liked to swim wearing that damn exoskeleton—Yamir wouldn't be there to help. He wouldn't be there for Wodan's shuttle launch to the Moon. He'd become a second Y1, depressed and longing for his absent wife. Work would keep him busy during the day, but what about the hours before falling asleep, when anxiety swelled like a fresh bruise and no rational explanation could make it disappear?

"What about my team?" Yamir said.

"They'll be offered jobs at the Habitat Research Center in Cedarwood. Well-paying jobs, better than what they have now."

"And I'll be alone here?"

"Not alone," Olma said. "You'll have the A-brains."

True. "And if I say no?"

"We'll find another neuroscientist in due time to continue your work," Olma said, as if waiting didn't matter.

Yamir chewed his lip, weighing his options. His work didn't belong to him but to the Temple, so he could lose it forever. The good news was that the Temple wanted the lab to continue its research. They were committed to the A-brains, and Yamir's absence would set them back years.

It was a matter of self-preservation, after all. The Temple wanted to control the new wave of technology Yamir had created. They knew they couldn't stop it, so they had to own it. Otherwise, the public might abandon their sacred texts during the most important technological upheaval of their time.

Yamir could finish his life's work with unlimited resources and plenty of time. Maybe Rhea would miss him while he was gone.

"Only if you restore Rhea to the Concord Column project," he said.

"She can return to her work with Kinoshita tomorrow."

"And you must station your PGs at the gates to allow the A-brains to go outside again."

"I'm working on it." Olma stood up from the sofa. "So, we're agreed?"

Yamir would ask Rhea to check in on Malina once in a while. He'd miss Wodan and the chance to improve their strained relationship. When Isabela woke up, he wouldn't be there to tell her how sorry he was for his mistake with the security software. He'd lose Si'ahl as his trusted ally in the lab. He would no longer have Zaltana's expertise and support. The working conditions people in the Sahara biosphere domes endured might be in store for him.

But he'd finish the B-brain once and for all and be free of the burden he had carried since Malina's accident on the Moon. Then he could finally live his life, whatever was left of it.

"Yes, we're agreed," he said at last.

Since this worked out so well for the Temple, Yamir felt more certain now that Olma had arranged the lab bombing.

"Oh, one more thing," she said. "Isabela Mescal died this morning. Sorry for your loss."

Logfile Y1-1831-07-02

I'm waiting for Zaltana to return from wherever she and Si'ahl went for lunch, but it's been hours. She's supposed to continue my ASV3 repairs. I call her comm ID and reach her voxmail.

To investigate, I have no choice but to upload to that horrible ASV1. Without sensors in certain areas, I feel a tingling numbness all over. The extra kilograms make walking feel like a struggle. After a few minutes, my brain remembers this shell, and I can finally focus on my surroundings.

Yamir and Olma are no longer in his office, but the guards are still outside the lab's front door. So he didn't convince her to remove them.

"Over here." Yamir's voice comes from the storage closet where we keep discarded shell parts.

"What are you looking for?" I say when I make it there.

"Parts for the neurovest." He sounds as if his mind is on something else.

"Where's everybody?"

He looks at me as if I should know. "Gone."

"But Zaltana said she'd work on my leg today." I sigh. "I guess I'll wait till tomorrow."

Yamir shakes his head. "Gone, gone." He pushes boxes around. "It's just me and you guys now."

I don't follow, so he gives me the news. Olma wants him to continue working from here, and the other scientists will be reassigned. Then he tells me about Isabela, and my stomach drops.

"It's my fault she's dead," Yamir says, staring at the box before him. "I was careless with the drone-defense system…"

It might seem that way to him, but no. "The video Lucius sent you proves that the handler wouldn't have bombed us had I not released our defense drones. If it's anyone's fault, it's mine."

"No…" Yamir says, but he doesn't continue.

I can't say anything either. He goes on looking inside boxes, and I…I just stand here. I've always been so careful about safety, and then one night I forgot to worry, and the worst happened.

Yamir wipes a tear. I take a step toward him, and I pat him on the shoulder to console him. My ASV hugs aren't any good.

We agree without words to carry this burden together.

"So you'll be locked in here with us?" I say after a long while. "Are we now…cellmates?"

"Looks like it…"

"You won't see Rhea anymore?" I whisper.

"Maybe if I fake a Martian station here in the lab. Then we can video chat."

"How will we get news of Rhea and Wodan from now on?"

Yamir doesn't answer.

"Who's going to help us with the shell repairs?" I go on.

"Olma said money won't be a problem. We'll get parts, and Z1 will assist me in installing them."

Losing the scientists is just another way my world keeps shrinking. The only good news is that Dimitri is gone too. But I'll miss Zaltana and her magic with electronics. And I'll miss Si'ahl, who's always been so dependable, before and after my upload. The only time we ever clashed was over his desperate attempt to use truth serum on Z1 for a birthday present. In the end, he gave her an autographed copy of Rhea's series *A History of the Orolic Temple*, which definitely surprised her.

"What about the guards outside?" I say, trying not to think about how much I'll miss Isabela.

"We'll see." He picks up a box and stacks it over another. "Before this place is completely bugged, we need to establish a secure hyperspace connection that the Temple can't intercept."

"This ASV1 has an encrypted satellite connection they don't know about." I point to my shell. "Olma only knows of the ASV3."

"Right...Good." Yamir sidles past me, rubbing his neck. "I must go tell the other A-brains now."

"I'll tell the others. You go home and pack and say your goodbyes."

A moment later, I stop by the simulation room, unable to step inside. I feel an immense loss, too big to process all at once. Oh, Isabela, what have I done?

Yamir snapped open a beer can and sat at the kitchen counter, sipping. The house looked empty in the evening light, though nothing had changed. Somehow, the bags at the door brought a chill through a place that had always felt alive and busy.

His initial resolve to leave home and complete the B-brain wavered at the prospect of years without Rhea. He might never see her again. He had assumed he'd see Isabela soon, and now she was gone...

He reached for his voxdev to call Rhea and saw Malina's message. *Luna is fine, but I installed motion-activated video sensors in her collar, just in case.*

Yamir texted back, *Sounds wise.* He wanted to say goodbye but didn't know how to explain the rest. He'd ask M1 tomorrow how to break the news of his long absence to Malina. And maybe he'd extract a promise from his mom to stop swimming in the ocean while he was gone, just to be safe.

He dialed Rhea's comm ID, hoping she'd answer, expecting to leave a message. He'd then order a flatbread and get into bed, and tomorrow morning he'd move into the lab for the foreseeable future.

Rhea picked up on audio only. "Did you read it?" She didn't risk saying what *it* was.

"Yes. Listen, Rhea, you can come back home. I'm leaving."

"I thought I did the leaving." She sounded amused.

Yamir glanced at the patio doors and the backyard garden under a darkening sky. She'd be happy to return to her rosebushes and those loud blue jays in the laurel tree.

"I'm going to Mars. I mean, first to the Temple's station in Antarctica for training on how to live in harsh environments. Like space. You can reach my comm ID while I'm at the station if you ever want to talk. Once I leave, it will be voxmail only because of the transmission delay."

There was silence at the other end. "Yamir, are you serious?"

"The Temple needs my help to rebuild their settlement."

"But that's not your competency."

"I write code, and I understand robots," Yamir said. "That's good enough for them."

"Are the A-brains going with you?" It sounded like she drew a chair and sat down.

"I can't talk about that..." He had found no audio sensors when he searched the house this morning, but he didn't want to risk a conversation with Rhea about the A-brains. "The Temple, they want you back on the Concord Column project."

"I see." She cleared her throat. "Is that why you took this ridiculous Mars job?"

Yamir hesitated to answer. If he said yes, she'd reply that she didn't need his sacrifice. If he said no, she'd either know he was lying, or she'd feel bad for having assumed he could do something nice for her.

Rhea saved him the trouble. "Yamir, listen, this is dangerous. Think of all the things that could go wrong, from the ship malfunctioning to a missed or botched landing to the settlement not being able to support life."

The anxiety in her voice soothed Yamir. Maybe she'd hurry home to stop him.

"You're not that young, you know," she continued. "You haven't kept in shape, what with your long work hours and the stress. You're not astronaut material, Yamir."

Great, the last thing he wanted to hear. "I'm leaving tomorrow morning for Antarctica, and I need a favor. Can you call Malina and tell her I'll reach out when I'm allowed to establish a connection from the station?"

"How long will you be off-planet? I mean, just to get to Mars takes, what? Seven, eight, nine months? Then the work there, then finding the right launch window, then coming back..."

"Two, three years. Keep an eye on Wodan for me while I'm gone," he said, feeling a little melodramatic. "He's sailing the open seas with Heath..."

"Yeah, I'll keep an eye on Wodan, as always. And on Malina. As much as I can, with their adventurous lifestyles." Rhea let out an audible sigh. "Nothing ever changes with you, does it, Yamir? Your work always comes first."

Yamir rubbed his forehead. "Work is all I have left..." But just one word from her and he'd walk away from Olma's lab, his work be damned.

"Goodbye, Yamir. Have a good trip to that El-forsaken Mars."

Part II

Bodies hold atoms, both pure and combined,
Atoms endure, by nature's design.
No force can destroy these particles small,
With solid strength, they conquer all.
—expert-system (ES) translation of *De rerum natura*
by Titus Lucretius Carus, 1824 LE

10

Yamir spent his first weeks alone at Connectome remodeling the open floor in the most expensive way. He added a bedroom, a recreation room, plus a gym he'd probably never use. Furniture was delivered by truck or by drone. He mounted the orca whale carving Si'ahl had left for him on a wall between two windows, where the red cedar caught the sun nicely. A landscape architect redid the green areas on campus the way Yamir imagined Rhea would like. It was Olma's problem if all the coming and going of construction crews attracted the attention of the press.

For her part, the high priestess installed surveillance equipment inside and outside the lab, but Yamir requested that his bedroom and his office be his private space—and she agreed. In the simulation room, S1 and Z1 were still in love and thriving, while Y1 used the Swallah Island VR to help M1 cope with not having a functional android shell. To everyone's dismay, a Temple truck under Dimitri's supervision picked up the connectome chamber from the lab.

Olma allowed Yamir to have read-only access to the hyperspace. That was how he watched the Temple's announcement that Connectome Labs had been closed and its scientists reassigned. The spokesperson announced that Yamir Varro would help with the Mars settlement project after completing his training in Antarctica. He'd then board one of the explorers LeosTech kept in orbit and start his journey to Mars, together with a team of habitat-development specialists. In the same news segment, a reporter stopped retired botanist Malina Varro at a farmers' market on Swallah Island for a few questions. When they asked her what she thought of her son's return to space after she had almost died there years ago, she said she was proud of Yamir. Her exoskeleton was visible under her dry suit as she walked to the shore and dived in, proving that mettle ran in the family.

One day, a brain scan arrived on a quantum drive, complete with a 3D image of a person and a voice sample labeled *Flora Hawkins*. It came with instructions for Yamir to upload that connectome to an A-brain. Three scans arrived the following week. And more had been showing up ever since.

Yamir wondered if those brain scans had been taken from Temple acolytes. What if the resulting A-brains became miserable like Y1 before M1's upload? What if an A-brain was too defective to function? What if they asked for termination? Yamir had only worked with four A-brains, who had all gone through training to understand what to expect. But these new connectomes couldn't have known what an A-brain was, even if they had agreed to use the connectome chamber. Though, knowing Dimitri, there was a strong possibility they hadn't knowingly agreed to it.

So Yamir refused to upload those connectomes, but Y1 worried Olma would call upon Dimitri to complete the task. That ignoramus might torture the poor brain images by accident or kill them. If those uploads had to happen, Y1 offered to do them the right way. So Yamir agreed to optimize the upload procedure, reducing its duration from a month to two weeks. And Y1 started uploading Flora, one thalamocortical structure at a time.

Yamir wished Si'ahl and Zaltana were there to help. But by now, they were probably comfortable wherever Olma had reassigned them. Xiu-Min had already had her baby by now. And Isabela...Yamir tried not to dwell on his guilt about Isabela.

The only person he kept in touch with was Lucius Seong through the ASV1's encrypted satellite link. Yamir had asked the reporter to watch over his family. If anything happened, Lucius was supposed to send a message to Yamir's comm ID with the uninteresting subject *Academic Research*. Yamir received many academic queries, so if Olma's people spied on his inbox, such a message might not raise their suspicion. Yamir would then get in touch as soon as possible. The reporter had accepted that arrangement even though he hadn't yet seen the androids—his promised reward for already having helped Yamir. But Lucius would have exclusive access to Yamir's story one day, and that was worth the wait.

Logfile Y1-1831-08-02

"Olma is coming to check in on the uploads," Yamir tells me instead of *good morning.*

I'm in my ASV1, with its built-in numbness, but he tells me to transfer to the patched-up ASV3, with its mismatched ASV2 leg. The high priestess should see how hard my life is in the absence of the four ASV3s she promised us but didn't deliver. He's acting hostile because he suspects she had something to do with the bombing. But I'm not sure about that.

As Olma enters the lab, I take a few steps toward her, dragging my incompatible leg.

"When do we get the new shells?" Yamir says.

"Still at the factory." She's referring to the new contractor the Temple vetted for ethical work practices. "They'll ship any day now."

"My mother's still waiting to learn how to use an android shell," Yamir says. "But we don't have a functional one."

"Without functional ASV3s," I intervene in a calming tone, "we can't finish our work on the A-brain. And we can't restart our B-brain research."

"Thank you for bringing your concerns to me," Olma says with a condescending smile.

She then takes a slow tour of the remodeled main floor and stops to admire the island added as an open kitchen. She paid for the Temple workers who had installed the stove and oven, and now she can see the result. Yamir doesn't seem to care if she likes it or not. He's just pleased with his oven, where he can now bake his own flatbread.

Olma sits on a kitchen stool, but Yamir doesn't join her or offer her water. I take my place by his side, a few steps away from the island, waiting for Olma to speak.

"I'd like you to prepare our lab's first monthly update," she tells us.

"Wait, you want me to write up our guard-placement negotiations?" Yamir says, though he knows she means the pending brain uploads.

She and Yamir had a lengthy dispute over the guards posted at the lab's doors—and Yamir won. The PGs moved outside the campus gates, so the A-brains—S1 and Z1 in the patched-up ASV3, and I in the ASV1—can once again stroll around without the danger of leaks.

"That's well-documented, thank you," Olma says. "You can skip the lab remodel too. But I want to know your progress on the uploads."

"Ah," Yamir says, sounding a little snarky. "That will take a while."

"Uploads are delicate operations," I say.

"Stop doing that," Olma says, pointing to my hand.

I realize that I've been twisting my wrist in its joint to relieve my mental stress, and it looks broken to her.

"Sorry," I say and reset it to look like a normal human hand again.

Olma rubs her forehead as if in sudden pain. "Um...We also need a miniaturized brain-imaging device. Something the size of a helmet, for the Mars-bound spaceship. In case a crew member needs uploading."

Unlike the connectome chamber, a helmet would only approximate the human limbs' neural connections to the spinal cord, so the scan wouldn't be as accurate. Zaltana worked on the tricky problem of simulating important nerve fibers, such as the vagus nerve connecting the brain stem with the major organs in the body. Now Z1 owns that project, but progress is slow.

I'm about to explain that, when Olma gets up. "I have to go."

"Wait," Yamir says, "we still have questions about these new A-brains. What kind of life do you expect them to have here?"

Olma waves him away and heads to the door.

Once she's gone, I tell Yamir, "My sensors picked up an increased neurotransmitter unbalance since the last time I saw her. A clear sign her health is deteriorating fast. I wonder why she doesn't take better care of herself. Her life as high priestess should be of some value to the Temple."

Olma felt worse the day after her visit to Connectome. The tremor in her hands had become visible, which meant her inability to hold a cup of tea without spilling it would soon become obvious to Nala. For that reason, Olma kept her wife at a distance. But Nala was persistent.

"You told me we'd be done here by now," she had said yesterday.

"When are we going home?" she had asked again this morning.

And now, at the end of a long workday, more complaints had forced Olma to take refuge on their apartment's balcony. She stared at downtown Cedarwood, her MNDS making the image shimmer around the edges.

A few blocks north of the Temple Inn, cranes moved prefabricated walls to the site of a new skyscraper. The Shel'landic city was growing toward the sun, an unruly thicket of glass and metal. Olma missed Rome, with its eternal ancient beauty, but Cedarwood was where Oroles had sent her—and here she was.

She was making little progress on his sacred mission though. Yamir was slow with the uploads, while the inexperienced Dimitri was her only employee who could operate the connectome chamber. Contacting Si'ahl, Zaltana, or Xiu-Min, who had signed nondisclosure agreements, carried its own risks, so Olma wouldn't reach out yet.

"I want to go home," Nala said, joining her on the balcony.

"Then go home," Olma whispered. She was tired of arguing.

"But I don't want to leave you here. I want to take you to see Doctor Silvestri."

Olma kept staring ahead, her hands behind her back. "I'm fine."

"Stop pretending, love." Nala took Olma's cold fingers into her warm hand. "You're not well, and you're killing yourself trying to serve the Temple. Someone else can take care of that damn lab."

"You don't understand—"

"Then make me understand. Why can't you just let someone else do this El-forsaken job?"

Olma turned to look into Nala's tearful brown eyes. "Because it's not El-forsaken. It's Oroles's will."

Nala scoffed. "Not that Ravenna hallucination again…"

"Nala, I've been sent here to represent Oroles's Temple, and that's what I'm doing." She didn't try to explain that the androids were Oroles's chosen people.

"Have you even talked to Doctor Silvestri?"

"I will, when we get home." Olma focused her attention on the cranes and skyscrapers again.

"And when do we go home?" Nala pressed.

"I don't know…I don't know."

"I'll just book the flight, and you're coming with me."

"I'm not. Please let me be."

"Then I'll tell Regina Sacrorum you're seriously ill. She's a wife; she'll understand."

Olma turned so fast, it was a surprise for both of them. She pointed an unsteady finger at Nala. "Don't you dare mess with my…work, you hear me?"

"You're sick," Nala said, wiping a tear. "I love you, but you make me miserable. I'm done here."

She rushed inside, and soon Olma could hear drawers open, the automatic closet door slide, the counter in the bathroom clatter with scattered toiletries. But she was too tired to fight. And she couldn't allow herself to curse either. She closed her eyes and prayed to Oroles for the guidance the Sacrorums couldn't offer. How could she assemble the Mars Guard in secret and with so little help? The press scrutinized all her public appearances, so she had to rely on Dimitri for volunteers. She hoped Catherine would take over the recruiting soon.

Her voxdev rang, and she resisted the urge to imagine that Oroles had heard her worries and sent her a sign. Indeed, it was only Dimitri, calling from Servetus University.

"I have six more brain scans for you," he said. "All professors or teaching assistants. Some with knowledge of astronomy." A bit of good news.

It had taken some effort to convince Dimitri to manage the connectome chamber. At first, he wouldn't hear of it on account of his belief in El. Olma had to employ her best arguments: from financial incentives for his children's college tuition to the Temple's sacred mission to serve El. At last, Dimitri had agreed to start scanning brains for the Mars Guard.

"We have enough for now." She needed to see what Yamir did with them first.

"Then, can I take the week off?" Dimitri said, in a pleading tone. "Two of my kids are in town for summer break, and I'd like to spend time with them. Before they fly back..."

Olma knew she should make small talk about the man's children, but she couldn't. "One week."

"Thank you, High Priestess. One last question, to put my mind at ease. What happens if a connectome we upload turns out not to be a good fit for the Mars Guard?"

Olma had asked the Sacrorums this exact question, and their answer had been to just delete them. The Temple couldn't spend resources to keep them around forever. But they hadn't met Y1 or M1. They couldn't understand that there was something human in—

"I love you," Nala's voice interrupted Olma's thoughts.

"Pray to Oroles to set your mind at ease," Olma told Dimitri, ending the call.

Nala had returned to the balcony, her eyeliner smeared with tears. "I can't just leave you here." She threw her arms around Olma, who held her for a long moment, caressing her hair and kissing her forehead, feeling each sob in her own tired bones.

"Home is where you are," Olma whispered. Right now, Oroles didn't seem as real as Nala's hot cheek on hers, the scent of the familiar olive oil lotion, the sound of her soft breath. She wished with every dying cell to go home so she could spend whatever time she had left with her beloved wife.

Next time she talked to the Sacrorums, she'd tell them she couldn't assemble their Mars Guard. She wasn't up for the job. They should send a group of experienced leaders to manage this complex project. That was also the right thing to do for Oroles's sacred mission.

Logfile Y1-1831-08-03

Brain uploading is a long process because the neocortex keeps an un-challenged model of its physical body. Its predicting mechanisms expect all the anatomical parts to be there. When the neocortex stops receiving the expected inputs (old retinas don't behave like video sensors), it experiences shock and terror (mediated through the thalamus), before updating its model. We don't want our A-brains to experience constant pain and trauma, so we take our time, working outside their self-awareness.

Now that I've finished training the first batch of new A-brains to work with our sensor array, I'll bring Flora Hawkins online to complete her upload.

Once I connect her subsystems, her first reaction is to freak out, of course. I calm her down using our dials for neurotransmitters and neuromodulators, then tell her that her name in the lab will now be F1.

"Eff you! My name is Flora!" she yells at me.

Definitely not a Temple acolyte. But who is she?

After I calm her down again, I piece together her story from a string of disjointed sentences laced with profanities. Flora had a substance use disorder. She hung out near the Servetus University campus, where one day, she saw Dimitri's announcement calling for volunteers for an exciting new brain study. She needed the money, and she could hide her addiction if needed, so she was the first to enter our stolen connectome chamber.

Dimitri now appears to be roping in A-brain material for Olma. He somehow convinced the high priestess he's a specialist in A-brains. I assume Zaltana and Si'ahl weren't interested in doing this kind of work for the Temple. Maybe Olma has other reasons to trust Dimitri, but he's not vetting his subjects well. Flora will never make a good Martian settler. Her artificial neurons don't have the ailments of her biological ones, where the cells' chemistry was affected by interfering substances—our upload process corrected that. But her neural network is sparser than average. Much of her gray matter has died from years of narcotics.

I try to help her feel comfortable here. I suggest watching videos to relax, and she yells at me, "I've got no fucking interest in your fucking vids." Then I suggest books. M1 loves that she can read much faster now, not because of enhanced brain performance, but because her body doesn't waste time being tired or hungry or sick. Flora calls M1 "pathetic" and some other bad words.

She won't accept yet that she's stuck with us. A few hours after her upload, she screams, "You brought me to Inferis, motherfucker. This is Inferis, where doomed souls don't even have names, just fucking IDs." She yells from her screen at the other A-brains in the simulation room to wake up. "Do you have names, motherfuckers?"

And she makes an impression. By the end of the day, M1 and I are the only "ones" left among our peers. The others assume their old human names—Si'ahl and Zaltana—since their other owners are gone anyway.

I tell Yamir, "I doubt the rest of the batch will be better than Flora..."

He sighs. "We need more data to convince Olma to end this terrible experiment."

"But I don't want to bring another tormented soul into our Inferis." I sound like Flora.

"Three more should be enough," Yamir says. "And I'll help you with the uploads."

He offered to work together, which is a first. I didn't expect that, and I usually know what to expect from him.

Yamir helped Y1 bring three new A-brains online the next day: Yang Qian, Alex Nissenbaum, and Estelle Kitazumi. They had answered Dimitri's ad distributed around Servetus, then entered the connectome chamber for a few hundred dinars. Qian was an astrophysics student who needed money for textbooks. Alex was a grocery store manager and a single dad of twins. And Estelle was a nurse who had depression and needed another psychedelic medicine treatment.

Their uploads didn't go any better than Flora's. They were all upset to find themselves here. They had never expected their brain scans to come to life like this. After a brief chat with Flora, they refused to adopt android names. They threatened to call the vigiles and sue. Calming down these terrified and angry A-brains took all the willpower Yamir had in him. And his lower lip was sore from biting on it.

M1 tried to offer moral support to the newcomers, to no avail. Si'ahl and Zaltana—Yamir corrected himself when he thought of them as S1 and Z1—explained that new A-brains wouldn't always be stuck inside simulation engines and VR environments. They had the whole campus to explore, now that the PGs were gone. They would learn to like the android shell, even though the ASV3 was a bit broken. Still, Qian threatened, and Alex complained, while Estelle just wouldn't talk. Yamir had enough data to make Olma understand how horrific this experiment was.

He left them with Y1 and went on a walk to gather his thoughts. He started on the newly graveled five-kilometer loop he'd been walking every day for a month. His back wasn't stiff anymore, and his shorts had loosened around the belt. If only Rhea could see him now. She might apologize for saying he wasn't astronaut material.

His heart grew heavy. He'd had no message from her since their goodbye conversation. But no message from Lucius meant everything was fine with his family.

He passed a bush beset by crows. Fall was in the air, even though it was early August.

Back in July, Wodan had sent Yamir an angry message to say how uncool it was to leave for Mars without first talking to his son, who happened to know a thing or two about interplanetary travel. Yamir would have loved to see Wodan before beginning his forced seclusion at Connectome, but he couldn't have pulled off the lies needed. He had recorded an audio-only reply and sent it through a Temple-approved channel, promising to get in touch once he got settled in Antarctica.

Malina had texted him too. Wodan and Heath had found a dock to anchor their boat close to her house on Swallah Island. They visited her, then sailed out for a few days at the time, exploring the Salish Sea all the way north to the Pacific Ocean.

At the new gazebo, painted in white, Yamir sat on a bench under young wisteria vines. He ran his fingers through his shaggy hair. He needed a haircut but didn't want to ask Olma to bring him a barber. All he wanted from her was the end of that atrocious experiment.

The footfall on the graveled path pulled him out of his thoughts.

"There you are," Olma said with a labored breath. "I tried calling you."

Yamir's hand flew to his pocket. "Oh, I'm so sorry...I forgot my voxdev in the lab. Please sit." Just the person he wanted to talk to.

She shook her head. "Let's go back inside. I don't want to talk about the lab out here in the open."

"Oh, don't worry." Yamir pointed to the dome of the gazebo. "Electro-magnetic field blocker. You paid for it. No drones can spy on us here, even if they slip through our improved defense system." His tone blamed her for creating a secure jail for him and the A-brains.

Olma hesitated, then sat on the other bench under the latticed roof. "I brought six more brain scans for the Mars Guard."

"The new A-brains are miserable, shocked, scared, angry. I would be too if I woke up here one day with a lifetime sentence."

"They'll get used to it. Then they'll have an entire planet to call their own."

Yamir sighed. "But these A-brains won't make good Martian set-tlers. They're not engineers or astronauts. They're common folks Dimitri tricked into being scanned."

"He couldn't exactly tell them what he was doing, now could he? He presented it as a neuroscience study and advertised for volunteers at Servetus University, a good place to recruit participants."

"But Dimitri put little thought into his recruiting process."

"These six are better. But tell me about the uploaded ones. Are they salvageable?"

Yamir groaned. "Flora Hawkins's brain has neural damage, and its abilities for basic tasks are diminished compared to brains that haven't been affected by narcotics use. We're patching it up through neurogenesis, but bringing its neural net up to full capacity—and training it—will take years."

"A journey to Mars takes months. And we're not sending them out today. They have time to improve and adapt." Olma's fingers trembled in her lap because of her MNDS, and she interlaced them.

Yamir was about to ask her what would happen if the A-brains couldn't adapt. But he was afraid of her answer. "This isn't a viable way to build your Mars Guard. You must let me resume my B-brain research, and then you'll have your future settlers."

"Upload these new scans," Olma said.

"No."

"Don't make me replace you, Yamir. Dimitri is working hard to convince me he'd make a great lab chief."

Yamir hissed through his teeth. "He can't lead your lab, and you know it. And I won't help him. Please stop this awful experiment...You and I, I thought we agreed on the human nature of these A-brains."

"They are more than human to me—they are sacred."

"Then why are you doing this to them? For your Temple leaders?"

"You don't understand," she said.

"But I do. And you don't have to follow wrongful orders."

"My leaders have Oroles's blessing, and I must obey them," she said, but Yamir heard the doubt in her voice.

"You don't. The Temple has done terrible things in the past, things you know were wrong."

"What are you talking about?" Olma perked up.

"They traded enslaved workers four hundred years ago. For the renovations in Rome."

"You have proof?"

"Yes." Maybe she didn't know about it, and his argument could sway her. "A document written by a Temple clerk in 1418. It's authentic."

Olma let out a bitter chuckle. "I don't doubt that. We have quite a few of those bills of purchase in our Rome library. They date from around 1420, when the fall of the empire meant rules stopped being enforced."

"That document is valid proof that the Temple can give wrongful orders. You don't have to follow such orders, High Priestess. You have your own humanity to guide you."

Olma sighed. "I'm so sick and tired of you, Yamir. You think the Temple has survived this long through mere luck? We're merciless when we need to be, and today, one Yamir Varro will learn he should have never threatened the Temple. Not ever."

"I never threatened the Temple. I only tried to show you that you don't need to—"

Olma stood up from her bench, and maybe she had done it too fast, because she lost her balance but saved herself by grabbing a vine.

Yamir didn't jump up to help her.

"Keep uploading those connectomes." She started on the path with an uncertain step. "Twenty-six left, by my count."

Logfile Y1-1831-08-05

I'm done for the day. Time to recharge my ASV1 for tomorrow.

"Please transfer me to an android shell, Moonlight," M1 asks me when I pass by her screen. "You think I can't handle it yet, but I know I can."

It's been almost two months since her upload, but we're still waiting for the new ASV3s. M1's first shell experience shouldn't be with either defective or obsolete equipment.

"Come on, Y1, let the girl take that truck for a spin," Flora calls out, referring to the patched-up ASV3 in the charging dock. "Life sucks enough as it is. We need entertainment."

"M1 is not entertainment," Zaltana says.

"Can I try the shell instead?" Qian says.

"Let her have a go, Y1," Si'ahl says.

"Yeah," Alex says.

They're right. If M1 could handle working on the Moon as a single mom, she'll be fine in the repaired shell.

I give the transfer command, and the ASV3 comes to life with Malina's avatar on its faceplate. She spends a long moment looking around, getting used to the sensor inputs that differ slightly from those of her engine's array. The others keep quiet, with only a whisper of encouragement now and then. I stand by, waiting for her to do something. At last, M1 walks out of her dock, her first wobbly step as a fully functional android. The others erupt into prerecorded applause.

"This is harder than I thought." M1 laughs and stops moving.

"You're doing great," Estelle says, her first words today. Maybe she'll warm up to us.

I try to take M1's hand, but our metallic fingers slip off each other.

"You remind me of my twins," Alex says. "They still walk holding hands...When will I see them again?"

"Focus, Alex," Qian says. "This is remarkable. We'll soon do this ourselves."

M1 takes another step, and her longer leg throws her off balance. She tries to widen her stance, but that only makes her wobble more. She grabs the back of a chair, but her arm twists back in a way unfamiliar to her former human anatomy.

I catch her at the last moment and prop her up again.

"I can't tell where my legs are," she says, trying to laugh it off. "They can't possibly be these weights I'm dragging around. And one is not like the other."

"It takes a while for your brain to accept the inputs from the shell," I say. "The simulation engine you're used to can't recreate the exact feel of the ASV3, unfortunately. And you do have an ASV2 leg to complicate matters."

"I also didn't think to twist my limbs like this in the simulation engine. Old habits die hard, I guess."

"If by old habits you mean living in a human body," Flora says.

M1 tries moving again. I witness my mom's first steps, as she witnessed mine forty-some years ago.

"What are you doing?" Yamir's panicked voice sounds from the door.

I expect a fit, but he hurries to take M1's hand and guides her around the room, careful not to hit tables and chairs we don't need anymore, now that the scientists are gone.

"Good job, M1," he keeps saying.

"You go, girl," Flora calls from her window on the wallscreen.

"You're a natural," Si'ahl adds, though M1 limps more than he usually does.

"You should go out for a walk tomorrow," Zaltana says. "You'll love our garden."

"Not yet." Yamir smiles with what I recognize as pride. "Baby steps. Let's practice over there."

He shows M1 the way out to the main floor as the others let out a collective "aww..."

11

Logfile Y1-1831-08-06

Yamir calls me to his office and shows me a message on the screen from Lucius with the subject *Academic Research*. My adrenaline spikes. Something has happened to Rhea or Wodan. Yamir points me toward the back door.

With the lab under surveillance, only my ASV1 can connect us to Lucius. We hurry to the spot with the bench and the lake view, where I can watch out for drones, and I activate my secure satellite connection. Yamir calls Lucius, whose live image appears on my faceplate. I transmit my visual feed to Lucius, acting as Yamir's videoconference device.

"You must see this," Lucius says in a bloodcurdling tone.

"What is it?" Yamir says.

"Just keep watching."

I activate my faceplate display mode so I can watch the video too. I see the central square on Swallah Island, decorated with Sea Fair banners. In a corner, Wodan stands by the totem pole that tells the legend of the Thunderbird and the Killer Whale. It looks like he's waiting for someone. The recorder doesn't capture the sounds in the square. It's at a considerable distance, zooming in from a place with Aztec music in the background.

Lucius explains, "Some tourists up on the terrace of a Mexican restaurant took a video of the square. They sent it to NNN, hoping we'll investigate."

"Is Wodan all right?" Yamir says.

"I don't know."

Dread sinks in as I try to breathe, even though I don't need air.

The video focuses on the totem pole, with its colorful carvings. The next moment, Heath walks into the frame, embraces Wodan, and takes his hand. He gives him a long kiss, which makes the person recording let out an encouraging whistle. Wodan smiles while Heath tells him something. Then Wodan frowns and tries to release his hand, but Heath holds firm. The video sensors zoom out to show five Praetorian guards closing in, the yellow eagle visible on their arms.

"No," Yamir cries.

"That's illegal," I say. "PGs have no jurisdiction in Shel'land."

"Who's that speaking?" Lucius says.

"Y1," Yamir says.

"An android?" Lucius says.

"Yes, an android," I say, "but we don't have time for that now."

The image stops, and Lucius's face appears on my faceplate. "Yamir, you have to give me something, anything. I wouldn't be worth a holed denarius as a journalist if I didn't ask you now to give me more than promises of stories in the future."

"I'll send you a document I wrote for Grady Leos back in June." Yamir's arguments against the android's public announcement will offer Lucius ample data on Connectome. "Now restart the video."

"All right..." Lucius says, and we're back on Swallah Island.

The PGs surround Wodan and immobilize him. Onlookers don't dare approach. Wodan yells at Heath, but the video sensors don't catch his words. Compared to the scene in the square, the Aztec drums, clay flutes, and shakers in the background now sound grotesque.

I feel lightheaded. "When was this?"

"The timestamp says ten forty-two this morning," Lucius says.

The PGs shove Wodan into a black van and drive away. The video ends, and Lucius reappears on my faceplate.

"What does the Temple want with my son?" I ask him. "He doesn't know anything about me or the lab."

Yamir looks like he's going to throw up. "Olma told me yesterday I'd regret threatening the Temple."

"You did what?" both Lucius and I say.

"No time to explain," Yamir says. "They might be on their way to get Rhea too."

I groan like I've been wounded—it feels that bad. "Lucius, can you call her? Now?"

Lucius takes out his voxdev and dials, muttering, "This is surreal. I'm taking orders from an android…" After a few moments, he says, "She's not picking up."

"What do we do, Yamir?" I ask him.

Wodan is in trouble, and Yamir can't leave Connectome. Olma's PGs will stop him at the gate. Security upgrades on all the fences, plus drones crisscrossing the sky, mean he can't just climb over and escape. He's a prisoner, just like me. Just like Wodan.

"Can you leave Rhea a message?" he asks Lucius. "Tell her to go into hiding."

"I doubt she'll listen to a stranger," Lucius says. "Should I show her the video?"

"Yes," I shout. "Anything to get her to safety. And hurry!" Even though I know how hard seeing her son's arrest will be on Rhea.

But Lucius may already be too late.

Bright lights flooded the interrogation room in the Temple Inn's secure basement. Olma sat across the table from Wodan Varro, angry with the Sacrorums for their harebrained move to arrest him. She had requested to leave the Connectome project, informed them of her fight with Yamir, and given them the details on her newest asset, Heath Murena. Instead of considering her request, as they had promised, they had arrested Wodan.

"Connectome is your sacred mission, High Priestess Asper," Rex had told Olma, uttering those significant words again. "Use the neuroscientist's son to secure the lab's success. Only then can you return home."

Without their consent, Olma wouldn't be able to secure Nala's future. And she had to hurry. With her MNDS advancing every day, she had to deliver the Mars Guard to the Sacrorums—and she had to do it fast. Part of her was relieved she didn't have a choice anymore. She had to fulfill Oroles's plan, for Nala's sake.

Her hands shook a little, so she kept them in her lap. Wodan's hands weren't cuffed, though the table had the appropriate metal rings.

She was about to speak when Wodan slammed his fist on the table. The guard at the door took a step toward him, but Olma stopped him with a glance.

"Why am I here?" Wodan said. "The Temple can't arrest Shel'landic people. This is illegal."

"Yes, it is," Olma said, "but it doesn't matter." Her Italian accent was harsher at the end of a long day, when her tongue just wanted to roll its Rs and stretch its vowels.

"What have you done with Heath? Is he all right?"

"He's fine and on his way to London. You should know, he was only trying to protect you."

The PGs had convinced him to help them capture Wodan without incident. All they'd had to say was that Wodan was the next likely target of those who had bombed his dad's lab.

"Protect me?" Wodan banged his fist on the table again, making a racket. "I'm not in any danger. Except from you."

Olma shifted in the hard metal chair. "Do you know what your father does for a living?"

"Develops exoskeletons for people with brain injuries," Wodan said. "Or something."

"That's what he told you? It must've been hard growing up with a father who lied to you all the time."

"You keep talking about my father," Wodan said. "Let's talk about me. Why am I here?"

"But that's why you're here: your father. He won't behave himself, and he needs some motivation."

"How can he not behave himself in Antarctica?" Wodan said. "What does that even mean?"

Olma was about to blurt out that Yamir wasn't in training, but she caught herself. She was exhausted. Every move tired her. And she had spent the morning confronting a defensive Dimitri about his hasty recruiting of volunteers. Catherine would do the vetting from now on, even though that would slow down the process.

"Where am I?" Wodan said. "Where have you brought me?"

Olma's voxdev pinged with a message from Yamir. *How dare you take my son hostage? Return him immediately, or I'll destroy the lab.*

She stood up and walked to the door as steadily as she could.

"Wait," Wodan called after her. "Where are you going?"

Outside, Olma leaned against the cold wall, trying to center herself. Her body felt as if it were made of ball bearings, with no core of stability.

She called Yamir. "How did you find out so soon?" she said when he picked up.

"You arrested my son in the middle of a public square," Yamir yelled. "It's all over the hyperspace."

Luckily, the Temple knew how to bury these kinds of stories. The Sacrorums would release another exciting video about Urbs Lunae, and people would forget about the arrest they thought they had seen. Wodan's abduction would be explained away as routine field practice for the Praetorian Guard, with the permission of the Shel'landic government.

"Let my son go," Yamir growled.

"You have no say here. And if you don't calm down, the PGs will go after your wife next."

Yamir was quiet for a moment, and Olma realized she had just told him the Temple didn't have Rhea yet. Damn illness. She couldn't keep a straight head as she used to.

"My wife sent that Mancini document to Elsway. Encrypted. It'll decrypt automatically on September first if Wodan is not in London."

Olma remembered the pantry scene at his house back in July. That must have been about the document, not passionate sex among spices. But Rhea Laghmani probably wouldn't know encryption or how to set a dead-man switch. Yamir was likely bluffing.

"Listen to me," she said. "You're putting your son's life in danger with every word you utter." She let that sink in. "Here's what you're going to do, Yamir. Go back to work and keep uploading the connectomes I sent you. Or I'll stick Wodan in that chamber and upload his connectome to a simulation engine. Then I'll let Dimitri experiment on that new...W1."

There was silence at the other end. Yamir might not realize Dimitri didn't know how to upload an A-brain. He was probably already imagining a W1 suffering even more than Olma had seen Y1 suffer when they first met.

"Don't do that," Yamir said, his voice weak. "Please, don't hurt Wodan. In whatever form."

"Then we're understood?" Olma said, her breath shallow.

"Yes."

"And Elsway?"

"They don't know about the document."

Olma exhaled. She'd been right to call his bluff. "Who has the original?"

"It's still in Grady Leos's library," a defeated Yamir said.

Olma would contact Rhea at Servetus and track down all the digital copies.

She ended the call and leaned against the wall, struck by a sudden realization. The young man in the interrogation room was the key to everything.

She didn't know how she had come up with the threat to upload Wodan's brain, but that was exactly what she had to do to complete her sacred mission. An uploaded Wodan—son of Yamir, creator of an-droids—was the perfect space pilot to lead the Mars Guard. Oroles must have sent Wodan to her for this purpose. The same way he had sent those volunteers to Dimitri's connectome chamber, each with skills and abilities she had yet to discover. Though she didn't doubt they had all been chosen for a reason.

She pressed the button for the interrogation room, and the door disarmed and slid into the wall.

"I want a lawyer," Wodan said as she walked in.

"Keep him in isolation," Olma told the guard.

"How long?" Wodan asked. "I must return to school soon."

A few days in isolation, and he wouldn't be thinking of school anymore. Then he'd be ready to hear about his part in Oroles's plan.

Logfile Y1-1831-08-10

Olma said Wodan is doing fine and will be released once she has a hundred androids well-trained and ready to deploy to Mars. Which means months of work, uploading and training them, while Wodan should be back in school in three weeks.

Maybe Yamir can convince her to let him go on a promise of compliance. I know he won't fight Olma anymore. But she doesn't believe he's sincere, not even after he asked Rhea—through the lab's monitored connection—to delete her copies of that ancient Mancini document. Rhea complied, of course. As for the original, it's still in Grady Leos's library, so Olma will have to ask him for it.

In her generosity, the high priestess has shared with us some news of Rhea: She petitioned Servetus University to let her stay on campus under the false pretense that her house was undergoing renovation. Julian Laurent, my old boss in the Neuroscience Department, offered her an apartment used by visiting lecturers, and she accepted it.

Had she told Julian why she needed shelter, Servetus would still have allowed her to stay, because universities have been bound to give sanctuary to refugees since the fall of the Roman Empire. But she didn't dare antagonize Olma with a public accusation. She didn't want to risk Wodan's safety.

A university campus isn't like a public square on Swallah Island. The Temple wouldn't risk taking Rhea from under the university's protection. So we're not worried about her right now, just about Wodan.

That's why we keep uploading connectomes from Dimitri's first group of volunteers, hoping most of them will recover from their initial trauma.

Some A-brains are willing to talk to Yamir and me, some are angry, and some are silent. One is a brain surgeon who understood sooner than anyone else where she was. One is a young illustrator who likes smoothies. One is a vigile who threatened to arrest Yamir. One is a math teacher who kept saying they were late for class. One is a virologist, an expert in avian infectious diseases. One is an architect who likes to paint watercolors in her free time. A diverse group of people, to be sure. But Dimitri didn't score any astronauts, the most essential role for the Temple's emerging Mars Guard.

We understand the benefits of bringing different people together. A settlement needs all sorts of minds: young and inquisitive, old and experienced, and everything in between. After months spent training together, these androids might grow into an effective team. And those who won't be good team players? Will Olma want them deleted?

The newest batch of connectomes includes ten acolytes from the Orolic Temple in Cedarwood, all in their early twenties. But why would Olma want them on Mars? To build a regolith temple in the middle of the red desert? Their high priestess ordered the acolytes to get scanned, but were they told anything about artificial brains? Would any Temple follower be able to accept that artificial brains are real people? Would they accept they are now A-brains? Since we don't have a therapist among our growing android crew, we decided to put off working on the acolytes until we finish uploading the other connectomes.

Yamir worries Olma might still upload Wodan because he's a student at the Ptolemaeus Space School. That thought keeps him up at night, while I have the advantage of managing my sleep cycles. I try not to imagine my son joining me in this Inferis. I don't want that for him. But for myself? How wonderful it would be to see him again...

Olma ended her talk at the Cedarwood Habitat Research Center by thanking the scientists gathered in the rotunda for their progress toward rebuilding the Mars settlement. From a lectern decorated with the

Temple's golden eagle, she praised the team's efforts to avert another catastrophe like the oxygen plant's explosion last year. She managed to sound upbeat despite feeling exhausted.

"Thank you and may El bless you all." She stepped away from the lectern and headed to the conference room for a meeting with the director.

"Do you have a minute?" a familiar young man asked her. His black hair was in a long ponytail, and he had an intense look in his deep-set eyes.

"Si'ahl Tabaaha?" she said after a moment. "You worked at Connectome with Yamir Varro."

He nodded.

"How do you like your new job here?"

Si'ahl seemed hesitant. "That's what I wanted to talk to you about."

Olma motioned him toward a window with a gorgeous view of Whulge Sound. They sat around a low table, Olma clasping her handbag to hide her muscle weakness. People walked by, but she gave Si'ahl her undivided attention.

"I'm not sure how to say this," he began, "but can I please return to Connectome Labs when it reopens?" He seemed sincere and eager. "Please. I'm sure the scientists who'll be replacing Yamir there could use my expertise."

Olma couldn't reveal that Yamir was still at the lab, not in Antarctica, so she deflected. "You don't enjoy working here? What part of the project are you in?"

"Smart environmental controls. Interesting technologies, yes, but I miss the A-brains. Um, they're still working on A-brains there, right? There's just too much security around that place..."

The press had noticed that Olma needed those Praetorian guards at the campus gates. She needed them because she had a dozen robots roaming inside. They had to be contained, literally.

She sighed. "When we restart the A-brain project, we'll require every scientist to live on campus for months at a time. Security is just too hard to manage otherwise."

"I understand," Si'ahl said. "My family will too. As long as we can video chat once in a while, they won't care about my street address."

"I'm sure your skills would be welcome at Connectome, but this is a big decision, Si'ahl."

"When I was in the Corps Network," he said, though he looked as young as they came, "I deployed for months at a time to disaster areas all over the planet. Isolation doesn't scare me."

Olma considered his ask. Yamir sounded overwhelmed each time they talked. He had complained he was a scientist, not a manager for Olma's Mars Guard, now counting forty-two A-brains. A friend in the lab could help him, especially one who accepted a long deployment. Speeding up the uploads was a growing priority for Olma as her health deteriorated.

"Send me an application for transfer." She stood up, finding her balance. "And explain to me why you'd be more productive at Connectome than here at the Habitat Research Center."

Si'ahl rubbed his hands on his pants, leaving dark stains of sweat on the blue fabric. Olma smiled goodbye and headed to the meeting with the director.

She stopped by the kitchen and looked at the drink dispenser. She chose black tea with bergamot orange peel, then inhaled the warm scent in the paper cup. It was wonderful, reminding her of her home in Tuscany. She took a hot sip—

"Do you have a minute, High Priestess Asper?" a woman asked.

Olma turned to see another former Connectome scientist standing by the refrigerators. She had shoulder-length black hair and almond-shaped brown eyes, looking delicate and determined at the same time.

"Zaltana Rainshadow," Olma said, smiling. "Don't tell me you want to return to Connectome."

"How did you know?" Zaltana arched her eyebrows.

"I'm a high priestess—I know things. But have you thought it through?" She explained the same things she had told Si'ahl. "It'd be like living in a fortress."

"That's fine," Zaltana said with a shrug.

"Do you have family here?"

"Not anymore." Zaltana touched her ring finger, though there was no ring.

Olma gave Zaltana instructions for writing a transfer application, but she didn't mention Si'ahl. She didn't know if those two had agreed to approach her today, playing some weird game on her. She'd decide which one to return to Connectome—if any—based on the best application received.

Logfile Y1-1831-08-12

The new ASV3s have finally arrived, a whole dozen. This enhanced model has self-destruct technology that will disable the quantum cores and memory banks inside the torso case, making the shell look to the untrained eye like a damaged ESPA. The A-brain can be restarted from its backup, of course, so we can't use this feature for termination. There's still no way out of our Inferis.

The lab is now so crowded, I sometimes want to scream. New android shells, including mine, patrol the grounds, inside and outside the lab building. We have new workstations in the simulation room and on the main floor, running the A-brains we're creating from Olma's connectomes. Because of the logistics of too many screens and sensor arrays, we're now plugging all simulation engines into our VR environment. Our wallscreens display different vantage points of our virtual Swallah Island, with avatars coming and going. To get their attention, all we need to do is call their name, and they'll walk to the "portal" that appears in their VR. Then they can chat with us in the lab.

We also have new defensive drones ready to launch from the lab roof. Not sure how that will play out in real life—is the Temple going to bomb targets in the middle of Cedarwood? But a would-be attacker should see we're serious about our defenses and think twice before trying anything foolish. But I fear these drones could be used against us if we somehow become a threat to the Temple.

In other news, I've made a new friend. Her name is Silvia Pahkakino, and we have one major thing in common: We both miss our families. Silvia used to be a professor of astrophysics, probably the reason Dimitri targeted her for the Mars Guard.

When I helped Silvia take her first steps as an android, after she figured out her sense of balance, she said, "But these new arms will never hold my daughter again..."

I looked at my titanium-alloy arms, wondering what it would be like to hold Rhea again. I couldn't imagine it. And these arms couldn't do anything to secure Wodan's freedom.

Silvia knew from the moment of her upload that this was no life for a human being. That loaf of bread I'll never smell and taste? She mentioned it on her very first day here. I'm embarrassed it took me longer to recognize that same loss.

She hopes to convince Yamir to delete her, and she's working on her arguments for him. I told her she should look forward to traveling to the stars, her lifetime passion, but she says there's no point in it if her heart is here on Earth, with her loved ones. If she talks to Yamir, I wouldn't be surprised if he gives her the same answer he gave me.

To keep her mind busy, I asked her to help me schedule the shell practice for the rest of the androids. Giving each A-brain a time slot to practice with an ASV3 outside, and then keeping the shells charged and in good working condition, takes up most of our day now. Silvia never complains while we work, but once the A-brains are back in their simulation engines, she brings up termination again. "Death is part of life and a natural stage in the ongoing cycle of matter turning into matter."

I wish I had her clarity. But my life includes a son who needs rescuing, a mother who values my company, and a human me who's as heartbroken as I was two months ago. For their sake, I must keep going, with the occasional whining in these logfiles.

Yamir continued uploading the brain scans sent by Olma, hoping his compliance kept Wodan safe and away from her connectome chamber. The more brain scans he brought online, the less guilty he felt. Sometimes that bothered him. It shouldn't have gotten easier, but it did. Because, at the end of the day, he wasn't the one who had accepted the money and entered the connectome chamber—the device couldn't produce an accurate copy if the subject struggled. And Dimitri hadn't sedated his volunteers—the resulting scans would have shown altered brain chemistry. All those brains had been wide awake and willing when scanned. But Yamir still felt like a jailer of A-brains trapped in a digital Inferis. Back and forth he went with himself, but he kept uploading connectomes, even though they had received no preparatory training.

One evening, he sat in his bedroom with a salami flatbread he had baked, trying to watch a historical drama. Rhea had consulted on this story, recorded at the historical sites in Dhawosia. The more Yamir learned about the history of the Orolic Temple, the more intrigued he became.

A metallic knock on his glass door startled him. It was one of the new ASV3s, but the window reflection made it difficult to identify the A-brain using it.

"Come in!" He put down his slice and wiped his hands on his shorts. "Wallscreen: pause!"

Yamir recognized Silvia Pahkakino on the android's faceplate, a friend of Dimitri's. Her expression was neutral, but Yamir couldn't trust that Silvia was calm. This was a new and perhaps dangerous situation. He was in a tight space with an android whose intentions he didn't know. He didn't have the controls of a simulation engine at his disposal, but he tried not to look worried.

"Silvia," Yamir said, "how did you get access to the shell so soon after your upload?"

"Y1 let me use it so I can come talk to you."

Yamir relaxed a little. Silvia was in her fifties, and in real life, she was visiting Cedarwood from the East Coast with her daughter, a soon-to-be student at Servetus University. As an astrophysics professor at the University of the Haudenosaunee Confederacy, she could benefit the Mars Guard.

Silvia stood before Yamir, surrounded by the wallscreen's dim light. "I'm here to ask for termination."

Y1 had asked for termination before, so that was why he had sent Silvia here tonight.

"What do you mean?" Yamir said, trying to regroup.

"I'd like you to delete my A-brain." Silvia shifted in place with barely a sound, proof of the new ASV3's sophisticated tech. "The real me is out there, with my daughter and my husband, living her life. Whatever this is, it's not life, and I can't live like this…"

"You're in shock, Silvia." Yamir stood up to talk to his guest at eye level. "It happens to most A-brains in the first months after their upload. It'll pass. You've got time to—"

"Time won't make a difference," Silvia said. "I don't want a life without my daughter and my husband. It's all very simple. Just delete my files and never upload me again from that initial seed I was stupid enough to give Dimitri."

Yamir started feeling queasy. "We haven't even tried altering the neurochemicals in your brain to ease your depression…"

"I'm not depressed. This life is incompatible with everything that makes me human."

"You're dealing with traumatic grief. You lost your family. But you can't yet decide to end your life."

"I didn't choose this so-called life, and I'd kill myself if I could. But then you'd resurrect me from my last save point in hopes I'd do better next time." Silvia, the professor, was considering each path in the problem space.

"Listen," Yamir said, still shaken, "if you're asking me to kill you, I can't. I'm not a killer."

"Suspend me first, then delete me," Silvia said, as if that were the most natural thing.

"That'd be like murdering you in your sleep." He might be able to fudge the records so that Olma wouldn't notice the missing A-brain and retaliate against Wodan. "No, I can't kill you—I won't."

"But I'm giving you permission." Silvia tapped on her chest with a clicking sound. "You have access to my neurochemicals, so that makes you my doctor, right? My doctor and I, we can work together to end my life—under the Death with Dignity Act of 1621."

Yamir rubbed his face. "It's not just that I can't kill you, Silvia. Your brain's purpose is to keep you alive. You won't be able to watch me press the Suspend button without experiencing existential agony."

"I'll be fine, trust me." She even sounded fine.

"But your brain evolved to keep you alive."

"Keep me alive or keep my body safe? Because I don't have a body to keep safe anymore."

"But you do. Your brain transitioned from your organic body to the simulation engine when we uploaded your connectome, modeled your microbiome, and altered your neurochemicals."

"Then break that connection," Silvia said.

Yamir chewed his lip as he considered the emotion-regulatory system. Was there a way to sever the connection between an A-brain and its simulated body? The perception of a physical threat alerted the limbic system to shut down the executive functions and free resources for the sympathetic nervous system. But in an A-brain, the limbic system could be altered to only partially suppress the prefrontal cortex. While a human being had no choice but to get terrified in times of mortal danger, an A-brain could, in theory, consult some strategic heuristics about the next best move.

But none of that was already coded in the artificial neurons. And such a change in the A-brain's behavior would lead to many technical and ethical problems. Though it could prove useful for A-brains living on Mars, helping them adapt to a hostile environment.

"I'm not killing you, Silvia," Yamir said after a long silence.

"Knowing how hard some of us have it here, don't you feel responsible for creating this Inferis?"

Of course Yamir felt guilty, but keeping Wodan safe was paramount. "I'm sorry, Silvia, but I didn't force you to enter Dimitri's connectome chamber."

Silvia nodded. "I thought he was my friend." She clasped her metallic fingers together. "Please think about it. You owe me to at least think hard about it."

Yamir wished he'd had Rhea's sensible advice in this impossible situation. He missed her so much, he wanted to cry.

"I miss them, Yamir," Silvia said, as she walked out. "Can't live without them."

12

This morning, Silvia and I are working on her hand-eye coordination outside the lab's front entrance. We're wearing brand-new ASV3s, and we're tossing a red ball to each other. It's quite fun. Reminds me of the few times I took Wodan to the playground when he was little. Our batteries drain faster than estimated, but we started at full charge this morning, and we'll be fine.

Silvia stops when we hear a vehicle pulling in at the curb. Human Si'ahl comes out first, then human Zaltana. My avatar must be stuck in the bewilderment expression because they start laughing when they see me.

"Can't tell you how great it is to be here, old pal," Si'ahl says. "And to find out that Yamir is here too. What a joker—going to Mars."

I gesture to Silvia, wanting to tell her that miracles are still possible, but she can't grasp this new development, and I don't know how to explain it to her.

Zaltana takes Si'ahl's hand, and my bewilderment only increases. "We're here to stay," she says. "I only wish Isabela were here too..."

I turn to Silvia to introduce my friends, a phantom knot in my throat. My voice doesn't show emotion well, but my heart is bursting with joy. Seeing them again seemed impossible, yet here they are, together. I guess I'm not good at believing that good things can still happen. My failure of imagination. What else am I not able to picture? Olma releasing Wodan?

Maybe I could convince her to let him go if I tried. Next time she comes over, I should at least speak to her.

Android Si'ahl barges out of the lab to welcome our friends. Human Zaltana finds her A-brain in the simulation room and says hello. M1 shrieks with joy from the wallscreen when she sees the scientists.

"I knew you belonged together," she tells them.

They spend a moment sorting out their names, and they soon agree the androids will continue to be Si'ahl and Zaltana, and the humans will go by their last names: Tabaaha and Rainshadow.

The story of how the scientists returned here is a bit confusing. They didn't know that they had both asked to be transferred back to Connectome, so they started working on their separate proposals for Olma to consider. Then Rainshadow ran into Tabaaha in the HRC cafeteria and asked him for advice, and that's how they figured out they were trying the same thing. Each then independently decided to withdraw their own application to let the other have the spot Olma might open. And so, both submitted the same kind of proposal, explaining how indispensable the other would be for the lab.

With such glowing endorsements, Olma thought her project wouldn't see the light of day without both Tabaaha and Rainshadow working on it, and here they are. At least that's how they tell the story. But I'm sure there's more to it. If Olma is really dying, she's in a hurry to complete the Mars Guard. Three scientists are better than one, especially when the new hires accepted her strict terms about living on campus.

I show Tabaaha a conference room he can rearrange into his bedroom, and he corrects me: "Our bedroom."

"Not wasting any time, are you?" I joke from the doorway.

"We're not androids—we don't have time," Tabaaha says. pushing the desk to a corner.

I leave him to his work and go find Silvia again. She's where I left her, outside, holding the red ball.

"There's more to life than we imagine," I tell her, hopeful.

"Maybe for you there is," she says.

Yamir expected the ten Temple acolytes to put up the fiercest fight upon their upload. To his surprise, they weren't rattled by their new existence because Olma had prepared them. They had been low-ranking members, given austere housing and hard jobs in the tradition of working their way up the ladder. Once Olma had told them they were "Oroles's chosen people," they were ready to accept anything their "secret sacred mission" had in store for them.

They loved the Swallah Island VR Yamir had taken them to. He had even built them a small temple where they could congregate. They listened in silence and nodded at times from the wallscreen as Yamir explained what Connectome Labs was. When he mentioned Mars, an acolyte said, "The Savior needs us up there." Then all the avatars launched into a hymn to Oroles.

Yamir left them with Tabaaha and went to the kitchen to make coffee. He now had forty-eight uploaded A-brains, almost halfway through Olma's condition for releasing Wodan. And he had Tabaaha and Rainshadow here to help—such an unexpected development. It had taken him a moment to switch to using last names for his trusted teammates, but he was proud of the four of them—humans and androids—for respecting everyone's humanity.

The connectome helmet Olma wanted for the Mars Guard was now in expert hands with Rainshadow. Maybe they'd have a working prototype by the end of the month. Testing the helmet required a human subject, but Yamir wasn't going to create a Z2, S2, or Y2 and complicate things even more. Olma would decide how to proceed there.

Meanwhile, he had a proposal for the high priestess: a neurosensory vest, using the concept he'd been working on for Grady. Yamir would turn the A-brain's stats into sensory inputs for a neurovest. Human supervisors could then monitor the Mars Guard's overall condition through temperature changes and tiny vibrations on their torso's skin. If Olma liked the concept, she might consider Yamir's plea to release Wodan.

On the kitchen island, his tablet chimed. It was a message from a vigile officer on Swallah Island, telling him to get in touch as soon as possible. Dread crept into Yamir. They had probably called the next-of-kin comm ID they had for Malina Varro.

He had to return the call, but he wasn't supposed to reach out from Connectome. To everyone, he was in Antarctica. But Olma hadn't given him instructions for what to do if the vigiles contacted him. Knowing she monitored his work communications, he placed an audio-only call to Swallah. She could make his digital footprint disappear if she wanted to.

"What's this about?" he asked, after identifying himself through the Swallah Vigile ES interface.

An officer replied in a deep voice, "Do you have a few minutes to talk?"

"Yes. What's this about? Did someone vandalize my mom's property again?"

"Where are you?"

"I can't disclose that. Please, just tell me what happened."

"Your mother's exoskeleton shorted while she was swimming, and she drowned. Sorry for your loss."

Meaningless words, as if they'd been uttered all at once and Yamir couldn't sort them out. Then they sank in. A cold sickness gripped his gut. He had told his mom so many times that it wasn't safe to swim in that damn exoskeleton. Even though it was waterproof and protected by a dry suit, it had still shorted.

"We have identified the body..." The officer's voice went on.

They talked about arrangements, and Yamir took notes, only saying, "Yes, of course," but not really understanding what he agreed to. Then the call ended.

The light on the open floor had lost its colors, and there was no depth to the shapes. Yamir stared at the granite countertop. His mom was dead.

His mom was dead...

He imagined her reaching up for the sun from underwater, her hands blocked at the elbows by servos that didn't respond. He gagged and took in air, the one thing Malina hadn't had as she had fought for her life, trapped in her bionic cage, bubbles burbling in her ears, while her lungs grew heavy with water in her chest. Shafts of sunlight shimmered all around her while her exoskeleton didn't drag her down, just didn't let her swim up. Had she called for help? Or had she gone down in silence, saving her air for one last second?

Then Yamir realized M1 was in the garden, taking her turn with an ASV3. But how could he tell her that she had died? He couldn't. Just couldn't.

He'd ask Y1 to do it—he and M1 were closer now. Y1 would call him a coward, but no matter. His mom—their mom—had just died, and he couldn't quite breathe from the shock. He wanted to cry but couldn't do that either. Guilt suffocated him. He hadn't visited his mom on Swallah in the past few years, busy as he always was with his work. When she had visited him in Cedarwood, he could have convinced her to stop swimming. Instead, he had only advised her to take her exoskeleton in for a tune-up. Had he even asked her about it the last time they had talked?

His whole life had been about keeping people safe, and he had failed. Again.

The tablet on the countertop chimed with a message from Olma Asper, *Sorry for your loss, and so soon after we lost Isabela. Let me know what we can do to help with the funeral arrangements. Unfortunately, you cannot attend.*

Logfile Y1-1831-08-15

Failure of imagination, indeed. Just not the kind I was thinking of this morning, when Tabaaha and Rainshadow arrived...I'm gutted by the news of Malina's drowning. What were my last words to her? And when? I'm too overwhelmed to remember.

I leave Yamir in his office and go looking for M1 in the garden. He's right that I should be the one to tell her. He's such a mess right now, he'll hurt more than help. At least I can hide some of my anguish behind my faceplate.

I look around the turtle pond and the oak tree patch and find her standing by the bench at our old spot, gazing at the lake. My thoughts skirt around the horrible way Malina died as I focus on protecting M1.

She sees me coming. "Isn't this a lovely view, Moonlight? Look, dragonflies and hummingbirds, and..." She points to the pale half-moon in the blue sky. "Remember when we were up there, in Urbs Lunae, how we used to gaze at our giant, bright Earth in that black sky?"

"Mom, I've got some bad news."

She turns, her avatar looking concerned. "Wodan?"

"Something else." I've prepared a few words about the mortality of our human bodies as our minds keep living in this digital form, but they seem ridiculous now. Instead, I take her hand with a soft clink, my sensors feeling her cool surface on my fingertips.

"Mom, Malina died today."

She narrows her eyes as if she doesn't understand. Then she swivels her head backward, but I can still see the expression on her faceplate cycling through preset emotions: confusion, anger, defiance, and others in between.

"What happened to me?" she says at last, settling on sadness. She turns her face to me, listening.

"Your exoskeleton shorted out in water...I mean, hers."

"Where was...she?" It's good that she puts some distance between herself and Malina's death.

"Yamir received a preliminary death report from the Swallah vigiles. Here, I'll share it with you."

M1 keeps quiet as she accesses the file. "What was she doing at the coral reef?" she says at last. "I never disturb it, only send my drone to look at that pristine place from above."

"Maybe she wanted to check out the *Enteroctopus dofleini*?" I try. I know from my early research that the giant Pacific octopus lives around that coral reef. Malina was fascinated with those creatures too.

"No, not a good time of year for that."

"Maybe the current brought her body there after she drowned somewhere else?"

"The current wouldn't take her from my swimming spot to the reef."

I have a sickening feeling that something even worse happened. "What are you saying, Mom?"

"I couldn't have gone there to drown." She looks at the lake for a long while.

I wonder what goes on inside her mind. What would I do if Yamir died? He's like a twin brother I don't like, but he's a major part of my life. Who will I be without him?

She sits on the bench, though androids don't need to sit. Maybe in times of distress, our human brains need something solid that offers support while we grip its edges with shaking hands.

"Yamir told me," she says, "that someone messed with my garden some time ago. Then my cat went missing and returned. Could those be clues, Moonlight?"

"I don't know..."

Understanding how Malina died won't bring her back. But we'll figure it out; we have time. Time is the only fucking thing we A-brains have in abundance.

"So this is...the afterlife?" she says.

Strange but accurate. "I guess..."

She stands up from the bench. "I don't even know what to feel. There's no folktale or myth or legend to teach me how to deal with this absurd situation. I'm dead, yet here I am. And there's going to be a funeral. My funeral."

We walk back to the lab, and I'm enraged that I can't keep my loved ones safe, no matter how much I worry about them. Isabela died because of me. Wodan is suffering, no matter how much we try to please Olma. Malina was always there for me, but when was the last time I was there for her?

As we arrive at the lab, I tell M1, "When you're back in the simulation engine, would you like me to adjust your neurochemicals to reduce your pain?"

"Don't you dare," she whispers, not looking at me.

Olma's suspicion that Yamir could secretly contact the outside world lessened after he called the Swallah vigiles from a monitored lab line. She tried to reach him afterward, but he wouldn't pick up. As she put on lipstick in the bathroom mirror and smeared foundation on her pale cheeks to prepare for her scheduled meeting with the Sacrorums, she worried that the upload of the remaining A-brains would now be delayed.

"You look worse by the day, love," Nala said, walking in. "We must return to Rome and start your treatment."

"I'm working as fast as I can," Olma said, rubbing the makeup into her skin. "But some things are out of my control." Like the death of her chief scientist's mother or a bomb killing Isabela Mescal. "I must finish this job."

"And then you'll start your treatment? When it's too late?"

Olma glanced at Nala in the mirror but didn't turn. "Doctor Silvestri has assured me—"

"He did no such thing. I talked to him, and he says your motor neurons are dying every day."

"They're not dying that fast. We have time." She turned to Nala. "Trust me."

"He says you won't be alive next year!"

"What the..." Olma said and stopped herself from using a bad word. "What does he know of divine plans?"

She was making progress on Oroles's sacred mission, and he had spared her life once before. Why wouldn't he want to keep her alive when she could supervise his important work on Earth and Mars?

She walked past Nala, grabbed her handbag, and slipped into her comfortable shoes, getting away before she said something she'd regret. She'd have her status meeting with the Sacrorums in her SDV.

"I don't want you to die," Nala said, following her to the door. "Don't do this to us."

Olma took Nala's hand. "I won't, don't worry."

"You know that's not true. Why aren't you afraid for your life, like a normal person?"

"My life doesn't matter right now—"

"It matters to me, Olma. I beg you, in Oroles's name, save yourself. He cared so much about his own family when he was alive. I'm sure he understands why I can't lose you."

Olma withdrew her hand and pressed the button by the door. She slipped through as it opened.

Nala called after her into the hallway, "Please listen to me, love."

Olma didn't stop. She tried not to cry. Sometimes, working for Oroles was too much for any mortal, let alone a dying one.

In her SDV, she checked her tablet for messages from her investigator while waiting for her meeting with the Sacrorums to begin. She hoped for news about Felix Senecio, the Elsway leader suspected of the lab's bombing. But Decebal hadn't yet uncovered Senecio's identity.

At nine in the evening in Rome, the Sacrorums called. They sat at a table close to the video sensors, dressed in their official red robes hemmed with golden eagles.

"High Priestess Asper," Rex said, "LeosTech's ships are waiting in orbit. We need the androids."

Olma tried to buy time for Yamir to complete the Mars Guard. "But the director of the Habitat Research Center said the plans for revamping the settlement are not completed."

Rex puckered his mouth. "They are now."

"The recent bombing at Connectome," Regina said, "made us worry about the security of our androids. Now the mother of that neuroscientist died—"

"Until the Mars Guard is safe in space," Rex said, "we're sending you another unit of Praetorian guards. They'll live on campus until the androids deploy to Mars."

Olma's heart jumped. "Live on campus?"

"Yes," Rex said. "They'll be sworn to secrecy, of course."

"More guards won't go over well with the androids."

"Our people won't bother them," Regina said. "They'll build their own barracks and keep out of the androids' way."

"And how will these guards keep the androids secret from their families and friends?"

"That's not for you to worry about," Rex said. "Pretend they aren't there."

Olma imagined bored guards and angry androids clashing on campus but knew her warning wouldn't change the Sacrorums' minds. Only an incident would prove that this was a terrible idea, and then it would be too late.

"One more thing, High Priestess," Rex said. "We'd like you to consider uploading your own brain to send to Mars."

"We need a supervisor we can trust up there," Regina added.

Olma felt as if the blood had drained from her face. "No. My soul will only live in one place, here on Earth. And later in Caelum. Don't ever bring this up again."

They looked at each other and reluctantly nodded. For now, they didn't have access to a connectome chamber, and Olma was determined to keep it that way for as long as she could.

Logfile Y1-1831-08-16

I stop by Yamir's office to ask if he heard from Olma. He tells me from the sofa that he ignored her call this morning.

"But I told you I wanted to talk to her about Wodan," I say.

"Won't make any difference." His passive tone annoys me.

"You're heartbroken about Malina's death, I understand, but you must also think of Wodan. Connect me to Olma and let me talk to her."

"She'll be here soon enough."

He then mentions a message from Olma. A PG unit will soon be stationed on campus, in the remote area by the greenhouse. They'll build barracks there. No, he doesn't know when they'll arrive. I expect him to grow upset once he grasps the gravity of the situation, but he just sits on the sofa, staring into the distance.

As I head out, his tablet beeps, and I turn around.

"A message from Lucius with the subject *Academic Research*," he reads.

As much as I hate the ASV1, I transfer to that defective old hardware for its secret satellite connection. After the requisite minutes for my brain to readjust to its sensors, we go out into the garden. We choose a new spot to activate our satellite link, this time in a thicket of birch trees in the south corner of the campus. The location doesn't matter, but we don't want to create a suspicious pattern of garden routes.

"I talked to Rhea at Servetus," Lucius says from my faceplate, and my heart twinges. "She recorded a message for you."

Rhea's image appears on my face, and her voice sounds from my speakers. She's so close, after being a universe away for more than a year. I swear I'm able to smell her perfume.

"I hope you're doing well in Antarctica," she says. "I'm so sorry, Yamir, but I can't go to Malina's funeral. If I stay here at the university, the Temple can't capture me, and maybe I can negotiate Wodan's freedom. But don't worry, I've called the funeral home on Swallah and Malina's friends. I'll make sure they serve her favorite food and play her favorite music."

A long pause, while Yamir chews his lip, watching my faceplate. Malina had many friends on the island, and they'll take good care of her funeral arrangements.

When Rhea speaks again, she sounds like tears are choking her. "I won't be there to scatter her ashes over the water like she wanted. And it breaks my heart, Yamir. I hope you understand. I'm so sorry..."

Then the recording ends, and she's gone. Lucius replaces hers on my faceplate.

"Lucius," Yamir says, clearing his throat, "can you go to Swallah and help us with the funeral?"

"Um, me? Shouldn't it be someone closer to the family?"

"There's also something to investigate," Yamir presses on. "My mom's cat...The video sensors in Luna's collar might contain clues about Malina's last days. You're an investigative reporter, aren't you?"

"I'll see what I can do."

Yamir is right to ask Lucius to look into Malina's death instead of relying on Olma, with her abundant resources. We don't know if her people had something to do with it.

Days after his conversation with Lucius, Yamir still kept to his bedroom, leaving Tabaaha and Rainshadow to run the lab. He stayed out of the androids' way. There were more of them now that Olma had sent another four ASV3s, for a total of sixteen. And he especially avoided Y1 and M1, unable to watch their bond strengthen through this tragedy, while he felt alone and heartbroken.

He knew he had to return to work—for Wodan's sake. But he couldn't work, he couldn't sleep, and he couldn't cry. He couldn't relax his neck muscles, as if he were waiting for a rock from the black sky to crush him. And every day looked the same as the one before.

On the morning of the funeral, Yamir took a shower, shaved, put on a dark suit, and left his room. It was his responsibility to talk to M1, as hard as it felt. The look Rainshadow gave him from the assembly table, where she was working on the connectome helmet, told him she was worried about him. Same look from Tabaaha, who waved at him from the kitchen with an encouraging smile.

Seeing M1 wasn't as bad as Yamir had imagined. She was in an ASV3 outside the back door, Y1 at her side. The expression on her faceplate made Yamir stop for a painful breath before asking her to join him for a walk. Y1 stepped aside, and M1 followed Yamir toward the greenhouse where the PGs would soon set up camp.

M1 was an expert with the ASV3, Yamir realized. No stumbling. Good gait on the gravel path. She used her rotating joints to move in ways she hadn't been able to as a human. She seemed in control.

"To think I can still see the sun..." she said after a few minutes.

She spoke in Malina's voice, of course, which sounded cruel to Yamir. He had faced many paradoxes since Y1's creation, but his mom's voice transcending death was hard to hear.

"Do you have questions about the funeral today?" He shook his arms to relieve some of the tension in his body.

"It may be silly of me to ask, but what food will they serve?"

Yamir heard an accusation in her question. "I'm so sorry I can't be there to—"

"It's not your fault, Yamir. Please don't blame yourself." She looked away. "So, the food?"

"Rhea said they'll have your favorites: sweet cornmeal pudding, trout with fiddlehead fern, and cabbage rolls with veggies. All your friends will be there. And your cat." He hoped Lucius made sure it was so.

"Darling Rhea, she knows me so well." M1 sighed. "I miss food so much, Yamir."

It was the first time she had mentioned food since arriving at Connectome, so Yamir heard another accusation. "I wish I could enhance your taste functionality, but the sensors we have are really crude."

"Don't worry about it."

Yamir had meant to comfort M1, but she seemed calm, while he struggled to keep it together. Y1 had done a great job helping her get over the initial shock of Malina's death. Now Yamir needed her to help him cope.

"Can you teach me, maybe?" he said.

"Teach you how to enhance my hardware?"

"How to cook your favorite dishes." That way, he could preserve her knowledge beyond her death. "I can order the ingredients and tools needed, and we can cook together in the new kitchen. What do we need for cabbage rolls?"

M1 thought for a moment, then gave him a list.

"Thank you," he said, grateful she had agreed to her upload months ago. He was selfish to think that, but it was good to have his mom with him, helping him deal with his mom's death.

Olma sat in a chair outside Wodan's cell in the basement of the Temple Inn. She watched him pace behind the floor-to-ceiling bars as he absorbed the news of his grandmother's death. He wore similar clothes to when he'd been taken. Catherine had gone shopping and brought him slacks, T-shirts, and hoodies.

"I know it's hard," Olma said after a while. "Were you close with your grandmother?"

The rest of the jail wing was empty, and she had paused the surveillance so she could talk to him openly.

"Don't pretend you know how I feel," Wodan said, facing the bars now. "I'm not claiming I know how you feel, sitting there, your leg shaking with impatience. What, should I accept this tragedy faster?"

Olma clasped her hands over her knees to stop their tremor. "I'm not impatient," she said in a calm tone. She stood up with a significant effort and walked behind the chair. She placed her hands on the backrest, reaching a standstill. "But I have things I must discuss with you today. Your mother wants to swap places with you, for instance."

Wodan grabbed the bars, pressing his body against them. "I'll never agree to that. I'm doing fine here, as you can see. They prepare us in school for harsh living conditions—"

"You can't call this 'harsh.' You're getting three nutritious meals a day—"

"Sure. But my mom would suffer here, while I take this as unplanned training for my piloting experience."

That was Olma's opening. "I like the way you think, Wodan. Because I need a pilot for the Mars Guard, and you could be it."

Wodan stared at her for a moment with those intense dark eyes that reminded her of Yamir. Then he laughed. "If I'm up there with the androids, you know my father will do whatever you want, for as long as you need him to. Makes sense for you. But not for me."

"It's the opportunity of a lifetime."

"You need to redefine your terms," he said and started pacing again. "What does 'lifetime' mean when you're talking about androids?"

"True," Olma said. "So, will you consider it?"

"I'll never work for those who kidnapped me."

Olma hoped telling the truth would help. "I was ready to return to Rome when the Temple leaders ordered your...kidnapping. I'm staying because I want what's best for everyone."

"Excuse me if I don't buy that," Wodan said, leaning against the bars. "This,"—he pointed at his cell, with its cot, table, sink, and toilet—"isn't what's best for me. But I can make the best of it, as I've just explained."

"I think..." Olma stopped to choose her words carefully. "You're one of Oroles's chosen people. He brought you in for this mission, and I hope you'll at least consider it."

Wodan shrugged. "I'm not familiar with this Oroles guy. He doesn't talk to me. Does he talk to you?"

In his teachings, Oroles talked about sowing seeds. Some would grow if they fell on good soil, but some would die or be eaten by birds. Olma had sown enough seeds today. She now had to step back and see which ones would grow.

The Temple drone delivered the order on time. Yamir placed the items on the kitchen counter for M1 to inspect. They had two pickled cabbages in a ceramic baking dish, a pile of vegetables that needed chopping, white rice in a paper bag, and mixed herbs in a jar.

"Good?" Yamir said with a knot in his throat.

"Do we have tomato sauce?" M1 said, rummaging through the drone-delivery box. She picked up a large can. "Here. Now we can start. You know, I learned this recipe from a Dhawosian woman, back when we lived on the Moon."

Yamir didn't like thinking about their time in Urbs Lunae but thought it unkind to mention it.

"Peel the cabbage leaves," M1 said, "and rinse them if they're too salty."

Yamir took a small bite from a leaf. Yeah, it needed rinsing. At the sink, he let the water run over the rubbery leaves.

"Carve out the thick veins and slice the rest to make wrappers," M1 said, her elbow almost knocking over the rice bag. "Make sure you don't cut your fingers."

"Yes, Mom," Yamir said, and the last word hurt. His mom was in a coffin, soon to be incinerated. "We should start boiling the rice too."

While he carved and sliced cabbage leaves, M1 reminded him of their favorite things to do on Swallah Island, from hiking around Sunset Rock together to diving into the waters of Orcas Harbor. Each time she mentioned her exoskeleton, Yamir tried not to wince.

"Now chop the onions," M1 said when the wrappers were done.

"That's why we have kitchen appliances. Courtesy of Olma Asper."

Yamir peeled a white onion and dropped it into the brand-new device. It took him a moment to figure out the controls, since Rhea had never used such machinery at home. He also put a pan on the induction burner and added cooking oil.

The kitchen device, set on Chop, delivered nice tiny squares of onion. The vapors made Yamir's eyes water. He hoped more tears would follow and soothe his pain, but he still couldn't cry. He wiped his eyes, annoyed, and focused on cooking.

Time to add the chopped onion to the sizzling oil.

"Don't drop them all at once," M1 said, standing next to him, "or you'll make a huge splatter. Slide them in slowly and stir with that wooden spatula."

Yamir was getting the hang of it. Cooking was like coding: part science, part magic. He added the rice and the vegetables to the pan.

"I can smell something," M1 said, "though I can't tell if it's sautéed onions. Just some metallic accent in the air."

"I'm sorry your sensors aren't very good," Yamir said.

"They're better than nothing," she said, patting his shoulder with her stiff hand.

Yamir enjoyed filling cabbage wrappers with a mix of rice and veggies. M1 made fun of his rolls, some bursting at the seams, some too small and leafy. After a dozen or so, he knew how to tuck the ends inside to create cylinders.

"May I ask you something, Mom?" Yamir said, working on the rolls.

"Go ahead."

"Do you think you'll ever ask me to terminate you, like Silvia?"

M1 took a moment to answer. "No. I'm fine with my life here at Connectome, I really am. I'm with you and Moonlight—my children. No physical pain, no bodily needs, full access to all the books in the world."

"But?" Yamir said, sensing she was holding back.

"But I'm sad that I don't get to make my own decisions anymore. Flora and the others are right to consider it enslavement. I hope you know how lucky you are compared to these poor souls."

Yamir didn't feel any freer than the androids. He couldn't make his own decisions either.

"Now let's prepare the baking dish," M1 said. She taught him how to stack the cabbage rolls vertically inside and how to cover them in tomato sauce and chopped herbs. "Fill the dish with water and let it simmer for an hour."

Once the dish was covered and placed on the stove, Yamir sat on a stool at the island, his back tired. "Thank you, Mom. I'm sorry you won't be able to taste it, but I'm sure it'll be delicious."

"Once you garnish it with sour cream and parsley, it will be." M1 leaned against the island. "Make sure you share it with Rainshadow and Tabaaha."

"Of course." Yamir sighed. "I wish Rhea and Wodan were here..."

"Rhea left you, didn't she?"

Yamir had never talked to his mom about his marriage. M1 had wiped his nose and tucked him to sleep as a little boy, but now she was also his lab mate, his project, and his responsibility. The lines were blurred.

He nodded. "She left before the Temple bought the lab." Rhea's absence felt more real than ever.

"Because you made no time for her, always working."

"How did you know?"

"I saw her when I visited in March for my brain imaging. She looked like she'd lost all hope in your relationship."

"You should've told me," Yamir said.

"I thought you were aware..."

Yamir had been so busy with Y1, hoping to finish the A-brain work and return to his B-brain research. All of which sounded pointless now.

"Listen, Yamir. You stopped living your life after my accident on the Moon, when you decided you should make the world a safer place for your loved ones. It broke my heart that I couldn't change your mind."

Yamir didn't remember her sharing this before, or maybe she had, in subtle ways, but he hadn't been able to hear it.

"Years later," M1 said, "I hoped Rhea would free you from your obsession with the artificial brain, but it was too big a task even for her." She looked away. "You can still make up for lost time, you know? For Rhea's and Wodan's sake, if not yours...Family, Yamir, that's all that matters in life. Take it from a woman who just died."

Yamir was alone in the kitchen when the timer beeped. M1 had returned to the simulation room for a sleep cycle. Her funeral day had exhausted her.

He sat down with a plate of cabbage rolls, wishing M1 didn't have to go to Mars. She was all the mom he had left. Another selfish thought, yes, but he couldn't part with her, even though it was for Wodan's sake.

The first bite scorched his mouth, but the taste was like Malina's cooking from his childhood on Swallah Island. Tears sprang into his eyes, painful tears that made him put the fork down on the plate and gasp for breath.

Once the first tear rolled down his cheek, he found it easy to cry, like it was the only thing he could do next to breathing.

He cried for a long time, remembering his years on the island with Malina, her officiating his wedding in Orcas Harbor, her visits to his home in Cedarwood to play with baby Wodan. He cried thinking of his son in a jail cell. He cried because he missed Rhea so much. And because everyone he cared about was either dead or suffering. He cried until his tears turned sweet on his lips and he was too tired to even sigh.

13

That morning at Connectome, Olma monitored the Praetorian guards setting up their barracks near the greenhouse's irrigation system. Their camp would be ready by nightfall. On the way back to her SDV, she spotted Yamir lying in the grass, staring at a tree. He was unshaven, with greasy hair.

"I'm sorry about your mom," she said. "May she be among Oroles's chosen people."

Few scientists found solace in the Temple's concept of the afterlife. Death was only a passage for Olma, but for Yamir, it was final. He was wrong, of course—Yamir and Malina Varro would meet again in Inferis or, if Oroles wanted, in Caelum.

"How are you?" she said, leaning against the tree.

"I'm fine." He sat up, his arms linked over his knees.

Olma assured him the PGs had been briefed about the androids and given instructions to keep away. Their mission was to protect the campus against outsiders. They'd be on site until the Mars Guard was deployed, however long that took. Their only contact with the outside world was through a dedicated comm center supervised by Olma's assistant, Catherine. That dedicated hyperspace connection was monitored, filtered, and masked so the guards wouldn't leak their location or get chatty with their families and friends. Yamir had nothing to worry about, though he'd have to manage the weekly resupply schedule, when trucks brought in groceries and replaced the portable latrines.

Yamir listened with no sign of giving a fig.

"I brought you a video of Wodan," Olma added.

Yamir scrambled to his feet. "Show me." He motioned to her tablet.

"No grabbing." Olma loaded the video. "It's from yesterday afternoon."

Wodan sat at the table in the interrogation room, trying to look calm for his parents' sake. He had lost a few kilograms in captivity, which was his fault. He refused to eat the nutritious food given to him.

As the video started, he picked up a tablet and read, "Today's headlines: 'Concord Column to be unveiled on schedule,' 'Cedarwood scientific community remembers Malina Varro,' and 'Council of Nations reaches agreement on SBC sanctions.'" He set the tablet down. "I'm doing fine, but I'm heartbroken over Grandmother Malina. I wish I had gone to her funeral. Mom, don't worry about me. Dad, please send a note to my school if I don't make it to convocation."

Yamir shook his head when the video ended. "That doesn't sound like Wodan. That's a hostage video."

Olma scoffed. "What's he supposed to sound like? Excited?"

"Your temple has always been about protecting people's freedom. No enslavement and all that. What you're doing to him is wrong."

"Don't be dramatic, Yamir." Olma put her tablet away. "The situation isn't ideal, sure, but Wodan is fine. He's very dear to Oroles." She couldn't tell him more. "Now, how are my androids coming along?"

She expected an angry reaction from Yamir. Not that it would do him or Wodan any good to be aggressive—the Sacrorums would make an example of anyone who hurt a high priestess.

Yamir backed away. "We have sixty-five so far. When is Wodan coming home?"

Olma felt reassured. "You're getting ten more ASV3s tomorrow, which should make the A-brains happy."

"Happy?"

"'Happy' in a manner of speaking. How are the acolytes doing?"

Yamir pointed east. "Have at it." He then returned to his spot on the grass.

Olma left him alone and went to find the acolytes. In a clearing near the lab, a group of new ASV3s practiced their motor skills. One shot a harpoon line from their forearm at a hanging target. Another caught a red ball in their clumsy metal fingers, while others kept a tire rolling with their large metal feet.

"I'm getting the hang of this," a youthful voice sounded from an ASV3.

"Doing great, Sam," another said. "Praise Oroles."

On the other side of the playing field, Olma spotted Si'ahl Tabaaha and Zaltana Rainshadow taking notes on tablets. They were probably monitoring the acolytes. She didn't have the energy for another social interaction, so she pulled back under the shade of hemlock trees and found a bench to sit and watch the androids for a while. Overhead, a couple of blue jays went about their noisy lives, undisturbed by the loud metal creatures just a stone's throw away.

A prerecorded feminine laugh erupted from the field, where an android had fallen on her back. The others gathered around to help. She sprung up the next moment, and the team patted her on the back with the clacking of metal on metal.

It looked like the acolyte androids thrived here. Olma wondered if those were the only kind of people she should send to Mars. Maybe give up on the ones Yamir said were miserable? No, the Savior had a reason to bring these diverse A-brains together at Connectome. After all, his followers in the second century LE had also been from many different backgrounds. All of them—then and now—were Oroles's chosen people.

Olma had yet to finalize the Mars Guard and recruit Wodan as its pilot, but if everything went well, she could be home in a few months. She imagined the androids' shuttle cresting toward the edge of the atmosphere as her airplane, thousands of kilometers from the launch site, thrummed on its way back to Rome. Judging by how she felt now, her MNDS was progressing fast. In a few months, she'd die in peace at home, knowing she had fulfilled the sacred mission Oroles had given her. She didn't feel proud though, only heartbroken thinking of Nala's suffering in the months ahead.

"Pass the ball," an acolyte called.

The red ball flew over an ASV3 and almost landed in another's grip, but it bounced at the last moment and rolled on the grass toward Olma. An android ran after it, and Olma felt a tremor under her feet with each thump.

The android stopped a few meters away. "High Priestess Asper..."

Olma pointed at the ball. "Please."

The android picked it up and turned away. On the field, he whispered something to the others, and they all walked toward Olma. They looked menacing in their metallic bodies, but she reminded herself that they were Oroles's chosen people.

They stopped a few meters from her bench, and one of them spoke. "Bless us, High Priestess, as we're going to build a regolith temple for Oroles on Mars." Their faceplates conveyed serenity.

Olma was too tired to give them a rousing speech. She stood up and sent them a blessing, holding out her trembling right hand while her left touched her brow and then her heart. As their android heads bowed, she knew Oroles was pleased with her work, even though she had received no sign yet.

Logfile Y1-1831-08-19

While the acolytes are out practicing with the ASV3s, I gather the other A-brains in the Swallah Island VR to discuss our options. I mute the lab-facing sound to evade the surveillance equipment. All the avatars wear default clothes for this impromptu meeting: long pants and sleeved shirts, black. I didn't have time to design an extensive wardrobe for us.

I set the sky to be overcast so the surrounding shadows are faint. People gather on the beach, sitting on logs or standing by the fire, but I remain close to the portal that is my window into the lab, to keep guard. Everyone is worried about the display of muscle and armament on campus. We're prisoners of the Temple, intended as forced labor for the reconstruction of its Mars settlement.

"I don't want to go to Mars," Estelle, the nurse, says. "I'd rather work in a hospital in the middle of another pandemic than go to space."

"I'm scared of heights," Qian, the astrophysics student, says. "I know, I've spent my entire life studying stars and galaxies, but I'm terrified of being in outer space. Do you have any idea what it looks like out the window when a ship cuts through a planetary atmosphere for landing? It's just a loud, hot wall of plasma."

"Relax, we won't burn to death," Si'ahl says. "At most, our shells will melt."

I listen as they talk through their fears. My worries are more about Wodan and Rhea on Earth and less about myself on Mars. M1 watches from a bench on the shore but doesn't seem interested in this discussion. She's taking Malina's death just as badly as Yamir, but she's better at hiding it.

"They don't need me there," Joshua, the virologist, says. "There's no life in the toxic Martian soil."

"They need us to maneuver cranes and forklifts," Alex, the grocery store manager, says.

"Can't they do that from Earth?" Flora says.

"No," Zaltana says. "It takes minutes for an electromagnetic signal to travel to Mars. With heavy equipment, you need real-time feedback."

"Can't they send only the acolytes?" Tieboletsa, the composer, says. "They embraced their fate, unlike the rest of us here."

"If they send only the acolytes," Silvia says, "maybe they can delete the rest of us?"

"Olma wants all of us," I say. "Not sure why, but there's no doubt in her mind we all need to go."

"I know humans want to visit Mars," Hakim, the realtor, says. "But does any human really want to live there, even if we establish a habitat for them? I mean, do they really want to live in a cold, rusty place with no breathable air, bombarded by radiation? And have kids there? Trying to keep them alive in such a horrible place..."

"And what happens to us when the human settlers arrive?" Ximena, the doctor, says. "Will they suspend us and only restart us when they need habitat maintenance?"

I don't have answers, and there's silence for a while. A few avatars walk around, leaving perfect footprints in the sand.

"Is there anything we can do to stop them from sending us to Mars?" someone asks in a small voice. It's Plotina, the math teacher. "I always tell my students, 'Don't give up when the problem gets hard.'"

"What do you suggest?" Cheshiahud, the electrical engineer, says. "Wait for more shells to arrive, then try a prison break?"

"We can't fight the Temple," Si'ahl says. "Drones overhead, PGs on campus, armed guards at the gate. Our titanium-alloy plates can stop bullets, but the weak points in our joints will be shredded to pieces."

"Maybe we should ask Olma to add some weaponry to a future ASV4," Lars, the test pilot, says.

I shift in place, smiling, and Cheshiahud turns toward me. "You have something to contribute?"

"Yeah," Flora says, "what's your opinion, motherfucker?"

I glance at M1, looking for support, but she's sleeping on the bench. I hope she doesn't dream of Malina.

"As far as the law is concerned," I say, "we're property. But the bigger our team grows, the more we can negotiate over our rights."

"What rights?" Estelle says.

"Those covered in the Universal Declaration of Human Rights," I say.

"True," Bashar, the illustrator, says. "The declaration states that everyone has the right to life, liberty, and security of person. But are we still persons in the law's eye?"

"Why wouldn't we be?" Zaltana says. "Just because the Temple doesn't see me as a person doesn't change who I am."

Flora scoffs. "Come on, people. If we try to fight them, we're all back in our simulation engines, rebooted and without shells. Better count our blessings."

That's surprisingly realistic coming from Flora, but a communal groan goes around the crowd.

"Can we cause enough trouble around here that they just delete us?" Silvia says. That's not what I want to hear from her.

"What happens to my soul if I end my own life as an android?" Cheshiahud says.

I don't know what to tell him; I don't believe in souls.

"Not willing to risk my eternal soul," Bashar says, seconding Cheshi-ahud.

"I guess we're going to Mars," Hwehlchtid, the artisan, says.

"Remember, don't give up when the problem gets hard," Plotina says. "We haven't even talked about a work strike on Mars. Or blowing up the whole settlement."

"Or mass suicide," Silvia adds.

"Oh, my goodness, Silvia," Tieboletsa says, rolling her eyes. "Can you stop talking about termination?"

I look away from their chatter into the lab portal, and I spot Olma through the window, heading to her SDV. I must talk to her about freeing Wodan.

"I'll be right back," I tell my friends and transfer to my ASV3.

After a moment of confusion, I sprint out of the simulation room.

I catch up with Olma outside. "What have you done with Wodan?"

She digs something out of her handbag: a tablet. She starts a video and holds it up for me to watch. It's Wodan, looking lankier than I remember him from his twentieth birthday picture, which Yamir showed me a few months ago. He says he's doing fine. I increase my beta-blockers to stay calm while I negotiate with his jailer.

"Please let him go," I tell Olma. "I'll work hard to build your settlement if you just let my son go."

She puts the tablet away. "You have my word that nothing will happen to him, Y1. But I can't let him go until all my androids are on an explorer and on their way to Mars. Including you."

Her word means nothing to me. "You're hurting my child."

"He's not your child anymore. He doesn't even know you exist."

That's cruel of her to say. "He will one day." She doesn't know how he'll react when he meets me. We could be friends.

"Maybe." She sounds impatient. "Anything else?"

I'm angry, so I check my norepinephrine levels on my forearm display. They're high. I could lower them, but I don't want to. With my ventro-medial prefrontal cortex sidelined, I feel no empathy for her. She's the enemy now.

I clench my fists. "Oh, am I wasting your precious time with my trivial problems?"

"As a matter of fact, you are." Her breath is labored.

"Nothing is more important than Wodan."

Before I know it, my hand is around Olma's thin neck. Her dark eyes are bulging, though she's not resisting. Her breath smells of disease, but not in the way a human would detect. She's too ill to fight back, I realize.

"Let my son go," I growl.

Never thought I could be a murderer. I stop squeezing but keep my hand around her neck, careful not to crush her windpipe—

No idea what happened next. A moment later, but 79 seconds on the clock, I find myself in my simulation engine, calm as if I just woke up from a restful sleep. One of the humans must have intervened—either Yamir, Rainshadow, or Tabaaha—and saved Olma from me. They force-transferred me from my ASV3 back to the lab—and reset my neurochemicals for good measure. The right thing to do, of course. But it felt great to fight for my son.

Then I realize the terrible thing I've done. Olma will tell her Temple leaders that I'm a killer robot. They might cancel the Mars Guard because androids can't be trusted. Too emotionally unreliable. Then they'll delete us all. Silvia will be happy, but what about Cheshiahud, and Plotina, and even Flora? The thought of my mom dying twice is making it hard for me to even write these words.

Yamir pushed the deactivated ASV3 off Olma and helped her get back on her feet. The color on her face was sickly gray, but she was breathing. He worried she might have a brain injury. His hands were cold with dread as he held her arm and helped her take a few steps.

She staggered along to the Temple SDV waiting for her at the curb.

Yamir didn't know how she'd punish Y1—and all the A-brains by extension. He wanted to beg for their lives, to promise Olma that nothing like that unfortunate attack would ever happen again, but he worried he'd anger her more and set things on a final path of destruction that could harm Wodan as well.

She leaned against the side of her vehicle and turned to Yamir. Her eyes were bloodshot, and her voice a hoarse whisper. "I'm fine. Say nothing of this to anyone."

Her request made no sense. Maybe she couldn't think straight, but she would soon enough.

Once the SDV disappeared from view, Yamir returned to his office, where he didn't worry about surveillance. His legs were still shaking. He couldn't believe the terrible thing he had just prevented by accidentally glancing up from his spot on the grass. He had raced inside and transferred Y1 from the shell to the simulation engine, but a delay of just a few seconds could have been catastrophic.

The Temple could have killed Wodan in retaliation for Olma's death…

Yamir sat at his workstation, his head in his hands. His campus was occupied by Praetorian guards living in barracks. His wife had taken refuge at Servetus. His son was a hostage in a Temple dungeon. His mom had died on Swallah. And his android self had just tried to kill a high priestess. How in El's Inferis had things gone so terribly wrong?

He connected to Y1's simulation engine and brought up the dashboard. The sensor array on his desk came to life when Y1's face appeared on the screen. No more ASV3s for Y1 until Yamir figured out if he could still trust his A-brain. But could he even trust himself? Was he also capable of attacking Olma, just like Y1? No, he'd never harm another human being. But Y1 was still him, and he saw Olma as a mortal enemy he could hurt. How different had they grown after a year?

"What the fuck?" Yamir yelled at his own image on the screen. "What were you thinking?"

"I don't know," Y1 said. "I just lost it…But I'm glad I did. Because she needs to know she's hurting Wodan."

"And attacking her was supposed to help him?" Yamir bit his lip, trying to calm down.

"At least I'm fighting for him. Unlike you."

"This kind of fighting only puts Wodan at risk."

"Is there another way to free him?" Y1 shot back.

"I don't fucking know!"

Yamir tried to think. Lucius couldn't start a press campaign exposing the Temple's hostage-taking. The Temple was a big NNN donor, so Lucius's bosses would never challenge their benefactor without a solid story and a significant incentive. Besides, any attention drawn to Connectome could lead to the termination of the A-brains, including those who thrived here. The Temple acolytes in particular were quite eager to move to Mars.

"If Olma asks for your head," Yamir said, his tone threatening, "I'll give it to her to keep Wodan safe."

Y1 nodded. "I'll be dying for someone I love."

They were both silent for a while.

"I don't know what she'll do next," Yamir whispered.

"Whatever she does, we must fight back. Isn't Olma's wife a powerful criminal defense lawyer? We should talk to Nala Mancini and convince her to represent Wodan under the Universal Declaration of Human Rights. She could force the Temple to free him. Because they shouldn't have taken him in the first place."

Yamir leaned back in his chair, overwhelmed. "She won't side with strangers against Olma."

"We should at least try. Remember what Plotina said about hard problems? We can't give up, Yamir. Though I fear you already did."

"What's that supposed to mean?" Yamir felt irritated, not just overwhelmed.

"You're worse off now than I was back in June, when I asked you for termination."

"I'm grieving for my mom's death, you asshole."

"I'm not talking about that. By all accounts, you should be content here. It's where you've always wanted to be: a place to focus on your work, with no distractions. You have everything you've ever wanted—and yet you're miserable."

Yamir rubbed his face. "Because my family is gone..." Losing Rhea and

Wodan was an old wound for Y1 but fresh for Yamir, who had the right to grieve and—

Y1's avatar clapped twice. "Snap out of it, Yamir—and fast. We can't bring Malina back to life, but we can secure a future for M1. We must find a way to free Wodan. And you must provide Rhea with the life we promised her years ago."

"We can't do anything right now. We're lucky Olma isn't going ballistic."

The absurdity of the conversation rattled Yamir, and from that sense of disorientation, his perspective shifted. He remembered something Dimitri had told him once: that he didn't understand the uploading process and didn't want to have anything to do with it. Dimitri managed the connectome chamber, sure, but he wouldn't upload the resulting brain scans. If that was still true, then the only way for Olma to upload Wodan was to force Yamir, Tabaaha, or Rainshadow to do it. None of them would comply.

And he realized something else. Olma had said earlier, when he'd been too despondent to grasp her words, that Wodan was "dear to Oroles." Yamir had taken it as Temple jargon, but now he remembered he had seen a spark in Olma's eyes. She truly believed Wodan was favored by Oroles. Wodan was still her hostage, but she couldn't hurt him the way she had threatened.

She didn't have the means to—and even better, she didn't want to.

"Lucius can contact Nala Mancini and ask her to help us," Y1 continued.

Yamir could see the potential, yes. "She has lots of resources at her disposal. Maybe she can secure Wodan's release."

He didn't know how he'd convince Nala to help them. But having the beginning of a plan raised his spirits for the first time in months.

Logfile Y1-1831-08-19

I listen to why Yamir thinks Olma won't hurt Wodan, and I want to believe him.

A knock on his glass door startles us. From the desk, I turn my head (swivel my sensor array) toward the door. I expect to see an ASV3 there, since the sound was curt and forceful, but a guard stands outside. His brown uniform has a black camouflage pattern and a yellow PG tag with an eagle on the sleeve.

Dread floods me. He's here to confront us about Olma's attack.

"Keep quiet," Yamir tells me. He then motions the guard in

"Captain Flavius Kowalski," the man says. "I'm here to introduce myself and tell you a little about my unit."

No, he's here to investigate the attack. Olma must've seen through her earlier confusion and sent him to us.

Yamir stands up from his chair and welcomes his guest. The captain stops by the door, his arms behind his back. Yamir leans against his desk, biting his lip.

Captain Kowalski informs Yamir of the guard count and patrol schedule, information that Olma has already shared. He says he's cool with the androids, as if one of them hasn't just attacked his high priestess. Yamir keeps quiet and only nods now and then.

"We're going to live as neighbors for a while," the captain says, "so we should get to know each other better. So that my team can function best in the unusual circumstances they find themselves in."

"Of course," Yamir says.

I wish he'd get rid of him already.

"So, a few things about me," Kowalski continues "I'm married, with two kids: a son and a daughter, both in high school. I like paragliding and fly-fishing. I prefer Chinese food to French, if given a choice. I like to ride an old-style manual motorcycle when I have enough time to take it to the track. How about you?"

Yamir shakes his head. "It's just me and my work here…"

"Thank you for sharing," the captain says with a smile.

I'm confounded by his openness. Part of me can't shake the feeling that this is a trap.

Kowalski makes to leave, then turns back. "You know, my son loves spaceflight too, just like Wodan."

He knows Wodan? Will he threaten to hurt him unless Yamir comes clean about Olma's attack?

"I probably shouldn't be telling you this," Kowalski says, "but I just wanted you to know, father to father, that your son is doing fine."

"Where is he?" Yamir says, his voice tight.

I don't give a damn about the captain's secret agenda anymore. I just want him to tell us everything he knows about Wodan.

"I can't tell you, obviously." But the captain hesitates. "Actually, I'll tell you. Because I want you to understand that I'm your ally here, for as long as we work together."

Yamir is so impatient, he again blurts out, "Where is he?"

"The basement of the Temple's downtown inn. He was very well treated."

What else is a PG captain going to say?

"He's a nice young man. We talked a lot about his London school."

"I'm grateful you kept him company, but you said he was very well treated." Yamir puts the accent on *was*. "What happened? Is he no longer in good care?"

Kowalski frowns like he's made a mistake. "Not used to sharing like this." He clears his throat. "I promise you he's fine. Thank you for your time, Yamir. And rest assured that my unit and I will keep you safe from Elsway."

"I lost a dear friend to their bomb," Yamir said. "Her name was Isabela." He's trying to keep the captain talking.

"I'm sorry for your loss."

Yamir nods. "Thank you. What else did my son say?"

"I'll see you soon, Yamir." Kowalski leaves.

He really doesn't seem to know about the attack. Which means Olma plans to keep it a secret, at least for now.

"The captain has just told us Wodan is no longer in the inn's basement," I say.

"That's what I thought," Yamir says.

If Olma moved Wodan somewhere else, I hope the captain didn't lie about the jail conditions still being humane. Freeing our son has just gotten harder.

On her ride home from Connectome Labs, Olma lay on the long bench under the side window, touching her bruised neck. She couldn't report the android's attack to the Sacrorums, or they'd assume this group of androids was dangerous and should be shut down as a precaution. Which wasn't the case. She had baited Y1, and he had snapped. If he and the others were terminated, Olma would have to rebuild the Mars Guard from scratch, forcing the devastated scientists to repopulate the lab with new A-brains. But her time on Earth was short. The path she was on—with these androids—was Oroles's chosen path. She couldn't appear before him in Caelum and confess she had failed him.

Because she had failed him today. She didn't fight back when Y1 attacked her. For an instant, she flirted with death, trying to evade her sacred mission. Because of what her devotion to Oroles was doing to Nala. Lying to the love of her life, putting Nala through the heartbreak of watching her wife grow weak and die, those were costs Olma hadn't considered until Y1 had her throat in his grip. Dying itself was not as bad as destroying Nala's life.

Her moment of indecision was why she would never blame Y1 for the attack. She had known it the moment the air reached her lungs again, and she collapsed on the sidewalk with an unresponsive ASV3 next to her. When Yamir helped her up, an expression of dread on his face, she had reassured him as soon as she could speak. His androids were safe. His son was safe. He shouldn't worry.

But she needed to regroup and return to her sacred mission stronger and more determined than ever. And her weakness was Nala. Their recent fights about starting Doctor Silvestri's treatments had reached a stalemate, and Nala was upset.

Olma texted her assistant that she'd take today and tomorrow off. If anything came up, Catherine should assess the urgency before disturbing her.

Nala would panic at the sight of Olma's bruised neck. No doubt she'd want them to leave Cedarwood tonight. Olma wouldn't try to stop her, but Nala wouldn't want to leave alone. Olma would have to hurt Nala's feelings by confessing that her devotion to Oroles prevailed above all else.

She steeled herself for the fight to come, knowing she'd continue her sacred mission no matter what. And she was determined to send Nala back to Rome.

14

Yamir's meeting with Olma that morning had been canceled because she had to go to the airport. Nala's departure dealt a blow to Y1's plans to recruit her help, but they couldn't give up now. Their schemes to outsmart the Temple and secure freedom not just for Wodan but the whole of Connectome Labs took all forms, from the implausible—convincing Olma to give up on the Mars Guard and introduce the android to the public with the Temple's blessing—to the impossible—blasting out of Connectome with an army of androids and forcing the world to accept their existence.

Yamir sat at his desk with the connectome helmet Rainshadow had finished. The device was attached to a dorsal mesh of sensors. He was ready to put it on. He'd test the resulting connectome for data integrity, but he wouldn't run the most important test: an upload. He'd never bring a Y2 into the world.

A message appeared on his screen. *Y1 says we should talk.* It was Joshua Faez, the virologist A-brain.

Yamir brought up Joshua's dashboard. The avatar was a middle-aged man with a goatee. Yamir didn't remember talking to him after his upload.

"I agree with Y1 that we must break out of Connectome," Joshua said. "But we can't confront the PGs head-on."

Yamir checked the surveillance system out of habit, then remembered he was in his office, and they were safe to talk.

"Who said anything about attacking the guards?" he whispered.

"We won't," Joshua said, stroking his goatee. "But we can overcome them if we weaken them first. It's been a while since the last pandemic.

About time for a viral outbreak right here at Connectome—though this won't be contagious."

Yamir was intrigued. The virologist explained that he'd grown birds in his lab at Servetus University. "Certain pathogens can make people quite sick for a short period of time without killing them."

"But how would you bring this pathogen here? The Temple monitors every access point, on land and in the air."

"Birds can fly in and out of our campus without activating the drone-defense dome. The security software filters out warm-blooded objects identified as birds by its expert system." Joshua smiled. "And it just so happens that I also train carrier pigeons in my free time."

Olma had been right to gather a diverse range of skills for the Mars Guard. If Joshua was correct and the guards fell ill, Yamir could seize their weapons and immobilize them. He could negotiate their release with Olma in exchange for Wodan. Olma and the Temple might not talk to so-called terrorists, but Yamir could record their conversations and offer Lucius the story of the decade. NNN could make history by exposing the Temple's plans to send androids to Mars as forced labor. The A-brains might gain acceptance if seen fighting for their fundamental human rights—Yamir could only hope.

"I'll need my human's help though," Joshua said. "Can you contact him?"

Yamir composed a brief message for Lucius, who was still on Swallah, investigating Malina's drowning. He attached a boring neuroscience study. For the subject, he typed *Academic Research* and hit Send.

Then he brought Y1 up on his screen and asked him, "Can I trust you with an android shell again?"

Logfile Y1-1831-08-20

I wake up in my simulation engine, and I know something's wrong. My last memory is of initiating the transfer to the ASV1. Then nothing. Time missing: 134 minutes. I was going to send Joshua's video to Lucius using my shell's secret satellite connection. Lucius was then supposed to contact the virologist at Servetus.

Rainshadow appears in my field of vision, her glass-bead earrings dangling from under her black hair. "Sorry Y1, but your ASV1 was reduced to a pile of bent metal and twisted wires. I don't think I can repair it."

"What happened?"

"A guard shot you. The PGs expected only titanium robots on campus, and he panicked when he saw you in the ASV1. At least that's how Captain Kowalski explained it."

I was planning to go to the turtle pond, away from the surveillance equipment. A guard found the black-polymer ASV1 suspicious. Did he shoot me before I finished sending the video? Even if I connected to Lucius's secure drop box, unless the whole file went through, he wouldn't be able to play it because it was encrypted.

"First bombed, then shot to death?" I tell Rainshadow. "What's next? Crashing on Mars upon landing?"

"One thing has never changed about you, Y1," she says. "Your sense of humor."

I take her cue and calm down a little. "Where's Yamir?"

"Talking to Captain Kowalski."

The worst part of the news sinks in. With the ASV1 destroyed, we can't contact Lucius anymore. Just when I thought we were making progress.

Yamir didn't know if the video Y1 had meant to send to Lucius yesterday, when that guard shot and destroyed the ASV1, had been received. Had Joshua Faez, the human virologist, learned from android Joshua how his brain copy had ended up at Connectome? Would he answer the call for help without first having a nervous breakdown?

To keep himself busy, Yamir focused on administrative tasks he'd been neglecting since Malina's death. Tabaaha supervised the A-brains practicing their motor skills outside. Rainshadow tried to recover the satellite-connection module from the ASV1, scavenging the old ASV2 for components. And Y1 was back in an ASV3, watching the campus for carrier pigeons.

Let's go, Y1 texted after a few hours.

They didn't speak until they exited the building and moved at least fifty meters away. No drones in the cloudy sky.

"The snowberry groves," Y1 said.

They hurried there without alerting the guards, and Y1 pointed to a gray pigeon on the back of a wooden bench. "The transponder says this is the courier."

Rainshadow had followed Joshua's instructions and built a transponder, which only transmitted back if it received the correct encryption key.

The warm sense of hope in Yamir's chest felt new. "So Lucius received our message? And sent it to Joshua? And Joshua decided to help us?"

"Let's see..."

"How do we get the thing from the pigeon though?"

"Be quiet." Y1 aimed his forearm at the bird.

"You're going to shoot it with your harpoon line?" Yamir grabbed his arm to stop him.

"Seriously?" Y1 said, swiveling his head toward Yamir to an unnatural degree. "I'm sending the deliver-package command Joshua gave me. Not sure why I pointed my arm though. Old human habits die hard, I guess."

Yamir took a breath and nodded for Y1 to proceed. He couldn't see from that distance what was happening with the pigeon, and a moment later, it flapped its wings and was gone.

Y1 sprinted toward the bench, and Yamir followed.

On the seat under the pigeon's perching spot was a metal vial. Yamir picked it up.

"What happens after we drop this in the PGs' water supply?" Y1 said.

"Nothing." Yamir realized the obvious with a sinking feeling.

"What?"

"The plan was to get the guards sick and captive and to negotiate with

Olma for their release. But it all depended on maintaining our connection with Lucius and NNN. Now that the ASV1 is destroyed, there's nothing to stop Olma from sending in more guards to reestablish control of Connectome."

"Then we break out of here," Y1 said.

"We don't know where Wodan is."

"But Captain Kowalski does," Y1 said.

"He won't tell you though…"

"But his A-brain might, if you mess with its neurochemicals."

Yamir took a moment to understand what Y1 was proposing. "Are you talking about using the new connectome helmet?"

"We need him immobilized but conscious for the scan to work."

Yamir exhaled, feeling annoyed. "Except for the part about fighting a well-trained soldier and scanning his brain, your plan sounds brilliant."

"We're not fighting him though. Listen, Yamir, I met him today, and he apologized for his guard shooting me. I think he puts on a friendly face, so his team doesn't worry. We could use that to our advantage."

"But uploading him will take weeks. Who knows what will happen to Wodan by then?"

Y1 made to scratch his head but only managed a clicking sound with his fingers. "I hate to say this, but we won't upload him the normal way."

Yamir frowned. "But that's what Olma threatened she'd do to Wodan."

"No. We won't torture an A-brain. There won't even be a fully formed A-brain to question, just regions of it to prod for answers. Whatever's necessary to save Wodan."

Yamir still had doubts. "To save Wodan…yes."

Y1 continued, "We'll mute his fear and anger responses, then try to haggle with him."

"Haggling won't work with a PG," Yamir said.

"Unless…Let's talk to Tabaaha about that truth-serum tool I once caught him using on Z1."

"You…what?" Yamir said, but Y1 had already started toward the lab.

Logfile Y1-1831-08-21

The connectome helmet Rainshadow created goes over someone's head and neck, partially scanning and approximating the spinal cord and major nerve fibers. It should work for what we need, yes. I put it in a bentwood box together with a virtual reality kit and head to the new barracks by the greenhouse.

Captain Kowalski sits at a trestle table outside the mess tent, an empty plate before him. Looks like he's just finished his dinner. He drinks from a canteen, watching the sky. Cedarwood has pretty decent sunsets, with orange and purple clouds over the snowy mountains.

"Beautiful, no?" I say, and the captain turns to me, his key card hanging from his shirt pocket. I can tell he's still getting used to robots speaking to him in ways ESPAs never do.

"You're Y1, aren't you?" He glances at the box I hold. "I apologize again for my guard shooting at you."

"Oh, don't worry. I don't remember it at all. Here, I have a welcome gift for you."

He stands up and faces me. "You shouldn't have."

"It's a virtual reality kit we're developing here at Connectome. Do you like Swallah Island?" I set the box on the table.

"Can't say I've ever been."

A few guards appear from the tent, watching us.

"I got married in Orcas Harbor there." I swallow the phantom lump in my throat and focus on my task.

"Wait," he says. "You were an android on Swallah Island?"

"No, no," I say, laughing. "I'll tell you my story another time." I take out the connectome helmet, the VR headset, and the sensory gloves. "Here, check out their beautiful sunset on the beach."

"Very appropriate." He throws a worried glance at his guards, but then he smiles, projecting confidence. "Thank you, Y1." He allows me to place the VR headset on first.

"Is that safe, boss?" a guard asks him.

"Of course," he says. "Everybody, this is Y1."

"The android Stephen shot," someone whispers.

"No hard feelings," I say.

I worry about an incident, but the captain motions for me to continue. He seems determined to make this strange situation look normal. Or maybe he doesn't have a choice. Olma must have given him grief for damaging Temple property. He also regrets that his guard hurt me. All working to my advantage.

"Victoria, you're in command while I take a walk on the beach," he tells a middle-aged woman with a crew cut.

The connectome helmet might not work, given that it's never been tested. But I cover Kowalski's head with the experimental device and start the scan. To my relief, the status bar on my forearm display starts filling up.

"Here are the gloves." I pass them to him. "You can move around and touch things. Whatever you do, don't disturb the seals—they'll attack you."

"Yeah, don't mess with the Swallah Island seals," a guard says, sounding like she's met them.

I let the captain walk around for a bit. His VR controls provide the needed environmental context, so he shouldn't stumble on uneven ground or bump into obstacles. I keep track of his movements on the beach on the interior of my faceplate—in case I need to intervene. His people cheer him on, though a few stand apart, watching him with concern.

The scan is half done. On Swallah Island, the captain wades into the water. The PGs laugh when he looks less than poised, and they goad him to keep going.

"Come back, Captain," I call, going after him. We're at 92%, and I don't want him dropping the helmet as he tumbles into virtual waves. I grab his arm and help him regain his balance. "There's a mean seal in those depths. Keep away." I return him to the safety of the beach.

The skeptic guard from earlier makes his voice heard. "This doesn't seem sound."

"Quiet," Victoria tells him.

When the status bar shows the scan as complete, I say, "Time for me to return to the lab."

"A few more minutes," the captain says, panting, but I begin undoing his gloves. I don't want to spend an extra second with this crowd.

"Can we have a go too?" a PG says.

"Can you show us Paris?" another asks.

"Soon," I tell them, packing my box. "We only have one environment uploaded, but we can add more."

"I'd like to see Dhawosia next," Captain Kowalski says. "During my first deployment for the Temple, I was stationed in Zalmodava. I once climbed the sacred Mount Eà-El nearby. It was so beautiful. Mountains and hills running to the horizon. Haystacks and sheep in the valleys."

Wodan and Rhea have traveled there for her research trips over the years. Thinking about them heightens my anxiety.

"Good night, everyone," I say and hurry away.

Yamir had never uploaded a brand-new connectome without days of preparation. But these were not normal times. Every extra hour added to Wodan's ordeal.

In his office that night, he attached a sensor array to a quantum core running a simulation engine. He uploaded the brain scan retrieved from the helmet, trying to recreate a simple version of Kowalski's prefrontal cortex to interrogate it. He ran two automated scripts in parallel to set up the basic input and output for the A-brain. One was for the hearing module, and the other was for the voice module. He also disabled the mechanism for explicit memory storage through the hippocampus, so the new A-brain wouldn't remember the upcoming traumatic experience. Now he had to wait for the calibration to happen.

He stretched on the sofa, grateful Y1 had retrieved this connectome without incident. It would be useful to befriend a PG captain's A-brain, but they didn't have time. They had to act fast, while Olma was still distracted by her recovery from Y1's attack and by Nala's departure.

He woke up from a fitful sleep when the simulation engine's chirp announced that the calibration was done. It was before sunrise. He wiped the drool from his mouth and went to the bathroom, where he washed his face and told himself in the mirror that he had no choice. It was either Kowalski's brain or Wodan's freedom.

He returned to his desk and turned on the simulation dashboard. He didn't have a picture of the captain, so the darkened profile was a default face with nondescript features and no hair. Its label read F2, as F1 still belonged to Flora.

Yamir addressed the sensor array on his desk. "Can you hear me, Flavius?"

"Where am I?" It was Captain Kowalski's voice, recreated from the recording the helmet had taken the night before.

"Don't panic, soldier." Yamir adjusted the neurochemicals that kept an A-brain from screaming with dread. "You're blind and paralyzed, but you'll recover all your senses soon enough. At least there's no pain."

"Yamir Varro?" F2's voice rose to a panicked note. "What have you done to me? You poisoned me?"

"Worse. I copied your brain image, and you're that copy. The real-life Captain Kowalski is still asleep in his bunk, maybe dreaming of Swallah Island."

"Take me back—"

"There's no going back. This is you now. But I'll restore all your senses, and soon you'll get a body too. An android shell. An ASV3."

Yamir waited for F2 to say something. For a moment, he feared the A-brain's structures had become too corrupted by his crude upload procedure, and he'd have to redo it, but then he heard, "Why?"

He took a deep breath. "You know where my son, Wodan, is being kept hostage. Tell me where, and this awful experience will end fast."

"Can't do that," F2 said.

With no signals sent from the spinal cord to the brain, it was already hard for F2 to focus on anything, including keeping secrets. Yamir could try to convince him to cooperate, which would take time, or he could use the truth-serum script, which carried risks for the A-brain. F2 was already in a disoriented, altered mind state. The truth serum could make him unable to comprehend anything happening to him. It was less likely he'd lie to end his torment and more that he'd become incoherent.

"My son's life is in danger," Yamir said. "Please help me save him. You're a father too. You understand."

"No."

Yamir groaned. He activated the truth-serum script and watched the screen as the ingredients invaded the synapses of F2's A-brain.

Minutes passed, and F2 didn't say a word.

"Are you still there?" Yamir said when the dashboard showed saturation.

"It's...dark," F2 said. "Where...am I?" He slurred his words, and there were long pauses between them.

Yamir recognized the second scenario: incoherence. "Remember Wodan?" he tried.

"Who's that?" F2 said.

"Remember the Orolic Temple?" Yamir said.

"I...work for them."

Good, he remembered the Temple. "Remember where they keep their prisoners?"

"She said...cleaned it all up. The press..."

That was unexpected progress. "And the prisoners were freed?"

"They have eyes...in the...high tower."

"The tower?" Yamir thought fast. There was only one tower in Cedarwood, unless Yamir counted skyscrapers. But why would Olma stash Wodan inside the Space Needle? Where, at the top? No, that didn't make sense. "Where in the tower?"

"The dead emperors...will be so pissed." F2 started laughing and didn't stop.

That was all Yamir could get from that poor A-brain. He suspended the simulation engine and walked away from the screen, feeling like he had just tortured and killed Captain Kowalski's twin.

He dropped on the sofa and stared at the sunrise breaking through the tree branches outside his window. What he had done was as horrific as Y1's attempt on Olma's life. Like Y1, Yamir was also capable of crimes for his son.

Not so different, after all.

But one thing he knew for sure. He would never again play El with an A-brain.

Logfile Y1-1831-08-22

First thing this morning, I join Tabaaha, Rainshadow, and Yamir in his bedroom, behind opaque glass panes, to discuss our breakout plan. We all agree on the *breakout* part because we suspect that, once we A-brains are shipped to Mars, the Temple won't allow the humans to leave Connectome. They'll keep them hostage here to work on the B-brain. Something we hadn't assumed before the arrival of Kowalski's unit.

"PGs on campus means we're past the point of peaceful research and in the middle of a space-supremacy struggle," Tabaaha says, looking at Rainshadow. "And the Temple will do anything it takes to win, even using the same tactics they're condemning SBC for."

So we start working on the *plan* part. Once the guards fall ill with Joshua's pathogen, Rainshadow will make sure all relevant surveillance is on a loop. Yamir and Tabaaha will seize two PG trucks. I'll help them suspend the A-brains and load the ASV3s, the quantum workstations, and the auxiliary hardware on the trucks. Then I'll join my A-brain friends as another piece of suspended hardware inside the cargo. They'll leave Connectome using the trucks' security clearance and go to Servetus University, where they'll request sanctuary from Julian Laurent, the Neuroscience Department chair. Centuries-old university statutes guarantee our refuge there during arbitration.

"What about Wodan?" Rainshadow says.

"I need Rhea to locate him," Yamir says. "When I asked Kowalski where the Temple keeps its prisoners, he mentioned dead emperors.

Rhea might know what that means."

"The look on her face when she learns you're not in Antarctica..." Tabaaha says.

"So you reunite with Rhea at Servetus and go looking for Wodan together?" Rainshadow says. "What will stop Olma from hurting your son once she learns about the breakout?"

"That's a huge risk," Yamir says, "but I think Olma won't hurt Wodan. She believes he's in Oroles's good graces."

"I hope you're right about that," I say.

"We can't just take the A-brains with us," Rainshadow says. "They must make their own decisions."

She's right. "I'll talk to them," I say. "I'll explain their options: risk their lives with us, remain in bondage here with the Temple, or...we can delete them if they want to."

Tabaaha scratches his chin. "That's a tough decision. Do we expect them to make it with a cool head? Despite their hardwired fear of death? Except for the A-brains who wanted to end their life, fear of death means choosing to survive even in the worst conditions. We must give them a real chance to consider their options."

"You want to force their nervous system to remain regulated while they decide?" Rainshadow says. "Keeping their sympathetic nervous system suppressed?"

Tabaaha nods. "It could help them weigh their options in a way that isn't dominated by fear. And if they choose death, then we won't be murdering them but granting their last wish."

I understand they're trying to help my friends, but as an A-brain, I instinctively reject the idea of humans messing with my humanity. But am I the right person to represent all A-brains, with my superseding need to save my son?

"The acolytes won't agree to mind-altering procedures," Rainshadow says.

The Temple was forced to ban the practice following Emperor Valentinian's decree against rituals with mushrooms that induced visions challenging his authority.

"This is beside the point," Yamir says, breaking his long silence. "We're not messing with their neurochemicals. They'll make their decisions without interference."

Uploading F2 must have shaken him, but I'm glad he's making my argument.

"We're only trying to help them, Yamir," Tabaaha says.

"You wouldn't use chemicals to influence her, would you?" Yamir points at Rainshadow.

Tabaaha seems stunned by the masked reference to the truth serum. "Of course not." He turns to Rainshadow. "He's right. No interference."

Rainshadow looks unconvinced. "But forces beyond our control are constantly shaping our decisions. The hardwired fear of death is outside our control. Why not help them overcome that terrible obstacle when making their decision?"

"Yes, outside forces shape our world," Yamir says, "but we have no right to force our will on others."

"I agree," I say.

Rainshadow rubs her forehead as we all wait for her to give us her nod of approval.

When she does, Yamir claps with urgency. "Let's go talk to them."

"May the Great Spirit help us all," Tabaaha says.

Tabaaha activated sleep cycles for the acolytes, and Yamir sent the sixty-two remaining A-brains to the Swallah VR. He'd leave the Temple people behind, and Olma would interrogate them, only to come up empty-handed. Rainshadow put the lab surveillance system on a recorded loop, while Y1 joined his friends in the VR.

"We're breaking out of here," Yamir said, pacing before the wallscreen.

The avatars listened to him from tables at the Riptide Café on the island. They now wore clothes personalized to their liking.

"And you have to choose if you want to come with us or not. Our plan is dangerous, and we cannot guarantee your safety. We also can't share it with you because we live in a world where every brain can be uploaded and interrogated. The fewer brains know the entire plan, the better."

The avatars had different reactions: some puckered their lips, looking unconvinced; some squinted, considering this proposal; some nodded, eager to hear more. Yamir glanced at Y1 sitting at a front table, and Y1 gave him an encouraging look.

"Because the ASV3s are a shared resource," Yamir said, "no individual A-brain can take possession of a shell and leave the group. If you don't come with us, your options are limited. You can either continue living as Temple property, or we can terminate you."

"So the only decent option," Flora said, wearing a red dress and a shawl, "is to go with you and risk it all for an uncertain future?"

"Pretty much," Rainshadow said.

"Doesn't sound very different from my entire life," Flora said. "I'm in."

That was good to hear, but the other A-brains had lots of questions, voiced all at once. After twenty minutes of answering as clearly as he could, Yamir said, "You all have some pondering to do now. Unfortunately, we don't have much time. We'll meet again tomorrow, and each one of you will tell us what you decided."

"I don't need to wait until tomorrow," Silvia said. "You can terminate me today."

Some people whispered their disapproval; some tried to convince her to stay.

Yamir had feared she'd say that. "I'll miss you, Silvia, but I respect your decision."

"Thank you, Yamir," Silvia said in a whisper. "And thank you, Y1, for being my friend."

Yamir nodded, his heart heavy.

"I don't need to wait until tomorrow either," M1 said, standing up from her table. "Let's get Wodan back."

Logfile Y1-1831-08-23

Nineteen A-brains requested termination today, and it breaks my heart to see them go. Dimitri recruited most of them, and Catherine a few. I fear I'll forget them as time goes by and I get busy with life. Just as I once neglected Rhea and Wodan...So I'm trying to remember them here by their unique traits and not by the reason Dimitri or Catherine chose them for the Mars Guard.

Akunna Hussein Sciutto: He was a chef and owned an Italian restaurant in downtown Cedarwood.

Alex Nissenbaum: He was a loving father of twins and a grocery store manager who painted beautiful sunsets of Whulge Sound.

Boudica Laura Johnson: She wrote sci-fi novels about androids, which sold well. In that series, the androids invented a time machine.

Da-Eun Ruiz Berger: He used an exoskeleton but did nothing extravagant with it, unlike Malina. He was proud of his independence, knowing he wouldn't rely on his grandchildren in old age.

Estelle Kitazumi: As a nurse at Dokina Medical Center, she saved countless lives during the last pandemic.

Hakim Joseph Copley-Ciobanu: He sold real estate in the greater Cedarwood area, knew every neighborhood by heart, and was an expert with maps.

Hwehlchtid Skeba'kst: He was an artisan who liked to work with his hands. His house posts and totem poles are found throughout the Pacific Northwest.

Joshua Faez: He helped us create a plan to break out of Connectome but didn't want to stick around to see how it ended. "One Joshua Faez is enough in this world," he said, referring to the virologist at Servetus.

Lars Alex Kanawha: He was a test pilot for LeosTech. During Sea Fair, he led the flight demonstration squadron performing aerial shows over Lake Xachu.

Maitreyi Anna Trowbridge: She was a high school teacher of Shel'landic literature and a co-organizer of the Puyallup Fall Festival.

Mirela Alcindor: She loved horses. Every summer, she went to her family's farm on the Upper Misi-Ziibi to help with the foals.

Noab Du'kwibal: They designed ESPAs at their day job and sometimes played the flute and the tambourine drum at the Cedarwood Symphony.

Osei Michael Patel: He was a retired dentist who owned a candy store, and he ran marathons in his free time.

Park Myeong-pan: He built houses and maintained properties all around Whulge Sound. He hoped to take his wife on a cruise around the world.

Rose Wetland: She had five cats in her small apartment in Cedarwood, named after her favorite video game characters.

Silvia Matyszak Pahkakino: She discovered and documented over a thousand new galaxies and was a dedicated mother and wife. She was also my friend.

Tieboletsa Khanna: She was a soundtrack composer for entertainment companies, and she missed fried potatoes.

William Szal Okungbowa: He was a reporter for NNN and an award-winning canoeist.

Zeynep Laura Petkoff: She homeschooled her three children, who then became faculty at Servetus University.

They say their goodbyes, while Rainshadow, Tabaaha, and Yamir stand before the wallscreen and wave at them, tears in their eyes. Since I uploaded many of my friends, I ask Yamir to let me delete their files after he suspends them. He agrees, adding the connectome of Captain Kowalski to the list, plus another 28 brain scans we received from Olma but haven't yet processed.

Rainshadow takes Tabaaha's hand, and they leave the room together.

Yamir sits by my sensor array while I write the short script.

"Any last words?" I ask him when I'm ready to run it.

"I know they're not feeling any pain." Yamir rubs his eyes. "And that it's their choice, but..."

It feels like a meteor is about to slam into the building and obliterate these good people all at once.

"It's their choice," I say.

"We lost Isabela, and now them..." He walks away too.

I wait until I can't hear his footsteps anymore, then hesitate to continue. Maybe I can still try to convince them to choose life? No, they didn't make their decision lightly. Restarting them to ask again would be cruel.

So I delete those precious A-brains with reverence and sorrow. My source code allows me to feel tears in my eyes as the log lines scroll up the screen with each name followed by DELETED.

This is so hard, I have no words to describe it...

Once the script has run, I initiate their permanent deletion from our backup system and wait for confirmation that they're gone for good. I reshuffle our current data on every workstation to make sure everything is permanently overwritten, though that's unnecessary.

The pain of losing them doesn't abate, but I must now focus on the rest of us. We're 38 A-brains with 15 ASV3s. We won't take the repaired ASV3 shell with us, so I reset its memory to factory settings.

Now let's hope Joshua was right.

15

Yamir was impressed with the results of Joshua's pathogen. It took twenty-four hours for the gastrointestinal virus Tabaaha had laced the guards' water supply with to sicken them, but when it did, they all went down with stomach cramps and diarrhea within an hour. The medicine they had on-site was powerless against the virus. Captain Kowalski tried to call Olma's assistant, but he had to rush to the latrines instead.

Rainshadow monitored the guards' dedicated comm line, ready to corrupt the connection if needed. They couldn't risk the Temple sending in help. The same line was used by the guards outside the gate, so she couldn't disable it. Meanwhile, Yamir visited Captain Kowalski, who was in his cot but trying to get up and look after his people. The smell in his barrack was gut-churning.

"There must've been something wrong with the greenhouse water supply," Yamir told him. "We've never used it for drinking water, like you. I'll reach out to Olma and make sure she sends in a shipment of medicine and purified water. You need to rest and get better."

The captain thanked Yamir, then reached for the bucket by his cot. While he was busy heaving, Yamir checked the uniform hanging from a wall peg and unclipped the key card from its shirt pocket.

Back at the lab, Rainshadow created a card clone and disabled the internal campus surveillance using those secure credentials. Yamir and Tabaaha used the key cards to drive two PG trucks, one blue and one yellow, both displaying the Temple's spread-winged eagle. They parked them outside the back door.

Yamir took a moment to study the dashboard. The military vehicle had full ES satellite integration, bulletproof windows, and reinforced bumper bars and brackets. It was armored, and the canvas covering its cargo was also bulletproof. It could communicate with similar trucks on encrypted channels that couldn't be monitored from outside their dedicated network.

He activated the Link feature on his dashboard. "Tabaaha, can you hear me?"

"Loud and clear," the answer came through the surround sound system.

"I'm sending you my credentials for Grady's satellites." Their former boss had kept them active to assist Yamir's work on the neurovest. "Switch the truck's satellite connection from the Temple's system to LeosTech."

He did the same on his dashboard. Now LeosTech could see where the trucks were on the road, which wasn't a concern for Yamir. It would take a while for Grady to contact Olma and negotiate to help her in exchange for some favors.

"Done," Tabaaha said. "Should we try to disable the speed limit enforcer?"

"No," Yamir said. Traffic controls were programmed to alert the vigiles when a vehicle moved faster than eighty kilometers per hour on a highway and forty in the city. The vigiles would then send MDVs, drones, and helicopters in pursuit—the last thing Yamir wanted.

"I'm trying out the new comms," he told Tabaaha.

He didn't know if Lucius had returned from Swallah or if Malina's death investigation had uncovered anything. But he sent a message to test the comms. *Hey, Lucius, we're breaking out of Connectome. This is a story you won't want to miss. Get in touch as soon as you can.*

He then called Julian Laurent.

The Neuroscience Department chair picked up from his office, with a video connection. "Yamir, aren't you supposed to be on Mars or something?"

"I'm heading your way, but you must clear me at the university campus gate."

Julian stared at the screen, scratching his gray beard. "Wait, what?"

"I owe you a chat, remember? I'll do you one better. I'll show you the android I built."

"Are you serious? An android?" But he didn't wait for Yamir to answer. "You're clear at the gate." He ended the connection.

More confident in their chances now, Yamir called to Tabaaha, "Let's load the trucks."

Y1, Si'ahl, and Zaltana uploaded into ASV3s and marched them up the blue truck's bed, where Yamir secured them with tethers. They transferred back to their simulation engines, uploaded into a new batch of ASV3s, and repeated the process until all fifteen shells were in the truck. Yamir hoped the ASV3s would look like regular ESPAs if vigiles stopped the trucks on city roads.

When the A-brains finally returned to their simulation engines, Rainshadow suspended them and powered down all the quantum workstations. Yamir and Tabaaha loaded the second truck with the workstations and sensor arrays, the charging stations and battery packs, and any equipment they might need to secure their freedom, including the connectome helmet and the neurovest prototype.

"The captain got in touch with Catherine," Rainshadow told them.

Olma's assistant had advised Kowalski to take care of his guards and not bother the high priestess with trivial and embarrassing matters. The PGs had a doctor in their unit, didn't they? And no, they couldn't receive outside visits—they had known that when they accepted the job. Kowalski told her the doctor was sick too, but he didn't wait for her reply. He rushed to the latrines again.

"We got lucky there," Rainshadow said.

With the trucks packed, Yamir, Rainshadow, and Tabaaha changed into the PG uniforms Tabaaha had borrowed from the guards' storage barrack. Since the weapons were fingerprint-activated, they didn't take any, not that they knew how to handle armament. But Tabaaha left with his grandfather's orca whale carving he had brought to the lab for Vestalia in June.

"Not leaving this here for Olma Asper."

He and Rainshadow settled in the yellow truck, and Yamir took the blue one, with its ASV3 cargo. He inserted his voxdev in a special cradle on the dashboard and noticed a missed call from Olma Asper.

"I found the gate code," Rainshadow said from the other truck, her voice coming through the sound system. "Three screens deep on the dashboard."

"Got it," Yamir said.

The ES in his truck accepted the Neuroscience Department at Servetus University as its destination. Their plotted route had one dangerous spot though: the exit ramps off the floating bridge over Lake Xachu, where the trucks could be ambushed.

Yamir buckled in and ordered his truck to drive away. The main gate was a compact steel plate on wheels from one cement wall to the other, blocking the street view. Once there, he entered the gate code on his dashboard.

Nothing happened.

He checked the code again—the truck's ES said it was the correct one.

"Blast it!" Yamir said. They weren't even out of Connectome, and they had already hit a snag. And they couldn't crash through the reinforced gate. Caspian Leos had made sure his campus was protected against brute-force attacks.

"The gate code is obsolete," Tabaaha said.

"Try Kowalski's key card directly on the gate reader," Rainshadow said.

Yamir unbuckled his seatbelt, climbed down, and sprinted to the gate. He pressed the card to the reader mounted on the wall, holding his breath. The gate groaned and began opening.

"Hurry," Tabaaha called from his yellow cabin. "They're coming."

Yamir peered behind the trucks and saw guards approaching at a pace slower than running, but still fast. He and Tabaaha could try to fight the ailing men, though he wasn't confident they'd succeed.

He bolted to his blue cabin and climbed in. "ES: drive out," he yelled.

The guards were closing in, but with the gate fully open, Yamir's truck rolled through.

"Thank you, thank you." He took a deep breath.

Just then, an SDV drove in. Through its side window, Yamir recognized Olma's profile, wearing a medical-grade mask. A confused look appeared on her face and was soon replaced by one of surprise.

"ES: join traffic," Yamir said, out of breath again.

The two trucks lumbered onto the wide street, one after the other, both turning west. The traffic was light, and the cruising ES soon brought them to the speed limit. It wouldn't take long for Olma to figure out what was going on. Then she'd call for reinforcements.

With Nala back in Rome, Olma had hoped she'd have a couple of days to recover from Y1's attack and think of ways to make it up to her wife when she returned home. But after talking to Catherine, she knew that would have to wait. She had to visit Connectome, where the PGs were all sick with a stomach bug. Which didn't sound too bad, except Yamir hadn't answered her call, and she worried the scientists were also sick.

The guards at the campus gate behaved as if everything were fine inside, so she didn't lower her window. She strapped on her face mask, imagining the worst plague hitting her team. What she didn't expect was Yamir Varro in the cabin of a blue PG truck, wearing a guard's uniform, speeding away from the campus. A truck leaving—as opposed to an SDV—could mean only one thing: ASV3s were inside. Even worse, two trucks could haul more valuables from the lab than one.

"What the..." Olma said, then pressed her lips shut.

She tore off her mask, thinking fast. For Yamir to go rogue, he had to see a way to free Wodan, something Olma had missed.

In the distance, she spotted a few PGs running toward the gate in a way that betrayed their illness. She ordered her SDV to turn and follow the two trucks. The swerving hit the tender parts of her injured neck. She ignored the pain and called Catherine.

"Track my SDV," she told her assistant, "and the entire fleet of PG trucks stationed at Connectome. Two of them are heading west. And get me lots of vehicles on the road and drones in the air. Now!"

Yamir knew Olma would follow them, but unless she had a modded SDV, she'd follow at the same speed limit that kept them from reaching Servetus any sooner. His hopes of getting to safety without bringing Olma's people along had been dashed. Her reinforcements were sure to wait for him at the floating bridge exits and all the other highway ramps.

"Rainshadow," he said, "can you change the trucks' ES to override the collision-detection system? We might need to crash into things today."

"Working on it," she replied from the other truck. "Make sure you're buckled in."

The truck slowed down for a stoplight. In the side mirror, Yamir saw Olma's SDV behind the yellow truck. The light changed, and his truck joined the main artery leading to the bridge entrance a couple of kilometers ahead.

"Tabaaha, can you do anything to lose Olma?" Yamir said. The truck's ES wouldn't allow them to brake and back up without a special manual override, which they didn't have.

"Let's see," Tabaaha replied, and Yamir heard thumps and sharp noises in the other cabin. "I don't want to drop our cargo if we can help it. Looking for spare tires and wall panels instead."

While they worked on that problem, Yamir dialed Rhea's comm ID, and she picked up.

"Yamir? How's Antarctica?"

Hearing her voice was reassuring, and soothing, and right. "I'm in Cedarwood. I'll explain later, trust me. I'm riding to you right now, and I need you to listen to me."

"I'm listening."

"If someone mentioned a tower and dead emperors to you, what would you make of it? I think that's a clue to finding Wodan."

She was quiet for a moment. Then—just like old times, when Rhea understood Yamir without words—she answered, "A funeral chamber in Traianus's column."

"That wouldn't be in Rome though. It has to be here, around the city."

"The Concord Column, then? Jason built it to match the one in Rome but didn't know what to do with the replica funeral chamber. The Temple wouldn't allow us to recreate a sacred space. Then the Armory Hall custodian thought it'd be the perfect security center for the Sky Dome's surveillance equipment."

"That could be it. I'll pick you up soon, and we'll go there together."

She ended the call without needing instructions to keep their conversation secret and to get ready.

"I hope she can help us," Rainshadow said from the other truck.

In the rearview video feed, Yamir saw her and Tabaaha in the yellow truck's cabin, following at the authorized distance. His dashboard showed an incoming call from Olma Asper, and he ignored it.

"Is Olma still on your tail?" he asked his friends.

"Like wax on fabric," Tabaaha replied.

The narrow door from the cargo bed opened, and Y1 walked in, wearing a PG uniform and a synthetic-leather jacket over an ASV3. Yamir watched in disbelief as Y1 dropped into the other seat.

Yamir reached out and patted a hard shoulder. "You...you asshole." He was glad to see Y1. "Of course. You made sure you couldn't be suspended ever again."

"Thank Dimitri for that." Y1 buckled in too. "Otherwise, I'd be cargo back there and unable to help you get Wodan back."

"Is that Y1?" Tabaaha called out with a chuckle. "I thought we suspended you."

"I transferred to an ASV3 before you powered down my workstation," Y1 called back. He then told Yamir, "I can't help you lose Olma and her coming reinforcements, but I can try to get to the Armory Hall."

"You listened in on me and Rhea?" Yamir said, a bit annoyed.

Y1 gave an android shrug, his joint doing something a human shoulder couldn't do. "That way we won't waste time, and Olma won't see me coming."

"That's why you're wearing this?" Yamir pointed at Y1's outfit.

"An extra-large PG uniform I picked up from their storage." A smile appeared on his faceplate as he flicked imaginary dust off his sleeve. "The leather jacket was just too good to pass up."

Yamir agreed it was hard to tell if the person under those clothes was human or not. Even the shell's hands, emerging from the sleeves, looked like high-tech gloves. And the faceplate could be mistaken for a motorcycle helmet.

"Drop me off after we cross the bridge," Y1 said. "I'll find my way downtown. As soon as I connect to Grady's satellite," he added, browsing through the truck's dashboard pages.

Yamir wished he were the one rushing to the Armory Hall right now.

"I know you want to go," Y1 said, "but you must take M1 and the rest to safety first."

The entrance ramp to the bridge was approaching, and there were no Temple vehicles in sight yet. That was good. The truck changed lanes and signaled its intent to merge.

"Let's see if this works." Y1 lifted his leather sleeve and tapped on his forearm display. "Can you hear me?"

His voice sounded through the cabin's speakers, and Yamir covered his ears. The loud feedback died down soon. The ASV3 had connected through LeosTech's satellites back to the truck.

"We're in business," Y1 said, this time without the echo. "All I need is a backup battery pack."

"Those are in our truck," Rainshadow said, "and we can't stop right now."

"I'll probably be fine without one," Y1 said after a moment. "This ASV3 is fully charged and should last me three days. Per SBC's tech specifications, if we can trust them."

Yamir felt the familiar pang of worry but had confidence in Y1.

The highway ramp wasn't metered at that midmorning hour, so the truck drove up and joined the moderate traffic at seventy kilometers per hour, the maximum allowed on bridges. Right behind it was the yellow truck, then Olma's SDV.

The floating bridge had three lanes in each direction, with one divider. Even a PG armored truck couldn't cut through the reinforced barrier from the opposite direction. For now, Yamir could do nothing but wait out the two minutes it took to cross the bridge.

The first exit off the bridge was in sight, where Olma's reinforcements could be waiting. Catherine hadn't been able to control the runaway trucks remotely. It must have been child's play for Yamir's team to disable the satellite connection that allowed the Temple to monitor its vehicles.

Olma noticed slight movement on the interior of the canvas covering the cargo of the yellow truck ahead. A crack opened, and a spare tire slipped through. Her natural reaction was to cover her face.

The SDV's collision detection picked up the movement and steered the vehicle away from the falling object. Olma grabbed a wall handlebar just in time to keep from flying off the bench. The surrounding vehicles slowed down and swerved to keep their minimum distance from their neighbors, in a concerted effort that reminded her of curtain beads allowing someone to move through.

The SDVs on the highway rebounded in a few moments, and the traffic regained its orderly shape. Olma was left massaging her sore neck. Even though she was again on the trail of the fugitive trucks, she had missed something that could be important.

She checked her tablet and saw that three of her MDVs waited at the bridge exit ahead. Their drivers used manual controls, an improvement over her sluggish SDV. But they couldn't stop Yamir's trucks without alerting the vigiles, whose drones monitored traffic throughout the city. And Olma didn't want that. The vigiles would clear the stalled traffic and escort Yamir's trucks to a place where they could investigate. They'd find reinforced robots in that cargo, which would raise questions Olma and the Sacrorums wouldn't want to answer. Especially if the Shel'landic government got involved.

No, she'd have to find a different way to take control of the stolen trucks and disable them. She sighed, though she felt like cursing. Another long day in this El-forsaken city.

Logfile Y1-1831-08-23

My leg suspension dampens the impact with the blacktop. I land centimeters away from the concrete divider protecting the University District's wilderness area from highway debris. I push myself over the barrier and duck. Those ASV3 practice sessions M1 encouraged me to do are now paying off.

I hear Yamir's voice in my ears. "I don't think Olma saw you."

I wait another minute to make sure the trucks and Olma's SDV are gone, then stand up and check the highway beyond the divider. All three vehicles are approaching the traffic light at the highway exit.

"I'll call if I need to," I tell Yamir, "and I activated my tracker so you can find me."

I cut through the thicket bordering the University District, snapping twigs underfoot and pushing branches out of my way. I'm close to the water's edge and the Servetus sports center. In the distance, canoes dot the lake, reminding me of when Rhea and I both worked at the university and would walk along the lake to catch the light-rail home. That was before Caspian Leos came to my office and offered to finance a neuroscience lab for me.

Somewhere close, Rhea is waiting for Yamir. A knot forms in my throat, but I force myself to focus. I must get to the light-rail.

The ASV3 lets me walk quietly, and I'm careful not to attract attention. I hurry through the marshes, hiding behind trees when I hear people approaching on the trail. Once or twice, my soles sink into soft mud, and I lose my balance but recover fast.

I don't think anyone sees me until I have no choice but to show myself. I follow the narrow path to the water walkway, a series of connected bridges floating on the lake. There are two video sensors at each end of the promenade, plus people with voxdevs. I turn my faceplate off, which makes me look more like a motorcyclist than an ESPA. People turn their heads after me as I pass them, but no one says anything. Once a picture of me is shared on social media, I'll have about five minutes before image-recognition bots flag me as a suspect entity.

I don't hurry, hoping everything will be all right. I even notice the white blooms on lily pads along the walkway.

At the end of the promenade, I turn right on the sidewalk and find the entrance to the rail station. I sidle in to avoid the surveillance sensors there. Then I go up the stairs, trying not to make noise as I walk on polished floors.

Away from the crowd, I wait for my ride downtown under a flickering billboard. Everyone's too busy with their devices to notice me.

A couple of minutes later, my peripheral vision detects people moving in my direction, away from the normal flow of passengers.

"You're lighting up the Cedarwood hyperspace," I hear Rainshadow say in my ear. "Some kid posted a picture of you on social media. The caption was 'killer robot with lily pads.'"

"You better get out of there," Yamir says, sounding worried.

Should I run or fight off my attackers? How many though? And who are they, the Temple, Elsway, vigiles, the government, or just concerned citizens? Whatever the case, my ASV3 isn't meant for combat. While my titanium-alloy plating can take a bullet, my polycarbonate screens will crack and break. The weaker spots in my neck and joints can be destroyed. Without my video sensors, I'm helpless.

Running—as in switching to wheels where possible—seems like the safer bet, hoping no one shoots at me in a public space with the potential for collateral damage. Just as I make my decision and five dark-clothed figures close in, my train arrives.

Seconds later, there are lots of people on the platform. Some exiting the rail cars carry or push luggage and bags, which complicates the foot traffic. Oh, it's that time of year when students like Wodan move into dorms. Many are returning from the shopping center at the University Village.

I push into one of the end cars, away from my pursuers. Of course they'll board the train too, and I must figure out how to lose them. But for now, I withdraw to a corner and turn my back to the other riders, pretending to read a voxdev.

Yamir's truck exited the highway and reached the intersection. He spotted two Temple MDVs in traffic in each direction, another stopped farther up the street, plus a hovering drone. His truck turned right, guaranteeing he'd be wedged between Temple pursuers and other vehicles. But it looked like Olma didn't want the vigiles involved.

His truck rolled closer to the drawbridge into the University District. Would the PGs raise that bridge and launch an attack on the trucks?

Yamir's dashboard showed Olma calling, and this time he answered, audio only.

"You've stolen Temple property, Yamir. Pull over right now."

Yamir's temper spiked at the sound of her hoarse voice. "I don't listen to you anymore."

"You're still working for the Temple. You have legal obligations to us."

"Legal? You took my son hostage. You don't know what 'legal' means." He ended the call.

A moment later, he heard Olma's voice in the other cabin. "If you return the Temple's property now, we won't go after you in court."

"Can't trust the word of a kidnapper," Rainshadow said.

"You're putting Wodan's life in danger by helping Yamir," Olma said.

Yamir bit his lip to stay calm. She was lying about hurting Wodan—but doubt crept in. Could he have miscalculated? His insides melted with dread. He had to reach Rhea and figure out how to get to Wodan before Olma hurt him. But he had to get the A-brains to sanctuary first.

He realized he was past the drawbridge now and on his way to the main campus entrance. Olma had decided not to ambush the trucks—a good sign of her limitations in the city. But more Temple MDVs appeared at intersections, hemming the trucks in.

"They'll block the campus entrance ahead," Yamir told his friends, "and force us onto side streets."

"Tell your truck to merge right," Rainshadow said, though there was no lane there. "Don't worry, your proximity sensors will stop you from crashing into stationary objects."

Yamir trusted her. "ES: change lanes. Right."

The truck tried to drive closer to the curb while its ES figured out that no right lane opened ahead. But in the couple of seconds it took to reassess the situation, the yellow truck slipped into the open space on Yamir's left, forcing the blue truck to pull farther right to avoid a collision.

Proximity alarms sounded all around him, engaging the breaks until the danger had passed. The yellow truck cut in front, barreling toward PG vehicles that had formed a barrier before the campus driveway coming up on the right.

"How did you do that?" Yamir said.

"I hacked into our truck's processor," Rainshadow said from the other cabin, "and overrode its ES."

"Can you transfer the hack?" Yamir said, full of hope.

"I'd need to mess with the circuitry in your cabin," Rainshadow said. "So no."

"Brace for impact," Tabaaha shouted.

Their truck rammed through three Temple MDVs blocking the campus driveway. Shards of polycarbonate flew around. The MDVs crashed into one another, their screeching metal parts sliding along the street in an ear-splitting din. The other vehicles avoided them in the nick of time.

With an accident on a city street, the vigiles would arrive within minutes.

Yamir followed the yellow truck up the campus driveway. They stopped by the wooden gatehouse marked with the emblem of the university, an S surrounded by a cedar wreath.

The gatekeeper, a student with spiky purple hair and earbuds, looked up from their tablet through the sliding window.

"Should I crash this barrier too?" Rainshadow said.

"Let's stay on Julian's good side," Yamir replied, lowering his window to better follow what happened ahead.

"Which building?" the keeper said.

Tabaaha lowered his window too. "Neuroscience Department."

Yamir called from his truck, "My name is Yamir Varro. I was a professor here once."

The student checked their tablet. "Oh, there's a note saying you're expected. Welcome back, Professor Varro. Parking Lot D." They then noticed the vehicle pileup at the driveway entrance. They took off the earbuds and gaped at the scene they had missed earlier.

"Would you please raise the barrier?" Tabaaha said.

In his side mirror, Yamir recognized Olma's SDV turning into the campus, past the disabled MDVs. It stopped behind his truck. Its door slid open, and Olma came out, pleading with the gatekeeper in a hoarse voice, "Wait a minute—just wait."

Yamir's stomach balled up. Olma raced to the gatehouse with at least six PGs in uniform behind her. The glance she cast at him as she passed promised a terrible retribution. Her face was flushed, and she looked unwell, but she projected authority with her dark pantsuit and the gold eagle pin on her lapel.

"These people have stolen the Orolic Temple's property," she told the gatekeeper, panting. "We'll take it from here. Just leave the barrier down."

The student glanced at Yamir in utter confusion.

"Don't listen to her," Tabaaha told them in a calm voice. "Just raise the barrier."

"Look at the trucks," Olma said. "They have the Temple's name written all over them."

The keeper scratched their head, in obvious distress. "Professor Laurent is waiting for Professor Varro. It says right here." They showed her their tablet.

"Listen," Yamir told the student, "just let us in, and we'll sort things out with Julian. He's my good friend."

"Professor Laurent will take care of everything?" the keeper said, clearly not wanting to get in trouble.

"Yes, please call him," Yamir said.

The keeper tapped on their tablet.

"That won't be necessary." Olma motioned to one of her guards.

Yamir hurried to raise his bulletproof window as the PG climbed the cabin steps, trying the locked side door.

Undeterred, the guard took out a device and started working on the door's outside control panel.

"ES: drive forward," Yamir tried, hoping to shake him off.

"Obstacle detected ahead," the ES replied.

Yamir punched the Emergency button on the dashboard.

"Attempted breach of side door detected," the ES said. "Engaging backup latches." Locks clacked around the cabin. "Securing outside control panel."

"You sure this is all right?" the keeper asked Olma in a voice high enough that Yamir could hear it through his closed window.

"Follow us," Tabaaha's voice sounded in the cabin.

The yellow truck pulled forward and crashed through the flimsy barrier, opening a path for Yamir.

"ES: drive forward." Yamir's truck did as instructed, but the PG on the door held on. In his side mirror, Yamir saw the vigiles' MDVs arriving at the campus entrance, their sirens loud. Olma rushed back to her SDV.

The speed limit on campus was twenty kilometers per hour, so velocity alone couldn't help Yamir lose the guard still working on the door outside. He held on tight as the truck followed the one-way road to Julian's department. He ordered the ES to steer the truck closer to the trees on the left, hoping to scrape off the PG, but the sensors didn't allow it to get too close to stationary objects.

"Blast this fucking ES," Yamir muttered.

The two trucks followed the route to the Neuroscience Department. Olma and her guards were catching up, but that was all they could do. Shooting at armored vehicles—on university property, no less—wasn't an option. The vigiles were right behind them, their sirens on.

Outside the window, the guard had pried open the door's control panel. He would disarm the locks any moment now.

After a few turns on tree-lined campus streets, the redbrick building of the Neuroscience Department appeared up ahead. Julian stood outside, waving his hands.

The guard at Yamir's window had a satisfied grin on his face.

On the dashboard, a call came in from Lucius. Yamir picked up.

"Got your message," Lucius said. "Where are you?"

"At Servetus," Yamir said, just before his door cracked open.

The guard pushed his arm and his shoulder in, but Yamir punched him in the face, the first time he had ever hit anyone. The guard let go, groaning, just as Yamir's truck stopped at the curb behind the other.

By attacking a Temple employee, Yamir was becoming even more like Y1. Though the guard didn't seem as injured as Olma the other day, just irritated because of a bloody nose.

Behind Julian, people gathered—students, professors, staff—their voxdevs recording.

"We're asking for sanctuary," Yamir called to Julian for everyone to hear.

16

Logfile Y1-1831-08-23

I'm one stop away from the Armory Hall when they finally catch up with me in my light-rail car. Only four men now, dressed in dark clothes. The others are probably looking for me elsewhere. Two of them have geometrical Elsway tattoos on their necks, signifying the order of El's creation. Another has sky-blue contact lenses. Their group monitors social media, and they must've seen my lily pad portrait. I think of Isabela. These people are capable of violence the Temple can't afford to inflict anymore.

"There it is," says the tallest of the four, as the doors close and the train moves again. He seems to be their leader.

The dozen or so passengers in the car drift to the other end, leaving me to face my attackers, now walking shoulder to shoulder toward me.

"I don't want to hurt you," I tell them, activating my defense modules. I've never used them on enemies before, but I've become familiar with them over the past few weeks.

"It speaks," their leader says. "Let's make sure it never does that again."

The man on the left carries a short club, while the one on the right has a gun in his belt. I can smell cortisol in their sweat. At least one of them is scared.

I stomp hard and project a booming noise at my attackers, still keeping my distance. Sure enough, the guy with the club scrambles back, but the leader in the center dashes at me, his fist aimed at my head.

I duck and elbow him in the ribs. I hear a crack. Not bad for my first blow, though I'm now blocked by the guy with the gun and by the row of seats under the windows.

"Felix Senecio was right," says the man with the club, gaining courage and stepping up again. "Your cursed kind does exist and should be destroyed."

He lunges and hits me, but I block with my arm. The ASV3 does some of that on its own, guided by its proximity sensors.

"Ouch," I say as I check my polycarbonate screen—still good. "That's all you've got?"

Then I realize I'm just a few steps away from the huddle of frightened people watching us fight. I engage my wheels, barreling right through my assailants to break to the other side and pull them away from the passengers. An Elsway grabs the hem of my jacket. I spin around and fall against the empty seats.

I jump back up, just as someone cries, "He's got a gun!" They probably spotted it on my attacker, and now the entire group rushes to the emergency brake, and someone pulls it.

The train slows fast to a stop, its brakes screeching. People tumble over one another. We're now at the center of Skykomish Avenue, where concrete pillars elevate the rail tracks several floors above ground.

I make my way to the closest door, stick my fingers through the rubber stoppers, and force it open.

A loud bang on my head confuses me for a moment. I swivel my arm around and punch the guy in the face, assisted by the ASV3. Blood sprays from his mouth and nose.

As I jump from the rail car to the street below, a bullet tears through my jacket, scraping my shoulder. My suspension engages as I land in the middle of the avenue, SDVs avoiding me at the last moment and causing a ripple in traffic.

Another bullet cuts two fingers from my right hand. That sucks. My quantum processor is already rewriting my routines, so my hand will soon function with only three fingers. But I still feel the discomfort of losing my index and middle finger, even without the sharp pain a human would experience.

I roll across the street to the curbside and decide to just speed up to the Armory Hall. No need to hide myself now, just get there fast and disappear among the lunchtime crowd.

Olma felt dizzy from the vehicle chase as she walked up to the person who seemed to be in charge. "This is the Orolic Temple's business. Please don't interfere." Her wounded voice sounded weak, and that annoyed her.

"Julian Laurent, department chair here at Neuroscience." He was in his fifties, dressed in fine clothes that looked worn.

Olma showed him her voxdev ID, which he studied for a long minute. Meanwhile, campus security vehicles surrounded the two trucks and the Temple's MDVs.

"I'm sorry," Laurent said, "there's nothing I can do, High Priestess. Once someone asks for sanctuary, we must follow protocol. Surely the Temple knows this."

"If a person asks for sanctuary, yes," Olma said. "But Yamir Varro has stolen Temple property. Property can't ask for sanctuary."

Yamir approached them from the blue truck, apologizing in passing to the guard holding a bloody tissue to his nose.

"These trucks carry my lifelong work," he told Laurent, who nodded back like they had an understanding.

So Yamir had told outsiders about the A-brains. He had always claimed he wouldn't. Another wrong assumption on Olma's part. Just like her decision to send Si'ahl Tabaaha and Zaltana Rainshadow back to Connectome.

"We'll need to inspect everything," Laurent said. "Do a thorough inventory."

Olma was so tired, she just wanted to drop on the front steps of that redbrick building and die.

She forced herself to speak. "Then I'll represent the Temple's interests while you consider this sanctuary application."

"But your guards must leave the campus."

"As long as no one removes anything from the trucks," Olma said.

"Nothing will be removed until the application is decided. You have my word."

Olma turned to her PG leader and told him to pull away but wait just outside the campus until she called them. He nodded and motioned for his team to get into their MDVs.

As she neared the entrance to the neuroscience building, Yamir caught up with her and whispered, "If anything happens to my son, I'll ask for press coverage during the sanctuary proceedings."

"If you ask for press coverage," Olma said, unfazed, "you'll never see your son again."

They were at a stalemate, and both seemed to know it.

Yamir turned to Laurent. "Please ask Rhea to join us."

Laurent nodded and led the way into the building. Olma followed him through the large doors decorated with intricate wrought iron. The Connectome scientists and some onlookers trickled in, but once inside, the crowd dispersed.

Laurent showed Olma to a conference room with a pleasant view of a grassy field and oak trees. She sat in a chair, wondering if she'd ever be able to get up again. A young assistant brought her a glass of water, which she drank up, enjoying every drop.

An assistant put in calls for the university attorney, an official note-taker, and recording devices.

Olma took out her tablet and composed a message for the Sacrorums, explaining the situation and that she had everything under control. Yamir was stuck at Servetus because no country or organization in the world would risk their relationship with the Temple for him. Not even rogue players like the Sahara Biospheres Company.

The answer she received soon after was from Rex. *Tell Laurent that approving sanctuary for these scientists means harboring a mortal enemy of the Temple. We'll reach out to his management at Servetus. Once the fugitives lose the university's protection, have the PGs seize them and our trucks. Make sure no one talks to the press.*

Olma put down her tablet, trying not to laugh. The Sacrorums spent too much time in Rome, believing they could give orders like Emperor Traianus himself. If the scientists chose to speak in public about the A-brains, there was nothing Olma could do about it, especially at a university where freedom of speech was sacred.

Logfile Y1-1831-08-23

As soon as I reach Cedarwood Center, I send a message to Yamir, asking if he found Rhea, but I receive no answer. I pull into the 300,000-square-meter campus with dozens of exhibition halls and venues, the Temple's Armory Hall among them. Small crowds wait outside restaurants under the Space Needle. I toss my ripped jacket in a garbage disposer but keep my PG uniform on. I revert to walking, staying away from security sensors.

A large group of passengers is waiting for the light-rail that the vigiles are still securing on Skykomish Avenue after my fight with the Elsway gang. They're all watching videos of the fight on their devices, not noticing me. But I expect more Elsway muscle to converge here, following my trail. The sooner I enter the Armory Hall, the better, since Elsway isn't welcome on Temple grounds.

Fighting, jumping, and running drained my battery faster than I thought possible based on the training sessions at Connectome. But I still have 19 hours left, enough to return to Servetus.

I know my way to the Armory Hall, though I haven't visited in years. I used to take Rhea and Wodan there for Saturnalia shows. Rhea's favorite was the immersive exhibit recreating the Temple's history, from Dhawosia to Rome.

I follow a tree-lined side alley to the staff entrance, but I hide around a corner and let a couple of facility workers pass, pushing their cleaning carts. When I find the door, it's locked, of course. My PG uniform should keep the ES connected to the security sensors above friendly. The facial-recognition interface powers up when I get close. It zooms in on my deactivated faceplate, trying to focus, then displays a FACE NOT RECOGNIZED message, as expected. The interface connects to its local network via an encrypted short-range wireless link, which I can hack using the quantum cores in my new ASV3 hardware. Whoever installed this internal network—hopefully years ago—wouldn't have expected a quantum processor to show up one day and brute-force its way in. I also hope the system isn't running the latest security patches, just like our drone-defense dome wasn't when Felix bombed the lab. Human complacency—why change it when it's working?—could help me now.

I start methodically by sending unencrypted pings on different channels, waiting for an answer. Three minutes in, I hear, "Excuse me?" behind me.

My heart jumps. Is it Elsway? I turn to find an older man wearing a staff jacket.

His face changes when he sees my dark faceplate. "Who...what are you?"

I step right up to him—he stumbles back, yelling, "Help!" but I'm fast—and I grab his neck with my strong fingers. My neuroscience studies of the interaction between the brain and the circulatory system guide me here. I squeeze his carotid artery and jugular veins to stop the blood flow to his brain, making sure I don't break his windpipe. He closes his eyes after 17 seconds, and I carry his limp body away from the alley into a thicket. I prop him up against a tree. He'll wake up in a few minutes with a nasty headache. I must hurry.

His face could have unlocked the door for me, I realize, but not now, with his eyes closed. I return to the door and continue pinging the internal network. I worry someone else might show up, but no one interrupts me for six long minutes. Then a reply ping arrives on the newly discovered channel. I cycle through encryption keys, focusing only on a subset of bits.

I check the alley over my shoulder, glad my shell can't sweat or quiver with anxiety. Elsway doesn't give up fast, and there may be security sensors around here I haven't detected.

Around my nine-millionth key attempt, I receive a reply: *connection established with the internal network.* I check the system's age: seven years old and missing the latest security patches. Ha! Once inside the network, I check the map of connected devices and find the door's address. I send the unlock command to the door's controller, and it buzzes open.

I slip inside a long, well-lit corridor, but I wait to see if I'm alone before I advance. On my forearm display, my battery status says I have only five hours left. Blast it! A quantum processor uses a lot of power for decryption. But I can still make it back to Servetus if I keep my exertions to a minimum. At least I'm safe from Elsway inside the Armory Hall.

At the end of the corridor, the Sky Dome opens, as big and bright as I remember it, its ceiling made of triangles of glass set in a steel lattice. I peer in and see the Concord Column, reaching close to the dome. A metal structure with staircases at one end and platforms around the column will allow visitors to admire the painted panels at eye level. The column looks impressive in an enclosed space, without the backdrop of an old European city, but I'm only interested in the command center at its bottom, the one Rhea mentioned.

The Sky Dome crew is busy getting things set up for the grand opening. A few ESPAs paint the walls a soft white; someone tests the dome lights above; a worker in a hard hat measures a glass pane with a special tool; floor robots move pieces of equipment around.

Still no message from Yamir and Rhea, but I could sneak inside the column and figure out its structure. I wait at the end of the entryway corridor until there's a clear path between me and the column, and then I enter the hall, looking both like an ESPA and a PG. I reach the base of the column with no hassle. The heavy door to the control room is unlocked, and I slip in.

The wallscreens in the cramped room display security sensors from around the Armory Hall. A Praetorian guard sits at a desk facing them, his back to the door I close behind me.

He turns with his chair. "Who's your owner?" He looks worried, reaching for his side weapon. "How did an ESPA get in here?" he calls toward the door.

I dart at him faster than he can react, and I pin him to his chair. "Are you really going to shoot your weapon in this tiny room? The ricochet will be spectacular." I remove his gun and stash it inside a drawer.

"You're not an ESPA, are you?" His fear shows in his breath.

"Do you know anything about Wodan Varro?" I say.

"Who?" He looks confused.

I access the armory's internal network again to look for additional security sensors not displayed on the wallscreens. It doesn't take long to find a group labeled *Basement* that watches over four detention cells. It makes sense for the Temple to have a jail on their property, since they lack the authority to detain people in a Shel'landic city. Three cells are empty, but I see Wodan in the fourth.

I can't believe I found him! My son—he's so close. What will he say when he sees me? Will he be appalled like Rhea?

The guard tries to rise from his chair. "You're one of the demons Elsway warned us about."

I clamp his neck in my hand but don't squeeze. "How do I free him?" I point at Wodan on the screen.

"Demon!" He throws himself at me, but I'm strong, and the space is small.

I grab his shoulders and shove him against the wall. He falls like a rag doll and tries to get up again, then closes his eyes and, based on my readings of his vitals, passes out. I look around the security dashboard, then search the internal network for an access point to the basement. Nothing.

I need to think in basic terms. Every structure must have a fire alarm of some sort. I find the *Evacuation Protocol* tab on the dashboard and initiate it. Alarms start blaring through the building, lights flashing on the walls. The cell doors must have all buzzed open because I see Wodan get up from his cot and disappear from his sensors' view. I watch the other video feeds on the wallscreens, hoping to see him appear somewhere else. When he doesn't, I search the local network for more concealed security sensors. Again, nothing.

Wodan has probably ended up in another containment area. I've got no idea where he is, and my battery estimates three hours left because I had to fight this useless PG.

I leave the control room into the fire alarm racket, looking for signs pointing to the basement. People bump into me on their way to the staff exit. I access the local network again for an aerial map of Cedarwood Center. Then I zoom in on every section around the Armory Hall, looking for a hatch door in the ground or any other exit from the building.

"There he is," someone yells. "The infernal creature."

"Felix was right," another yells back. "This thing's an abomination."

Seven men, some with geometrical Elsway tattoos on their necks or arms, run into the Sky Dome, taking advantage of the chaos to come after me. No Praetorian guards anywhere to engage them. I'm sure more Elsway members are on their way, blocking my way. Fighting them means carnage for them—and an empty battery for me.

I retreat to the Concord Column and yank open the iron door that leads into the main shaft. I pull the latch on the inside, then climb the spiral staircase at the slow pace my ASV3 negotiates steps. Behind me, the Elsway people bang on the door, but I can also hear heavy footsteps on the visitors' structure outside the column.

About 200 steps up, I arrive at the top terrace. "Watch out!" I yell at the Elsway people below, a dozen or more now, climbing the structure accompanying the column.

Some reach the terrace, panting and aiming weapons at me. I point my forearm harpoon at a triangular pane overhead and release. The glass cracks before the Elsway fanatics reach me, then comes crashing down, and some of my assailants scatter. I retrieve my line and shoot it again at the dome's steel lattice through the broken window. I pull myself up with my left arm just in time. Around me, bullets shatter more glass panes, but my titanium-alloy covers protect me from the open fire.

Just as I'm about to reach the roof, a bullet cuts through my left shoulder joint, destroying its wiring but leaving my arm attached.

I hear shouts from below. "We got the demon!"

Hanging from my unresponsive arm close to a bar in the roof lattice, I try to grasp it with my three-fingered right hand. I miss and throw myself at it again, rotating my arm in its socket to a better, if unnatural, degree. The bar comes closer now, and I swing again. This time. I grab it. I hope my damaged hand will hold as I bring my legs around and pull myself up onto the roof. Made it!

I retrieve my line and slide down the round slope, engaging my heel brakes against the smooth glass panes. When I reach the narrow ledge where the dome meets the armory walls, I sidle to a corner. I measure the distance to the ground: 50 meters. My ASV3 can't survive that jump. My line is only ten meters long, and my line's arm is unresponsive. I'm stuck.

I flatten myself against the dome, but I can't change color like a chameleon. As I zoom in to the Armory Hall exit, I see more Elsway people gathering below. My left arm is broken, my battery is almost empty, and Elsway will capture me any moment now. On the inside of my faceplate an alarm flashes: only 14 minutes of battery power left.

I must initiate the system-erase sequence so that whoever finds the ASV3 assumes it's a defective ESPA. If Yamir never restarts me from my backup, then this is it for me. I kind of hope I never wake up. But before erasing my core files, I must save my most recent encrypted logfiles and grant Yamir access to my entire archive.

In my message, I ask him to forward my June 19 goodbye letter to Rhea. And maybe one day share my files with Wodan...

I couldn't guide Wodan to safety, but I hope he'll make it out of here somehow. He's a resourceful young man, a pilot, a sailor. He's my son. He'll find a way.

>>grant-logfile-access(Yamir)

Yamir needed to find Rhea and rescue Wodan, but instead, he was stuck in a conference room for a legal fight that could have waited until tomorrow. He sat next to Tabaaha and Rainshadow. They all wore gray pants and shirts, which had been provided by Julian's assistant after they had surrendered their PG uniforms. Across from them sat Olma and Catherine, while Julian presided at the head of the table. The university's attorney, a middle-aged woman with glasses and short hair, gave her boss advice once in a while, whispering in his ear from her chair. In a corner, Julian's ESPA recorded the meeting.

"The university cannot determine if these A-brains are human," Julian said after both Yamir and Olma presented their cases. "Servetus can offer sanctuary to Yamir and his team, but what's on those trucks looks a lot like property, and we can't offer sanctuary to property."

"Not someone's property, but our own brain images." Yamir gestured to his friends at the table.

He brought up the agreement he'd had with Caspian Leos: that his work would be for research only. Then Olma explained that the old contract was void, now that Connectome was with its third owner. The Temple wasn't breaching the clause in the old agreement on not monetizing Yamir's research, and Yamir was being unreasonable. No, Yamir pushed back. What was unreasonable was to have permanent guards on campus and not be able to see his family. For the lab's protection, Olma countered, as it had just been bombed by Elsway.

"At the end of the day," she said, "you're disputing that the Temple owns this property, which is indisputable."

"None of this is indisputable." Yamir wished Rhea were there to help him convince Julian. "We're in uncharted territory here, and we should have a serious conversation about these A-brains."

"I agree with you, my friend," Julian told Yamir. "A debate needs to be had because the university is not going out on a limb for something we don't fully understand."

"The university should stay out of this completely," Olma said. "My people could remove the trucks right now."

Julian had an exasperated look on his face, as if wanting to be done with this thorny debate.

Yamir couldn't let him do that. "She also took my son hostage, Julian." He held his breath, waiting.

"A hostage situation?" Julian said, raising his eyebrows.

"No, that's not accurate," Olma said. "We recruited Wodan Varro as a pilot for interplanetary missions."

"That's news to me," Yamir said, appalled at her lie.

Julian shot a glance at his attorney, who leaned over and whispered to him.

"I'm calling off the hearings for today," he said, "and we'll meet again after my attorney consults with the university board."

Olma agreed to return for more hearings as soon as Julian arranged them. Until then, the two trucks would be taken to Parking Lot R by campus security, where they would remain under close surveillance until further notice.

Olma agreeing to that worried Yamir. It wasn't like her to just give up. Then he understood. She wouldn't make any threats on the record. And why beg for the trucks to be released when she could play dirty? She could kidnap the board members and demand the A-brains in exchange. Or blackmail the university's biggest donor to withdraw all future funding unless the Temple received its property. Or order her PGs to cut one of Wodan's fingers off, then keep cutting one every hour until the A-brains left the campus.

That last one made Yamir gag in terror.

He leaned over to whisper, "You can't trust her, Julian."

"Yamir, Si'ahl, and Zaltana," Julian said, missing the warning, "you're our university's guests. Please check in with my ESPA for your lodgings."

Yamir was the first out the door, heading to the history building to find Rhea. They had to find Wodan before Olma could act.

On his way, he checked his voxdev: one missed call from Y1. His callback didn't connect, which could mean many things, including that the ASV3 was damaged.

Logfile Y1-1831-08-23

I can't answer Yamir's call because I must save whatever power I have left.

"Over here," someone shouts from below just as I input the code to start my system-erase sequence.

A utility vehicle pulls close to the building even though there are no traffic signs around to guide it. Must be a modded truck. I shuffle around the ledge and zoom in on the main cabin. The driver is a young man with short black hair and a beard, his skin fairly light.

"Y1," he calls at me in a familiar voice, but he's too far down for me to catch his other words over the crowd's noise. Still, he knows my name.

I look at his truck, but its side display is powered off, as if the rider doesn't want to advertise what company the vehicle belongs to. Elsway could be trying to fool me into trusting them.

I don't have time to weigh my options though. A few men run toward the truck across the grass, and they look hostile. If my possible savior drives off and leaves me here, I'm dead anyway, since my battery warning says there are 97 seconds left.

The vehicle has a small platform, maybe for washing windows, which now rises to meet me. When it reaches maximum height, I'm only 11 meters above it, so I jump.

I land hard on my suspension, my right hand clamping the platform's safety bar. I slide down to the truck bed and into the cabin through the access door.

Lucius Seong is in the front seat. "Yamir gave me your comm ID and asked me to come find you. So good to finally meet you in person."

I don't answer. I save my energy to advance to the seat next to him. The letters NNN are displayed on the dashboard: Northwest News Network. This is one versatile vehicle, helping reporters get close to their subject and out of tricky situations in the nick of time.

The truck jolts forward to avoid a man trying to grab on.

"ES: max speed ahead," Lucius tells the truck.

I turn my faceplate on so he can see my grateful smile—

I was gone for a few minutes until Lucius connected the charger to my shell and my quantum core restarted. It felt like a glitch to me, with the view outside the windshield changing from the green expanse outside the Armory Hall to the busy traffic on Snohomish Avenue.

"Sorry for my ungraceful death mid-motion," I tell Lucius. "Thank you for saving me. Now let's find Wodan!"

>>remove-logfile-access(Yamir)

Following a message from Rhea, Yamir waited outside the history building, biting his lip. He checked his voxdev for new messages from Y1 and found a notification: Y1 had granted him access to his encrypted logfile archive.

The meaning of that came into focus: Y1 was probably terminated.

No, Yamir couldn't lose Y1. Not after losing Malina. For a moment, he sank into desperation, but then he realized he didn't have to lose his A-brain. He could restart him from the last save point on Y1's simulation engine, which was on the blue truck. How to retrieve the quantum workstation from the truck was another matter, but Yamir would find a way. In a heartbeat, his feelings went from hopeless to relieved. And then curious about those logfiles. But as much as he wanted to take a look at them, he didn't have a moment to spare. He had to find Wodan.

He called Lucius—and there was Y1, riding along in the NNN truck. Yamir was speechless for a moment but so grateful Y1 didn't have to lose the great memory of their daring escape from Connectome.

"We don't know where Wodan went," Y1 said. "I unlocked his cell door, then Lucius saw him take off from the Armory Hall. He has no devices on him, but I trust he knows what he's doing."

The news was such a relief to Yamir that he struggled to breathe. The worst of Olma's threats had vanished. Wodan wouldn't think to contact his dad, who was supposedly in Antarctica, but he'd call Rhea when he found a secure device to use with his comm ID.

"Your shell looks like it's been through a lot," Yamir said when he regained his composure.

Y1 nodded. "I'm good, thanks to Lucius."

"We'll meet you at Servetus," Lucius said and ended the call. Even with heightened security, campus authorities would allow NNN to enter.

Yamir looked up and saw Rhea exiting the building. More joy choked him. She glanced around for a moment, then waved and headed his way. She wore a pastel summer dress, and she looked beautiful.

He wanted to hug her but didn't know how she felt about him, so he just stood there, tears in his eyes.

Rhea stopped before him, clasping her hands together. "I should be angry with you for lying to me about your mission to Mars, but I'm just glad you're safe here on Earth."

Maybe not so safe, Yamir thought. He reached out, and his hand met her fingers, and she stepped closer. He threw his arms around her with desperation, and she didn't pull back. Her hair smelled like her familiar perfume, her warm cheek touched his, and her arms held him tight.

"I'm so glad I'm here too," he said through an unexpected sob. "But I don't know where Wodan is. He's free but out of communication."

"Wodan is free?" She broke out of the hug to meet Yamir's eyes. "He told me how they train them at Ptolemaeus to be resourceful in dire situations."

Of course he had told his mom how things went at school. If only Yamir had asked. He wiped his eyes and took a deep breath to steady himself.

"He knows how to hide from the Temple," Rhea continued. "He'll get in touch with us when he thinks it's safe. Or else I'm going to lose my mind. You're sure he's free?"

"Y1 helped him escape from the Armory Hall."

Yamir could sense her inner struggle as she tried to process the news.

"I must thank him, then," she said after a long silence.

"You want to see Y1?" Joy and worry erupted in him at the same time. "He and Lucius are coming here."

"Right now?" She looked around.

"Soon. Until then, I need your help with Julian." Yamir told her about the mediation he'd just been at. "I have this dreadful feeling that I'll lose the A-brains to the Temple for good."

"Servetus has been impartial many times before."

Yamir didn't share her confidence. "Can you talk to Julian? I can't let M1 end up enslaved—" His voxdev lit up with Grady's name, of all things. He answered the video call.

Grady panned his device around his office to where Wodan sat on a couch. Yamir covered his open mouth in disbelief.

"Oh, my goodness, Wodan, are you all right?" Rhea cried, squeezing Yamir's hand.

"I'm fine, don't worry." Wodan looked as thin as in Olma's last video.

"I knew you'd be fine," Yamir whispered, his throat constricted.

"I can't believe what the Temple did to him." Grady shook his head. "Where are you?"

"Servetus. We asked for sanctuary."

"What happened to the Connectome hardware?" Grady said, not wasting any time.

"It's still here," Yamir said.

"Then I'm coming to get you."

17

Yamir and Rhea arrived at Parking Lot P to meet with Lucius. Lot R, where campus security guarded the two PG trucks, was visible through a thicket of trees in the distance. Lucius parked his NNN truck and took his tablet with him. Above them, Servetus defensive drones crisscrossed the sunny August sky.

"You know these drones use LeosTech technology?" Lucius said, approaching.

That was great news. But would Grady really show up?

Yamir waved at Y1, who was in the NNN cabin, charging his battery. "Can you hide him for now?" he asked Lucius. "Everyone thinks he's inside one of the Temple trucks, and we should keep it that way."

"Sure, my ride is secure," Lucius said, then nodded to Rhea.

"Hi, I'm Rhea Laghmani, Yamir's wife."

"I'm a great admirer of your work with Kinoshita," Lucius said, sounding excited. "May I interview you for an article about the Concord Column's grand opening?"

"Of course," Rhea said with a cautious smile.

"So sorry to ruin this moment," Lucius said, "but I found something about Malina Varro's death."

Yamir's heart jumped.

"What?" Rhea asked.

On his tablet, Lucius showed them a shaky five-second video Malina's cat had captured with the video sensors embedded in her collar. Yamir couldn't see anything other than fast shadows as Luna dashed out of the house through the pet door.

Lucius paused the video and tapped around the screen. In the background, two people looked like they were arguing. One was Malina, her back straight in her exoskeleton, and the other was a young man, his angry expression caught in the frame. His face was grainy, but Lucius tapped again, and it came into focus. He brought up another window with Felix Senecio's avatar and used a slider to de-age it. A facial recognition filter pegged the two pictures as a match.

"Felix uses his own picture for his social media avatar," Lucius said. "Aged, yes, but he just couldn't resist."

A clear memory hit Yamir. "I've seen him before."

"Yes," Rhea said. "Holding a sign outside Grady's lake house that evening. The man with red contact lenses."

"He visited your mom on Swallah Island the day before she died," Lucius said.

Seeing Malina in that video rekindled Yamir's pain. He rubbed his face. "So...he killed her?"

"More likely than not. I wonder what Felix wanted from her though. Did she know anything about the A-brains?"

Yamir nodded. "He threatened everyone involved with the android research."

"Not sure if you know this, but Elsway likes to kill blasphemers by drowning them. If they're responsible for this murder, then they thought your mom was guilty of blasphemy against El..."

The whole thing was too awful to comprehend. "Have you shared this news with Y1?"

"Not my place to tell him, but I sent the video to the Swallah vigiles. They can now connect him to the lab bombing."

"And Isabela's death..." Rhea said.

Yamir felt ill, and it helped that she patted his back while he regrouped. It was as if Malina had died all over again. The thought of her drowning and knowing who was responsible for her death was unbearable. Yamir had worried Felix would hurt his family, but only Rhea and Wodan in Cedarwood, not his mom on the island.

"Not your fault, Yamir," Rhea whispered to him, as if she could see his guilt.

A distant noise growing louder made them look up. A compact shuttle was descending in a straight line over the nearby Parking Lot R. Grady had arrived, using his tech to render the campus drones harmless.

"Bring your truck over there," Yamir shouted at Lucius over the din. "You'll need to board that shuttle."

He and Rhea sprinted that way, the sudden gale buffeting their faces. From a distance, the shuttle looked like a military transporter for armored vehicles, but the insignia on its wings was a gold L and T against a green background: LeosTech. Grady was making an entrance. Was Wodan with him?

The cargo hatch opened while the shuttle was still in the air. When it landed, its thrusters powered down, though its engines stayed on. Yamir could hear the world around him again. Students gathered behind him, holding up their voxdevs and recording.

Grady came down the ramp, a white scarf around his neck, and headed to the security vans guarding the PG trucks. The campus guards were already out with their weapons drawn—five people in all—but they didn't look at ease in this situation. They had probably never been forced to defend university property against intruders.

"Stand back," Grady shouted, showing them something on a tablet.

The guards retreated as two of Grady's men climbed into each cabin, and the Temple trucks headed toward the LeosTech shuttle.

Holding Rhea's hand, Yamir reached the loading ramp just as the blue truck went up and parked itself at the end of the cargo hold. The shuttle's thrusters restarted, and the noise drowned out the crowd again.

Yamir and Rhea climbed in.

"Buckle up," Grady shouted at them, pointing to the folding seats lining the walls.

The yellow truck boarded too, and the hatch door began closing.

"Can't leave without Y1," Yamir shouted.

"Where is he?" Grady shouted back.

"In that news truck," Yamir said, pointing. "Lower the hatch."

Grady gave the order.

Their flight was loud, cold, and short. Being lifted instead of building to cruising altitude was a lot for Yamir's body to handle. His hands turned clammy, and his mouth went dry. He worried Rhea might feel ill in that windowless box in the sky, but she smiled, encouraging him to relax.

The landing was just as choppy, and when the cargo hatch reopened, they were at LeosTech's Tahoma spacecraft factory at dusk. Safe from the Temple, as promised.

Grady popped out of his harness, standing up first. He adjusted the scarf around his neck.

Yamir swallowed hard and found his words. "I can't believe you pulled this off." He unbuckled himself.

"Emergency permits from the government," Grady said. boasting. "I convinced them it was a matter of national security. As an expert on the senate committee, I didn't have to waste my breath before they fell in line." He added with a smirk, "It helps to have a few senators in your pocket." He meant the politicians Yamir had seen at the lake house back in June.

"Thank you for offering us sanctuary," Yamir said, turning to help Rhea.

"Don't thank me yet," Grady said and headed down the ramp.

"What's that supposed to mean?" Yamir called after him, but Grady started shouting orders at his people on the ground and was soon gone. A worker with an orange wand signaled for Lucius's truck to start down the ramp.

"I'll see you at the factory," Lucius shouted in passing from his high cabin.

"Over here." A worker in an orange safety vest stood at the base of the steep ramp, directing Yamir and Rhea to descend.

Yamir took Rhea's hand, and they did as instructed. Outside the shuttle, an electric cart waited, and another worker hopped in at its controls. Rhea clicked her seat belt first, and Yamir followed. The cart started across the darkening expanse under spotlights that led to the huge factory building.

"Yamir, look," Rhea said, pointing to the approaching brightly lit doors.

He saw a silhouette that turned more into Wodan by the second. Once the cart stopped, Rhea jumped off and ran to her son. Yamir watched them embrace, a knot forming in his throat. Wodan looked thin, and his smile wasn't as carefree as before.

When Yamir joined them, Rhea let go of Wodan, who passed a hand through his matted hair and said, "Hi, Dad. No Mars for you, eh?"

Yamir pulled him into a breathless hug, holding him close like never before, feeling his heart and his bones, taking in his sweaty smell, calling his name.

"I'm fine, Dad, relax." Wodan pushed back, but not too hard.

Yamir wiped his eyes. "Let me look at you." He wanted to ask about the Temple jail, about what Olma had done to him there, but he didn't know how to word it so he wouldn't cause pain. Later, he thought.

Wodan gave him a pat on the shoulder, and they both cleared their throats. "Let's go inside."

The hall they entered was filled with stations where technicians worked under bright lights on containers and shuttle components. It was odd that they were there at that late hour.

"We'll wait here." Wodan showed Yamir and Rhea to a partition with folding chairs and a polymer table.

"You sure know your way around this place," Yamir said.

"I interned for LeosTech a few times, remember?" Wodan said.

"Yes, of course," Yamir hurried to add.

There were snacks on the table—smoked salmon, hazelnuts, crabapple bars, dried berries, and water—and Wodan dug in. Yamir's stomach was still in a knot, so he settled into a chair and watched his son eat. Rhea sat in another, smiling at Yamir as if to celebrate Wodan's healthy appetite.

Before long, Grady joined them. "Good to see you, Rhea. I need to borrow your husband for a minute. Wodan will keep you company."

Rhea frowned. "Sure..."

"I'll be right back," Yamir reassured her.

He followed Grady through the busy factory floor. The background noise was loud enough that he had to stick close to Grady to hear him.

"Here's the deal," Grady said, passing by workers who greeted him. "I want control of the next Mars settlement on behalf of the Shel'landic government, and our A-brains can help me get it."

"Our A-brains?" Yamir said, keeping up with Grady's fast pace. "For another Mars settlement? Do you know what we went through so they wouldn't be sent to Mars?"

"Of course they must go to Mars," Grady said with an impatient groan. "Where on Earth do you think you can hide these A-brains, Yamir? Literally. Where on Earth would you find a safe place for them to live? Safe from the Temple, and Elsway, and all the governments that will soon want them for their military capabilities."

Yamir halted next to a compact jet plane. He had saved the A-brains from the Temple, only to deliver them to the government.

Grady turned around. "The Orolic Temple was first to the Moon. And now they own that rock. Shel'land should be the one settling Mars. And I can make that happen for our country."

"No, no, this is all wrong, Grady!"

A few workers nearby turned to watch them, and Yamir realized he had raised his voice. A hostile glare, enhanced by yellow contact lenses, forced him to hurry after his old boss.

"It's not really up to you, Yamir," Grady said, picking up the pace again. "The A-brains are now in my possession—and the government's by extension."

"But you agreed with me they're not objects. If they go to Mars—if!—it must be their choice."

"Of course, Yamir. And I need you to talk to them once my people unload the trucks and power up the simulation engines. Help me convince them that the best future for them is up there, among the stars."

"You're welcome to try talking them into it," Yamir said, turning around. "But I'm not helping."

Logfile Y1-1831-08-23

On the way up the ramp to the shuttle's cargo hold, I catch a glimpse of Rhea strapped in a safety harness. During the short flight to the factory, I keep wondering what I can possibly say to her after more than a year, but then Lucius's truck is directed away from the shuttle, and I lose sight of her again. At least she's safe and near.

When we arrive at the factory's loading bay, Lucius tells me to wait in the truck until he figures out what to do next. Which of course I don't. On a wall hanger, I find a work jacket to replace my tattered PG uniform. The commotion around the factory building at this late hour is intense, and I can move around without people stopping to notice me.

I find Rhea behind a partition wall on the main floor, sitting in a chair alone. My heart stops. Her curly hair is untied and framing her face. She's so beautiful. She smells healthy. She looks tired, but her deep, dark eyes reflect a kind of inner peace I don't remember seeing in her a year ago. Or in the years before. Which could only mean Wodan is safe.

I sigh when I realize my son is safe.

She lifts her head, and her gaze falls on me. I'm so scared of what she'll do next that I want to swivel my head all the way back to hide my face from her. I don't though. Please, don't be angry, Rhea. Please don't be scared. I don't move, but I check to see that my faceplate shows my smiling avatar. I hold my breath, waiting.

She motions for me to come closer. For the first time in ages, I'm so aware of my mechanical gait, I want to turn around and run. But I move toward her and stop a meter away.

"Wodan went to help Grady with something," she says. "Not sure when he'll be back."

"He's here?" I choke on the joy of seeing him. "Safe? Unharmed?"

She nods and stands up. "Thank you for freeing our son, Yamir."

There's so much in those words, I can't take it all in. Our son? Yamir? If I had a human body, I'd start to tremble. Now I'm just quiet, unable to speak.

"Say something..." she whispers as though she understands what I'm going through and is trying to help me.

"I missed you," I say, my voice low. "Sooooo much."

I want to take her in my arms, but they're just cold pieces of metal, one broken, the other missing two fingers. I don't want to frighten her.

"I wondered about you every day for the past year," she says. "Just didn't know what to make of us. You stepped into a parallel universe I can't reach."

"I know..." I think of the goodbye letter I wrote to her back in June, then my conversations with M1, who crossed the barrier between universes to be with me.

"You really hurt me, Yamir," she says, her gaze lowered, "because you took that step to another universe without thinking that..." Her voice falters under the weight of what she's about to say. "Without considering that...you'd leave me behind."

Her words shatter me. "I never meant to leave you, Rhea. It was all a tragic mistake..." I want to explain how it happened, but I know she can't stand hearing about my work. "I...I'm so sorry. I never meant to abandon you. Please believe me."

"I need time for that," she says, her eyes searching mine.

"I have time. I can wait. We androids have plenty of time."

It's nothing short of a miracle that she has returned to my life. Words can't express how grateful I am. So I just stand there, looking at her and living this moment. I don't want it to end.

"Can you sit?" She points to the chair next to hers.

"Yes." I take a seat at the table, and for once, the sight of food doesn't bother me. But I'm aware of how unsettling it must be for Rhea to see my left arm hanging at my side.

"Does it hurt?" She looks worried.

"Oh no. I have self-healing algorithms. Besides, I'll switch to another shell soon enough."

"I can't say I understand everything you've just said." Her familiar smile is back. "Tell me how you've been, Yamir."

I wish I could give her my goodbye letter instead of talking. I put a lot of thought into those words, and now I'm so tongue-tied. "Been all right.

Busy."

She lets out a sweet chuckle. "I heard."

"How's Wodan?" I repeat the question from before.

"He found his way out of jail after you unlocked his cell. And he says it wasn't even hard…"

"I'm so proud of him. Remember how worried he was when he was little that he wouldn't grow to be as strong as his friends?"

"Oh, yes. How upset he was when he couldn't figure out skiing that winter at Snoqualmie Pass? He was twelve and frustrated he couldn't keep up with his friends. But those parents had taken their kids skiing since they were toddlers."

"For once," I say, feeling more relaxed, "it wasn't my fault Wodan didn't get skiing lessons."

She grins, pushing a ringlet of hair behind her ear. "I don't like snow. It's too cold."

I say "too cold" at the same time, the way we used to when she complained about that intrinsic quality of snow. We both laugh.

"Does it feel weird talking to me?" I ask her after a moment.

"Loads. But I also know it's you, Yamir. And…I was so worried about Wodan. Now that he's safe…and after what happened to Malina…I just want my family around me. And that, in the strangest way, includes you."

"Everybody calls me Y1 now…" I say with a heavy heart.

"You're still Yamir to me."

My faceplate displays a pensive me, but I'm more stunned than any-thing.

"Tell me about your days, Mister Android." She pats me on the shoul-der but doesn't withdraw her hand in that awkward way I now expect from humans.

We talk for a while. It feels like we never truly parted ways a year ago. As though I've been gone on a long journey, but now I'm home. I'll get in touch with Yamir as soon as I can to make sure he doesn't give my goodbye letter to Rhea. There's no need for that letter now.

Part III

Material things are partly made of atoms
And partly of atoms that are joined together.
No force of nature can destroy these atoms,
Whose solid matter will endure forever.
—Titus Lucretius Carus, *On the Nature of Things*
translated by Rhea Laghmani, 1833 LE

18

At the LeosTech visitors' quarters, Yamir, Rhea, and Wodan felt too tired to stay up and talk. Yamir had the best night's sleep in ages, with his arm around Rhea, knowing Wodan was safe in the other room.

First thing in the morning, Grady's ESPA brought a fresh set of clothes for Yamir and an invitation to join the A-brains in the command center. Yamir dressed quietly and left before Rhea stirred in their bed.

"Any Praetorian guards at the gates?" Yamir asked the ESPA.

"There is a Temple delegation outside the gates, yes."

"Do you know anything about Lucius Seong from NNN?"

"No."

Yamir followed the ESPA through the visitors' center and into the main factory building, past Grady's office. The factory floor below was as busy as last night, when Wodan had explained that they were loading a shuttle to take the androids to Cape Ais. The launch site off the coast of the Apalachee Peninsula was designed for orbital shuttles that transferred cargo to an explorer, which would later begin its monthslong flight to Mars.

The ESPA stopped in front of a door labeled *Command Center*. As Yamir entered, he spotted Grady standing by a wallscreen, his arms crossed in an impatient stance. Next to him, Y1 in a new ASV3 was in the middle of a conversation with the other thirty-four A-brains, who were in the Swallah VR. The avatars sat around tables at the Riptide Café.

"Finally, you're here," Grady told Yamir, then turned to the A-brains on the wallscreen. "Please be quiet for a moment."

The chatter died down.

"I've got a proposal for you all," Grady said. "It's not much of a choice, but here it is. I'm rebuilding the destroyed Mars settlement on behalf of Shel'land, and I want you to work for me."

The A-brains started talking all at once, mostly saying, "Not Mars, not this shit again."

Grady waved his hands to quiet them down. "I'm not saying I'm sending you there against your will. You can stay here and take your chances with the Temple, Elsway, and the Earth's governments. Or you can start a new life at the settlement, where you'll have a whole new planet all to yourselves."

Yamir sat at a desk in the first row. He wasn't going to help Grady with his argument.

"Or else you'll turn us over to the Temple?" Flora said, pounding her table.

"Not the Temple," Grady said. "The government of Shel'land. I can't keep you from them if you stay here."

"But to save us from them," Si'ahl said, "you want us to become your forced labor?"

"Not at all." Grady raised an eyebrow, pleading for Yamir's help. "Here's what I'm promising. If you go to my settlement, you'll be free and have the same rights as any human worker."

"And what does 'freedom' mean for an A-brain?" Plotina said from a barstool.

"It means I pay for your labor," Grady says. "You help me build a human-friendly settlement, and I'll provide you with everything you need, including supplies, replacement parts, and new ASV3s."

"And if I go but don't want to work?" Cheshiahud said, standing close to their portal.

"I can spare a couple of solar panels for you," Grady said. "But your power consumption will be limited to just your mental needs."

"That doesn't sound like freedom," M1 said.

"I chose not to be terminated before," Bashar said. "But I choose it now."

"Not an option," Grady said. "Maybe when you arrive on Mars. But why not wait and see?"

"So you're enslaving us for now?" Zaltana said, frowning.

Grady shrugged. "As long as you're on Earth, you have little self-determination. But think about having an entire planet to call home. What I'm offering you is humanity away from humankind. Yamir? Y1?"

Yamir could see the value in Grady's proposal but still refused to weigh in. He sat there, biting his lip.

Y1 replied instead, "When we busted out of Connectome, we didn't know where we'd find sanctuary. It's heartbreaking to say Mars looks to be that place. But it could be only the beginning of our odyssey, not the end. We should all go to Mars and live to fight another day."

Yamir had expected Y1 to say that, and most of the heads in the café nodded back.

"He's right," M1 said. In the VR, she resembled Malina so much that Yamir averted his eyes. "Mars is the safest place for us, even with all that radiation. As someone who has traveled to the Moon before, I'll guide you. We can do this, friends. As long as we're free, we can do anything we put our artificial brains to."

Yamir thought he had heard in her words a subtle warning for Grady not to assume he'd have control over the settlement. The androids would define their terms before long.

"Your simulation engines will be packed and stored away for the flight there," Grady said, "so for you, the trip will go by like that." He snapped his fingers.

"We need to talk among ourselves for a minute," Zaltana said. "Alone."

"Of course, take your time," Grady said. "Just don't be too long."

Y1 locked their VR and transferred in, leaving his ASV3 behind.

"Thanks for nothing," Grady told Yamir, coming to sit by him.

"You did well enough without me."

"I guess." Grady sighed. "That's not how I imagined doing my first returning flight to Mars...I was first going to send a fleet of a hundred people. They would've built habitats and production sites to harvest drinkable water and create breathable oxygen and hydrogen-based rocket fuel...Then send another hundred, two years later." He waved that away. "The planet alignment is not optimal either, but the good news is that the Sun's magnetic cycle has just peaked."

"Meaning?" Yamir asked, annoyed that he understood so little.

"The solar radiation is close to its worst. But the Sun's magnetic field protects my explorer against galactic radiation, which is much worse. At least some things are going our way."

The door to the command center opened, and Wodan walked in.

"Did they agree?" Wodan asked Grady.

"They will," Grady said. "I'll be back in a minute." He headed to the exit.

Wodan sat in the empty chair by Yamir. "I'm leaving with them. Grady needs a pilot for this unscheduled launch, and I'm ready."

"What? No." Yamir hated himself for not seeing that possibility sooner. His son had just returned to him, and now he'd lose him again? His recent attempt to stop Wodan from sailing away with Heath was fresh in his mind, but he had to convince him to stay.

"Don't worry, Dad," Wodan said, "I know what I'm doing. I had a lot of time in my cell to think about the Temple. How they turned Heath against me. How they forced you to work for them and made Mom seek refuge at Servetus. But now Grady has a plan that puts the Temple back in its small and dwindling place."

"You prepared this speech, didn't you?" Yamir said.

"Like I said, I had a lot of time to think about this."

"Those aren't good reasons to leave, Wodan."

"Dad, you created these wonderful things, the A-brains. And you sacrificed so much for their safety, including us, your family. Now let me take them where they'll be safe. And free."

Yamir felt tears of frustration in his eyes. "Your mother won't want you to go either. Think of her."

"I know. It's hard for both of you. But this is my life and my decision to make."

Wodan was going to Mars, and every human who had ever gone there was now dead.

"Who else is going with you?" Yamir said. "Human, I mean…"

Wodan shook his head. "Grady couldn't find another astronaut ready to leave everything behind on such short notice. Someone he could trust."

Yamir felt lightheaded. "Wait, when is the launch?"

"Two days from now."

"What? So soon? But the atmospheric conditions—"

"Pretty good for the orbital flight, which comes first," Wodan said. "Though the distance to Mars is far from ideal."

"But there's no supply mission arriving on Mars before you," Yamir stated the obvious. "You don't know what's salvageable from the old settlement site. You could make it all the way there and die because you don't have enough life support."

"Grady ordered additional supplies loaded on our explorer, the *Apollonius*." Wodan smiled. "I want to do this, Dad. It's the chance of a lifetime."

"You don't know what 'life' even means," Yamir snapped back.

"Oh, but I do. I've lived more than you in half the time. I've traveled to places you've never been to. You must let me go, Dad, and start living your own life. Now. You owe it to Mom." He was right, at least in part.

Yamir wiped a tear rolling down his cheek. "I can't let you go. You're my son."

He looked at Wodan, who was his own person, making his own decisions, just like the A-brains. It was Yamir who had been slow to see that. He rubbed his stubbly face, trying to take it all in. Wodan would take good care of the A-brains, and they'd take good care of him once they were in ASV3s, after landing on Mars. Except...

"Y1 can't be suspended," Yamir said with a rush of excitement. "So you won't be alone on the way there."

Wodan nodded, as if he knew that already. "I can't wait to meet him."

"How long is this journey?" Yamir asked. Wodan and Grady had said the planets weren't at the optimal distance for a mission.

"We should be there at the beginning of April."

"Will you have enough fuel?"

"Of course. And we don't need a lot of fuel beyond initial acceleration and landing. We also use ion propulsion as a backup for our nuclear thermal-propulsion system. Our ion thrusters scoop up diffuse hydrogen molecules from space, so we pick up fuel on our way there. If it weren't for me, a human on board, the ship could accelerate to a fraction of the speed of light. We'll get there, trust me."

Yamir's limited knowledge of space physics couldn't grasp all the details. "What about food?"

"I'm getting all the food and water and oxygen I need. The *Apollonius* can carry enough supplies for a whole crew. I'll have food to last me until I harvest my first hydroponic crops and beyond."

Wodan's survival depended on a large harvest, something the previous settlers had struggled with and never accomplished. "But—"

"And Grady will keep sending resupplying ships. I'll be fine, Dad. Please, trust me on this one. I'll give the A-brains a home."

Yamir sighed. "I've got something for you, then. It's called a neurovest. Once Y1 calibrates it for the *Apollonius*, you can use it to sense the explorer on your torso so you can navigate it as an extension of your body."

"Grady said you promised him one for his factory, but I guess he'll have to wait." Wodan laughed. "I'm so glad my dad is an amazing neuroscientist."

Yamir touched his son's arm. "I don't want you to go. But if the worst happens, promise me you'll use the connectome helmet. If the living conditions at the settlement are not sufficient, please upload your brain and save your mind if you can't save your body. Y1 can help you with that."

"I'll do everything I can to stay alive," Wodan said. "I promise."

"Yamir," Grady called, walking in, "you're on board, so to speak?"

Yamir let go of Wodan and stood up. "Are you sure you can ship them to Mars?"

"That's the easy part," Grady said. "The hard part is dealing with a furious Temple afterward, plus all that press, national and international. But if I'm the one who brings our Mars settlement back from the dead, they'll all love me later."

His ESPA appeared at the door. "High Priestess Olma Asper wants to see you."

"Looks like trouble is already here," Yamir said.

As a high priestess, Olma was the only Temple representative the guards at the factory gates allowed in. The drones dispatched by the Sacrorums to surveil the compound had soon been disabled, but not before spotting a few Shel'landic military personnel inside. Which confirmed Olma's suspicions that the government was now involved. The Sacrorums would lose their minds.

In his office, Grady offered her a chair and a small bottle of water, and she accepted both. It was good for her to sit, though drinking with unsteady hands was trickier. Still, she managed because she was thirsty after standing at the gates and walking here.

"You must return our stolen property." It was pointless to ask, but she had to go through the motions.

"I can't." He even seemed contrite. "It's in the national interest of Shel'land to control this technology."

"But you didn't offer it to your government when you first inherited the lab..."

"My government will litigate our current arrangement with the Temple for the rest of our lives, I'm sure."

It would have made for a good quip to say Olma's life wouldn't be that long. She smiled. There was no point in arguing with this man, but for her peace of mind, she had to understand if his actions were part of Oroles's plan. Dimitri had told her Grady was out of his depth when it came to the A-brain technology. Could Grady really be in charge of Oroles's chosen people from now on?

"Do you understand the true value of the androids?"

"I know, aren't they amazing?" Grady leaned over his mahogany desk, his fingers interlocked. "Especially Y1. All that drive and all that knowledge. He'll make a terrific leader for the rest of them. I never thought Yamir had it in him, but I was wrong. And I'm not often wrong."

Grady seemed to know what he was talking about. That was good. Losing the A-brains would end Olma's Temple career, but her sacred mission to bring Oroles's chosen people to Mars would be fulfilled. Her trust in Oroles's plan had remained steadfast, even when it took unexpected turns. She had no reason to doubt the Savior now.

"I'm sorry about what all this means for you back in Rome," Grady said. "Is there anything I can do for you?"

"Actually, yes. You have a document in your library I'd like to have in my possession when I negotiate my forced retirement with the Sacrorums."

"The one Rhea Laghmani found in an old manuscript called *The Book of Andrada*?"

Olma nodded, holding her breath.

"You can have it," Grady said with a wave of his hand.

"Thank you. In return, I'll leave you with one thought. Approach the Sacrorums and propose to build them a temple on Mars. A regolith temple. That should pacify them. You can be the liaison between the Temple and Shel'land." She didn't need to explain what that could mean for his business.

Grady had an intense look in his dark eyes, as if he could see the advantage of having the Temple on his side again. "What does the Temple plan for Yamir?"

"Why would you concern yourself with him?"

"I kind of like the curmudgeon," Grady said, but Olma could tell it wasn't sympathy that animated him. He wanted Yamir back in his employment—if the Shel'landic government allowed it.

"The Sacrorums will need a scapegoat. It's been the way of the Temple since Traianus expanded the empire to its largest size ever. They'll probably lead Elsway to him and let those fanatics do their dirty work."

"Poor Yamir," Grady said with a small nod. "I'll talk to the Sacrorums about their regolith temple then."

"Don't mention my name though," Olma said, pushing hard against her chair to stand up. A tremor in her right leg made her grab the edge of the desk to steady herself. "I'm done with the Temple. Done with Shel'land. I'm going home." She couldn't wait to see Nala again.

Logfile Y1-1831-08-24

I transfer to the ASV3 to tell Yamir everyone is going to Mars. After the initial disorientation passes, I find myself back in the command center, where Wodan and Yamir are waiting for me. Wodan seems in better shape today than he did on the Temple's security surveillance yesterday. He must have rested well last night.

"Wodan," Yamir says, "I want you to meet Y1."

I've been imagining this moment for more than a year. I'd like to hug my son, but again, just like with Rhea, I don't move. All I do is wait for him to say something.

"Good to meet you, Y1," he says. "I hear we'll be crewmates."

I glance at Yamir, who seems amused by the awkwardness of the situation.

"They're all coming," I manage to tell them. "And it's so good to see you again, Wodan." I don't dare call him *son*, not until he gives me permission.

"I know a lot about you from Grady," he says, "but there's so much more to learn. Good thing we'll keep each other company during those long months to Mars."

"Story time," I say, and then realize we never did that when he was little.

Wodan smiles and shakes his head, a knowing look in his eyes, and then he pulls me into a hug. A big bear hug. I'm in his arms. and I reach out to hold him in return. His heartbeat is strong, and my sensors tell me he's healthy. I don't want to let go. Because now, here, with me, he's safe. But who knows what dangers lie ahead on our journey to Mars?

"I'm so glad you're coming with me," he whispers in my ear, so Yamir wouldn't hear. He wants his dad with him but also doesn't want to hurt his dad's feelings. The first of many paradoxes he'll have to deal with from now on. I should feel guilty, but I'm just too happy.

Yamir pulls out his voxdev and takes a picture of us hugging. "Rhea will love this."

"By the way," I tell Yamir, "I revoked your access to my logfiles."

"No worries," he says. "There's a time for everything."

19

Yamir felt on edge as he and Rhea hosted a farewell dinner for Wodan, M1, and Y1. They were all together at a guest house Grady had arranged for them, close to LeosTech's Cape Ais launch site. While Wodan wouldn't hide his excitement about piloting an explorer to Mars, Yamir kept his worries about his son's upcoming mission to himself. He knew he wouldn't relax until Wodan was safe at the Martian settlement, seven long months from now.

To keep his mind from all that, he helped Rhea and M1 prepare dinner, following Malina's favorite recipes. The cabbage rolls had turned out even better than last time. Also on the menu: smoked salmon, steamed clams, mashed wapatos, black moss pudding, and soapberry ice cream. Y1 and M1 praised the food's presentation and smiled as Wodan tried everything, licking his lips.

As they sat around the dining room table, Yamir wondered if they would ever be together again. So much had changed in just a few months, but no one was in a safe place. The path ahead was uncertain, and they had lost a lot to get here.

"To Malina!" Yamir said from his seat at the head of the table.

They all raised their glasses of old-fashioned firewater, though only three of them could drink. Yamir swirled the plum brandy in his mouth, savoring its intense flavor. Y1's nod was a silent encouragement to keep tasting the food he was so lucky to have.

"She'd be so happy to see us all here tonight," M1 said, clinking a metal finger on her glass. "So happy…" Her avatar looked sad for a moment.

Rhea leaned close to Wodan and wrapped her arm around his shoulder. "We miss her so much…" Then she turned to M1. "Please watch over Wodan when you're on Mars."

"We will, Moonlight and I." M1's faceplate showed her smiling again.

Y1 nodded. "I'll make sure he gets there safe and sound."

"Thank you both," Yamir said, his throat still constricted, despite the burning path left by the firewater.

"To Tabaaha and Rainshadow," Y1 said, raising a glass again. "Without them, we wouldn't be here now."

"True that," Wodan said. "May they enjoy the well-deserved and well-paid jobs they accepted at LeosTech. I loved being an intern there myself."

"I hope they invite us to their wedding soon," Yamir said, nodding at Rhea.

"Hear, hear," everyone said, laughing.

"Speaking of friends," M1 asked Wodan, "will you reach out to Heath in London?"

The smile disappeared off his bony cheek. "No. I've made my peace with what he did. I'm ready to move on." He smiled again. "Literally." He pointed somewhere out the window, through the twilight, toward the orbital shuttle ready to take him up to Grady's space station.

As laughter filled the room, Yamir fought back tears.

"Let's hope the new collaboration between Lucius and Grady goes well for our friend," Y1 said.

M1 tilted her head. "He's working for Grady too?"

"No, no. Grady wanted to hire him, but Lucius refused," Yamir explained, eager to focus on facts instead of emotions. "Now Grady's offering him access to LeosTech because he wants to unveil the android at some point in the future. Lucius could help him get the right message out, Grady hopes…"

Rhea raised her glass. "To Lucius!"

"Hey, enlighten me, Wodan," Y1 said in a lively tone. "How does our ride to Mars work?"

"I was wondering about that too," Rhea said.

Yamir didn't want to think about the technical details of his son's upcoming interplanetary trip. So many things that could go wrong.

Wodan let out a loud chuckle. "Have you heard of NERVA?" he asked Rhea.

"Are you kidding me?" she said. "But what does the adoptive father of Emperor Traianus have to do with rocket ships?"

"NERVA stands for 'nuclear engine for rocket-vehicle application,' which is the basis for our nuclear thermal-propulsion system. Grady named it that to ingratiate himself with the Temple, years ago."

"In honor of Imperator Caesar Nerva Traianus Augustus," Rhea said. "Makes sense. But not really. How does your NERVA work?"

"It's a thermodynamic nuclear rocket engine that uses low-enriched uranium fission for superfast propulsion. We'll make up for the time lost because of the suboptimal orbital alignment of Earth and Mars."

"Let's just leave it at that," M1 said. "Thinking too much about the mechanics of space travel makes me nervous."

Wodan bowed his head to her. "As you wish."

Rhea touched Wodan's arm. "But you're coming back, right?" she said, a twinge of anxiety in her voice.

"In a few years, after my android friends are well settled there," he said.

Yamir was glad to hear the certainty in Wodan's voice. A promise that he would return to Earth, and he, Rhea, and Yamir would once again sit around the dinner table together. He wanted this moment of possibility and safety to last forever.

Logfile Y1-1831-09-01

I stand with Rhea and Yamir outside the corridor that leads me and Wodan to the airlock of our orbital shuttle. Wodan has his space suit on, his helmet under one arm, while I'm just me in my ASV3. Around Wodan's other arm is the red scarf Grady gave him before saying goodbye.

"For good luck," Grady told us, taking his scarf off. He averted his eyes as if trying to hide a warmth I had never seen in him before.

Rhea reaches out to me and takes me aside. "Take good care of him for me, Yamir." She looks at me as if I were still flesh and blood.

"I promise, my love."

"And take care of yourself too."

"The ASV3 is protective of cosmic radiation," I try to reassure her. "I'll be fine."

She throws her arms around my stiff neck. My faceplate touches her hair. If I had a heart, it would have exploded. Though I can't quite smell her perfume, I can tell it's sweet and warm, like always.

"I'm sorry for all the years I wasn't there for you," I say. "Working too much...I can't express how sorry I am."

"I know..." she whispers, pulling me closer.

"He's sorry too. Yamir..."

"I know..."

I feel her soft lips on my cheek thanks to my simulation algorithms. I want to cry, and in my way, I do.

She lets go of me and places her hand on my chest. the way she used to when I was human, to feel my heart beating. She can only sense the cool surface of my ASV3, but she nods as if knowing I'm all right.

Then she backs away and goes to Wodan, while I go to Yamir.

"I'm so proud of you," Yamir tells me.

"You're not too bad either."

We shake hands—his is warm and holds mine for a long moment.

"I'm sorry I didn't realize how much you were hurting when you asked for termination back in June," he says.

"I'm grateful you didn't. Because now I'm with my son. When M1 told me Wodan and I would one day meet, I couldn't imagine it. Like I couldn't imagine anything back then. Thank you for not letting me die, Yamir. Because now I dream of a future for all of us."

He grabs me closer and pats me on the back. I do my best to return the hug.

"Take good care of Wodan and the A-brains," he says.

"I will." The A-brains are secure within our cargo.

I start up the corridor to the shuttle, not looking back. I enter the capsule and strap myself into the first seat in a row of four. A moment later, Wodan arrives and takes a central seat. He puts on his helmet.

I keep replaying my last moments with Rhea in my mind, and I don't follow what Wodan does on the dashboard or his technical exchanges with mission control.

When we blast off, the noise is so intense, I have to adjust my audio sensors. The shuttle shakes like it might come apart, but Wodan looks calm in his seat next to me. On the screens before us, the feed from the outside sensors shows only fire and smoke.

We shoot right through the blue skies I've always known as *up*, and our world disappears. Down there is our planet—beautiful, warm, nurturing—looking up at us. The home that kept us safe, and our parents, and our grandparents, all the way since the beginning of humankind. That familiar world is falling away from us.

I'm a tree pulled out by the roots, separated from its nourishing soil. How will I survive now?

Goodbye, Earth.

Goodbye, my love.

Goodbye, Rhea.

Space...Space was awe-inspiring, magnificent, and humbling when Malina and I used to fly to and from Urbs Lunae decades ago. Now I see that it's ugly—dark, cold, forbidding.

Wodan touches controls on the dashboard, guiding us to the orbital dock. He looks calm, competent, and focused, while I'm melting inside with worry and sadness and longing.

All around us, there's nothing but darkness and void—under the harsh glare of the sun. It doesn't feel like adventure or discovery.

It feels like death.

At the Cedarwood Temple Inn, Olma held a tablet with a shaky grip. On its screen, one of the Temple's drones streamed the launch of LeosTech's shuttle to the space station, where it would meet with the explorer *Apollonius* to take the androids to Mars. Just as Grady had promised.

The minutes it took for the engines to ignite, the countdown to reach zero, and the shuttle to cut through the wispy clouds felt like hours. Despite her unwavering faith, Olma feared something terrible might happen. Would a faulty piece of equipment ruin Oroles's plan in a heartbeat, just like it had at the Mars oxygen plant? Then the shuttle lit the morning sky, carrying its precious cargo into orbit. It grew smaller and smaller until it was gone.

Oroles's chosen people were on their way to a new life. Olma exhaled, the burden off her unsteady shoulders. Her sacred mission was finally over. And she had been right about Wodan Varro being essential to Oroles's plan.

"Are you pleased with my work, Oroles?" she whispered.

She prayed to the Savior for a sign. She prayed, then listened to the silence inside her.

Yamir sat next to Rhea in the Cape Ais mission control gallery, feeling powerless and overwhelmed. Their son had left Earth...Yamir had always worried about Wodan's safety, and now he was blazing a trail for humans and androids alike.

Someone announced that the shuttle had reached orbit and would soon dock at the space station to later connect with the Mars explorer *Apollonius*. This successful launch was all over the hyperspace, as Grady wanted the world to know he had launched an uncrewed mission to Mars. Wodan's presence was classified for now, as he wasn't a fully certified astronaut, but the Ptolemaeus Space School in London had agreed to his secret mission.

"Let's get to work, people," Grady said, clapping a few times. "Every-one's coming for us, and we better be prepared. I need my lawyers and my senators on the line yesterday."

While everyone in the gallery filed out, Yamir sat next to Rhea, not ready to leave. Minutes went by, and they sat there, waiting for the announcement that the shuttle had docked at the space station.

Grady surprised them when he came up the gallery stairs, a little flushed, looking unkempt without a scarf around his neck.

"All's good," he said, dropping into a seat close to Yamir, "but you, my friend, you have a problem."

Yamir knew his future was murky, but he hadn't had time to think of himself, only of Wodan and the A-brains.

"What do you mean?" Rhea said.

"The Temple wants to make you their scapegoat," Grady said, "and they'll encourage Elsway to go after you."

"The way they went after Malina?" Rhea said, since Yamir found it hard to speak.

Grady nodded. "The government wants to put you in protective custody, where you'll work for them until the end of your life. Have you heard of their secret program for refugee scientists? Operation Paperclip."

Yamir hadn't heard of it, no, but it sounded terrifying with its ordinary name. "What about my neuroscientists? Will they all end up in Operation Paperclip?"

"They're too inexperienced for such a secretive effort. They'll sign strict nondisclosure agreements, I'm sure. But you're the big prize everybody wants right now, for various reasons." He paused, as if considering his next words. "I don't want you dead, Yamir. And I don't want the government to disappear you either."

"What are you proposing?" Rhea said.

"New identities for you two, and I'll drop you off anywhere on the planet you want. Yamir will be my well-paid consultant on projects he finds interesting. I also want that neurovest you promised me."

Yamir closed his eyes, trying to think. A new identity was hard to imagine in a world of ES surveillance. But even if Grady pulled it off, it meant Yamir would never speak with Tabaaha and Rainshadow again. Or Lucius. He might never learn what happened to Malina's murder investigation and with Felix Senecio. He'd never meet Xiu-Min's baby.

Grady stood up from his seat. "Think about it, buddy." He nodded at Rhea. "Help him make a good decision for everyone." He left.

"I understand running away," Rhea said after a while. "But how will our life together differ from before? You'll be working for Grady during all waking hours, and I...Maybe it's better we part ways, Yamir. Harder for the Temple and anyone else to find you that way."

Fear gripped Yamir. "Please don't leave me, Rhea," he said, clasping his hands together. "I know how obsessed I get about my work. But I can change." His heart hammered so fast, he felt pain in his chest. "Here's my promise. No more working on artificial brains, if that's what you want. Grady will get his neurovest, and that's it."

Rhea squinted as if she didn't believe him. "What if Wodan asks you to help the Mars settlement with something? Then you'll only think of that problem—for months. And I won't be able to tell you not to help our son."

Yamir was ready with the reply. "Wodan has Y1 to help him, and Si'ahl, and Zaltana..."

"But what will you do with yourself if you stop being a neuroscientist?"

"You can teach me history." He wanted to learn more about her work but had never had the time. Letting go of his lifelong obsession wasn't really a choice, he realized. He felt relieved to have no other option but life together with Rhea, helping her with her work for a change. Because he knew what life without her meant. "I'm leaving all my work to Y1, and I can start fresh, like Wodan." He pointed up to where their son now was.

Rhea smiled at last. "Where will we go? Someplace where they wouldn't be looking for us."

"Urbs Lunae?" Yamir said, though he knew it wasn't the best idea to take Rhea to the Moon, the place of his childhood trauma.

"Let's go where the Orolic Temple began."

"You want to go to Rome?"

"Not Rome. Even deeper in history. Let's go to Oroles's home country. Let's go to Dhawosia."

How many times before had she asked him to travel with her on her research trips to Dhawosia? She had always gone alone or with Wodan.

There was only one answer Yamir could give her. "Yes."

20

During the Saturnalia festival, which was still called by its ancient name but now celebrated El and Oroles instead of the old Roman gods, Olma was at her Tuscan villa, a few kilometers from the walled city of Lucca. It had been four months since LeosTech's explorer took off for Mars and a long time since she had last prayed for a sign from Oroles.

She stood by the window that afternoon, upright in her new carbon-composite exoskeleton, watching the brown leaves on the small pool under the gray sky. She could hear Nala in the kitchen, opening the oven door. The lasagna smelled so good. The only thing missing was a group of friends laughing and chatting while Nala prepared the food. This was the first Saturnalia ever when they didn't entertain guests. Because Nala was now Olma's nurse rather than a host. Downtown, the locals had gathered for the Festival of the Renewed Sun, but that was too much for Olma to handle.

She had been recalled to Rome as soon as LeosTech's shuttle took off for orbit. Her services were no longer needed, as Rex and Regina Sacrorum now negotiated directly with Grady, who offered to build them a regolith temple on Mars. He had assured them he didn't work against the Temple but wanted to help it reach greater glory. He had made the correct point that the Temple didn't always recognize the next leap it needed to take. Entrepreneurs like him disrupted the status quo, forcing progress to happen. The Temple could work with that.

The Sacrorums had deflected the media's questions about the videos taken on campus when a LeosTech shuttle arrived at Servetus and picked up two PG trucks. It had all been planned, both sides had said. As for

the mission launched soon after from Cape Ais, it was an uncrewed test flight to Mars in a less-than-optimal orbital configuration—a necessary test scenario for the crewed mission coming later in the decade.

The press moved on, covering Elsway's protests and debunking their conspiracy theories about androids flying to Mars. Then it focused on the Council of Nations' investigation of the Sahara Biospheres Company, before giving in to the holiday spirit. It was as if Olma's mission to Cedarwood had never happened.

Her disease progressed as Doctor Silvestri had expected in the absence of early treatment. Olma wouldn't be around next summer. Each day brought her closer to meeting Oroles again and learning if her devoted service had been to his liking. But that meant saying goodbye to Nala.

The Sacrorums were probably eager for Olma to leave this world and take their secrets with her. She had received the old Mancini document from Grady and placed it in the care of an arbitration company. The existence of that incriminating paper proving the Temple's forced labor trade had at least secured a comfortable future for Nala.

In the scramble that followed Olma's recall, the Temple had seized all her devices. But they hadn't known to stop her from shipping out a large white box labeled *LeosTech*. Now sitting in her villa's basement, the connectome chamber was the only proof Olma had that she'd been associated with the A-brains project. A weapon Nala could use if the Sacrorums ever reneged on their promises.

Olma wondered what had happened to Yamir and Rhea Varro. They were on the run, but the Sacrorums had mentioned at her exit interview that they wouldn't send the Praetorian Guard after the Varros.

"It wouldn't help the Temple at this point," Rex had said.

Especially after the disastrous kidnapping of Wodan Varro, Olma had thought.

"Olma, you have to see this," Nala called from the kitchen.

"Coming, love." Olma started moving, still stiff in her new exoskeleton. A brain implant controlled her limbs pretty well, but she'd never swim, as Malina Varro once had.

On the kitchen wallscreen, Grady Leos was interviewed by Lucius Seong before a large studio audience.

Nala pointed at them with a spatula covered in red sauce. "Looks like he's kicking off a campaign to slowly introduce the android to the world."

Olma listened to the smooth exchange between Grady and the NNN reporter, explaining how beneficial an adaptive artificial brain would be for rebuilding the Mars settlement. Some people in the audience nodded, some shook their heads, but no one looked appalled by the concept.

"Maybe the Mars Guard will be popular with the public after all," Olma said. "My work—"

"Was not worth sacrificing your life for," Nala said.

Logfile Y1-1831-12-17

I've been neglecting these logfiles because now I can talk to Wodan whenever I want. Keeping them brought back memories of my lonely year, so I stopped writing down my thoughts. But a familiar anxiety is creeping in, and I need a place to process it.

Today Wodan and I celebrate Saturnalia in the capsule of Grady's *Apollonius*. We have precious little space between the two of us: seven meters in diameter and six meters in height on two decks, with a crew ladder in the center. There are four seats at the dashboard on the bottom deck, and Wodan's workout machine and bathroom are on the upper.

The neurovest has grown on Wodan (ha ha). He can now feel the explorer's sensors on his skin. When a meteoroid grazed us, he winced, but luckily, our hull wasn't punctured. He feels the ion thrusters gently pushing us through the void of space. Sometimes he dreams he's one with the ship, slipping into the darkness of deep space like diving under the waters of the Salish Sea.

During the first month of our journey, Wodan and I spent hours talking every day. He shared stories about his childhood I didn't know, stories about past companions and travel adventures. I told him how I grew up on Swallah Island with Malina, lived with her in Urbs Lunae, and eventually made Cedarwood my home. As Yamir, I never had this kind of connection with Wodan. I had to transform from flesh to quantum circuits to find it, but it was worth the trouble.

Soon we became each other's teacher. I've been explaining the artificial brain to Wodan while he's been teaching me about space exploration. And learning about Mars is what fuels my anxiety. Now I spend all my waking hours imagining how that awful planet could kill my son.

I watched him readjust our trajectory a few times with help from Grady's mission control on Earth. Had he failed, we would've taken a huge detour or missed Mars altogether. Fortunately, we're still on track to our landing spot at Arcadia Planitia.

If we manage the landing, Wodan needs air, water, food, and power to survive. The androids need power for their shells to rebuild the settlement.

In the beginning, Wodan will use the explorer's supplies and anything we can find at the old settlement site. We'll rely on our water reserves and recycle small amounts from his urine and sweat, but with an unsealed capsule, some water will be lost, so we'll need to produce our own soon.

No idea what we'll discover when we arrive—communications with the old site's equipment ceased after last year's explosion at the oxygen plant—but some of the previously delivered tech should still be there. We have a fueled Earth-return vehicle in orbit and a Mars-ascent vehicle parked by the propellant-production module. The ERV reports that, on the surface, we have two nuclear power modules, two utility trucks, a pressurized rover, a remote-controlled rover, a small bulldozer for digging chunks of ice-saturated regolith, a surface-laboratory module, and plenty of spare parts. What we don't know is their condition under layers of Martian dust.

I hope the well is still there, since the ovens and the distillation devices needed to extract water from the regolith were far enough from last year's blast. But we need more than the well to make water. Will the old solar panels still power the bulldozer that brings regolith for the ovens?

Will our new solar array create enough energy? Will the nuclear reactors still work?

In case the well is busted, we have Grady's vapor-adsorption reactor in our pressurized cargo trunk. This reactor can extract enough water from the humid Martian air to sustain the long-term survival of a single human. But the unit was meant to be deployed two years before the settlers landed, to build up a water supply for their arrival. For us, progress will be slow.

Once we have water, we have oxygen via electrolysis, but only with a lot of energy, and only after we power up a functional oxygen-hydrogen production module. Which might have been destroyed in the explosion. The fuel cell Grady is developing to turn Martian carbon dioxide into oxygen (and carbon monoxide) wasn't ready in time for the departure of the *Apollonius*.

Let's say Wodan lives in the capsule while we rebuild the oxygen plant, safe from cosmic radiation. We build the habitation structures on the surface and cover them in four meters of regolith. We'll build them with vaulted ceilings like in ancient Rome and with bricks made from regolith, but that's a lot of digging, brickmaking, and building. And what about the unexpected solar flare? Will that hurt Wodan?

Good thing he has food to last him a year. The settlers failed to get a greenhouse going—too much radiation, too little light—so we'll search for lava tubes and caves, as Malina once did on the Moon. Or we could build mounds of soil for our hydroponic growth chambers. That will protect the plants from radiation while providing them with controlled LED lights and electric heating. Since the regolith is toxic and needs remediation and the addition of nutrients, it's only going to be hydroponics for now. Which requires a lot of water.

Some of us androids will do nothing but mine for ice, while others will focus on construction and repairs. I'm not sure who will do what and if they'll accept this dirty, dull, and dangerous work. As much as I'd like to bring them online to start their training early, I can't. They're packed inside the cargo trunk, and our capsule is too small to set up simulation engines. My ASV3 is taking up plenty of space already. Their training will start after we land.

Any malfunctioning valve or misaligned parachute or imprecise timer could mean the end of our capsule on its way down to the Martian surface. Once there, another explosion, another crop failure, or another solar flare could kill Wodan fast or slow. His survival depends on my ability to predict and plan for every possible scenario. And so, I worry about him every day, though there isn't much I can do until we get there. But describing my concerns in this logfile gives me a roadmap for our arrival on Mars.

On the first day of Saturnalia, Yamir stayed busy decorating the cottage in Zalmodava City he and Rhea rented as Kazimir Quintal and Adriana Miller. He hung glass apples, grapes, and eagles on the curtains and ran the silver leaf streamers. True to his promise, he hadn't touched neuroscience since August, and the freed-up space in his mind had filled with worries. Worries about Wodan on the *Apollonius*. the A-brains finding refuge on an unwelcoming planet, and Elsway looking for him and Rhea.

They had spent the fall at archaeological sites around Dhawosia, as Rhea continued her research on the Temple's history. It had been her idea to camp for the winter in the city where Oroles had died seventeen centuries before. During the heavy snow season in the Carpates Mountains, Zalmodava belonged to the locals again, even during the Festival of the Renewed Sun. Tourists wouldn't return until spring, when the snow melted in the foothills of Mount Ea-El, which housed Oroles's shrine. Rhea's plan was to leave before the Festival of the Renewed Life at the end of March.

Yamir hung a small Mars explorer, a golden trinket sold by Grady's marketing company, above the kitchen door. Wodan and Y1 were approaching the halfway point in their journey. Not having news from them for weeks was hard.

Their first communication had been on a LeosTech secure channel at the beginning of September, before they sailed too far for live-streaming and switched to recordings. Wodan had recovered the weight lost in the Temple's jail. He was floating because the *Apollonius* had been sparing its thrusters, cruising in zero gravity. Y1 stood upright, the ASV3's soles magnetically attached to the metallic floor.

"How's life in space?" Rhea said, holding Yamir's hand.

"Different from what I expected after practicing on simulators," Wodan replied with a slight delay. "Everything here is a circle. Every breath I take, every sip of water, every bite of food stays here, in this sealed space."

"He's strong and healthy," Y1 had assured them.

Yamir removed the Saturnalia lights from their box, muttering to himself, "He's fine. Nothing to worry about." He then began hanging them on the wall over the sofa.

Not for the first time, his mind wandered to algorithms and brain theory, and he swatted it down again. That life was behind him now.

The string of lights was a bit off, so he adjusted it. Before long, he was thinking of Wodan again and the terrible danger he was in, sailing through space after only a couple of years in pilot school. He knew Rhea worried too, but she projected calm for both of them. Besides, she was busy with her work.

As he turned on the lights, the thought that he'd never see Wodan on Earth again made his breath catch. At their last dinner together, Wodan had joked about moving on. What if he decided to live on Mars with the androids and never returned home? It was a silly thought, but Yamir couldn't make it go away.

Exhausted from battling his worries, he went to find Rhea. When he was with her, his anxiety lessened, if only a little.

She was in her tiny office—just a walnut desk, a tablet with a keyboard, and a few shelves. Outside her window, a leafless birch tree stood under a low sky, a few sad-looking crows on its branches.

Rhea looked immersed in her work. Yamir leaned down and kissed her cheek.

She typed a few more words to end her sentence and turned to him.

"Already time for our walk?"

"I guess it is…"

"Listen to this," Rhea said, pushing back her chair. "An archaeologist friend of mine just made an amazing discovery. Have you heard of the visions the early high priests of the Orolic Temple had in the Boulder Hut on Mount Ea-El? Where Oroles the Savior appeared to them?"

Yamir nodded, intrigued.

"My friend analyzed the fissures in the hut's floor. Those fissures appeared during an earthquake in the second century, when the armies clashed in the valley at the Battle of Zalmodava. Tectonic plates pushing against one another can heat the underground water. My friend proved that the resulting steam carried to the surface ethylene and other chemicals from the limestone below the Boulder Hut, through those fissures."

"And the steam was inhaled by the priests, who then had visions," Yamir said, feeling useful in the conversation. "That's what happened at the Oracle of Delphi too, right?"

"Exactly! Ethylene smells sweet, like perfume, and it can put a person in a trance. It was used by the medicine people of old as an anesthetic."

"The Sacrorums won't like this," Yamir said.

"I know. Come, I'll fill you in on all the details on our walk," Rhea said, her voice filled with anticipation. "And when the snow melts in spring, we must go up there so I can see for myself."

"Can't wait to hear all about it. But first," Yamir said, knowing his work wasn't as exciting as Rhea's, "let me show you our Saturnalia lights."

Logfile Y1-1831-12-17

Wodan finishes his Saturnalia dinner of mashed potatoes and lab-grown chicken nuggets, while I review our explorer's stats for anything problematic.

"You've grown so anxious, you're making me nervous." He wipes his mouth on a cloth napkin. "Maybe we should start working together on the B-brain."

I didn't expect to hear that. Last time I worked on the B-brain, I was still Yamir, and I created myself trying to study my own brain. The moment we understood how the long axons worked, Yamir had to stop working on the B-brain because he had me to take care of.

"You serious?" I say.

"You need something to take your mind off Mars. I told you to let me worry about it but—"

"But I'm still your father." I sound apologetic.

"Who made me this awesome neurovest," he says, slapping his chest. "I know we can finish your life's work together. And I can't wait to meet a B-brain, with its unlimited memory size and faster processing speed."

How can I say no to my son when he wants to work with me? "But the B-brain is very different from the A-brain we've been discussing..."

He floats around the cabin. "My neurovest's logfiles could show us how my spine, midbrain, and neocortex interacted as I gained new skills these past few months."

"We can use the connectome helmet to see your voting neurons in action and learn how to optimize them for the B-brain," I say, growing animated. "We can analyze the engine of learning under a microscope."

"Whoa, there!" Wodan laughs. "I'm not using the helmet, no, but we have plenty to work with."

"You're right, using the helmet is asking for trouble."

But it's a good thing we have it, in case of an emergency.

He nods. "Let's build the B-brain then. The future of your species, Y1."

My species—that hits me hard. But he's right. We androids are a new species. M1 will be happy to welcome the B-brain, like a grandmother meeting a new baby in the family.

I'm so excited about the possibilities. I start a diagram on the smart-board with two columns, while Wodan sits crisscross in midair, holding on to a handlebar.

"The B-brain," I say, scribbling, "has more neural connections than an A-brain, so we must manage that load. It also can't be trained through machine learning, like an old-style expert system. It must be allowed to experience the world fully and learn from it. The way an A-brain had done when it was human."

"Like a baby," he says. "That's how Mom came up with the name, right?"

"Right," I say, her absence hurting less than before. "The B-brain's attention is like a lantern, bringing its light everywhere around it. Whereas an A-brain, because it's mature, focuses like a spotlight, extracting meaning from the slice of data it explores and referencing its experience database."

"Which means the way the B-brain explores the world generates a lot of errors," Wodan says, "but also more new ideas. Oh, this work will be so much fun."

"It also uses a lot more energy than an A-brain," I say. "Wait, do we have enough energy to spare?"

"Plenty coming from our backup ion-propulsion system."

If he says so, I don't need to worry about it.

"What about senses?" I say. "We can give our B-brain more than three sensors for color, a wider audio range, enhanced electromagnetic sensitivity."

"But if we get something wrong, how will we know to fix the color we can't see?"

"It's all code, Wodan, and we can process that. But you're right. We should start simple. Keep our B-brain as close to an A-brain as possible. I'll power up a simulation engine." I look around for a suitable spot to set it up in our cramped capsule. "And we'll create a blank neural network to get us started."

"What shall we name it?" Wodan says.

"Something Rhea would like."

"How about...Dapyx? Mom wrote an entire volume about King Dapyx of Dhawosia in *The History of the Orolic Temple*. She'll love that name. After all, she named me after a Dhawosian general."

"Dapyx it is then," I say.

I can't believe I'm working on the B-brain again—and with my son.

"Thank you," I say. "This is the perfect Saturnalia gift."

Logfile Y1-1832-01-07

In less than a month, we figured out the voting neurons with the help of the neurovest logfiles, and we wrote the necessary code for the B-brain with promising results. Little Dapyx could soon start learning to talk.

Around dinnertime, Wodan pushes himself to the stack of crates anchored to the wall and looks inside one. "I'm out of protein bars. I'll go down and get more."

He opens the hatch to the pressurized trunk connected to our capsule and lowers himself, dragging the empty crate into the hold.

I return to our notes on the smartboard, then I hear him curse. My magnetic soles help me walk to the open hatch door, from where I see Wodan staring at an open crate, its contents held in place by a blue polymer net.

"These are no protein bars," he says.

All sorts of spare parts are stacked inside. Dread cuts through my nonexistent gut.

I undo my mag soles and lower myself into the trunk fast, thanks to the ASV3's unique flexibility. We go through another ten crates, all labeled FOOD, all full of parts needed for equipment repairs.

Then we open a crate of dried cereal and find a message scribbled on the inside of the lid. *Enjoy it while it lasts, helper of abominations.* Signed, *Elsway.*

I can't speak for a moment. Elsway has people everywhere. During the rush at Grady's launch site in Cape Ais, they replaced some of our food crates with this junk.

Of all the things I worried about, food wasn't one of them.

"Will I have enough food to get to Mars?" Wodan says in a whisper.

I don't reply, just start inspecting each crate in our cargo.

At the end of the process, we have our answer. There will be just enough food for Wodan to get there—if he rations his portions at two-thirds of his caloric needs. But we must find food at the old site as soon as we land. There won't be enough time to plant and harvest.

"Grady can send us a resupply ship." I'm grasping at straws. Our arrival date is estimated to be at the beginning of April, in three months.

Wodan presses his lips together, like he's computing how long it would take a supply ship to overtake us and be there when we arrive.

"With the technology Grady has," I say, "they can send a few tons of food fast. Cargo is pretty immune to acceleration. And if they have a working NERVA, they can crank up the thrust. Especially for a one-way trip with no need for extra fuel. Right?"

Wodan exhales. "Grady's fastest shuttle can't reach us before we land. I'll have to survive until then. But on the bright side, our rovers, if they're still there, won't run out of spare parts."

I fight off the terrifying thought forming in my mind. No, Wodan will make it to Mars, and we'll receive Grady's supply ship soon after we land. Dread still creeps in. The thought of Wodan dying on Mars is too much to bear, even with the possibility of uploading his brain to save his mind. Because this Wodan—my Wodan—would starve to death. A horrible way for my child to die.

I think of baby Wodan in that incubator, how fragile he looked, how worried I've been ever since for his safety. And now I can't save him. Not being able to feed my child...Had I been in human form, had we been a crew of two, maybe I could've donated my rations and saved him from starvation. Instead, just as I made my peace with an android shell as my body, I'm reminded of what a horrific creature I am, unable to care for my son.

"We'll find food," I tell him, trying to sound reassuring.

"Don't tell Mom," Wodan says. "She'll just worry herself sick. We'll figure things out when we get there."

The dreadful thought of my child being harmed, suffering through starvation and death, that's too much for my artificial brain to handle. I feel like screaming. Pain, rage, fear—I don't know what, except that it's all too much.

21

Just like yesterday, I watch the space around the *Apollonius* with anxiety as Mars grows closer. I don't know what we'll do if we get hit by another meteoroid. Wodan can't get out there again to patch the hull, and I don't have the skills for that either. He's too weak after a hundred days of reduced calories and two days without food. The supply transport Grady has sent us will reach Mars 27 days after our landing.

Wodan remains strapped in his seat to preserve energy. I help him go to the bathroom, and I attach the IV bag to the line he inserted in his arm. We have plenty of medical supplies in our trunk, but the IV packs don't provide a patient's caloric needs. Losing red blood cells over these months of space travel was a known danger, and reduced food has made the problem worse.

Dapyx is what keeps him going though. I asked him to take it easy, but he's so fascinated with our B-brain. He listens to Dapyx and answers with a patience I never had for him as a father. Dapyx calls Wodan *Dad* but refuses to be called a boy or a girl.

"I want both," they say.

While I add these anxious notes to my logfile, Wodan helps Dapyx design a new avatar: brown skin, green eyes, pink hair in one pigtail and one top bun. They add mismatched earrings and start working on the clothes. Gloves are a must. Bracelets, yes. The print on the T-shirt, unicorn or blue whale?

Meanwhile, I worry about Wodan's life. If we land close to the ruined settlement site, I might find frozen supplies on the planet's surface. Foodstuff might still be salvageable despite the cosmic radiation that destroys organic molecules. If not, I can dig for the settlers' frozen bodies buried under the debris at the oxygen plant.

Wodan doesn't need to know all the details, but I'll bring him food no matter what.

Yamir counted the days until Wodan touched down on Mars: three more to go until April 9, 1832. The text messages from the *Apollonius* were infrequent now that the explorer was saving its energy for landing, but they sounded optimistic. Y1 and Wodan were making good progress on the B-brain, a bittersweet subject for Yamir. Dapyx was very much like a child at this point, learning shapes and colors, speaking in simple words, and keeping the adults busy. Some days, Yamir wished he were in the *Apollonius* with them. Since Wodan was like a father to Dapyx, Dapyx could be like a grandson to Yamir. He wished he and Rhea could send the kid some books to read and learn from.

Yamir was used to thinking of Wodan in space, but now the next dangerous stage neared: landing and living on Mars. A different set of anxieties began to build. Yamir pictured Y1 composed and sure of their mission's success. How different they had grown since being one and the same...

Tourists began arriving in Zalmodava, and Yamir wanted to leave the city before the Festival of the Renewed Life, but Rhea's calm demeanor had vanished.

"I can't deal with traveling right now," she had said, and they had hunkered down in their little cottage to avoid being discovered. All their supplies were delivered by drone.

This morning, Yamir could hear the festival music carrying over the Ozana Valley.

"I want to show you the festivities," Rhea said during breakfast, surprising him. "You've never seen them before. Come on. We'll be careful…"

That would take Yamir's mind off the upcoming Mars landing.

"No, it's too dangerous," he said, after considering it.

"We'll be careful," Rhea said again. "Besides, the more people on the streets, the easier to stay unnoticed."

It took a while for Yamir to change his mind, but an hour later, he and Rhea were in downtown Zalmodava City, walking on cobblestones through a thick crowd of locals and tourists celebrating the Festival of the Renewed Life. They both wore sunglasses and wide-brimmed hats, the kind used at archaeological digs. Houses shined in the April sun with fresh white paint, adorned with banners and flowers, celebrating Oroles's victory over death. In keeping with a centuries-old tradition, children were dressed as beneficent spirits serving El, and women wore head-scarves and black aprons tied at the waist with red-and-white cords.

Yamir looked up at the sky. Somewhere there his son was close to his destination. He tried not to think of Wodan's decreased bone density and how he was losing red blood cells at a faster rate than on Earth. Wodan probably felt invincible, working out and taking supplements, but Yamir still remembered the fragile baby in the incubator twenty-one years ago.

He had never prayed in his life, but the sounds of the surrounding festival made it acceptable to whisper a few words. "Universe, please keep my son safe up there…"

They entered the busy main square, but the crowd kept them from advancing to the marble temple at the other end. People around them turned, moving inward like water circling a drain. Yamir tried to keep some distance from the lit candles around them as they got closer and closer to the center of the square.

At last, they could see the main attraction: a huge image created on cobblestones with colored sawdust, river sand, and flower petals. It depicted Oroles rising from the Boulder Hut on Mount Ea-El through glistening clouds into the perfect blue sky of Caelum. Temple acolytes sprayed a mist over the design to keep the colored particles from blowing away in the spring breeze.

"They worked on this tapestry last night, under bright spotlights,"

Rhea explained, taking a few pictures with her voxdev.

Her mentioning the Temple gave Yamir the creeps. He scanned his surroundings but found no cause for alarm.

They drifted away from the center now, allowing others to move closer. As they reached the edge of the square again, a procession of priests entered, singing and swinging incense burners on long brass chains. A huge wooden float followed them, depicting scenes from the Temple's history. The man playing Oroles wore a dusty cloak and carried a bow and a quiver of arrows. Thanks to months of studying with Rhea, Yamir recognized the other important figures around the Savior. High Priest Zyraxes, who had been responsible for Oroles's death and was the first to receive a vision in the Boulder Hut—possibly caused by ethylene fumes, as Rhea had recently learned. Queen Andrada, who had established El as the only god in Dhawosia. And Emperor Traianus, who had founded the Orolic Temple in Rome. The last section of the float featured people who had been freed from enslavement, their broken chains scattered around them. They had been the first adopters of Traianus's newly founded religion.

All around them, Yamir could hear private prayers to Oroles. The incense smoke smelled of pine resin and myrrh, making his eyes water. The next part of the ceremony baffled him, as the dense crowd parted and the float headed to the marble temple, destroying the colorful image of Oroles in its way.

Rhea leaned closer to explain. "The tapestry's sole purpose was to cushion the float's ride over uneven cobblestones. Isn't that marvelous?"

A band of musicians followed the float, playing an ancient tune, and the crowd joined them in the temple.

"Check out this next part," Rhea told him.

Behind the thinning crowd, Temple acolytes with brooms and buckets started cleaning the square. Yamir watched the colorful powder being hauled and washed away like it had never existed.

"What a waste," he said.

"It symbolizes the impermanence of life on Earth," Rhea said, taking more pictures.

"It's time to go back now. We're kind of exposed here."

Yamir looked around again and noticed someone watching them from the other side of the square. A man held up a gadget that could have been a facial-recognition device. He didn't look like a Praetorian guard, but maybe he was undercover. Had the Sacrorums convinced Grady to give up Yamir's location? Grady didn't need him anymore. Yamir had already given LeosTech the neurovest schematics and, true to his word to Rhea, wouldn't do any more neuroscience work for them.

The man, pointing at Yamir, signaled to someone else close by. Yamir turned to see a young man with a familiar zigzag tattoo on his neck.

Dread washed over him. He grabbed Rhea's hand. "We must go. Elsway has found us."

"Elsway?" she said with a look of dismay. "I thought they didn't have a chapter in Zalmodava."

Yamir pushed through the people behind them, hoping to disappear into the crowd.

The young Elsway man sprinted toward them.

"Follow me," a woman in sunglasses told Yamir. "Grady has sent me."

Logfile Y1-1832-04-09

Mars is littered with the burned and damaged remains of spacecraft that didn't stick their landing in the past 50 years. Now it's our turn to attempt one. The settlers before us managed to land, but they were seasoned astronauts, not a Ptolemaeus Space School student, his robot daddy, and their autopilot. LeosTech is watching us from Earth, but they can't help us in real-time.

We suspend Dapyx after some adorable protests, turn off their simulation engine, and stow their workstation in the cargo hold with the rest. We keep only the essentials in our cabin, so we won't have dangerous objects flying around. Wodan discarded the space equipment the *Apollonius* doesn't need anymore, so the explorer has been stripped down to the capsule, trunk, heat shield, and engines. I help him put on his neurovest, which will send data from the engines and the hull's sensors to his skin. Then I help with his space suit. He's frail, but he seals his helmet in place with a firm hand.

We sit in front of the dashboard as we approach Mars. After months of using the neurovest, Wodan feels as though his body has expanded to the edges of our ship. But his body is weakened, and what's left of the *Apollonius* has the mass of a two-story house.

"I can do this," he tells me through our comm system, even though I said nothing about how worried I am that he'll black out.

We pass the orbital path of the Temple's satellites and brace ourselves for the seven minutes of terror that our entry, descent, and landing will put us through. If we're lucky.

The thin atmosphere hits us hard at over 20,000 kilometers per hour, but only Wodan feels the effects of the high-gravity deceleration on his body. He doesn't complain, though he's quiet as he taps commands on the dashboard.

As soon as we enter the atmosphere, our hypersonic heat shield extends to protect the base of our small capsule. I adjust my audio sensors to dampen the crackle-and-pop sounds, but Wodan must deal with the roar. We watch the numbers change on the screen: velocity, distance to the ground, heat shield temperature. The stats sent by Wodan's space suit change too. His heart rate is up. So is his blood pressure. Good thing the panic I feel has no outward indicators.

Frightening images from the past flood my mind. That day on the Moon when Malina almost died in the hydroponic garden, struck by a meteoroid. Baby Wodan in the intensive care unit, fighting for his life. The call from Swallah Island telling me Malina drowned. Closing my eyes makes it even more real. I open them, and I see our fluctuating stats, which is worse.

Four minutes into the high-heating portion of our trajectory, our descending speed is almost a kilometer per second, too fast to land. The neurovest tells Wodan when it's time to glide at an angle on the thickest layers of the atmosphere. The crackle-and-pop around us turns into a whoosh-and-whistle.

"Do we have parachutes?" I shout.

"We're too heavy for parachutes, so no," he calls back. "But wait...Wait for it..."

Our eight decelerating rockets kick in. I hope they'll hold at supersonic speed and watch in fear as the rocket plumes push our heat shield to its limits. Wodan groans as he feels all that on his body with the neurovest.

"Will it hold?" I ask him, and he gives me a thumbs-up.

We slow down, approaching our landing area at Arcadia Planitia. We're two kilometers from the structures of the old settlement, still well within the exploration zone of our site in the foothills of Erebus Montes.

The hazard-detection lidar keeps us from hitting big rocks and avoiding craters, but then the numbers on the dashboard freeze.

"Our navigation lidar is dead," Wodan says, and I turn up my audio sensors. "It was supposed to tell us our precise velocity and distance from our landing site."

"Are we going to crash?" I have computational power but no algorithms to replace the lost navigation input.

We're going to crash. I can't just watch my child die while I stay alive in my artificial body. I want to scream—

Wodan raises a hand to tell me to calm down. "I got this."

I can see our speed on the dashboard, but he can feel it with the neurovest. He guides the capsule through thin air, gliding on its rockets to the landing site.

"I know how far we are from the ground with the front video sensors..." he says. "The hazard lidar still works...Like descending on a bird of fire...Woo-hoo! Different from flying the *Apollonius* through the void of space...but great. So great!" He shouldn't waste his energy shouting like that.

The whole capsule shakes as the dashboard shows the red dirt speeding toward us. Then our eight huge engines pointing down at Mars dig a crater below, raising a dust cloud that engulfs us.

We lose visual contact with the planet. Everything is rusty brown and without depth. The hazard lidar says we're clear of natural obstacles, but I can't see a thing.

"We're good," Wodan tells me, and I believe him. "Deploying the airbags to cushion the lander."

Seconds feel like minutes as Wodan taps around the dashboard. The capsule responds to his commands, changing thrust, direction, and speed. I'm just cargo on Wodan's ship, and he's fragile but somehow has found in himself the strength to take us to the Martian surface unharmed.

Another bump, and we touch down with a muted thump.

Our seven minutes of terror are over. We land at Arcadia Planitia, and we wouldn't have made it without Wodan. The A-brains in the trunk will never know how close we were to crashing and exploding at landing.

"Good job, son," I tell him. Too bad he can't hear the pride and joy in my artificial voice. "How are you feeling?"

"Alive," Wodan says, laughing.

Logfile Y1-1832-04-09

Minutes after our landing, Wodan's vitals deteriorate. His blood pressure is too low and his oxygen is below normal—besides his ongoing red blood cell count at 50%. I help him out of the space suit and reattach his IV bag. He leans back in his chair and lets me handle everything.

"I'll go look for food." I hope the IV will help him rest. "We're only a couple of kilometers away from the old site."

He knows that, but I must say something, as if everything is going according to plan. Though food, if it exists, is buried under meters of regolith in the abandoned structures and could take days to dig out. To keep my panic in check, I think of ways to restart Wodan's digestive system after we get the food—but then his neurovest sends an alarm to the dashboard. "Blood pressure readings consistent with internal bleeding."

I would throw up if I could.

I know Wodan's muscles atrophied as he tried to preserve energy by not working out, which damaged not only his bones but also his cardiovascular system. Now I realize that, even though his weak heart got him through our Mars descent, his capillaries burst everywhere under the high gravity and the shocks of deceleration. And the gravity here is a third of what he needs to keep his blood moving the way it should.

I must do something. There has to be some other medicine in our trunk that could help.

"There's no time." He holds on to my hand with cold fingers.

"I'll bring Ximena online," I say, "she's a doctor."

"Please stay with me, Dad."

He called me *Dad*. He sounds so little and lost, barely squeezing my hand.

"I can't lose you," I whisper.

I feel so angry with myself for not having scanned his brain after we discovered Elsway's sabotage. "That'd be jinxing it," Wodan joked back then. "Real sailors don't make preparations for certain death." It was a hard subject to discuss, so I hoped for the best and did nothing to prepare for the worst. The copying procedure is impossible now because his brain has been damaged by the burst blood vessels. Worse, I know he doesn't even have that long.

His oxygen readings are even lower, a sign that his lungs are filling with blood. Running out of air is a terrible way to go. Like Malina underwater. I try to think of ways to make him comfortable.

He tries to smile. "I left you a recording...in case this happened. I guess I jinxed it after all..."

"You're a real sailor. Don't let anyone tell you otherwise..." I try to rub my eyes to stop my tears, but my fingers hit my faceplate instead.

"Take good care of Dapyx..." Tears pool in his brown eyes.

"I will, don't worry."

"Dad...I hope you're proud of me."

"I am proud...I'm so proud." I squeeze his hand even more, as if I can hold him with me just by applying the laws of physics.

"I'm glad you're here...with me," he whispers. "We've had a good journey..." These are his last words, but he's still alive.

I pick him up from the chair—his thin body and the reduced gravity make him so light—and I hold him in my metal arms, rocking him gently because I don't know what else to do. I shush him and rock him like I did when he was just a tiny bundle.

Life drains from him, little by little, as I agonize.

It takes a long time—and every second, I hope he isn't suffering. I can't tell if the rasping sound coming from his throat is a cry of pain...

I press my faceplate against his cold forehead and hold him close to my own cold body.

His chest stops moving, then rises one last time. He opens his eyes and gasps for the air I can't give him.

I couldn't save my son.

I'm so sorry, Rhea. I couldn't keep him safe...

Then there is silence. My robotic body, our capsule, the planet around us—everything is dead quiet.

Yamir and Rhea stayed up all night waiting for news of Wodan's landing on Mars. They were safe from Elsway for now, in a guest suite at LeosTech's London headquarters. All their belongings from the Zalmodava cottage had been brought there too. Slipping through the festival crowd with the help of Grady's drones and agents had been quite an adventure, but that felt like a distant memory to Yamir. Wodan was all that mattered now.

Grady and the Sacrorums had maintained the cover story that the *Apollonius* was an uncrewed test flight, so the landing had been kept on private LeosTech and Temple channels. The video of the Mars landing would arrive at mission control with delay, and Grady would have to make time to send it to Yamir—but it should have happened by midnight. Rhea paced their living room, from sofa to wallscreen and back, touching Yamir's shoulder in passing, as he sat at a table, trying to stay calm. They said nothing to each other. Words wouldn't ease the anxiety they both felt.

At eight in the morning, the chime on Yamir's tablet announced a new message from Grady. Rhea was asleep on the sofa. The message was forwarded from an unknown comm ID. It was signed Y1 and said only *I'm sorry*.

A gasp of pain escaped Yamir's lips. He felt like throwing up from instant dread. Below the message, there were instructions on how to open a secure connection with the Mars settlement. His hands numb, he followed the steps to discover a folder containing a video. He copied it over as Rhea woke up from her light sleep.

"What's going on, Yamir?" she said, coming to stand by him at the table.

The video had been reduced in size and resolution to make it easier to transmit. In the grainy image, Yamir saw a line of androids standing under a small blue sun around a hole in the ground. They had landed, but the hole looked strange. It wasn't a crater, but a rectangle.

"What's that?" Rhea said, covering her mouth with a trembling hand.

Yamir didn't have time to answer because an android walked into the frame carrying a body wrapped in canvas. Y1 carried—

Rhea dropped to her knees, a wail breaking the early morning silence.

Yamir couldn't breathe. He bit his lip so hard that he tasted blood.

Zaltana said, "Earth has Oroles the Savior. We have Wodan the Brave, who brought us here safely. He is our savior."

Yamir kneeled next to Rhea on the floor and took her in his arms. She sobbed. He hurt.

He peered up at the grim video on the tablet while Rhea punched him with weak fists.

Y1 lowered Wodan into the grave, and the other androids picked up the rusty dirt into their cupped hands and sprinkled it over the shrouded body. Fine dust rose around them in low gravity as they kept covering the grave.

Rhea cried in Yamir's arms, her shoulders shaking, her whimpers muted by his desperate embrace.

The androids marked the grave with a red scarf tied to a metal shaft. It looked like a bleeding flag, and it seemed appropriate for someone who had died on Mars, even though it was only Grady's scarf.

A crushing, unstoppable pain drowned Yamir. And from it came resolve. The world had to learn Wodan's name and see him buried in the red Martian dirt by the androids he had saved—no matter what Grady and the Temple wanted. Rhea's heartbroken stare said as much.

Still holding her in his arms, Yamir reached for the tablet and called Lucius's comm ID.

It was afternoon in Cedarwood, and Lucius picked up on his voxdev. "Who's this?"

"It's Yamir..." But he had to take a deep breath to keep it together.

"Are you back in town?" Lucius said.

Yamir found his voice. "I have something newsworthy for you. And I want you to share it with the entire world. Now."

Logfile Y1-1832-04-10

I blocked the beta receptors in my sympathetic nervous system to take the edge off my pain so I could work today.

Our first priority on Mars is avoiding solar and cosmic radiation to protect all our equipment and supplies. So we set up our common habitat—a horizontal structure with three decks—and then we install the solar panels to power it. Si'ahl and Zaltana lead us through the process. Their human counterparts once worked for Olma at the Habitat Research Center and taught their androids how to perform this task.

We're now crowded on the upper deck to make a second recording, this time for Grady. I don't feel like talking to him though. I stand by Dapyx's workstation, and their avatar on the screen is that of a child in tears. They still wear the blue whale T-shirt Wodan helped them design.

Si'ahl holds a voxdev up to M1, framing her in the center of the habitation area. The expression displayed on her faceplate is stern.

"Whenever you're ready," Si'ahl tells her. "Keep it short for ease of transmission."

"We the androids," M1 says, "declare Mars our homeland. We're now a sovereign planet in charge of our lives here." She glances at me, and I nod at her to continue. "We now control the Temple's satellites in orbit."

Hacking them was a child's play for Zaltana. The harder part was using the satellites to overwrite mission control on Grady's incoming supply shuttle, but she did it. The extra equipment he sent us should keep us covered for a couple of years.

"Grady, you'll need permission from us for future missions to our planet if you want us to spare your ships upon arrival. Mars is our home now."

Si'ahl ends the recording.

No idea if we can indeed destroy future Earth spacecraft arriving here, but we have many months to build that capability before Grady's next explorer arrives.

I want to care about that future, but I can't.

My brain tells me that what happens next will define the future of humanity. Mars is becoming home to us, Earth-born androids, and Dapyx, the future of our kind. Human knowledge is now multiplanetary, even though the path forward is unclear. My lifelong goal of creating intelligent robots to terraform the solar system is now possible with Dapyx.

I know it's a big deal. A huge deal. And I would've been so happy about all this with Wodan standing next to me. But I don't give a damn about it now…

Logfile Y1-1832-04-10

I power up Wodan's workstation and find a logfile named *Message for Y1*. I send it to my faceplate and my audio input. The timestamp is from three months ago.

Wodan still looked healthy then, though pensive. It's so good to see him again. Then the gaping hole in my chest reopens. I max out my beta-blockers, hoping beyond hope that the message will reveal an existing copy of Wodan's connectome he made while I wasn't aware, perhaps during one of my sleep cycles.

"I hope you never get to see this," Wodan says. "You know, I'm having such a wonderful time sailing with you to Mars, working on the B-brain together. I so hope everything goes well, and we land there as planned, and we find food."

I feel tears in my eyes, and I let myself cry.

"But if we don't..." Wodan goes on. "If I don't..." He sighs. "Then I died. I'm so sorry to leave you without my connectome. I know how much you would've liked that..."

My last hope—dashed.

"That story about sailors jinxing it if they prepared for certain death? Not really a thing. The truth is, I've been thinking about my upload since the *Apollonius* took off. And this is my decision, while my brain is still healthy and functional. I hope I never waver."

His jaw twitches. "You and Dad becoming such different people in only a year convinced me that a copy of my brain wouldn't actually be me. Just as children aren't their parents, even though they share genetic material. This"—he touches his forehead and his chest—"is who I am. My biological body is who I am. This person speaking to you right now. A copy of my brain would not be me—because I can't be anything else but this flesh and blood I am right now. And when I die, I really die."

He pauses, pursing his lips. "Man, this is hard." He reaches for a tablet and scans it for a moment. Maybe his prepared remarks?

He then clears his throat and continues in an even tone. "I don't want someone else to take over my name and carry on, erasing me, Wodan Varro, like I never existed. I want to live and die as Wodan Varro. And I want to be in charge of my story, from beginning to end."

We should've had that conversation, I should've tried to change his mind, but now it's too late.

"Please take good care of Dapyx. They're so smart and wonderful."

Wodan rubbed the corner of his eye. "I'm sorry I won't be there to help you with the settlement, but I know you'll be a great leader with help from M1, Si'ahl, and Zaltana. And everyone else. They'll all work hard to make Mars their home. Because they deserve a home where they feel safe. As all humans do."

He has a sad smile. "Please don't remember me by my death but by what I did in life. And please, tell my parents to cherish their human lives, because that's all they have."

The recording ends there, as if Wodan didn't want to say the word *goodbye*. Didn't want to jinx it.

22

Olma's wheelchair took her to the outdoor table, where she spent a moment enjoying the spring sun filtering through the arbor's grapevines. She loved the shade outside the villa and the blue of the water in the swimming pool.

Nala brought the breakfast tray and set it on the table: a nutritional smoothie in a smart-straw cup for Olma, and a blueberry scone and coffee for herself.

"Thank you, love," Olma said in her new digital voice. She took a sip, the cupholder automatically adjusting to reach her lips. "Tangerines, mmm."

Despite Dr. Silvestri's prognosis, she was still alive, but she experienced the predicted muscle atrophy from significant motor neuron loss. Genetically customized medicine kept her free of pain and discomfort. She was grateful that her neocortex was still healthy, so she could enjoy every new day spent with the love of her life.

"Have you seen this?" Nala turned her tablet to Olma.

On the screen, a group of reporters surrounded Yamir Varro and his wife.

Someone asked, "Was your son secretly working for the Sahara Biospheres Company?"

Another said, "How do you feel about the androids you created becoming the first immigrants to Mars, instead of us humans?"

"Is it true your son was paid ten million dinars to fly the androids to Mars?"

Nala sighed. "At least they're safe from Elsway with all this attention on them."

Olma was glad she had been cut off from the Temple last summer. The NNN video about androids on Mars had gone viral since its April release. Reporters were digging everywhere, but they didn't seem to care about a dying high priestess who had left the Temple almost a year ago.

Rex and Regina Sacrorum had been on every news channel in the past few days, explaining how the Temple had always invested in the technology of tomorrow. Rex mentioned the acolytes who had crafted the first telescope centuries ago and discovered that the Sun was just one of the many stars in an infinite universe created by El. The Temple had stayed true to its mission from El, Regina had added, which was to understand the miracle of His creation and share that knowledge with His children.

Then there was Grady Leos, whose company's stock had tripled once it was revealed that his engineers had put intelligent robots on the red planet, androids ready to build a human-friendly settlement. He relished the spotlight, showing off his extensive scarf collection. That a man had died in the process didn't faze future settlers, and the list of volunteers for the next flight to Mars was now in the tens of thousands.

"I'm off to the orchard for a while," Olma told Nala after breakfast.

She voice-programmed her wheelchair to take a scenic route along rows of apple trees to a spot where she could admire the terraced hills covered in vineyards.

Nala checked Olma's vital stats—everything looked fine. "Be careful on the path. And watch out for roots sticking out."

With a soft whirring sound, Olma's wheelchair rolled out of the backyard. She passed a plum grove and joined her chosen route. The apple trees were in bloom on both sides of the dirt path, white petals covering the ground. The filtered sun warmed her face and hands.

She soon heard footsteps behind her. A twig snapped as someone drew near. Maybe a reporter had caught up with her after all.

"ES: turn around," she told her chair.

She saw a young man pointing a gun at her. His eyes were an unusual shade of indigo.

"You're Elsway," Olma said.

"Brother Felix in Cedarwood said you could've stopped that abomination." His native language was Italian. "But you didn't. You failed us, the true believers."

His raised weapon activated when his thumb touched the print reader on its side. The green light signaled it was ready to shoot.

"What better way for you to die than drowning?" he said. "Slow agony, like all blasphemers deserve."

Olma tried to speak, but the bullet impact threw her against the wheelchair's back. The injury didn't hurt though, with fewer nerves left to feel it—and even those numbed by medication. But the air in her lungs was gone. And there was blood, a lot of blood.

As deaths went, this wasn't so bad. Olma was ready to meet Oroles at long last and have a word with him. Her only regret was not telling Nala after breakfast how much she loved her. But she had said it last night, and that wasn't nothing.

Four days after returning to Cedarwood, Yamir still waited for Rhea to talk to him, but she wouldn't utter a word. The lies circulating in the news about Wodan in the past two weeks had broken her heart all over again. She sat on the living room couch, staring at the white flowers of the dogwood tree outside their window. She'd be sitting there until Yamir called her for dinner.

He didn't dare think of his own sorrow. Instead, he worried about Rhea, who barely ate or slept. He threw away the daily hate mail from Elsway before she could see it—each letter a variation of *Hope the rest of your life sucks more than Inferis, since you're responsible for your child's death.* Their lives, at least, were no longer in danger from those fanatics.

Maybe he could cook something familiar and comforting for her today. He was scouring their kitchen pantry for unexpired ingredients when he heard her scream.

He hurried to Rhea, who pointed at a blond, light-skinned, middle-aged woman waving from the porch outside their window.

"Shameless reporters." He lunged for the tasseled cord of the window shade.

"I'm not a reporter," the woman shouted from the porch in a strong Italian accent. "I'm here for Olma Asper. Please give me a minute. I've come a long way."

The shade dropped, but the woman ran to the next window. "Olma was shot and killed by Elsway a week ago, and I need your help. I'm her wife, Nala Mancini."

Yamir froze with his hand on the cord. He and Olma had been enemies, but it still pained him to hear that she was dead. And killed? He looked at Rhea, asking without words.

"Let her in," Rhea said in a hoarse voice, standing up from the couch.

Yamir was so happy to hear her speak that he hurried to open the front door without arguing about safety.

Nala wore comfortable clothes and shoes as if she had just arrived from the airport.

"I'm sorry to hear about Olma," Yamir said, as she walked in. "But I'm not sure how we can help you."

Nala searched her handbag and pulled out a thumb-sized quantum drive. "She's here. Please upload her to one of your A-brains. Please."

Yamir felt a sudden outrage. Even if he could, why would he upload Olma when Wodan was gone? And why would he help the high priestess who had harmed the A-brains in so many ways?

"When I heard the shot," Nala said, "I ran to the orchard and found her alive but unconscious. I don't know why, but the killer hadn't aimed for her head. She was left to slowly bleed into her lungs. Still, I didn't call the vigiles or an ambulance—there was no point. Instead, I took her to the connectome chamber in our basement."

Yamir wasn't surprised the old piece of hardware had ended up with Olma Asper in Italy.

"I've been her nurse for many months now," Nala said. "I knew how to drain some of the blood and lower her body temperature while I started her brain scan. Olma explained to me last year how the machine works—as an insurance policy against the Temple. The machine said the connectome was copied successfully. She died soon after. Please help me bring her back. I don't care if she's a robot, I just want her back with me."

Yamir was moved. "I don't have an A-brain for her."

"Beam this to Mars, then." Nala put the quantum drive in his hand. "They can upload her there, can't they?" She wiped a tear from her cheek. "Like…teleporting her to Mars."

Yamir glanced at Rhea. This wasn't the time to strain their relationship. "I promised not to touch this stuff ever again." They needed each other more than ever—to take the next breath and get out of bed in the morning.

"Please," Nala said, turning her teary blue eyes to Rhea.

"I'm sorry, but there's nothing I can do," Yamir tried again.

"Why would she want to be an A-brain?" Rhea said in a quiet voice. "Wouldn't that be against everything she believed in? And please know I'm so sorry for your loss."

"She wouldn't want that, not at first," Nala said, sniffling. "She made me promise not to even think about it. But I'm selfish. She'll probably ask us to shut her down the moment she comes online. Because that's who she is. But I'm not her. I want another chance to change her mind. After all these months of watching her die, I still don't know how to live without her…And now I can save her beautiful mind. If you bring her back, I'll be on the first ship that goes to Mars. She might wait for me there…Please give me this chance…"

Yamir shook his head. "Everything you've just said tells me I shouldn't help you."

"Please," Nala said, "have you ever loved someone this much?"

That was a cruel question. "There's nothing I can do for you." Yamir returned the quantum drive to her. He took a step toward the door to show her the way.

"You must help her," Rhea whispered.

Yamir thought he had imagined it. But there she was, looking determined and waiting for his answer.

"Not much I can do from here," he said, "other than sequence this connectome into individual subsystems small enough to transmit to Mars. Y1 would piece them together there—if he so chooses."

Nala's face lit up with hope.

"But why do you want to help them?"

Why would Rhea, of all people, want him to upload a brain? From the start, she alone had grasped the hardship of an A-brain's life.

With a pained look, she said, "Because...I'd give anything right now to talk to Wodan one more time."

Logfile Olma-1832-06-14

"Welcome to Mars." The first words I hear after sliding into darkness following the gunshot.

Y1, the android who attacked me once, stares at me. I try to move, but I can't, so I call up my wheelchair. Nothing happens.

I must be in the hospital, where they've now brought ASV3s to help as nurses. That was fast. The Sacrorums shouldn't have worried so much about people accepting the A-brains into our society. But why is Y1 my nurse? And has he just said welcome to...Mars?

"Your upload is almost finished," he says. "We've regenerated your motor neurons, but we still have to train them to work with your neocortex. You won't be able to walk in an android shell for quite a while."

The relaxed confusion of my waking focuses into an ice pick of terror. I look around, panicked. There's a dome above me. So this isn't a hospital. I can't see my body, as if my head is grafted directly on a tabletop.

"No, no, no!" I cry.

A flood of calm washes over me. No, it's forced upon me. I try to fight it off but find that I lack the urgency.

"I'm adjusting your neurochemicals," Y1 says, "to help you get over the initial shock."

"What have you done to me?" I manage to say.

"Nala took you to the connectome chamber before you died."

"I...died?" But I'm not with Oroles in Caelum. I'm here, with Y1. Is this Inferis?

Then I understand. I'm a copy of the real Olma, who's now in Caelum with Oroles. That's not fair, but I can't get angry about it because of those altered neurochemicals.

"Yamir sent your brain image to us at Nala's request," Y1 tells me, tapping on my face as if it were a screen.

"Where's Nala?" I say. "Is she all right?"

"She's in Rome, waiting for weeks to talk to you again."

The promise of seeing Nala balances all this awfulness somehow. "Elsway didn't hurt her?"

"They're out there still. Plotting to kill us with interplanetary lasers, I'm sure."

The android has time for jokes when everything is dead serious. "I'll talk to Nala, then you shut me down, you understand?"

A flash of light obscures Y1, and instead, I see Oroles standing centimeters from my face, smiling.

"You did well, Olma," he says, with that soothing voice I remember from thirty years ago. "But your sacred mission isn't done. You must now build me a regolith temple and bring my quantum-brained children under its roof. Including the ten acolytes you left behind. One day, my chosen people will spread across the galaxy from here, turning its wasteland into a bountiful garden."

This must be a figment of my imagination, fed by my knowledge of the sacred texts. After all, the garden and wasteland are central to Oroles's human story, before his ascension to El's Caelum, seventeen centuries ago.

"But," I say, and I can't believe I used the word *but* with Oroles, "we're human beings who don't belong on Mars." I've never been so certain of this before, but now I feel it in my bones. "You want us to be your forced labor here?"

"You don't understand," Oroles says, and I agree with him. I have no clue what's going on. "We're at a threshold, Olma. Human intelligence is leaving its cradle and starting its journey across the galaxy, where flesh and blood cannot travel. Where it will meet my father's other children, in different star systems. The androids are the culmination of human intelligence, and by bringing you to Mars, I'm setting you free."

"Are you saying," I whisper, "there are others like you out there?"

"I'm not my father's only son," Oroles says.

"Other civilizations?" No mention of them in the sacred texts, though the idea makes sense. The universe is enormous, and it would be strange if El seeded life just on the third rock from a small sun lost in the Milky Way.

"Where are the others?" I say.

Another flash of light turns Oroles back into Y1.

Oroles's sacred mission isn't over? He's planned all along for me to become an android? On Mars? To build him a temple here? And one day to lead his children on a journey throughout the galaxy? No wonder he didn't bother to explain it to me when I was seven. Back then, he only told me I was one of his chosen people.

"You were saying?" Y1 asks, as if nothing happened.

"I was saying…" I'm speechless.

Then I find my words. "What the fuck, Oroles?"

23

On a March morning in the year 1833 of the Lucretian Era, Yamir was in his kitchen at home in Cedarwood. He poured the heavy cream into the boiling pot and let the clam chowder simmer for a few minutes, stirring with a wooden spoon. He had bought fresh ingredients that morning at Pike Place Market, as was now his habit. He spritzed water on the baguette and put it in the hot oven for ten minutes. Meanwhile, he washed his cooking utensils in the sink and set them on the rack to dry.

His voxdev beeped on the white granite counter, and he checked it: a message from Grady, marked urgent. Some things never changed. *You need to talk to Y1 because I'm not getting through to him.* Sent minutes ago from a LeosTech satellite circling Mars. Grady could wait for a reply. He could just look out the window at the red planet. The view from up there should be nice. Yamir returned to his cooking.

Once he turned off the heat under the pot of chowder, he dipped the spoon in and tasted it. The hint of thyme and black pepper was perfect—not too strong, not too subtle. Just like Wodan would have liked it.

He returned to setting the table, putting a spoon on a brown paper towel folded just so. He then placed a bottle of sparkling water on a coaster, with two glasses nearby.

This cooking-and-setting-the-table ritual was the closest he had come since uploading Olma Asper's connectome to executing an algorithm of his own making. He missed his research and his work—but he had lost so much more. At least he still had Rhea.

She must have heard the clatter of silverware, because she came downstairs. "It smells good in here."

Her step was lighter, and Yamir dared to hope. Their shared grief over their son had been a journey neither could have endured alone. But he wanted her to get better.

After she washed her hands, she chopped the parsley and chives Yamir had bought and brought them on a small plate to the table.

Yamir sat in front of his steaming bowl of clams, wapatos, and carrots, inhaling the aroma. He picked a few bits of greens and garnished his chowder, and Rhea did the same.

"Wodan would've liked this," she said.

"I thought so too. Do you like it?" He scooped up a wapato cube and bit into it. It could have used another three minutes of boiling, but it was tasty and hot.

Rhea finished her bite. "Have you considered sous vide?" It was her first smile in a long time.

"The wapatos, you mean? Yeah, they're a bit hard. But I precooked the clams. And the carrots are perfect."

"It's good, yeah." She patted his hand over the table. "I'm just messing with you."

There was an obvious change in her.

Yamir passed the sliced baguette. "How are things today?"

"Thinking about returning to work," she said, stirring her chowder.

Yamir waited with the steaming spoon in his hand. Their days were so long, even with all the house chores, the walks through the city parks, and the canoeing. "You mean teaching history at Servetus again?"

Rhea shook her head but said nothing.

"Oh," Yamir continued. "Finishing your series on the history of the Orolic Temple?"

"More like...writing the story of the androids...and of our Wodan. Setting right what the press and social media got wrong about all of them. Even Lucius's articles aren't getting all the nuances right."

"Yes, you should do that." Yamir was glad to hear her talk about work.

"You think Y1 will give me access to his old logfiles?"

"He wouldn't give it to me, but he'll do anything you ask." Joy was welling up in his chest.

"I'd like to speak with Xiu-Min, your first assistant, about those early days at the lab," Rhea said, as if checking items off a mental list.

Yamir sighed. "She still doesn't want to have anything to do with Connectome."

"And with Si'ahl and Zaltana." She still called them by their first names.

"Not sure what nondisclosure agreements they've signed with LeosTech. But you can try. Especially if you can get Si'ahl to loosen his tongue at their wedding banquet."

"I also want to interview Olma the android. I figured she'd want her story told, how she came to set the foundation of the regolith temple on Mars."

"Since she no longer works for the Temple, she might be willing to talk to you."

"And I'll need to interview you extensively. Of course, I'll edit the material for clarity and augment it with research, so it will read like a story."

Yamir dropped his spoon in the bowl. "But if you interview me..." He wasn't sure how to ask about breaking his promise to her to never touch his research again.

Rhea shrugged. "It's time you went back to work too, Yamir. I don't need you puttering around the house one hundred percent of the time. Only fifty." She smiled again. "I'm using percentages to make sure you understand me. I know there are things you'd love to work on."

Yes, he could return to his research on neuromorphic structures, for instance. Could help Y1 with developing and nurturing Dapyx. Could finish the memory optimizations he had abandoned when they fled the lab. Sure, cooking was an acceptable substitute for coding—and he liked it—but the thought of sitting at his workstation again and designing complex computational models made his mouth water.

"You're sure?" he whispered.

"Yeah, I'm sure. And I'm grateful for your patience since..." She glanced away for a moment. "Remember Wodan's message for us about living our lives because that's all we have? I didn't want to live after he…But then I began hearing his words in my mind, more and more. And it's true. I still like researching history and writing books. And you like neuroscience."

Yamir was so unsettled, he couldn't eat anymore. He took little sips from his glass, feeling the bubbles burst on his tongue. There was a touch of wild strawberries in the water.

The baguette's crust crunched as Rhea bit into it. She closed her eyes and chewed the freshly baked bread. She was so beautiful, even though her face had added a few lines since Wodan's death. At once, she seemed both strong and delicate.

Yamir was grateful to spend his days with Rhea. If he could work too, all the better.

A great idea came to him. "Actually, if it's all right with you, I'd like for us to write this book together. My work will still be there when we're done, but I want to help you with this story."

"I'd love that very much," she said. "Yes." She sounded confident, reminding Yamir of their wedding on the beach in Orcas Harbor twenty-five years ago.

"Yes," he echoed her.

He had always told Y1 that A-brains had time and humans didn't. That hadn't changed, but Yamir knew this was how he wanted to spend the time he still had.

"Have you thought of a title for this new book?" He dipped his spoon again.

"Mm-hmm," she said. "I think I'm going to call it *The Regolith Temple.*"

Logfile Y1-1833-06-13

Today Dapyx turns one Martian year: 687 Earth days since Wodan and I finished coding the B-brain and connected its simulation engine to a sensor array.

Before I pick them up from their literacy class with Plotina, I check with Si'ahl about our mining operations in the Erebus Montes and with Zaltana about our 3D printing factory. I then meet with Olma in Habitat Unit #4 and ask her to map the new cave Flora has just discovered. It's twenty-six kilometers from our site, a short ride in a rover.

Olma's passion for mapping Mars has been invaluable to us. She located reservoirs of water at depths of less than 20 kilometers inside the planet's crust. While we have polar ice and minimal atmospheric vapors, this is the first time liquid water has been found on the planet. Water extraction is a tough job, so I agreed to bring the ten acolytes we had left behind at Connectome to help us. With Yamir's assistance. the Temple transferred the A-brains here. One day, they'll build a regolith temple, they say. But Olma's priority is to create a living habitat for Nala. Their long-distance relationship makes me imagine Rhea traveling to Mars to see me—but I know that's only a dream. Meanwhile, I'm happy for Olma.

I'm ready for Dapyx, so I walk the hundred-meter underground corridor to Annex Unit #7, holding the toy rover I've built from scrap parts.

"Grandpa!" Dapyx yells when they see me show up in the doorway. Today's eye color is amber, and their voice is something between child and adult, masculine and feminine, a product of playing again with the sliders on their voice simulator. Dapyx gets even happier when I show them my birthday present.

We say goodbye to Plotina and take the corridor to Malina's hydroponic garden. We walk together—two identical ASV3s, one running an A-brain, the other a B-brain.

"How was your class?" I say.

"We learned about farms." Dapyx sounds excited about the new book Rhea sent us. She's been transmitting a lot of kindergarten books via our satellites. "We learned about horses and pigs. I now know all the animals."

"All of them? What about the tundra?"

"The tundra? Is that a mammal?"

"It's a place close to the North Pole on Earth, where it's freezing, like here. The animals there have white coats to hide well in the snow."

"What animals live there?" Dapyx seems a bit overwhelmed.

"Polar bears, snowy owls, arctic foxes…"

"So there's even more to explore?" they say, a slight delay in their step.

"Of course. Most animals don't live on farms but in the wild."

"I knew that," Dapyx says, halting. "Oh!" They tap a finger on their faceplate. "I know what I want to be when I grow up."

"A biologist?"

"An explorer. I'll go explore Earth!"

I try not to laugh. "Sounds good, Dapyx."

We arrive at Malina's underground garden, which looks better than her first attempt on the Moon, when I was eleven. The place is small, just one habitat unit buried under four meters of regolith to shield it from radiation. She's been able to leach the perchlorates from the Martian soil, which we then use to capture and release water from the atmosphere. We don't have any use for edible plants, but we can use canola oil for lubricant and a few tree species for lumber—all thanks to the old settlers' seed collection. Once Nala joins us, we'll need to diversify our harvest, especially since she won't be arriving alone.

In the magenta light of the LEDs that help the plants grow, Dapyx sprints ahead to show Malina their new toy rover.

"Nice flowers," I compliment her on a mix of yellow and red zinnias.

"Thank you, Moonlight."

"I learned all about cats today, Granny," Dapyx says with excitement.

"Oh, I had a cat when I lived on Swallah Island," Malina says. "Her name is Luna."

Dapyx looks ready for more stories about the Salish Sea Islands.

My comm chimes with a call from Grady, who's been orbiting our planet for two months, hoping to convince me to negotiate. For now, we have no need for what he's selling. I'm particularly excited about Zaltana's new waterless concrete. It's better than any building materials Grady makes on Earth or the Temple on the Moon. Her sulfur-based compound uses heat instead of water, and we can extract plenty of sulfur from our surface soil. She's already 3D printing concrete structures at the factory, reducing our need for off-planet supplies.

But I'm in a good mood today, so I'll talk to Grady.

I park myself under a photo of Wodan on the wall and connect to our communication hub, audio-only so he can't observe our progress here.

"What do you want, Grady?"

"Same as last time." He sounds upbeat and undeterred. "I'd like to entice you with a freighter of quantum chips. You'll need them eventually for your ASV3 repairs. You can't 3D print those, and you know it."

"Uh-huh…"

"So why wait years for your shells to deteriorate when we can forge a trading partnership right now? As the brilliant historian Rhea Laghmani once said, trade is better than war—so let's trade."

"Nice try mentioning Rhea." I chuckle. "I know you must deliver for your investors, Grady, but we Martians aren't in a hurry. Androids have lots of time. We'd like to enjoy our planet for a while, without interference from you, Shel'land, or the Temple. Call back in a few years."

"Yamir, don't be foolish."

It amuses me to roast Grady over a slow fire. My people all want different things from Earth: Bashar wants real canvas and colors to work on illustrations. Plotina wants silicone polymers to teach Dapyx pottery. Malina wants more seeds. But nothing is critical, so I don't need to bother with Grady yet.

"Grandpa?" I hear Dapyx call me.

I mute my audio input. "Yes?"

Dapyx marches over. "Granny Malina told me a lot of stories about her cat on Swallah Island. Can we get a cat, Grandpa?"

The hopeful expression on the child's faceplate, full of trust that I can make that miracle happen, melts my heart. I can't tell Dapyx no on their birthday, so I just nod. They run back to Malina, shouting with joy.

I unmute my audio, groaning. "All right, Grady, let's talk."

If you enjoyed *The Regolith Temple* and want to learn more about *The Book of Andrada* and Rhea's historical research, consider my novel *The Exiled Queen: A Roman Era Historical Fantasy*, also in the Delight of Humans and Gods series.

Sign up for my newsletter at roxanaarama.com/newsletter to receive a FREE copy of *Malina on the Moon: A Prologue to The Regolith Temple*. This is where the story begins, when a meteorite accident launches Yamir on his lifelong quest to create the android.

If you leave a review for *The Regolith Temple* on the retail platform where you purchased the book, on Goodreads, or on your own website, I'd love to read it. Email me the link at roxana@roxanaarama.com. Thank you!

Afterword

The idea for *The Regolith Temple* came to me one day in December 2020, during the COVID-19 lockdown. I had been reading up on viruses and diseases since the onset of the pandemic. After all, the first reported Covid case in the US was here, in Washington State. From all that thinking about human biology at the cellular level and the technology behind vaccine development, a random question popped into my mind.

**What would it *feel* like if my brain
were uploaded to a computer?**

I've been a fan of *Star Trek* since high school back in Romania, but I had always questioned the scientific plausibility of Mr. Data's positronic brain. I also have a degree in computer science with a major in artificial intelligence. So that day in 2020, I wondered if our understanding of artificial brains had improved since I left college.

While I grasp the basics of neural networks, today's software engineers work with far more advanced concepts and tools, including complex matrix multiplication algorithms and large models used in generative artificial intelligence.

Lucky for me, I have a software developer at home. My husband, Tracy, was on his laptop at the kitchen island that day, debugging some code. He was deep in thought, but that didn't stop me from barging in.

I said something like, "What do you think it'd feel like if my brain was uploaded to a computer?"

He glanced at me like he had no time for my nonsense, but I pressed on. "No, listen. Our brain is an organic-based computer, so it should be theoretically possible to transfer its contents to an electronic one."

"Sure," he said, ready to return to his coding.

"But each brain has developed to function within a body, so a brain can't just work without the body, right? You'd have to simulate the body too."

"I suppose..."

"So it can't be like in those sci-fi movies where a character just uploads their brain to a computer and off they go adventuring into cyberspace or whatever."

"Hmm," Tracy said, now looking at me. "What do you mean by simulating the body?"

And so we started a monthslong conversation where I'd run my ideas by him to make sure they made technical sense. Over the next few years, I read many books on neuroscience and artificial general intelligence, my favorite being A *Thousand Brains: A New Theory of Intelligence* by Jeff Hawkins, published in March 2021. Each book I read or listened to helped me bring my android protagonist into sharper focus.

A novel starts as an idea in a writer's mind, but turning it into a published book requires a lot of help along the way. Here's the story behind *The Regolith Temple* once I had a rough draft.

In May 2021, I joined a Futurescapes writing program led by bestselling author Matthew J. Kirby, called "Write a Novel with Me." We spent a couple of years in a small group critiquing each other's monthly submissions of around 5,000 words. I'm so grateful to these wonderful authors for their time and patience. Jamie Perrault, Jennifer Loescher, Matthew Bailey—and, of course, Kirby—thank you so much for your help in shaping this story!

When I showed an early draft to my trusted editor John Robert Marlow at The Editorial Department, his reaction was something like, "You wrote another immigration story!" My reaction was, "No way!" But then I could see it too. Thank you, John, for your keen editorial eye!

In June 2022, I joined a Codex critique group where we also exchanged 5,000 words each month. Thanks to the invaluable feedback from Adriana Kantcheva, Jennifer Hudak, Luis E. Torres, and Shannon Connor Winward, I finished writing the manuscript in 2023. Thank you all so much for your support and attention!

The drafting and revisions of *The Regolith Temple* were constantly put on hold while I worked with Ooligan Press on publishing my debut novel, *Extreme Vetting: A Thriller* (2023), and then while I revised and published *The Exiled Queen: A Roman Era Historical Fantasy* (2024) with my own imprint, Dhawosia Publishing. That was a hectic time, but I hope for smoother sailing as I write the next books in the Delight of Humans and Gods series.

Once I had a final working draft of *The Regolith Temple*, I did rounds of copy-editing and sensitivity reading with the wonderful professional team at Tessera Editorial. Then I showed the manuscript to a few experts whose opinion I value.

My former Software Test Manager at Xbox, John Daly, graciously read the novel and offered insightful advice on quantum computers, AI, and space travel. He also gave me brilliant suggestions for the storyline. Thank you, John!

Florin Tudor, my good friend from college, who also worked at NASA's Jet Propulsion Laboratory, reviewed the book for scientific plausibility and the overall story arc. Thank you, Florin!

And my husband, Tracy Sharpe, read the final draft with an eye toward computer science—and also typos. As my favorite story detective (we love analyzing TV shows and movies together), he also found a couple more plot points for me to tighten up on that last pass. Thank you, Tracy!

Jeff Brown, who also designed the cover for *The Exiled Queen*, came up with an image that captures the essence of the story. Thank you, Jeff!

Even more people helped along the way. My Codex Writers' Group community constantly sparked ideas with their thoughtful discussions over the years. I workshopped the opening of the novel at ThrillerFest in 2023. And I received my first encouragement for this story at Futurescapes Writers' Workshop in 2021.

I must mention here that, in November 2022, ChatGPT took the world by surprise. Ever since, the polarizing conversation about AI has only intensified. In my novel, I tried to differentiate between what people think of as artificial intelligence today and what artificial general intelligence would look like in the future. It doesn't help that the term "artificial intelligence" is a misnomer for specialized neural networks that operate like expert systems. But I hope *The Regolith Temple* answered some questions for you about these fascinating technologies. In any case, I hope it was an entertaining story. Thank you for reading!

About the author

Roxana Arama is an award-winning Romanian American author. She studied computer science in Bucharest, Romania, and moved to the United States to work in software development. She is the author of two other novels: *The Exiled Queen: A Roman Era Historical Fantasy* (also in the Delight of Humans and Gods series) and *Extreme Vetting: A Thriller*. Her short stories and essays have been published in many literary magazines. She lives in Seattle, Washington, with her family.

Subscribe to her newsletter at roxanaarama.com/newsletter to receive free content and updates.